MISTRESS
OF JUSTICE

MISTRESS OF JUSTICE

Jeffery Wilds Deaver

A PERFECT CRIME BOOK
DOUBLEDAY
NEW YORK LONDON TORONTO SYDNEY AUCKLAND

A PERFECT CRIME BOOK
PUBLISHED BY DOUBLEDAY
a division of Bantam Doubleday Dell Publishing Group, Inc.
666 Fifth Avenue, New York, New York 10103

DOUBLEDAY is a trademark of Doubleday,
a division of Bantam Doubleday Dell
Publishing Group, Inc.

This is a work of fiction. The characters, events, and institutions
depicted are wholly fictional or are used fictitiously. Any
apparent resemblance to any person alive or dead, to any actual
events, and to any actual institutions is entirely coincidental.

BOOK DESIGN BY TASHA HALL

Library of Congress Cataloging-in-Publication Data
Deaver, Jeff.
Mistress of justice / by Jeffery Wilds Deaver.
p.   cm.
"A Perfect crime book."
ISBN 0-385-42377-2
I. Title.
PS3554.E1755M57   1992
813'.54—dc20   91-45714
                                   CIP

MISTRESS
OF JUSTICE

prologue

At night, a law firm sleeps.

Shadowy but not dark, quiet but not silent, the firm is unlike other offices, unlike banks and corporations, unlike museums, concert halls, unlike the brood of anonymous apartments, large and small, filling the island of Manhattan. The firm differs from these sites because it persists, animated, even after its occupants are no longer present. Like a gothic manor, these halls have their own lineage —a genealogy of history, will, ambition, deceit.

Here, down a wide wallpapered corridor, is a portrait of a man in stern sideburns, a man who left his partnership to become governor of the state of New York.

Here, in a small foyer decorated with fresh flowers, is an exquisite Fragonard oil painting, unprotected by alarms or thick glass.

Here, in a conference room, are reams of papers that contain the magic words the law requires to begin a lawsuit for 160 million dollars, and in a similar room down the hall sits roughly the same amount of paper, assembled in solemn blue binders, that will create a charitable trust to fund private AIDS research.

Here, in a locked safe file room, rests the last will and testament of the tenth-richest man in the world.

Tonight, the law firm sleeps, a being unto itself, its sonorous breath the white noise of power and money and brilliance. You can hear this noise, even now, late Saturday night.

Suddenly, though, a disturbance: A harsh sound reverberates through the dry air. The noise is a loud, resonating snap of metal—an ugly sound, like an impetuous shout in a dream. Then there is the soft hiss of a door closing, followed by the whisper of footsteps in quick retreat on carpet, as someone escapes through the moody corridors, which are unaccustomed to urgency like this.

Another door closes, and peace returns. The dream, or nightmare, is over, and the firm returns to its stately, contented, yet watchful sleep.

one

—

When she got the phone call, Taylor Lockwood had been reflecting on why the fifteenth floor was called Halsted Street.

Sometime in the seventies, the firm had wooed a young law school grad—University of Chicago, law review, Seventh Circuit clerk, *magna cum,* the whole business. Eager to have the boy join them, the senior attorneys gave him a tour of the firm. He walked down the marble staircase to the fifteenth floor, squinted at the forty cubicles of chest-high dividers where the firm's paralegals worked, and said, "Ha, looks like Halsted Street to me." He smiled. The other lawyers smiled. No one had the presence, or the courage, to ask what he meant.

By the time he declined the job offer several days later, the mysterious name had spread throughout the firm with the speed of telepathy; Halsted Street was now the permanent synonym for the paralegal pool.

Taylor subscribed to the majority theory behind the name—that the kid must have been referring to the labyrinth of pens in the old stockyards on Chicago's South Side. This morning, sitting in her own cubicle, she knew this theory was the correct one. It was eight-thirty, the Tuesday after the Thanksgiving holiday, and she had been at work since three A.M., stalking back and forth from the copier room to a conference room, editing, assembling, and stapling several hundred documents for a business closing that afternoon. When the attorney she was assisting told her to take a break, she fled here, where she now slouched in her comfy red swivel chair, downed her fifth cup of black coffee, and sucked on a paper cut while she tried to rid her mind of a persistent image: cattle marching into pens, cattle marching out.

The phone rang. Wearily, Taylor lifted it. *A half hour. He said a half hour. It's been ten minutes. Ten minutes is not a half hour. . . .*

It was not, however, the voice of the lawyer, but that of the Keeper of the Stockyards: the paralegal supervisor, a woman of thirty with the fastidious habits of a librarian and the delicacy of a funeral director. She said, "Taylor, would you mind, I hate to ask, but would you mind terribly going off the SBI deal?"

"I beg your pardon?"

"Would you consider it? Off SBI?"

Taylor, astonished, said, "The closing's at two today. I've been working on this deal for three weeks."

"Would it be terribly upsetting?" the woman asked. The question obviously pained her.

"What's the alternative?"

"Actually," the word stretched into more syllables than it had, "there is no alternative. I've sent a replacement to work with Mr. Bradshaw."

Taylor spun her chair one way, then the other. The paper cut had started to bleed again, and she wrapped her finger in a napkin with a happy turkey printed on it, a remnant from a firm cocktail party the week before. "Did I do something wrong?"

"Mitchell Reece wants you to help him on a project."

"Reece? I've never worked for him."

"Apparently your reputation has preceded you." She sounded wary, as if she hadn't known that Taylor had a reputation. "He said you and only you."

"Uh, you'll recall, I'm scheduled to go skiing next week."

"You can negotiate with Mr. Reece. I mentioned that fact to him."

"What was his reaction?"

"He didn't seem overly concerned."

"Why would he be? He's not the one going skiing." Blood seeping through the napkin had stained the turkey's smiling face. She pitched it out.

"Be in his office in an hour."

"Should I call Mr. Bradshaw?"

"It's all taken care of. Be in Mr. Reece's office—"

"—in an hour." She hung up.

Taylor walked through the carpeted cubicles to Halsted Street's one window. Outside, the Financial District was bathed in early-morning, overcast light. She didn't care much for the scenery today. Too much old grimy stone, like mountains pushed up abruptly by some powerful force and now weathered, abandoned, eerie. In one window of a building across the way, a maintenance man was struggling to erect a Christmas tree. It seemed out of place in the huge, cold marble lobby. She thought it odd that the color of the tree, not the gray stone, disturbed her. It was very dark; its color was to green what dried blood was to red.

She focused on the window in front of her and realized she was looking at her own reflection.

Taylor Lockwood was not heavy, but neither was she fashionably bony or angular. Earthy. That was how she thought of herself. When asked her height, she would answer five-five (she was five-four and a quarter), and she had a dense black tangle of hair that added another three inches. A boyfriend once said that with her hair hanging frizzy and loose she looked like she belonged in a pre-Raphaelite painting.

Taylor hardly believed that. On days when she was in a good mood, she believed she resembled a young Mary Pickford. On not-so-good days, she felt like a thirty-year-old little girl, standing pigeon-toed, impatiently waiting for the arrival of maturity, decisiveness, authority. (Still occasionally crying, *I'm grown up, I'm grown up!* with real tears.)

Taylor Lockwood thought she looked her best in imperfect reflections, like storefronts painted black.

Or Wall Street law firm windows.

She turned away and walked back to her cubicle. It was now close to nine, and the firm was revving up. Other paralegals were arriving. Shouts of greetings—and warnings of impending crises—were criss-crossing Halsted Street, talk of subway snarls and traffic jams were exchanged. She sat in her chair and thought about how abruptly the course of life can change, and at someone else's whim. Then those dramatic observations vanished and she went to find a Band-Aid for the paper cut.

On a warm morning in April of 1887, a balding, thirty-two-year-old sideburned lawyer named Frederick Phyle Hubbard walked into a small office on lower Broadway, slipped his silk hat and Prince Albert coat onto a hook, and said to his partner, "Good morning, Mr. White. Have you any clients yet?"

The life of a law firm began.

Both Hubbard and George C. T. White graduated from Columbia Law School and had promptly come under the acutely probing eye of Walter Carter, Esquire, the senior partner at Carter, Hughes & Cravath. Carter hired them without pay for a year, then turned them into professionals at the end of their probation by paying them the going salary of twenty dollars a month.

Six years later, the two men—as ambitious as Carter shrewdly pegged them to be—borrowed three thousand dollars from White's father, hired one law clerk and a male secretary, and opened their own firm.

Though they dreamed of offices in the Equitable Building at 120 Broadway, they settled for less. Rent in the old building they chose near Trinity Church was sixty-four dollars a month, which bought the partners two dark rooms. Still, their quarters had central heat (though they kept the office's two fireplaces going throughout most of January and February) and an elevator that one operated by pulling a thick rope running through the middle of the car, with pieces of tapestry carpeting Hubbard's wife had cut and stitched; the felt pads provided by the building management were, Hubbard felt, inelegant, and he feared they might "impress clients adversely."

The office had other amenities. Over lunch at Delmonico's on Fifth Avenue, where Hubbard and White sunk many of their first profits feeding existing and would-be clients, they could brag about the firm's new letterpress, which used a damp cloth to make copies of firm correspondence. The men had looked at, though rejected, a telephone —it would have cost ten dollars a month (besides, there was no one to call but court clerks and a few government officials). The firm had a typewriter, but the men wrote most of their correspondence with steel pens. Hubbard and White both insisted that their secretary fill the firm's ink-blotting shakers with Lake Champlain black sand.

In school, both men had dreamed of becoming great trial lawyers, and during their clerking days at Carter, Hughes, they'd spent many hours in courtrooms watching famous litigators cajole, plead with, and terrorize juries and witnesses alike. But in their own practice, economics could not be ignored, and the lucrative field of corporate law became the mainstay of their young practice. They billed at fifty-two cents an hour, though they added arbitrary and generous bonuses for certain assignments. Those were the days before income tax, the Antitrust Division of the Justice Department, and the SEC; corporations rode like Assyrians over the landscape of American free enterprise. Messrs. Hubbard and White were their tacticians, and as their clients became exceedingly wealthy, so did they. A third senior partner, Colonel Benjamin Willis, joined the firm in 1920. He died several years later of pneumonia related to a World War One mustard gassing. As his legacy to the firm, Willis left behind a railroad, a bank, and several major utilities. Messrs. Hubbard and White also inherited the matter of what to do with his name—appending it to theirs had been the price for both the colonel and his fat clients. Nothing of the bargain was in writing, but after his death, the partners kept their word; the firm was then and would forever be known as a triumvirate.

By the time the mantles passed, in the late twenties, Hubbard, White & Willis had grown to thirty-eight attorneys and had moved into its cherished Equitable Building. Banking, securities, and litigation made up the bulk of the work, which was still performed as it had been in the nineteenth century—by gentlemen, and a certain type of gentleman only. Attorneys who were in fact or by appearance Jewish, Italian, or Irish were interviewed with interest and cordiality and were never offered positions.

Women were always welcome; good stenographers were hard to find.

The firm continued to grow, occasionally spinning off satellite firms or political careers, which not too curiously were invariably Republican. Several attorneys general were born from Hubbard, White & Willis, as were an SEC commissioner, a senator, and two governors.

Yet the firm, unlike many of its size and prestige, wasn't a political breeding ground. It was common knowledge that politics was power without money, and the partners at Hubbard, White saw no reason to forsake one reward of Wall Street practice when they could have both.

The current Hubbard, White & Willis had over two hundred attorneys and three hundred support employees, placing it in the medium-size category of Manhattan firms. Of the eighty-four partners, eleven were women, ten were Jewish (including five of the women), one was oriental American, and three were black (one of whom was, to the great delight of the executive committee, Hispanic as well). In response to the challenges from the press or minority lawyers' associations, a firm spokeswoman would recite, "Hubbard, White & Willis is not concerned with racial, gender, sexual preference, national or ethnic distinctions; our policy is to hire only the best legal minds in the country." It would also be pointed out that the firm had one of the most active pro bono, minority-rights programs in the city.

Hubbard, White & Willis was now big business. Overhead ran over $2 million a month, and the partners had upped the billing rates considerably higher than Frederick Hubbard's. An hour of a partner's time could hit $450, and in big transactions a premium (referred to by associates as a no-fuck-up charge) of perhaps $250,000 would be added to the client's final tab. Twenty-five-year-old associates fresh out of law school made $95,000 a year.

The present-day partners were true descendants of Messrs. Hubbard and White—brilliant, stable, responsible, culture-supporting, low-risk-takers. They were counselors and scribes rather than entrepreneurs. Kings of Meadowbrook and the Creek Club. The younger partners were a curious mix of the present and past centuries. They wore suspenders under their Hart Schaffner & Marx suits, they loved the woody collegiateness of the Yale Club, their palms grew moist with excitement as they planned municipal financings and leveraged buyouts. But they were also up to speed on high-density lipoproteins and body-fat ratios. They jogged a collective nine hundred miles a week, and more than one male partner had scheduled closings while taking into account that his wife was supervising an underwriting for Salomon Brothers or Merrill Lynch, and it was his turn to escort Paul, Jr., or young Atkins to the Dalton School.

The firm had moved from limestone into glass and metal. It now occupied three floors in a skyscraper near the World Trade Center. An interior designer had been paid three quarters of a million dollars to awe clients with dramatic understatement. The theme was lavender and burgundy and sea blue, smoky glass, brushed metal, stone, and dark wood with a satin finish. Spiral marble staircases connected the floors, and the library was a three-story atrium with fifty-foot windows offering a stunning view of New York Harbor. The numerous iron and bronze sculptures (one or two tastefully erotic), the textile hangings and Kozo silk screens were not as memorable as the Calders, Pollacks, Monets, and Matisses, but nonetheless helped bring in an appraisal of the firm's collection at about eight million dollars.

Within this combination MOMA and *Interior Design* centerfold, Conference Room 16-2 was the only one large enough to hold all the partners of the firm. This Tuesday morning, two men were sitting here, at the end of a U-shaped conference table, surfaced with dark red marble and edged in rosewood. Amid an aroma of baseboard heat and brewing coffee, they together read a single sheet of paper.

Donald Burdick had been for the past twelve years the head of the firm's executive committee. At sixty-seven, he was lean and had sleek gray hair trimmed short by a barber who visited Burdick's office fortnightly, the old Italian brought 'round to the firm in the partner's Silver Cloud—fetched, as Burdick said. (When summoned to Burdick's office, one often had a sense that he had been fetched.) People referred to the partner as dapper, a description that seemed appropriate but was usually offered by those who did not know him well; "dapper" belied power, and Donald Burdick was a powerful man, more powerful than his remarkable resemblance to Laurence Olivier and his suede-glove manners suggested.

His was a power that could not be wholly quantified—it was an amalgam of old money and old friends in strategic places and old favors owed. One aspect of his power, however, did lend itself to calculation: the complicated formula of partnership interest in Hubbard, White & Willis. Which was not in fact so mysterious at all if you remembered that the votes you got to cast and the income you took home varied according to the number of clients you brought to the firm and how much they spent.

Donald Burdick's salary was close to two million dollars a year.

He slid the paper away, relinquished it into the tough grasp of

William Winston Stanley. Sixty-five years old, Stanley was stout, ruddy, scowling, grim. You could see him in Pilgrim's garb, cheeks puffing out steam on a frigid New England morning. You could see him reading an indictment to a witch.

Burdick was Dartmouth and Harvard Law; Stanley had gone to Fordham Law School at night while working in the Hubbard, White mailroom. By a crafty mix of charm, bluntness, and natural brilliance for business, he'd fought his way up through a firm of men with addresses (Locust Valley and Westport) as foreign to him as his (Williamsburg in Brooklyn) was to them. His saving grace, quite literally, was membership in an Episcopalian church.

For over a decade, Hubbard, White & Willis had lived under the guidance of these two men. At one time a more literate group of associates had called them the Ravens, after the birds whose presence assures the survival of the Tower of London. More recent associates, if they referred to Burdick and Stanley at all, called them the Old Men.

Burdick asked, "Is that accurate?"

Stanley looked at the list. "It's an informal poll my boys put together. Who knows how the vote will go."

"I'm astonished. How did he do it? How did he get this many in his camp without our hearing?"

Stanley laughed in a thick rasp. "We just *have* heard."

"Bastard." Burdick's narrow, dry hand snatched up the paper. For a moment it seemed he would crumple it into a tight ball, but he folded the paper slowly and slipped it into the inside pocket of his trim-fitting suit.

two

"**I** have a breakfast meeting in half an hour, then the partnership meeting for the rest of the morning," Wendall Clayton snapped. "*You* handle it."

"You bet, Wendall." The young associate nodded confidently to mask the distilled terror he felt.

"And when you call them back, aristocratize them."

"Will do." The boy nodded vigorously and scurried out of the man's office, trying to figure out what the hell he meant.

Aristocratize the bastards. Sometimes Clayton would write it in the margin of a memo one of his flock had written. Then watch the girl or boy, flustered, trying to pronounce it. Ar-is-*toc*-ra-tize . . . he'd made up the phrase himself. It had to do with attitude mostly. Much of it was knowing the law, of course, and much was circumstance. But mostly, attitude. Clayton practiced often, and he was superb at aristocratizing.

The low, Tuesday morning sunlight poured into his office, the corner office he was doubly proud of. Proud of the atmosphere, courtesy of his wife, an amateur decorator. And proud of the room's location and size. On executive row, the seventeenth floor, it measured twenty-seven by twenty—a size that by rights should have gone to a partner more senior than Clayton. When it fell vacant, however, the room was assigned to him. No one was quite sure why.

The sunlight. He liked the way it hit low and golden on the rugs, the Chippendale chairs, the Sheraton cabinet, the set of Paduan apothecary jars, a Dutch tin-glazed earthenware tile painting, the nineteenth-century Swedish astrolabe, the solid brass urns, the Steuben ashtray.

Clayton was a handsome man. Not big—under six feet—but solid from running (he did not jog; he ran) and tennis and skippering the thirty-six-foot *Ginnie May* around Newport every other weekend from April through September. He had a thick bundle of Harvard professor hair, and he wore European suits, slitless in the back (some even double-breasted!), forgoing the burdened sacks of dark pinstripe that cloaked most of the pear-shaped men of the firm. Killer looks, the women in the firm said. Another three inches and he could have been a model. Clayton worked hard at his image. A duke had to be handsome. A duke enjoyed dusting his suits with pig-bristle brushes, and getting a glow on his burgundy-colored Bally's. He took great pleasures in the small rituals of fastidiousness.

Clayton glanced at the Tiffany nautical clock on his desk. Nearly time. He rocked back in his chair, his throne, a huge construction of oak and red leather he had bought in England for two thousand pounds.

Aristocratize.

Wendall Clayton looked out the window. The sun squatted over Brooklyn, making all the garbage in the air fiery and dramatic. The red light fell on his face. He believed he felt warmth, though that did not seem possible with such a low November sun. He rubbed the flesh under his eyes. He was exhausted. At six P.M. the previous Friday, Clayton had been sitting at Murphy's with some young associates. Clayton was treating them to drinks and laughing at mildly dirty jokes, telling a few of his own and arguing football when his beeper had sounded. One of his clients was in a panic. His company had been served with a temporary restraining order. Clayton was a corporate, not a trial, lawyer and had only vague ideas how to vacate TROs, but the company was *his* client, and within three hours he'd extracted a litigation partner from his pretheater dinner, rounded up two fresh associates, and was at work putting together the case to have the TRO lifted.

They had finished the paperwork at midnight Monday, and just half an hour ago the litigator had presented his case before an accommodating judge in the Southern District. The judge ruled for Clayton's client and vacated the restraining order.

Clayton had just delivered the good news to the client, who was astonished that Hubbard, White had managed to win the case even before the start of business. Clayton accepted the man's accolades and avoided mentioning that the bill for the weekend's work would come to sixty thousand dollars.

Now, looking out his office window, bathed in golden light and the afterglow of the courtroom win, Clayton was relaxed and more or less content.

He felt this way even as he wondered—he did frequently nowadays—if he should quit his $415,000-a-year job and kiss Hubbard, White & Willis good-bye. A duke did not turn tail, of course. A duke's first responsibility was his clients. That is, his *subjects*. But a smart duke did not wait until the king fucked up so badly the kingdom was overrun. Dukes had balls. The metaphor got a little complicated, and Clayton found it easier to think not about kings and nobility, but about Donald Burdick and the firm, and himself.

Goddamn him, Burdick, that pompous dowager.

Goddamn the man! Clayton's fist clenched and his substantial arm trembled with anger.

His phone rang. The limo was downstairs. Clayton stood, pulled on the jacket of his suit, then his overcoat, and stepped into the ominously quiet halls. He had an appointment uptown—an engagement as important to him as the partnership meeting scheduled for later that morning. But first he had another task that he considered more crucial than either—Wendall Clayton was going to thank personally the associates who had sacrificed their holiday weekend for his client, and for him.

"You ever been here, Wendall?" the man across the burnished copper table asked.

When Clayton spoke, however, it was to the captain of the Carleton Hotel on Fifty-ninth Street, off Fifth. "The nova?"

"No, Mr. Clayton." The captain shook his head. "Not today."

"Thank you, Henri. I'll have two scrambled and a croissant. A rasher of bacon."

"Very good, Mr. Clayton."

"Ha," John Perelli gave an explosive laugh and ordered the same, with a fruit cup. Perelli was stocky and dark, with a long face. He wore a navy pinstripe suit.

Clayton shot his cuffs, revealing eighteen-karat Wedgwood cuff links, and said, "I feel, in answer to your question, right at home here."

Though this was not completely true. Wendall Clayton was from shy money. He owned an eight-room apartment on upper Fifth Avenue; a summer house in Redding, Connecticut; and a ten-room cabin in Newport. He had a stock portfolio worth, on a good day, three million. Hanging on the oak paneling in his Upper East Side den were two Picassos, three Klees, a Mondrian, and a Magritte. He traded in his Jaguar for a Mercedes station wagon because he didn't like the ride of the Brit wheels. Yet his wealth was of the hushed, Victorian sort: a third inherited, a third earned at the practice of law (and cautious investment of the proceeds), the rest from his wife.

Wendall Clayton was not unique in this tripartite wealth, but here, in Midtown, he was surrounded by a different genre of money. It was loud money. Acquired from new wellsprings. Oh, the men and women who possessed these funds had taste no worse than his; that wasn't the issue. The point was the source. This money was from media, from advertising, from public relations, from junk bonds, from LBO's, from alligator spreads and dividend-snatching. Commission money. Sales money. Real-estate money. Italian money. Jewish money. Japanese money.

Clayton's wealth was money with cobwebs, and therefore here it was, ironically, suspect. *The more respectable, the less acceptable,* he would think with a grimace, reciting his own coined phrase.

He tried not to give a damn. He'd been to Cornell, he'd been to Harvard, he'd served with the U.S. attorney's office, he'd risen through Hubbard, White & Willis, he'd brought money into a marriage of money. He was as powerful as anyone in the room.

Yet here he sat in a restaurant where he was known intimately by the help, and he did not feel at home. Witness Perelli, who had assumed Clayton was a stranger here. Clayton felt like an immigrant in steerage, as if *he* were the one without passport. This irked him and made him defensive.

Clayton asked, "So, John, do you want a law firm, or not?"

"I might. . . . We might. We want to see your numbers, of course, but, hell, what do you want me to say? The rumor is your fees are low, you're top-heavy in partnership draw, you've got a skewed incentive bonus, and there's a lot of fat."

"And we've got the loyalest client base of any firm in the city, a lease that's up next year so there'll be no buyout, and incoming classes from the best schools. Four partners are authors of textbooks or treatises, and five are adjunct professors at Fordham, Columbia, and NYU."

"You've got a word processing system on long-term lease . . ."

"John."

". . . that was outmoded two years ago."

"John."

"I'm listening."

Clayton was patient. "We wouldn't be here breaking bread if we didn't want to climb into the sack together. The question is, what is that fuck going to cost you, and what's it going to cost me?"

The waiter set the plates on the table. Clayton hunched over the soft mounds of eggs and ate hungrily, cutting the food into small bites.

Perelli waited until the waiter was gone then said, "So cut the bullshit is what you're saying? Fine. That's the way this here boy likes to operate. We're definitely interested, Wendall. We've got labor clients we want to parlay into SEC. We've got products liability cases that are gold mines. You've got corporate people and litigators who'd be a natural fit. Obviously we want your banking department, and you want our real estate group. In theory, it's perfect."

"What makes it untheoretical?"

"One of the two of our firms is going to have deadwood. And I hope it's no shock to you that we aren't real happy about letting any of our people go."

Clayton signaled for more ground pepper. They paused while the waiter twisted the huge mill and the smell of juniper rose from Clayton's plate. "So fire some of ours."

Perelli laughed, then realized Clayton wasn't joking. "Just like that?"

"No," Clayton said with a grunt. "Not quite like that. I've made it easy for you." He handed Perelli a piece of paper.

Perelli read, then looked up, questioningly.

"That," Clayton tapped the paper dramatically, "is who should go."

"There are, what?, fifty names here?" Perelli read. "Donald Burdick, Bill Stanley, Woody Crenshaw, Lamar Fredericks, Ralph Dudley . . . Wendall, these men *are* Hubbard, White & Willis. This is a hit list."

"That's exactly what it is."

"These people must know they're at risk. You think the firm will approve—what do you need? two-thirds—you think you can get the vote to approve the merger?"

"If you guarantee me that they'll go, I'll get the votes. I have . . ." Clayton's voice faded. He wondered how candid he could be with this man. "I'm making certain arrangements to ensure the votes. But I want a few other things: one, a seat on your executive committee; two, guaranteed partnership within two years for no more than ten Hubbard, White associates of my selection—"

"Ten? Wendall, that's close to two million dollars of commitment you're talking."

"Look, these are my boys. They've busted their balls for eight years. When a client says he wants somebody fucked, they ask only two questions: first, 'Who?' second, 'When do you want them in the barrel?' "

Perelli laughed and eyed Clayton's bacon hungrily. Clayton waved his palm toward it, and Perelli lifted a piece to his mouth with his fingers. He said, "Burdick is a big name. He represents a big chunk of your client base."

"Look at his clients and look at their work. He's got one bank; the rest are old manufacturing companies and rich old pricks that may be worth a bundle, but are mostly doling out some low-fee T&E work."

"What about MacMillan Holdings?"

"What about it?"

"It's a huge chunk of revenue," Perelli said. "Got to be millions . . ." The lawyer watched Clayton's face for confirmation of this classified information, and when he got no response continued, "And Burdick's like family with them, isn't he?"

"Families get estranged. It happens rather frequently. MacMillan knows Burdick's old, they've probably considered he'll be retiring soon. It's a risk. What can I say?"

Perelli didn't smile. "MacMillan . . . I'd hate to lose that client."

They sipped coffee as they talked about deals they were working, speaking in guarded terms and euphemisms, the waltzing of attorneys respecting the attorney-client privilege. When they had both finished their second cups, Clayton brushing croissant crumbs off his slacks and waving for the check, Perelli said, "Just tell me: If I insisted that Burdick stay, would you still be willing to proceed?"

Clayton signed his name to the check. He offered no credit card. The waiter swept past, picked it up, and vanished.

"Let me tell you something, John. In 1971, Donald Burdick was asked by Nixon to head a special committee looking into abuses in the steel industry."

"The Justice Department was involved."

"That's right. Burdick was picked because he was known in both Albany and Washington. The executive committee at Hubbard, White —it was called a steering committee then—was ecstatic. Publicity for the firm, a chance for Burdick to do some serious stroking on the Hill. Afterwards, a triumphant return. More publicity, new clients. Donald Burdick told the committee he'd accept the appointment on one condition. That when he returned he and a man of his choosing would be placed on the executive committee, and three particular partners would be asked to leave. Now, John, that was in the 1970s. Law firms did not fire partners. It simply was not done."

"And?"

"Three months later, a memo went around the office congratulating three partners who were unexpectedly leaving Hubbard, White and starting their own firm." Clayton pushed back from the table. "The answer to your question is this: The only way this deal works is without Burdick and everyone else on that list. That's the quid pro quo. What do you say?"

Perelli slipped a cigar out of a tube, handed it to Clayton, then took another for himself. He opened a small silver knife and began working on the tip. "I say we exchange vital statistics and get to work on a goddamn merger."

three

"Wat it is, I've been robbed," Mitchell Reece said. He swiveled back in his black leather chair. The mechanism gave a soft ring as a spring worked.

Taylor Lockwood asked, "As in what they do to you on the subway, or what they do at the IRS?"

"We're talking"—Reece's square jaw shifted; he laughed bitterly —"burglary."

Reece stood up slowly, as if he'd been sitting in one position for hours, and walked to the door to shut it. Taylor again swallowed the yawn that had been trying to escape for five minutes and rubbed her stinging eyes. The time was ten A.M. and she was waiting for her second wind; she suspected it had come and gone unannounced.

What she knew about Reece: The trial lawyer, with dark straight hair a touch long to go unnoticed by the more conservative partners, was in his mid thirties. He specialized in complex corporate litigation. The firm's clients loved him because he won cases; the firm itself loved him because he ran up huge tabs doing so. *The only cure for law is more law,* he would say, quoting Professor Karl Llewellyn. He worked fifteen, eighteen hours a day. (Taylor had heard that he'd once billed twenty-six hours in a single day; working on a flight to L.A., he had taken advantage of the time zones.) Young associates idolized him, and they burned out working for him. Partners were uncomfortable supervising Reece; the briefs and motion papers he wrote under their names were often beyond their skill. He also participated in the firm's pro bono program, volunteering much of his time to represent indigent clients in criminal cases.

More relevant to the paralegal pen: Reece was a hunk ("Hey, Taylor, check out John Jr. over there.") And better than that: He was single. And straight (the proof wasn't conclusive—a divorce, but the ladies were willing to accept that circumstantial evidence as entirely credible). He had had affairs with at least two women at the firm, or so the rumor went.

He returned to his chair. It was hot in the office, and Taylor slipped off her navy suit jacket. She ran her hands through her tangle of curls. She sensed Reece's eyes scan her figure, her white blouse with an explosion of bow at her throat.

His office was a mess. A hundred files—bulging manila folders and Redwelds stuffed with documents—filled the floor, the credenza, his desk. Stacks of legal magazines, waiting to be read, filled the spaces between the files. She smelled food, and saw the remains of a delivered Chinese food dinner sitting in a greasy bag beside the door.

Reece poured coffee from an automatic maker on his credenza and turned to face her. He wore a two-tone shirt, dark blue with white collar and cuffs, navy wool slacks and black penny loafers. He didn't look real spiffy; under his eyes were shadows like smudges of pencil lead, and the whites had visible red veins. His hair was mussed. His skin was pale, and she wondered if he'd ever had a tan. He yawned so hard his eyes watered. Taylor stifled another one of her own.

Reece asked her, "What do you know about banking law?"

"The fee for bounced checks is ten dollars."

"That's all?"

"I'm afraid so." She paused, then added, "But I'm a fast learner."

Reece said seriously, "I hope so. Here's your first lesson. One of the firm's clients is the U.S. subsidiary of Banque Industrielle de Genève. You ever work for them?"

"No." Taylor took a steno pad out of her purse and uncapped a pen. She began to write.

"Last year, they loaned twenty-five million to—"

"Francs?"

"Dollars," Reece said. "To a company in Midtown. Hanover & Stiver, Inc. Why are you taking notes?"

"I always take notes."

"Don't," he commanded.

Taylor hesitated, then dropped the pad on the floor beside her.

"Hanover & Stiver do environmental cleanup, waste disposal, and trucking. Well, nobody did much due diligence before the loan, and the company turns out to be run by real sleazoids. Right away they were late on all the loan payments, they came up with excuses, their customers aren't paying, blah-blah-blah. Finally, they tell Banque Genève, 'Hey, sorry, we don't have the money to pay.' And bang, they default on the note."

"Note?"

Reece looked at her uncertainly, "You *don't* know banking law, do you? When a bank loans money, the borrower signs a promissory note. It's like a check."

"A check worth twenty-five million," she said. "Got it."

Reece continued, "Banque Genève decides to sue Hanover & Stiver, and I get the case. When you're going to sue to recover money on a note, you have to produce the note in court. The bank couriered it to me, but there was a delay in trial, a postponement for two weeks, and—"

Shocked, Taylor said, "It wasn't?"

Reece said in a low voice, "Somebody took it right out of my fucking file cabinet. Just walked right in and stole it."

"You need the original? Can't you use a copy?"

"It can be done, but I don't have enough time. The defendant's in a bad way financially—that's why we're suing in the first place—and by the time I can establish the authenticity of a copy, they won't have a penny left." His voice was bitter. He massaged his eyes and the bridge of his nose. "Banque Genève is one of Donald Burdick's biggest clients. I lose them their money, they'll walk."

"But it wasn't your fault. How could you guess somebody'd steal the thing?"

"It *is* my fault. I went home to get some sleep. . . ." He brought his palm down on the polished table, hard, then smiled weakly as if to show his anger was not aimed at her tender of sympathy. "When I got back to the firm, it was gone."

"Maybe it was misplaced," Taylor said, and she immediately regretted the stupidity of the remark. Reece mildly nodded at the deep gouge in the file cabinet, and the broken lock.

"And you didn't call the police?"

"How could I? There'd be press. Burdick would find out that the note is missing; the client would, too. The newspapers . . ." He held her eyes. "So I guess you know why I asked you here."

Vague objections formed in her thoughts. "You want me to find out who took it?"

"Actually, I'd like you to *find* it. I don't really much care who did it."

"But why me?" she asked to buy time. "I mean, why not you?"

Reece leaned back in his chair; the singing metal rang again. He looked at ease, as if she had already accepted his offer. "Whoever took it will know I can't go to the cops, and he'll be expecting me to search for him. I need somebody else. I need you."

"I just—"

"I know about your ski trip. I'm sorry. You'd have to postpone it." *Some negotiations.*

"Mitchell, I don't know. I'm flattered you called me, but I don't have any experience at this sort of thing."

"Well, let me just say one thing. I've worked with a lot of detectives, you know, private eyes—"

"Sam Spade, sure."

"No, not at all. This's what I'm saying: The best detectives're women. They're quiet, attractive, smart. They don't dominate the conversation. They let the subjects do the talking while they listen. They're sexy. . . . Can I say that?"

"I'm not going to stop you." The blush started fast and swept over her face. She felt foolish, responding with a flirt to a comment that wasn't meant to be flirtatious.

"Sexy is distracting," Reece said. "And if you want another reason, I trust you."

"You don't trust anybody at Hubbard, White & Willis but me? I've never worked for you. For all you know, I could have been the one. . . ." Her voice faded and she asked, "When did they steal it?"

Reece was grinning. "Saturday. You had an alibi. You were out of town."

"I'm just a paralegal. I copy things, I file papers, I read depositions."

"And you've got"—he paused, and she looked at him quizzically —"the grapevine says you've got balls."

"Does it now?" Taylor asked, frowning and feeling immensely pleased.

"Will you help me?"

Taylor looked out the window and felt, more than saw, the triple glance that men give women: face, tits, legs. Instead of the usual resentment, she felt a low, pleasing twist in her belly. The sun went behind thick clouds, and the sky became as dark as its reflection in the choppy harbor. "I love views," she said. "In my apartment, you can see the Empire State Building. Provided you lean out the bathroom window."

"And I'm keeping you from a beautiful view of the mountains."

"Mostly," she said, "I stand at the top, I see Blue Shield claim forms."

Silence. Reece brushed his hair aside, then rubbed his eyes with his knuckles. Another yawn was stifled. The clock on his desk ticked softly.

Taylor said, "I'll help you. I don't know what to do, but I'll help you."

He leaned forward suddenly, emotionally, then stopped. There is a code of chastity within law firms. Whatever liaisons occurred in hotel rooms or attorneys' apartments, when you were within the four walls of the office, cheeks were not kissed, much less lips. Reece's concession to gratitude was taking Taylor's hand in both of his. She felt a heat, like friction, between their hands.

"I guess the first question is," she said quickly, "do you have any idea what happened." She withdrew her hand from his.

"The bank messengered the note to me at three P.M. on Friday. . . ."

Just around the time I was watching a soap opera and force-feeding myself a turkey and dressing sandwich.

". . . I locked it in my file at four. I worked all day Friday and Saturday, and it was still there when I left at eight. I came back at nine on Sunday morning, and it was gone."

"Did you see anyone here that Saturday?"

"I was reading transcripts all day. I was aware of some people, but I didn't talk to anyone. I can't remember who was in."

"Who at the bank knew you had it?"

"Only the one vice president who worked on the deal."

"And him?"

Reece said, "Couldn't have been. If the bank doesn't collect on this note, his career is over."

"What about your secretary?"

"She's been on maternity leave for two months. I'm having the steno pool do all my work till she gets back."

"Who here knew you were working on the case?"

Reece laughed. He slid a memo across to her.

FROM: M. A. Reece.

TO: Attorneys of Hubbard, White & Willis

RE: CONFLICT OF INTEREST

I AM REPRESENTING OUR CLIENT BANQUE INDUSTRIELLE DE GENÈVE IN A SUIT AGAINST HANOVER & STIVER, INC. PLEASE ADVISE IF YOU HAVE EVER REPRESENTED HANOVER & STIVER OR HAVE ANY OTHER CONFLICTS OF INTEREST INVOLVING THESE COMPANIES OF WHICH THE FIRM SHOULD BE AWARE.

"You follow? This is the standard conflicts memo. To let everybody know who we're suing; if anybody in the firm has ever represented Hanover, we have to drop the case. So *everybody* knew what I was doing. And by checking copies of my correspondence in the file room, they could figure out when I'd probably have the note."

Taylor prodded the conflicts memo with the fork of her fingers. Twenty-five million dollars. She was trying to think of important questions. "Why steal it? Could anybody cash it?"

"I think that somebody at Hanover bribed someone here to lose the note for a while. Probably until they've paid off heavy debts the company owes its officers and directors. Then, after the company's bled, the note can resurface, and we can sue to our heart's content. But there won't be a cent left to collect."

"It sounds so extreme—stealing something from a Wall Street law firm."

"The CEO of Hanover & Stiver, Lloyd Hanover, is unadulterated scum. He thinks he's some kind of smooth operator. You know the kind—late fifties, crew-cut, tanned. Has like three mistresses. Wears so much gold jewelry, he'd never get through a metal detector."

"That's not a crime," Taylor said.

Reece snapped back with, "No, but his three SEC violations and two RICO convictions were."

"Ah."

Reece was pulling a file folder off his credenza.

Taylor asked, "Why don't you get Hanover himself in on a deposition? Grill him."

The V where Reece's thin lips joined tightened. Taylor tried to preempt him, "Of course, he'd just deny it." Reece nodded. She said, "I was just thinking that that way, he'd perjure himself."

"Taylor, the D.A. does not give particularly high priority to perjury suits."

"No. Of course not."

If you can only ask dumb questions, girl, don't ask anything.

Taylor sat forward and examined the file that Reece was opening. On top was a copy of the computer key entry ledger for the firm's front door. It showed the code numbers of everyone who had entered the firm on Saturday. He ran his finger along it. "There were fifteen people here on Saturday. But everybody had left by five or six. I was the only one here later than that. See, that's me, when I checked out, at eight-ten. But then somebody came back in at nine-thirty, and only stayed for two hours. Why would he do that? It's a curious amount of time for somebody to be in a law firm on a Saturday night. If he'd forgotten something, he'd just pick it up and leave. If he was doing serious research, he'd stay for longer than two hours, and probably not come in Saturday evening at all. Two hours. What it's long enough for is to find the note and take it."

"Whose key is it?"

"That's the problem." Reece turned to the back of the printout. "I have the number, but I don't know who it's assigned to. I can't get into the computer. Do you know how?"

She shook her head. "No idea."

"So that's your first step, I suppose. Find out who has that card."

"There are other ways to get into the firm, Mitchell, you know. Maybe somebody from the outside just broke in."

He noticed a fleck of dust on his brilliant cuff and flicked it into space. "There's an old trial lawyers' story about the cop who kept finding bodies of hobos murdered out by the railroad tracks. Their bodies were all beat up. He had this elaborate theory of a cult murderer whose father had been a bum and who was seeking revenge for a deprived childhood. The cop spent all his time out by the tracks looking for the killer."

"What happened?"

"He got hit by a train on the blind curve, just like the bums. The moral: Don't go looking for the elaborate when the obvious will do. Sure, there are lots of things that could have happened. Stick with the probabilities." Reece took out his wallet and handed her a thousand dollars in hundreds.

She looked at it with a funny smile, embarrassed, curious.

"For expenses."

"Expenses."

Reece was impatient. "Bribes. It's for bribes."

Taylor held the bills awkwardly for a moment, then slipped them into her purse. She looked up into Reece's somber face as he slid a piece of paper toward her. She squinted at the sheet, which was legal-sized and pale green—the color of corridors in old hospitals and government buildings. She recognized it as the court calendar the managing attorney of Hubbard, White circulated throughout the firm daily. It contained a grid of thirty days beginning with today. Filling these squares were the times and locations of all court appearances scheduled for the firm's litigators. Reece took out a pen and slowly circled two squares. Today, November 26. And, two weeks later, Monday, December 9. He pointed to the latter date and said, "Read that."

She leaned forward.

Reece said, "Out loud."

She glanced at him, then said, "Banque Industrielle de Genève *v.* Hanover & Stiver, Inc. Trial. Ten A.M. No continuance."

"I have two weeks to find that note, Taylor."

She was flustered. "I'll do my best, Mitchell." She took the calendar memo. "Can I keep this?"

"Of course." He looked at his watch. "Let's talk again tomorrow. But I don't think we should meet in the firm. How's the Vista at nine-thirty?"

"The hotel? Sure."

"We can always get together at my place, or yours." His eyes sideslipped to a stack of papers. "Yours is okay, isn't it?"

She said, "I'm sort of between boyfriends." She wondered if he noticed the blush.

Reece said, "I know. I heard."

"Oh."

Reece laughed. "Don't look so surprised, Taylor. You think there are any secrets in a law firm?"

Who are these men and women?

What do I know of them other than the baldest facts of their wealth, their brilliance, their aspirations?

In the hall on the south side of the sixteenth floor, Donald Burdick hears the grandfather clock chime the Westminster and begin its ringing climb toward eleven A.M. The partners are arriving. Most carry foolscap pads or stacks of files and their ubiquitous leather personal calendars.

As I have administered the law with them over the years, I have seen glimpses of stubbornness, and sometimes brutality, and sometimes cruelty.

And generosity and sacrifice.

But what is in their hearts?

They take their places around the table in the dark conference room. Some, the less confident, the newcomers, examine nicks in the rosewood and trace the pattern of the marble with their fingers; they wear jackets with their suits. Others, the veterans, are in shirtsleeves, and have no time for the administrivia of meetings like this. They appear inconvenienced.

A congregation of brilliant, ambitious people, all bound together by the fascia of a thirty-two-page Articles of Partnership. Even as they assemble, associates scurry in and out with urgent messages. The young men and women take their whispered instructions, nod eagerly, and hurry off. The conversation among the partners is informal and does nothing to hide the drone of speculation.

My partners . . . and how many are my friends?

Burdick, sitting at the apogee of the table, however, understands that this is not a relevant question. More important: *How many who are my friends will betray me?* If the tally that Bill Stanley had showed him earlier is accurate, the answer to this question is that many will. Burdick surveys the faces, probing behind bifocals and tortoise-rimmed glasses at eyes that are placid and untimid. Yet often, when one of the partners inadvertently returns his gaze, his eyes dart away like a guilty child's.

To Stanley, Burdick whispers, "Nearly fifteen'll be missing. That could swing it one way or another."

"Wendall may have killed them," Stanley says with a growl. "And we'll never find the bodies."

At eleven-fifteen, the last partner arrives, and Burdick nods to him to close the door. The mechanism gives a solid click. It seems to Burdick that the pressure in the room has changed, and they are sealed in as if they were in a chamber in the Great Pyramid. Burdick calls the meeting to order. Minutes are read and not heard, a report from the executive committee goes ignored. Committee reports are recited at breakneck speed, with surprisingly few interruptions and little debate.

"Do you want to hear about the hiring committee's schedule?" asks a sanguine young partner who has probably stayed up half the night to prepare it.

"We do not," Burdick said evenly, and—seeing several partners smile—decides the royal pronoun is an unfortunate slip.

There is silence in the room, punctuated by the popping of soda cans, and papers being quietly organized. Dozens of pens make graffiti on legal pads. Donald Burdick studies the agenda for a moment, and Wendall Clayton slips his suit jacket off, opens a file, and says, "May I have the floor?"

Burdick nods in his direction. In a rehearsed baritone, Clayton says, "Several members of the firm and myself have been approached by the executive committee of Sullivan & Perelli to consider a merger of our firms. . . ."

Burdick scans faces. He sees shock, which in turns astonishes him. He had assumed that everyone knew about Perelli.

"And why didn't they approach our executive committee?" Bill Stanley's rumbled comment is perfunctory.

As is Clayton's dismissive, "I can't answer for them."

Work has stopped. Doodling has stopped. Coffee cups are lifted to lips only to buy time.

"Wendall," Stanley says petulantly, "you're not even on the planning committee."

Clayton looks surprised. A slight smile curves across his face. "Perhaps they felt they would not get a full hearing."

Burdick says, "Well, what exactly is their proposal?"

"They don't have one yet. They simply want to see our balance sheet and P&L statement, client and personnel lists. They'll give us the same."

"But that's all classified," one partner says from the far reaches of the table. Now that the issue is drawn, the others are bolder.

"Our P&L's?" someone else asks in surprise.

Wendall says, "They want a nondisclosure agreement so we can both release data."

Another voice calls, "Can we discuss this? What do we know about this firm?"

More voices join in, and a tide of comments and tension-breaking laughter fills the room. Clayton's clear, steady voice silences this. "Sullivan & Perelli has two hundred and thirty attorneys. They specialize in real estate, labor, ERISA. A lot of city and state government."

Although Burdick knows every public fact—and a few nonpublic —about John Perelli, he now shakes his head in dismay, as if disappointed at Clayton's answer. "City government . . ."

Clayton draws a mouthful of cigar smoke and fires it at the ceiling. "Sullivan & Perelli has been quite successful. I understand they grossed seventy-eight million last year. And profits were rather evenly distributed. There's seven hundred fifty thousand cap on senior partner shares."

This intensifies the silence in the room. Hubbard, White & Willis has no such cap, which was the reason that the most-senior partners— such as Burdick and Stanley—earned 28 percent of the firm's income, and junior partners often earned less than they did as salaried associates.

"City, state, labor," Stanley says. "That's blue-collar law."

"Perelli went to Yale," Clayton counters.

Burdick, contrary as a sour schoolmarm, says, "I don't care about Perelli's academic career. You're talking about grafting a scrub pine to an oak tree."

Clayton laughs, fast and involuntarily—the sound is a sniper round he had not wished to fire at the elder partner. "We'll have plenty of opportunity to debate the merits of the merger. Right now the only issue is whether we exchange information."

A new partner at the end of the table speaks. His dialect puts him within five minutes of the Charles River. "It's not inappropriate to talk about the substance of the merger now, I think. Word is bound to get out, and you know what the press thinks about law firm mergers. In a week we'll see an article in *The National Lawyer* about the demise of Hubbard, White & Willis."

Clayton says patiently, "Some of the most respectable firms in the city have grown by merger. . . . But that's not the issue. The nondis-closure agreement will contain a complete prohibition on leaks. And if word does get out, well, so what? We've had a public-relations firm on retainer, doing nothing, for how long?" His flecked green eyes sweep toward Burdick. "When did you hire them, Donald, over a year ago? Let them earn their keep for a while."

Burdick says, dismissingly, "If you want a vote, Wendall, put it on the table. It makes no sense to me, but if two thirds are in favor of it—"

"A simple majority, Donald."

Burdick frowns, then shakes his head. A trace of confusion crosses his face. "Majority? No, Wendall, I don't think so. The issue is a merger of the law firm, and that requires a vote of two thirds."

Clayton says, "The issue—I keep explaining this—the issue isn't a merger, it's signing a simple nondisclosure agreement."

Burdick is patient. "Yes, but it's a nondisclosure whose whole point is to ascertain if a merger is practical."

A tennis match. Faces move right to left and back again, watching Clayton and Burdick volleying. The other partners are embarrassed for Burdick, with his churlish argument. They are angry at Clayton for requiring them to go on record as supporting one partner or the other in this perilous matter.

"But it is not a merger. . . ."

"It's a vote *pertaining* to a merger. . . ."

In the end, Clayton wins. Burdick grimaces, tired of the jousting, and sounds magnanimous as he says, "All right, we'll be here all day at this rate. Go ahead, make your motion. Let's vote."

Burdick had scowled, but it was a facade. He believes that Clayton is absolutely correct about the majority vote. That, however, is irrelevant to his needs at the moment, which are simply to make absolutely clear—in front of the men and women of the firm—where he stands on the merger, for the sake of the naive, the newcomers, the oblivious. This has been done, and now he will with great interest take the pulse of his influence.

As Stanley growls off names, the votes come in. Burdick sits calmly, pretending to edit a letter. He does, however, keep score in his head. The "Fors" and "Againsts" are called off, and Burdick counts them in his perfect memory. His mood goes from despairing to elated to coolly relieved. In the end, it is clear that Clayton will win this battle. But not by a strong margin. The list of traitors Stanley had shown Burdick earlier was not accurate. Clayton is strong, but not as strong as Burdick feared. He has won the preliminary vote, but does not yet have enough people in his pocket to consummate the merger.

Clayton looks at Burdick, studying his opponent from behind the Great Stone Face, the distracted precision of royalty. His gold pen dances on a pad. "I'll do a draft of the nondisclosure and circulate it. I think we should also form a committee to review the Perelli financials, and prepare a report for the firm."

There is no sense in making an issue of it, and Burdick says, "Fine, Wendall. Good idea. I think it should include our auditors and the planning committee members. Anyone else?"

Clayton shrugs.

Burdick asks, "I suppose you'd like to be included?"

"It had occurred to me."

"I think that's an excellent idea, too." Burdick smiles. "Shall we vote?"

four

"**D**imitri." Her voice was a whisper. "Don't say satin touch. Please."

"Hey, they like it," said the deep, Greek-accented voice. "They like to you know, fantasize?"

"It's embarrassing."

"It's sexy," he said.

"No, it's not."

"Yes, it is."

"The lechers go nuts, they hear that."

"Hey, so do I. You got the lights?"

She sighed and said, "Yeah, I got the lights."

From the amplifier: "Ladies and gentlemen, Miracle's Pub is pleased to bring you the silky and oh-so-smooth satin touch of Taylor Lockwood on the keys. A warm round of applause please. And don't forget to ask your waitress about the Miracle menu of exotic drinks."

Oh-so-smooth?

It wasn't a bad gig. The sullen owner of the club in the West Village figured some ambiguous blend of sex and music would sell bad food and had hired her for Tuesday nights, hers exclusively subject only to sporadic pre-emption by Dimitri's son-in-law's balalaika orchestra.

With her day job at the firm and this gig, Taylor had managed to find a schizophrenic harmony. Music was her pure sensual love; her paralegal job gave her the pleasures of intellect, organization, function. Sitting at the piano, she missed the sanity and order of the firm. In her cubicle, she found herself thinking of the freedom of music, the adrenaline of performing, the smoky lure of bars. She sometimes felt like those men with two wives and families who know nothing of the other. Maybe someday she'd get nailed, but so far the secret was safe.

Taylor was doing the bridge to "Anything Goes" when the front door swung open with its D to B-flat squeak. The woman who entered was in her midtwenties, with a round, sweet, big-sister face, framed by hair pulled back in a ponytail. She wore a sweater decorated with reindeer, black ski pants, L. L. Bean Top-Siders. She smiled nervously and waved broadly to Taylor, then stopped suddenly, afraid of disrupting the show. Taylor announced a break then sat down next to the L. L. Bean girl. "Carrie, you made it."

The young girl's eyes sparkled. "You are *so* good. I didn't know you were a musician. Where did you study, like Juilliard?"

Taylor sipped her Seagram's and soda. "Juilliard? Try Mrs. Cuikova's. A famous music school. You never heard of it? Freddy Bigelow went there. And Bunny Grundel."

"I never heard of them, either."

"Nobody has. We were all in the same grade school. We'd go to Frau Cuikova's in Glen Cove every Tuesday and Thursday at four to be abused about arpeggios and finger position. . . ." She looked at the girl's Coach attaché case. "You've got some paper there, looks like."

"I feel like a, you know, spy. This is like too weird. I'm kind of nervous about it, Taylor."

"Carrie, I wouldn't have asked if it weren't important. I would have done it myself, but I don't know the computers. Are these the door key logs?"

"Yeah."

"How do I find out who's got key number two-eleven?"

Carrie read the list. "It was checked out to attorney number eighty-five two years ago."

"And who was that?"

Carrie looked at another ream of printouts. She frowned. "Douglas Keller."

"Who's he?"

"He left about a year ago." She looked up. "They recirculate the computer keys. They cost like twenty dollars each. So when somebody leaves, they reissue them."

"Who'd this one go to?"

Carrie plowed through more green-and-white-striped computer printouts. "It was reissued in January. To Thom Sebastian."

"Sebastian." Taylor focused beyond the table. She tried to picture him. So many of the young associates looked alike. "What do you know about him?"

"He's like a true party animal. Goes out every night, dates a different girl every week. But he's a little grabby, you know. We went out once, and he couldn't keep his hands to himself."

"Is he around?"

"When I left the firm, maybe a half hour ago, he was still working. But he'll probably be going out later. I think he goes to clubs every night."

"You know where he hangs out?"

"There's a club called The Space. . . ."

Taylor said, "Sure, I've been there. Anyplace else?"

"That's the only one I know about."

"Did you bring copies of the time sheets from the Hanover & Stiver case?"

Carrie slid a thick wad of Xerox copies to Taylor, who thumbed through them and said, "God, look at the hours Reece worked. Fifteen hours in one day, sixteen hours, ten hours. It goes back a year."

"That's why I like being a corporate paralegal," Carrie said, sounding as if she devoutly meant it. "You do trial work, you could be on the same case for two years."

"Look at this. Linda Davidoff worked on the case."

Carrie said, "Wasn't that sad? I didn't go to the funeral. Were you there?"

"Yes, I was. Did you know her?"

"Not real well. She was kind of a mystery." Carrie laughed. "Like you in a way. I didn't know you were a musician. Linda was a poet. Looking back, she seems like a poet."

Taylor said, "She worked almost as much as Reece."

"He's dreamy, huh? Mitchell Reece, I mean. I flirted with him when I first started, but he wasn't interested. I felt kind of bad. Guess I'm not exactly his type."

"This is odd," Taylor said. "In July, Linda stopped working on the case. Bang. Just like that. Why would that be? She went from working eight to ten hours a day, down to nothing. Sean Lillick took over for her as paralegal."

"Sean? He's a strange boy. I think he's a musician, too. He's a little skinny, but I like him. He kind of ignores me a lot. Mitchell's cuter." Carrie played with the pearls around her neck, and her voice flattened to a gossipy hush. "I heard you were with him all day."

Taylor didn't glance up. "With who?" she asked absently, feeling her heart gallop.

"Mitchell Reece."

"How'd you hear that?" *You think there are any secrets in a law firm?*

"Just the rumor around the paralegal pen. Some of the girls were jealous. They're dying to work for him."

Who the hell saw them?

Who the hell would care?

Taylor said, "Nobody knows you have this stuff? The files?"

"No. I'm sure."

"Can I keep them?"

"Sure, they're copies."

"Where do they keep the time sheets in the firm?" Taylor asked.

"In the file room. They're filed by attorney."

"Are they locked up?"

"No."

"And the key entrance records?"

"In the computer. One of the girls can get them for you. Uh, Taylor, can you like tell me what's going on?"

"Well, there was some mix-up on the Banque Genève bill. It was kind of embarrassing. Mitchell wanted me to revise it. On the Q.T."

"I won't say a word."

Taylor put the papers into the attaché case that contained her music.

The lights dimmed.

"Got to go pay the rent," she said and climbed back under the homemade spotlight—a pineapple can painted black. A trickle charge of ambiguous fear ran through her as she began to play.

Who the hell saw us?

Who the hell cares?

She couldn't answer either question, and decided she was being paranoid. She smiled then laughed out loud, softly, when she realized the title of the tune she found herself playing, selected by some subconscious hiccup. The song was "Someone to Watch Over Me."

"You can call me Sly."

The young woman glanced at the chubby young man. His smooth baby-fat skin, the newscaster hair, the gray suit, wing tips, Cartier watch. He looked back at her: red angular dress, paisley black stockings, black hat and veil. Small breasts, he noticed, but a lot of skin was exposed.

"What?" she shouted. The music in the club was at jet-exhaust decibels.

"Sly." It was a line he used a lot. They usually laughed right away and said, "Fuck off." This one was taking her time. She watched him sending out Morse code with something in his hand, tapping it against the bar absently, while he stared at her.

Tap, tap, tap.

"I'm a lot of times mistaken for Stallone on the street. It's an embarrassment, really," he said, this young man with a swell of double chin and a belly leaning over his Tripler's alligator belt.

They were lines that he knew how to deliver. The process was like negotiating. You had to play a role, act, be somebody else. It was a shame, of course, that they didn't go all soft-eyed when he'd mention the Athletic Club or the Junior League Ball at the armory, tennis at Piping Rock (*Now, that is a turbo club for you, my darling, a turbo club.*) But he was Downtown, and you had to know your market. Right? The club was an old warehouse turned inside out; the approach was on streets worn through and cobblestoned, deserted, except for the limos and cabs pulling up to drop off the supplicants who clustered in front of the baggy-jacket doormen, who selected Those Who Might Enter with a grudging flick of finger.

Tap, tap, tap.

Mostly they'd tell him to fuck off. But then a lot of times they did what she was doing now—looking down at the telegraph key. A dark brown vial.

And then they'd say:

"Hi, I'm Veronica."

He counted seven colors on her face, and he wondered how long it had taken her to put on all that Revlon. Hours, at least. You add all that effort up, over a couple of weeks and maybe you could produced a some no-shit heavy-duty work of art. How long, he wondered, did it take Picasso to do *Guernica?*

"And what do you do, Veronica?"

"As much as I can. And how about you, Sylvester, when you're not, you know, making films?" The Brooklyn lilt in her voice saddened him immensely.

"I go by the name of Thom Sebastian, and I'm a lawyer."

The speakers, as tall as the six-foot-six, blue-gowned transvestite dancing in front of them, sent fluttering bass sound waves against their faces. The smell was a pungent mix of cigarette smoke and a gassy, ozonelike scent—the effluence of the machine that made fake fog.

Vibrant Veronica, vivacious Veronica, very available Veronica. Veronica of various talents. Veronica who'd go down on whoever filled her nose or belly.

Tap, tap, tap.

He offered his boyish grin, while she rambled on about careers— she sold clothes at an import shop in SoHo and wanted to get into modeling. Sebastian nodded and murmured single-word encourage- ments and tumbled into a soft avalanche of déjà vu. He saw the evening unfold before him, and he smiled a vibrating smile of anticipation. They'd hit the john, duck into a stall, and do a fast line or two. No nookie yet; nor would he expect any (there was a protocol of pacing). Then they would go for pasta and salad. Then back here maybe, or another club. After that, when it was pushing three A.M., he'd ask her with mock trepidation if she ever went north of Fourteenth. *I'll be your bearer, your white hunter, don't you worry, dear, the natives are restless, but I'll get you up there. God forgive me, but yes, we'll go Uptown.*

They'd grab a cab, show her the apartment, give her a fast tour. Do an alligator line. She wouldn't, however, freebase or do crack; the words alone would terrify her. They'd jockey around the sexual thing: *Your condom or mine?*

And later, after a Val or 'Lude to come down, they'd sleep. Up at eight-thirty the next morning, share the shower, take turns with the hairdryer, give her a kiss. She'd cab it home.

"Knock, knock, Veronica, very luscious. . . ."

Tap, tap, tap.

She was laughing.

". . . Little brown jug, just you and me?" He took a sip of his V&T. He said, "I never mix drugs and booze. I finish my drink first, then I do drugs."

Laughter flowing from her crimson lips.

Tap, tap, tap.

But there was some disturbance. Another incarnation of Veronica appeared. A young woman walking toward them. Different clothes; the same high solemn cheeks, pale flesh, laces, silks, a flea market's worth of costume jewelry. A waft of floral perfume. They were interchangeable. They kissed cheeks. Behind Veronica II stood a pair of quiet, preoccupied young Japanese men, hair greased and spiked high like porcupine quills. One wore a medal studded with rhinestones. Sebastian suddenly detested them not because of the impending kidnap of his new love, but for no reason he could figure out. He wanted to lean forward and ask if he'd won the medal at Iwo Jima. The foursome vanished in the mist. Veronica lifted her eyebrows with regret and a smile that belied it.

Tap, tap, tap.

"*Quo vadis,* Veronica?" Sebastian whispered, pronouncing the v's like w's the way his Latin professor in Cambridge had instructed the class.

He glanced up and saw a face in the mirror, that of a pretty woman in a black dress. She ordered a rum and Coke and impulsively said to Sebastian, "Can you save me? That woman over there? She's decided I'm her soul mate. I don't know what she wants, but I don't think it's healthy."

Instinctively he glanced across the room, then back. "Don't worry. I know something you don't."

"What's that?"

"It's not a *her,*" Sebastian said.

"No!"

"But you better sit here for a while. No telling what it has in mind."

"I'm not bothering you?"

"*Au contraire.* Cheer me up. My true love just left me."

"Mine just stood me up," she said.

His mind raced. Where did he know her from? Here? The Harvard Club? Piping Rock? He wondered if he'd slept with her, and, if he had, whether he'd enjoyed it.

She was saying, "I couldn't believe it. The bouncer wasn't going to let me in. It took all my political pull."

"Political?"

"A portrait of Alexander Hamilton." She slung out the words, and Sebastian thought he heard something akin to mockery in her voice, as if he weren't quick enough to catch the punch line.

"Gotcha," Sebastian said.

"This drink sucks. The Coke tastes moldy."

For a moment he felt offended, as if they were on a date and she was criticizing his choice of club. He sipped his own drink and wondered how to get back control.

"Look, I know I know you. You're—"

"Insulted is what I am. I thought my name was emblazoned on everyone's lips. Taylor Lockwood. Where *do* I know you from?" She squinted.

They shook hands. "Thom Sebastian." His mind made the connection. "Hubbard, White."

"Sure." She seemed moderately pleased to place him. "You ever fraternize with the paralegals?"

"Only if we blow this joint. There's nothing happening here."

The transvestite began a striptease in front of them.

"There isn't?" Taylor asked.

Sebastian smiled, took her hand, and led her through the crowd.

The man listened to the buzz of the lock as he slipped the computer key, as official-looking as a driver's license, into the metal plate beside the massive oak front door.

It was midnight. The man, who was short but solid under his gray overalls and had the bubble of a thick scar on his neck, walked casually down the halls of Hubbard, White & Willis, pushing a canvas cart ahead of him. On the side was stenciled, "AAA Drapery."

This man had been in many different offices at all hours of the day and night. Insurance companies with rows of gray desks bathed in sickly fluorescence. CEOs' offices like the finest comp suites in Vegas casinos. Hotel rooms. Even some government office buildings. But his was an industry that had like many others reached the era of specialization, and he generally now worked only in banks and investment and law firms. Hubbard, White & Willis had at first impressed him. He found it old but elegant. Jewel-like.

But now, pushing the cart through quiet corridors, he felt belittled. He sensed contempt for people like him, sensed it from the halls themselves; the way, for instance, the carpet swallowed up any sound of his steps. To these mere halls, let alone to the people who worked here, he was nothing. His neck prickled as he walked past a dark portrait of some old man. He wanted to pull out his knife and slash the canvas. He felt the eyes of powerful ghosts glance at him, snicker, then look away.

The drapery man's face was full of vessels burst in fistfights, and his muscles were dense as a bull's. If any of these scrawny pricks, hunched over stacks of books in the offices he passed (no glances, no nods, no smiles, fuck you!) if any of them challenged him, he would have been tough, and if it went farther than that, he would have been dangerous.

Eventually his anger faded, as he pushed the cart down the dark corridors, checking out the modern paintings, which he couldn't make any sense out of but which he figured were worth a bundle. He thought they'd look nice on the wall of his Florida co-op, and this cheered him, finding that he had taste that was similar to men who lived such a lavish life.

He checked names on the offices as he passed, and believed he was moving in the right direction, and had to stop only once to check the map he'd been given. He stopped once more because he had heard voices nearby. Young lawyers joking with tired voices. His hand slipped into the pocket where he kept the half-inch socket wrench that weighed a pound. He was reluctant to use it tonight, though, because he'd been instructed to avoid violence. (He had, however, considered the terse instructions, and concluded that *avoid violence* didn't mean he couldn't crush somebody's jaw if forced to.)

The voices faded, and he continued on until he found the office he sought.

Knock, knock, who's there?

Not Mr. Reece.

The drapery man clicked on the light (more incriminating to get caught with a flashlight than in a lit room), and wearing thin cotton gloves, went to work. It was hard. The drapes were heavy and the weave much thicker than he'd thought. He repeated to himself—one of his favorite private jokes—how hard it was to make a dishonest dollar.

When he was finished, he spent another three or four minutes arranging the drapes so they looked bunched up but natural. That was always the problem. Getting the cloth thick enough for concealment, but not so thick the mike wouldn't pick up the conversation throughout the room. He wished he could use a telephone mike, but this was a law firm, and attorneys' phone lines were regularly monitored for bugs.

The drapes would have to do.

He tested it. The battery would only be good for another two weeks, which he had been told was sufficient life.

He peeled off the gloves and walked out into the halls, which greeted him once again with their silence and their real, or imagined, disdain.

five

"I suffer from the fallacy of the beautiful woman."

The Lincoln Town Car limo crashed through the meat-packing district near the river. Taylor leaned sideways to hear Thom Sebastian over the crackly sound of the talk show on the driver's AM radio.

He continued, "Which is this: That because a woman is attractive, she can do no wrong. You think, Oh-my-ever-loving-Lord, the way she lights a cigarette is the right way, the restaurants she picks are the right restaurants, the way she fakes an orgasm—pardon my French —is the right way, so *I* must be doing something wrong. For instance, we're going to Meg's. You know anything about it?"

"Absolutely no idea."

"There, my point. I'm thinking, Christ almighty, I'm doing something wrong. Taylor is a primo woman, she doesn't know about this club, I've fucked up. I've got it wrong!"

Taylor smirked. "Does that usually work?"

Sebastian paused, then slouched back in the cab seat and lit a cigarette. "What?"

"That line? The one you're trying to use on me now?"

Sebastian waited a few more seconds. "You'd be surprised what you can get mileage out of. The thing is *women* suffer from the fallacy of the man who knows what he's doing. We never do, of course." He gave her what might pass for a sincere glance and said, "I like you."

They drove for ten blocks, and pulled up in front of nothing. A row of warehouses, small factories, not a streetlight in sight, only the distant aurora borealis of industrial Jersey across the Hudson, reflecting off the low clouds. Sebastian led them through an unguarded, unmarked door into what looked like a Victorian bordello. The walls were covered with dark tapestry. The tables were marble and brass. Oak columns and sideboards were draped with tooling and floral chintz. Tiffanyesque lamps were everywhere. The uniform for men was tuxedo or Italian suits. For the women, dark, close-fitted dresses with necklines that required pure willpower to keep nipples hidden. The rooms were chockablock with high-level celebs and politicos, the sort that regularly make *New York* magazine and Liz Smith.

Sebastian whispered, "Three little piggies," and pointed out a trio of young novelists that a *Times* critic had just vivisected in an article called "Id as Art: The Care and Feeding of Self-Indulgence." Emaciated, loose-dressed women hovered around the threesome. Sebastian eyed the women with dismay and said, "Why are they wasting time with those dudes? Didn't they see the article?"

Taylor said dryly, "You assume they can read." And bumped into the arm of a Hollywood actor she'd been in awe of for years. He glanced at her with a polite acknowledgment, apologized, and continued on.

"He's here." She gasped, staring at his broad back.

"Yes," Sebastian said, and sighed. "But so are we."

The music wasn't as loud as at the other club, and the pace was less frantic. Sebastian waved to some people. The bartender shouted, "Hey, Sly, how's *Rocky Sixteen* coming?"

"They don't have Guatemalan soft drinks here," Sebastian told Taylor. "It's the real stuff. Whatcha want?"

"Stick with R&C."

They sipped their drinks for a few minutes. Sebastian leaned over again and asked, "What's your biggest passion? After handsome men, I mean."

"Music and skiing."

"Skiing? Sliding down a mountain, getting wet and cold and breaking bones, is that it?"

"Breaking bones is my favorite part."

"I got some exercise once," Sebastian said, shaking his head.

She studied him in the mirror. He didn't look good. His eyes were puffy and red. He blew his nose often, and his posture was terrible. He seemed deflated as he hunched over his drink, sucking through the thin brown straw. Suddenly he straightened, slipped his arm around her shoulders, and kissed her hair. "Does anyone ever get lost in there?"

She kept the smile but didn't lean into him. She said, "The thing is, about my boyfriend. He stood me up, but he *is* a boyfriend."

"And I'm happy for him. I'd like to meet him someday. Of course, not here, not now."

"Just want the ground rules understood."

He left his arm where it was for a noncommittal sixty seconds, then dropped it. *Nolo contendere. I'm not guilty, and I'm not innocent. All rights reserved.* "This is Tuesday night, you gotta tell your honey if he's going to stand you up, he should do it on Thursdays. That is *the* night to club."

"You go out a lot?"

"Work hard and play hard. By the time I burn out at forty-five . . ." His voice faded and he was looking her way expectantly.

Tap, tap, tap.

She saw his hand swinging against the bar. A brown vial.

"You want to retire to the WC with me? I want to build a strong body twelve ways."

"Not me. I have to keep in shape for breaking bones."

He blinked, surprised. "Yeah? Okay. Excuse me for a minute."

When Sebastian returned, he was with another man, similar in appearance but thinner, shorter, a few years younger. He wore a conservative gray suit and bright red sunglasses, from which dangled a green peeper-keeper cord. Their conversation was serious, they studied the floor as they walked. Sebastian said, "Hey, Taylor, Bosk. Hey, Bosk, Taylor." They shook hands.

"Will you marry me?" Bosk asked her.

"I'm betrothed."

"Story of my life." He turned back to Sebastian. "How leveraged?"

He said, "I can come in with a hundred. You, seventy-five. We'll syndicate out the rest. I make it with fees and the commission, we'll need seven-fifty."

"That's more than we thought."

Sebastian lifted his hands in frustration and slapped them against his solid thighs. "Fine. Great."

"Sea Bass, come on. . . ."

"You got some other deal that's got a net-net this good? You got a bankrupt nursing home you want to buy from the RTC? Hey, how 'bout a nice K Mart? Such a deal—"

"Don't be such a fucking wuss."

Sebastian grinned and grabbed Bosk, swung him into a neck lock, then rapped him on the head. Bosk broke away and shouted, "You're a cow chip, you know that?"

"But I am fucking lovable, no?"

"Cow chip," Bosk said, and rearranged his sunglasses. "Now, I've been talking to Dennis about the other—"

Taylor had turned away, but she caught the fast warning that Sebastian made with his index finger.

"Later," Sebastian said.

"Uh, sure," Bosk said, recovering quickly. "Hey, come on out to the camp this Saturday? Get fed, get lit, get laid. . . . The man'll be there."

A pocket calendar appeared in Sebastian's pudgy hand. He did some mental rearranging. "Can do, dude," he said at last. They slapped palms, and Bosk vanished.

"Primo guy," Sebastian said.

"Business?" Taylor asked.

"We're doing a little deal."

"Like real estate?" Taylor asked.

He was distracted. "Yeah."

Taylor turned back to her drink. "I'd like to do some investing. But I got one problem. No money."

"Technicality," Sebastian said. "Use somebody else's. It's the only way."

"Hubbard, White lets you work on your own? Don't you have to clear it with somebody?"

Sebastian laughed, a sharp exhalation of bitterness. "We aren't on such good terms lately, Messrs. Hubbard, White and Willis and my-self." He chewed air as if words wouldn't form, then said calmly, "They passed me over for partner." His lips tightened into a bleak smile.

"I'm sorry."

"After they told me, I tried to convince myself I didn't really want to be partner. I mean, Christ, you can make more money at real estate or investment banking. I said, 'Fuck it.' Who needs them? It's just a bunch of old men. . . . Well, that's what I told myself. But t'ain't true. I wanted it bad. I'm a lawyer, not a banker. I've worked fifty, sixty hours a week for years. And this is what they do to me?"

"Did they tell you why?"

His pale jaw, round with fat, trembled. "Finances was what they said. 'Effecting economies,' if I may quote. But that wasn't the reason." He turned to her and said, "Look at me. . . ." Taylor did. He said, "What do you think my c.v. are?"

Taylor shrugged. "Phillips Exeter, Princeton, Yale . . . No, you're more Harvard Law."

"*Ve-ri-tas,*" Sebastian said sourly. "One out of three ain't too good. Harvard Law, true. But I muscled my way in, with seven-eighty on the LSAT and a three-point-seven GPA from Ohio State. And I went to St. Mark's high school. See, I don't fit the HW&W stereotype. I'm a country boy. I put myself through law school. *My* after-the-bar trip to Europe I paid for myself, and I backpacked not because it was cool, but because I had to." Sebastian blew his nose with a cocktail napkin. "I loathe self-pity," he said, "though not all the time."

Taylor said, "It *is* bullshit, though, isn't it? Just because you're not a blue blood?"

"Those things are important to Wendall."

"Wendall Clayton? What did he have to do with it?"

"I'm not one of his chosen few. Most of the partnership slots this year got filled with his boys and girls."

"But Clayton's not even on the executive committee," Taylor said.

"Ha, doesn't matter to him. He's got ten times more power than Burdick or Stanley think. He's going to ramrod the merger through."

"The merger?" she said. "That's just a rumor. It's been going around for weeks."

Sebastian looked at her, frowning at her naïveté. "Just a rumor? You think that, then you don't know Wendall Clayton. A year from now, you won't be able to recognize our firm. . . ." His voice dwindled. "Our firm. I should say, *your* firm. Ain't mine anymore."

"What's going to happen to you now?"

"They'll let me stay while I look for a new job. A year tops, I suppose."

"Then why are you working so hard?" Taylor asked, blasé, avoiding his eyes. "I mean, you're still putting in long hours. You were in last Saturday, weren't you?"

A slight hesitation. "Saturday? Me? No. I was here all night."

She frowned casually. "No, wait, I'm sure you were. I was doing some billing for, who was it? I don't remember. Anyway, I saw your key card number."

He looked at her for a long moment. His face was completely blank, but she sensed that the mechanism was grinding hard and fast. Slowly, he shook his head. "Ralph Dudley."

"Grandpa?"

"Yeah. He had my key all week. He said he found it in the library last week, and he returned it yesterday." He looked toward the men's room again. *"Excusez-moi."*

After he disappeared, Taylor motioned the bartender over to her and said, "You working last Saturday?"

He normally didn't get questions like this. He polished glasses. "Yeah."

"Was Thom in here?"

"I don't remember."

She slid the two twenties toward him furtively. He blinked. This only happened in movies, and he seemed to be considering how his favorite actor would handle it. The bills disappeared into the man's tight black jeans. "I don't think so, no. I was surprised."

"He's usually here Saturdays?"

"Clockwork."

When Sebastian returned, he took her purse and slipped it around her—over one shoulder and under the other arm—the way paranoid tourists do. "Come on. I'm wound, I'm flying like a bird. I gotta dance. . . ."

"But—"

He pulled her onto the small floor. After fifteen minutes, her hair was down, streaming in thick, sweaty tangles. Her toes were on fire, her calves ached. Sebastian kept jerking away in time to the reggae beat, eyes closed, lost in the catharsis of the motion and sound and the coke. Taylor collapsed on his shoulder. "Enough."

"I thought you were a skier."

"Exhausted." She was gasping.

His brow arched, and the surprise in his eyes was genuine. "But we haven't eaten yet."

Taylor said, "It's one A.M. I've been up for nearly twenty-four hours."

"Time for penne!"

"But—"

"Come on. One plate of darling little squigglies of pasta in *crème fraîche* with cilantro and basil, one teeny endive salad, one bottle of Mersault."

Taylor was weakening.

"*Belgium* endive!"

"I'm not that hungry."

"Okay," Sebastian the negotiator was now speaking. "How's this for a deal: We have dinner, and you can tell me about the Pine Breath Inn in Vermont or wherever the hell it is you ski, and we'll call it a night. Or I can take you home now and you'll have to fight off my frontal assault at your door. Few women have been able to resist."

"Thom—"

"I take no prisoners."

She lowered her head on his shoulder, then straightened up, smiling and resigned. "Does this place have spaghetti and meat balls with thick red sauce, à la Ragú?"

"I'll never be able to show my face there again. But if you want it, I'll force the chef to make it."

"Let me fix my makeup."

"At your leisure. The night is ours."

six

——

The alarm clock wailed like a smoke detector.

Taylor Lockwood opened one eye. Was this the worst headache of her life? She lay still for five minutes, while the votes rolled in. Maybe not. She sat up. The agony claimed its victory. She slammed her palm down on the alarm, then scooted gingerly to the edge of the bed. She still wore her pantyhose and bra; the elastic bands had cut deep purple lines into her skin, and she wondered if she would be permanently discolored. Taylor sent her tongue around her parched mouth; she didn't enjoy the trip it took, and she wove into the bathroom, where she downed two glasses of water and brushed her teeth twice. She wandered around the apartment, locating the rest of her clothes.

She squinted at the clock. Eight-thirty. Wednesday morning. *Let's see, home at three forty-five . . . We're talking about four and a half hours' sleep.*

And it hadn't been quality time.

Taylor lived in two small rooms in the Fifth Avenue Hotel, a dark, gothic building distinguished only by its address and its site as the place Judge Crater was supposedly destined for when he disappeared. Her apartment was furnished in postcollegiate—Conran's, Crate &

Barrel, Pottery Barn. A lot of fake stone Formica, black-and-white plastic. A huge pillow sofa. Canvas chairs that, looked at straight on, seemed to be grinning.

She kneaded her belly, which swelled slightly over the top of her panties. There're a hundred fifty calories in each glass of wine. . . . She squeezed her temples. Her vision swam. What a trip, being drunk in the morning. She felt a burst of hatred for wine, winemakers, vineyards, and grapes. She wondered if it were possible to keep from being sick by strength of will alone.

Okay, girl, twenty minutes to get yourself beautiful. Go for it. She rose slowly to her feet.

Sitting before Mitchell Reece was a plate of scrambled eggs, hash browns, bacon, and a bagel. Taylor was nursing a grapefruit juice and seltzer. She had lifted the same piece of dry toast to her lips three times and had not yet taken a bite.

Reece said, "You feeling okay?"

"I was out dancing last night."

"All work and no play . . ."

Taylor grunted. The juice was reviving traces of Bordeaux lurking in her bloodstream. This resuscitation was not pleasant. She frowned. "Very funny. I was with a suspect. Thom Sebastian. It was his computer key." She unsteadily took another Advil.

"Sebastian?" Reece tried to place him. "In the corporate group, right?"

"I'm not sure what to make of him. He was passed over for partner, and he's got a grudge against the firm."

"Grudge." Reece's face showed the same fatigue-dulled skin and damp red eyes that Taylor knew matched hers. Still, his suit of textured charcoal wool was perfectly pressed and his shirt was as even and white as the napkin that lay across her lap. His dark hair was combed back, slick and smooth from either a recent shower or some perfumeless lotion. He sat comfortable and upright at the table and ate heartily. "Anything else about him?"

Taylor braved the toast again and managed to eat a small piece. "He's planning some deal of his own. He was real secret about it. He claims he was in a club on Saturday, but the bartender there said he wasn't. He also claims Ralph Dudley took the computer door key."

"Old man Dudley? Impossible," Reece said quickly, then reconsidered. "Funny, though, I heard Dudley had money problems. He's borrowed against his partnership equity."

Taylor said, "How do you know?"

Reece seemed surprised at the question. "Always know the rich partners from the poor ones."

She nodded. "I'll find out if Dudley really did use the card."

"If he did, he was up to something. Dudley hasn't worked a weekend in his life. But I doubt he's our thief. He's a sweet old guy. And he's got that granddaughter of his he's looking after. Have you ever met her?"

"That cute little girl he brought to the outing last year? About fourteen or fifteen?"

"His son abandoned her, or the parents were killed, or something. Anyway, she's in a home somewhere and he takes care of her. God, having kids. I can't even think of it at my age. Let alone his."

Taylor asked, "You don't think you'd want a family?"

No, no, dear, there are times for questions like this, but now is not one of them. Get your bod out of here. Go look for your Maltese Falcon. . . .

But Reece answered, "I just haven't met anyone I wanted to have a family with. I thought I did with my wife. She wasn't so inclined. And, after all, it does take two, you know."

"I think when I hit thirty-eight—"

"A couple of decades from now . . ."

"No comment. When I hit thirty-eight, I'm going to find a genetically acceptable man, get pregnant, and send him on his way."

"You could always try marriage, of course."

"Miracles happen."

He looked at her for a moment, and he started laughing.

She asked, "What?"

"I was thinking, we should start an organization."

"What's that?"

"The Visine Club," he said, motioning to her eyes, then his.

"I can get by with six hours' sleep. Four, no way."

Reece said, "Four's pretty much standard for me." He finished the bacon and held a forkful of eggs toward her. She smiled, fought down the nausea, and shook her head. She noticed, behind the bar, a stack of wine bottles and felt her stomach twist. Reece asked, "Where you from?"

"Burbs of St. Louis. Nobody ever heard of it. Ladue."

"Sure. Used to go with a girl from University City."

"Yeah, that's closer to downtown. Nice place."

"Nasty in the summer. Humidity."

She said, "I was born on Long Island, but my parents moved. My father inherited a business in St. Louis."

"A business?"

She sipped the coffee, avoiding the question. The only significant unwanted stigma she carried from childhood was her father's career. Funeral director. *(To Taylor on Valentine's Day. I'd give you my heart, but your father can get you a fresh one.—Anonymous.)* She wanted to confide, she felt a sudden urge to look into his dark, bloodshot eyes and tell him all her secrets. But she said, "Just a mom-and-pop kind of thing."

"So how'd you end up here?"

"Came East to school—"

"Which was?"

"Dartmouth. . . . I wanted to be a famous musician."

"Musician?"

She was suddenly embarrassed. "I play piano." And felt like an idiot as she held her fingers in position and tapped the tabletop, as if she were illustrating to a foreigner who didn't speak English. "Jazz mostly."

He asked, "Who do you listen to?"

"Billy Taylor's my fave, I guess. But there's something about the fifties and sixties. Cal Tjader, Desmond, Brubeck."

Reece shook his head, and Taylor felt a pop of disappointment, but then he said, "I'm mostly into horn. Dexter Gordon, Javon Jackson."

Perfectly acceptable to me. I forgive you. She said, "I love Jabbo Smith."

He continued, "I'm a big Burrell fan."

She nodded. "Guitar? I still like Montgomery, I've got to admit. For a while I was into a Howard Roberts phase."

Reece said, "I've heard him. Too avant-garde for me."

"Oh, yeah, I hear you. A melody. You gotta have a tune. A movie's got to have a story, a piece of music's got to have a tune. . . ." She paused, realizing that she'd slipped into her musician's persona.

"You perform?"

Taylor didn't want him to see her onstage. Not yet. She said, "A little. Mostly I'm trying to get a record contract. I do some composing. I just dropped a bundle making a demo. I rented a studio, hired union backup."

"Yeah?" He seemed excited. "Give me a copy. You have an extra?"

She laughed. "I've got plenty, even after I give them away as Christmas presents this year."

"How's the response?"

"Next question?" she asked, shaking her head. "I've sent out ninety-six tapes—to agents, record companies, producers, some musicians I like. So far, I've gotten eighty-four rejections. But I did get one *maybe.* The company's going to present it to their A&R committee."

"Well, good luck."

"Luck, yeah."

The waitress asked if they wanted anything else. They shook their heads. "You women, always dieting," Reece said, eyeing her untouched toast.

We women, always trying not to throw up in front of handsome young attorneys. . . .

Taylor leaned forward and said, "There is one thing I wanted to ask you about. Linda Davidoff worked on Hanover & Stiver, right?"

"Linda? Yeah, she was my paralegal until, when was it? July or August, I guess. Just before she died."

"Well, she stopped working on the case all of a sudden."

"She got sick; didn't you hear? Maybe it was a breakdown, or something. But she died months before the note disappeared. She couldn't have anything to do with it."

"It's curious, don't you think, that someone works on a case day and night for three months, then stops, then kills herself, then the note disappears?"

Her voice faded as he extracted a folded sheet of green paper from his pocket. He slid it toward her across the table. She looked at him cautiously, then unfolded the paper. She knew what it was—today's court calendar memo. She looked at the circled Banque Genève *v.*

Hanover & Stiver, Inc. "You have a lot of choices, Taylor. You have to pick carefully. There's very little time. Twelve days." He tapped the sheet, and his gesture disturbed her. Not so much because she felt him prodding her, but because it ruined the fragile inroads into their personal lives they had made this morning. She had almost believed the two of them were on a date. The memo had bluntly opened the gate to reality; she remembered that what was just an assignment to her was the thread that Mitchell Reece's career hung by.

He touched her arm. He had a firm, warm grip. "Whatever happens, Taylor, I know I made the right choice." Their eyes held for a moment. She broke off first. He paid the check.

She said, "Maybe we could do this tomorrow. I could give you a status report. Like on a regular basis."

He shook his head. "I've got that trial tomorrow at nine." He stood up. "I've got to prep witnesses now, speaking of which . . ."

Taylor remained seated. She said, "You leave first, so no one will notice." He seemed impressed with this bit of espionage.

"Call me or stop by if you want to talk," he said.

"You think it's safe?"

"Positively. Last week I had my office swept for bugs."

Taylor Lockwood sat in her cubicle in Halsted Street and dialed a number. She let the telephone ring ten times. When the system shifted the call over to the main switchboard, she hung up, left her desk, and wandered down the halls casually, like a teenager window-shopping. Up a flight of stairs, she turned down a corridor that led past the lunchroom, then the forms room, where copies of prototype contracts and pleadings were filed. At the end was a single office, one smaller than most in the firm. Inside were crammed an Italian Renaissance desk, a tall bookcase, two shabby leather chairs, prints of nineteenth-century sailing ships and eighteenth-century fox hunts. Through a small window you could see a brick wall and a sliver of the harbor. On the desk rested a large brass ashtray, a picture of a little girl in an oval frame, a dozen Metropolitan Opera *Playbills,* a datebook, and one law book—a *Supreme Court Reporter.*

Taylor Lockwood opened the book and bent over it. Her eyes,

though, camouflaged by her fallen hair, were not reading the twin columns of type, but rather Ralph Dudley's scuffed leather datebook, opened to the present week. She noticed *W.S.* penned into the box of Saturday evening, the night the note disappeared. She flipped through the pages of the diary. The same letters appeared once or twice a week. They were also written in the ten P.M. slot for Friday of this week. She turned to the address portion of the calendar. There was no one listed with those initials.

"Can I help you?"

Taylor forced herself not to jump. She kept her finger on the *Reporter* to mark her spot and looked up slowly.

A young man she didn't recognize stood in the doorway. Blond, scrubbed, chubby. And peeved.

"Ralph had this *Reporter* checked out," she said, hearing each word shake with a beat of her heart. "I needed it. Who're you?"

"Todd Stanton. I work for Mr. Dudley." He squinted. "You're an attorney?"

"I'm Taylor Lockwood. A paralegal." She forced indignation into her voice.

"Oh. A paralegal." The timbre was dismissing. "Does he know you're here?"

"No."

"If you need anything, you can ask me for it. Mr. Dudley doesn't like"—he sought the least disparaging term—"people he doesn't work with in his office when he's not here."

Taylor turned back to the book and finished reading a long paragraph. Stanton shifted, then said with irritation, "Excuse me. . . ."

Taylor closed the book softly and walked out the door. "Okay," she said, passing him without a glance, "you're excused."

He was, before anything else, a gentleman.

For instance, Ralph Dudley rarely left his apartment on East Seventy-second Street without wearing a tie, and this was true whether he was heading for a stroll through the park or to a local discount drugstore or to a function at the Carlyle. He never reflected on whether or not he *should* wear a tie. He merely selected one and put it on. The same unquestioning habit that made him polish his shoes every Sunday and organize his cuff links and buy no more than three days' worth of bread at a time.

Gentlemen wore ties.

And in the office, they wore dark suits and white shirts and socks with calf garters. They carried attaché cases, not shoulder bags, and if they smoked, they lit their cigarettes with sterling silver lighters, not disposable plastic ones, and never let the ash grow more than a quarter inch long.

Ralph Dudley was sixty-three. Thin and tall, he stood with military posture, and kept what little was left of his white hair brushed back straight with Brylcreem.

That Wednesday afternoon he was sitting not in Hubbard, White & Willis, but in another law firm, in Midtown. He was looking across the table at men he knew were not gentlemen.

He felt the advantage; he smiled.

These three men were lawyers, but they were also something else. They were thugs.

Moreover, they were thugs of a particular derivation. As a gentleman, Ralph Dudley would never in public comment upon anyone's religion or ethnicity. But he had noted, and had not forgotten, that they were members of a firm whose names ended in the suffixes *-ein* and *-itz*.

"Ralph," one of them said, "it's probably as plain as the nose on my face, but *why* can't your client just let us have this one point? A small concession. It's not unreasonable."

Dudley frowned. "I tried, Sol, I did. I talked all night. But my client simply isn't agreeing. We've given you A, we've given you B. We aren't giving you C. That's what he said."

They scowled and sat back. In their thugs' hearts, they were frustrated, confused, angry. In their thugs' eyes, Dudley was naive, foolish, uninformed.

In fact Dudley had absolutely no idea why they could not or should not have what they wanted. It had something to do with tax recapture, a concept he had tried to understand, but simply gave up on as too complicated. His associate from Hubbard, White—the boy who had actually put together the whole deal—had explained to him that if they agreed to what the thugs wanted, Dudley's client would lose some major write-off, although one it wasn't entitled to.

"We've got to talk about this, Ralph," one thug said.

Which was the last thing Ralph Dudley wanted. He simply could not discuss it. If he had tried, they would have understood immediately that they were correct: He *was* naive and foolish and completely uninformed.

"Where is that boy?" Dudley looked at the door. His young associate, the one who could talk quite articulately and annoyingly about the tax issue, had left ten minutes before to call the office.

"Ralph, this is fucking frustrating. . . ."

Dudley quashed a frown. (*A gentleman speaks in a gentlemanly manner.*)

"We've spent a month on this deal."

And Dudley, whose attention had been riveted solely on the pacing of the conversation, was very pleased that this comment occurred at this moment. He uncrossed his legs, leaned forward, and refilled everyone's coffee cup, carefully pouring from a silver pot. "A month's nothing! I was talking to a friend of mine at Abbott, Miller. . . ."

Dudley sensed one of the thugs, the head thug, the ringleader, turning to him. "Who do you know there?"

"Phil Abbott."

The thug laughed. "You know Phil?"

"We play cards at his club. I spent a lot of time with him after his wife passed away."

"Phil's my mother's cousin."

"No!" Dudley appeared delighted. "What a small world. Nice man. Sharp as a firecracker, too. So you're related?"

"Sure, he was always over to the house in Brooklyn."

Dudley said, "We had lunch, let's see, just last Friday, after Thanksgiving. He's gotten over Gertie's death well, I think. When Emma died, that was my wife, I got to know him pretty well. Just after Gertie passed away, we'd spend hours, oh, my, hours and hours talking."

"He really loved her." The thug was watching Dudley closely, his eyes roaming up and down across his face. "They fought, you know, but sometimes that's a part of love."

"I'm my granddaughter's guardian. I tell you, bringing up a child is what teaches you about love. Sometimes it's heaven, sometimes it's a battle. Phil told me about the children he used to play with. Maybe you were one of them."

"Yeah, I was. Sure, Uncle Phil we called him. You can't really call him cousin. He was, what would it be?, twenty years older. Yeah, we used to play all the time. I remember one Passover, when Elijah is supposed to come and drink the wine—kind of like Santa Claus drinking the milk the kids left—he'd rig up these great effects with fishing line. So we'd be sitting at the table, and there'd be this noise in one room and we kids run in there, and he'd get up, drink the wine, and sit down before we raced back. He got us good there. Sweet old man."

"Salt of the earth," Dudley said, looking around. "Now where is that boy of mine? . . . So what were we discussing? Just that one tax point?"

The head thug sighed and glanced at his lieutenant thug, who motioned with irritation at his heavy Rolex. The head thug said in a conspiratorial voice, "Ralph, okay, tell you what, you want the tax provision out, it's out. I can talk my people into it. We've diddled around enough on this deal."

"Well, that's good of you, Sol."

"We talk the same language. You sure there're no surprises in the woodpile, Ralph? You're sure you're *goyim?*"

"Well, if not, the archbishop of Canterbury's having a good laugh, since I've been putting envelopes in his basket for fifty years."

"What's the difference between a reform Jew and an Episcopalian?"

"What's that?"

"About a quarter inch."

The thugs laughed.

Dudley closed his eyes with a smile and rocked back in his chair. Was this supposed to be funny? What did he mean? Was it a reference to being circumcised? It was certainly not a gentleman's joke. Dudley looked at his watch. "Oh, I'm afraid I've got to get going. I'll track down that young man and send him right in so you can finish the nits."

Outside the conference room, he found the associate leaning against the wall, sipping coffee.

"We got it," Dudley said, pulling on his overcoat and setting his gray felt hat on his head.

The associate blinked in astonishment and said, "Ralph, you got them to take out the recapture clause?"

"I'm sorry I kept you waiting this long," Dudley apologized. "Can you go in there and finish up?"

"There was no way they'd agree to it. How'd you do it?"

"The law is logic," Dudley answered solemnly. "Never forget that." And he touched the brim of his hat as an attractive young woman walked past.

seven

"Month of Sundays since I heard from you," Willy Lansdowne said. The tall, muscular black man hopped off his unicycle and bent down to kiss Taylor Lockwood on the cheek, studying her eyes. "Wassup? You got man problems?"

"Do not," Taylor said fast.

Lansdowne frowned at the barren outdoor café of Dobro's restaurant on St. Mark's Place. They walked inside, and he asked the waitress, "You closed up outside? Can't we sit there?"

"It's November," she snapped.

"It's Wednesday, November 27, which in numerology combines to nine, an extremely significant number."

The waitress led them to an inside table, dropped menus on the tabletop and disappeared.

"Ah," he said.

To Taylor Lockwood, Willy Lansdowne was an Influential Person. Not the sort who have connections in business or City Hall, but the more important kind, the ones who take a fast look at your life and know with absolute, instantaneous certainty what you ought to be doing with it.

Lansdowne wore a Walkman headset everywhere and guided his

life by music the way Caesar relied on entrails. He had the most fun of anyone Taylor had ever known. Whatever he did, he would enjoy, lying in the sun, bicycling against traffic on Sixth Avenue, playing gigs on odd, hairy musical instruments and erotically shaped pipes (a master *berimbau* player), working restaurants, practicing the Latin American dance like martial art of *capoeira*. Sleeping he enjoyed. Walking, eating.

He read books she had never heard of—*The European Roots of Reconstructionist Politics. The Social History of Dining. Mixolydian Modality as Symbol in Greek Culture.*

("Willy, you don't really read that stuff, do you?"

"Shit, Taylor, gotta read it, ain't no pictures.")

After she had been in New York a while, several people had told her that having an intellectual black friend was very chic. She had quickly recognized this as a bit of misogyny when she realized that both Lansdowne and she belonged to a raceless class of New Yorkers. Not in some sappy sixties greeting card way, but in a more important sense. Taylor Lockwood understood that Willy Lansdowne was a person —just like her—who had every opportunity to be someone with a Tradition, yet was not. Lansdowne was smart, so he'd have picked up right away how far he'd go with the North Carolina affluent business-man persona that could have kicked white ass to hell and gone on Madison Avenue or Wall Street. But for obscure reasons, both Willy Lansdowne and Taylor Lockwood had jettisoned the past and plowed into New York as if the liner had missed Ellis Island completely and beached in Greenwich Village.

Willy Lansdowne was a corporeal spirit guide, a person she lis-tened to, and she was particularly receptive to his cosmic prescriptions, especially so one afternoon three years ago. She had then been in the city for six months, was selling women's shoes at Macy's, and was as broke and depressed as she had ever been in her life. Walking home along Tenth Street after a Wednesday Super Sale, she had heard the double squeal of Lansdowne's navel-high ten-speed as it braked to a crawl beside her.

"Hey, heard you play teeth."

"What?"

He mimed a piano player. "Keyboard, dig?"

"Sorta."

"Whatcha mean? You play or not?"

"I play."

"Where you gigging now?"

"No work." She shrugged.

"No, no, no. What's your day job?"

"Macy's."

"Oooo," he said with a moan, making a face. "Uh-huh, love. Don't want to do that. Lissen up. Here's what you're going to do."

A notebook appeared, then a pen that wrote in gold ink. "Call *this* man 'bout a job. *This* one's got a gig. Don't get 'em mixed up. Keep the left hand and right hand separate. Fret players don't have that problem; you play keys so you got to watch it, hear me?" He handed her two slips of paper.

He sounded so certain and confident, she said "Okay" before she asked, "Who are these guys?"

"One teaches a paralegal course. Pay a couple hundred, but you come out earning good bread. Dignity, you know. Be important. The other one's a club, tell him I recommended you. He'll let you play some shit night. Wednesday, probably. But be better than nothing. You can move up the ladder you any good."

"Willy . . ." Tears welled.

"Hey, when you rich and famous and got your own recording company, you just 'member Mr. L."

The audition lasted two measures and got her the job. The paralegal course took three months, and when she got her certificate (which looked like a refrigerator warranty), she landed work in a big Midtown law firm. She moved to Hubbard, White & Willis a year after that. She'd been there ever since.

Lansdowne dropped into and out of her life that way. She wouldn't hear from him for six months, then he'd reappear and it was as if they were carrying on yesterday's conversation.

Today, sitting in Dobro's, he said, "Now, 'bout men, what stories you be telling me?" Lansdowne stretched out his long elegant legs, encased in startlingly blue biking shorts.

Taylor said, "Well, maybe everything isn't too copacetic, but that's not what I've got to ask you about." The waitress hovered long enough to take their orders, then wove her way through tables of earnest and sleepy artists who hunched over afternoon breakfasts of eggs or chili.

Lansdowne told her that after Christmas he was taking three months off to travel through India and Nepal.

She said, "Not a bad little vacation. Which lottery was it?"

"Green?" he laughed. "You still worried about the green? It work out. Somehow, you don't worry, it work out." And he told her about his new sleeping bag, which weighed three pounds.

His eyes shone when the waitress brought the salad. "Oh, you got some of those little brown breadsticks with the seeds on them? The ones that look like little fingers?"

The waitress sighed and went to find them.

"I love those little breadsticks."

For five minutes he ate with unrestrained devotion, subdividing his salad, organizing it, and eating the bits slowly. He asked for more butter, breadsticks, salad dressing, and hot peppers. ("Sinuses, dig?") Then he looked at Taylor. "So, it isn't men, what is it?"

"You worked for a security company, didn't you?"

"I was a guard, yeah. It was a kick. I carried around this big billy club. What you do is you hang it from a steel guitar string, take a, say, B or high E, and tap it with drumsticks or a spoon. Man, what a sound. . . ."

"You know somebody there I can talk to?"

"What kind of problem you *got?*" He looked concerned.

"I just want to learn a thing or two about the business. Discreetly, you know."

Lansdowne said, "Know a guy you might rap with for a while. John Three Names. Yeah, he's okay."

"What is he, an Indian?"

"That's what I call him. His real name is John Silbert Hemming. Man's in the clouds. . . . Wait'll you meet him. In the clouds, I'm saying. Most of those security dudes, they're ex-cops or FBI. Deficient in the humor department. And their minds, they're always someplace else, like they're worrying about a pot on a burner somewhere, you dig? But John Three Names, he's okay. I'll make the call, tell him you're real people."

"Great, Willy."

"So what's with the man problems? Tell me all about it."

"Oh, you don't want to know."

"You still with Gary?"

"Nope."

"You got somebody in the wings?"

"Nope."

"You wanta become a nun and forget the whole thing?"

"You got it."

For the fifth time that day, Ralph Dudley thought about the merger of the law firms.

The exhilaration of the day's victory at the House of Thugs had vanished. He sat sullen and agitated on a bench in Central Park, which was warmed to sixty degrees by a renegade southern breeze. Dudley's long index finger and knobby thumb rose to his face, and he gripped a pinch of soft skin beside his mouth. He rolled it absently, feeling both the satisfaction from a careful job of shaving that morning, and the despair of self-knowledge.

This awareness was not news to him, yet it tended not to surface except at moments like this. The knowledge was this: He liked the *idea* of law more than the actual practice of it. When he considered the profession, he did so in a glowing romantic light. He said that he had "read the law" in Michigan, using the term that nineteenth-century lawyers used to describe legal studying. He liked phrases like *force majeure* and *laches* and *res ipsa loquitur.* On one of his many trips to London, he had sat outside Grey's Inn and read a book about Francis Bacon, coming close to tears at the part where the high chancellor was ousted for taking bribes.

Dudley liked the law of the old days, the days before it became big business, before it became so excruciatingly complex. Before computers and disk readers and fax machines. Even his desk telephone with its dozens of incomprehensible controls intimidated him.

Long ago.

Before mergers.

Before men like Wendall Clayton.

Dudley was scared of Clayton, who was a thoroughly coarse thug. He believed that Clayton had the power to force the merger through, a virtual rape, which Dudley believed would have cataclysmic results. What disturbed him most about the merger was not the shattering of the Hubbard, White & Willis tradition, which was sorrowful enough to him, but the impact of the merger on two people. Himself, and the girl he now watched sail along the sidewalk on Rollerblades.

She was fifteen, tall, pretty, though she wore too much makeup and her eyes would narrow in a cool way that made the word "pretty" inaccurate. Coldness is compatible with beauty, not with prettiness, and Junie had moments of great coldness.

Ralph Dudley knew, without a doubt, that if the merger occurred, he would lose his job. Dudley knew this because although he felt almost tearfully emotional about the law, although he could recite Latin phrases as if he were a classics professor, although he could charm even the most insufferable thugs, he was not a good lawyer. Indeed, he was perhaps the most unemployable attorney in the city of New York. His talents were nebulous and nonnegotiable—his ability to spin a good yarn, for instance—and they had no value in the world of late-twentieth-century Wall Street law.

Dudley's financial equity in the firm partnership was heavily borrowed against, and he did so little direct work for clients that he never received more than the modest draw that was for most partners at Hubbard, White just a starting point that they quickly soared beyond. Nor did he have enough cash to take advantage of the real-estate investments and limited partnerships that the clients were always offering partners. To lose his job now would mean disaster. His savings account would vanish in a month or two, and life as he had lived it for thirty years would disintegrate before his eyes.

He sat on a park bench that was unevenly thick with dark green paint and felt the slats of wood against his spine. He felt, too, the encroaching sense of doom that inevitably threatens people like him—those who, mostly through luck, have found a series of narrow toeholds in the world's epicenter of power and prestige.

That delicate life was threatened.

He watched Junie stare down a boy her age—shorter, but heavy and bully-browed. The boy stalked off.

Oh, for the brashness, for the clarity, for the invulnerability of children, for their courage, which is as boundless as they need it to be. . . .

Dudley was suddenly cold. He stood up. Junie saw him, and she skated slowly to his side.

·   ·   ·

"Dactyloscopy," the man said. *"Répétez après moi:* dactyloscopy."

Taylor did.

"Good," he said. "Now you know the first thing about finger-printing. It's called dactyloscopy. The second is that it is a royal pain in the butt."

She sat in the office of John Silbert Hemming. His card explained that he was director of Corporate Security Services at Manhattan Allied Security, Inc. When he'd come to meet her in the reception area, she blinked and looked up. Hemming was six-feet-eleven ("In the clouds," Willy had said). His height had led, he had explained on their way back to his office, to his becoming a backroom security man—the company technical expert.

"You've got to be unobtrusive in private detective work. A lot of what we do is follow people."

Taylor said, "Tailing."

"Pardon?"

"Don't you say tailing? You know, like you tail somebody?"

"No, we say 'following.' "

"Oh."

"If you stand out like me, that's not so good. When we recruit, we have a space on our evaluation form that says 'Ordinary?' We mean 'boring.' "

His hair was sandy and unruly and Taylor's impression of Hemming was that he was a huge little boy. He had eyes that seemed perpetually amused and belied a face that was dramatically long—what else, given that it was atop a body like his? She supposed he was attractive, but lately, against her better judgment, she'd been comparing all men with Mitchell Reece; the result here was no contest.

When she had arrived, Taylor looked around the halls of the Midtown office building, disappointed. "I expected more. I don't know, Bogie, Raymond Chandler."

"What? We look like a, forgive the expression, business?" Hemming had looked down at her. "You expected dark oak, bumpy glass partitions, and trench coats. A fifth of scotch in the drawer . . . Wait, wait!" Hemming had dug into his desk. "Best I can do." He set a bottle of mineral water on the desktop. "Times have changed, Miss Lock-wood."

"Taylor."

He nodded. "We do about ten million dollars a year. Our investigators are mostly ex-police or -FBI, accountants, former lawyers. I have a law degree. We mostly work for corporations, and a lot of our work is very technical. Auditing, uncovering insider trading leaks, embezzlements, theft, cocaine use or dealing. Gathering information for takeovers or proxy fights. You know, of course, that the police don't have much more authority than anyone else."

"Of course."

"A citizen can make an arrest that's just as valid as a policeman's. We're in the midst of a big sting operation that's identical to Abscam. Some employees of a big ad agency are taking kickbacks, and we're trying to find out who and how long it's been going on. Half our people have carry permits."

"Carry?"

"Guns."

That was when he'd paused for a sip of Perrier, and she had said, "Tell me everything you know about fingerprinting." He'd fired back with, "Dactyloscopy."

Now, John Silbert Hemming was aiming a startlingly long finger at her and saying, "I hope you mean that, about wanting to know everything. Because there's a lot, and here it comes. Let's start with: What are fingerprints?"

"Uh—"

"I know. *You* paid the money, *I've* got the answers. But I like people to participate, I like interaction. Time's up. No idea? Okay, fingerprints are the impressions left by the papillary ridges of the fingers and thumb, primarily in perspiration. There are no sebaceous glands in the fingertips themselves, but people sometimes leave fingerprints in human oils picked up elsewhere on the body. Yes, in answer to the first most-often-asked question, they are all different. Even more different than snowflakes, because for hundreds of years people have been collecting fingerprints all over the world and comparing them, and nobody—none of my close friends, I'll tell you—have been doing that with snowflakes. Go ahead ask the next most popular question."

"Uh, do animals have fingerprints?"

"Primates do, but who cares? That's not the question. The question is twins."

"Twins?"

"And the answer is that twins, quadruplets, duodeceplets—they all have different fingerprints. Now, who first discovered fingerprints?"

"I have a feeling you're going to tell me?"

"Guess."

"Scotland Yard," Taylor offered.

"Prehistoric tribes in France were aware of fingerprints and used them as cave decorations. In the sixteen and seventeen hundreds they were used as graphic designs and trademarks, and the first attempt to study them seriously was in 1823—Dr. J. E. Purkinje, an anatomy professor, came up with a crude classification system. Fingerprints became sexy in the late 1800s. Sir Francis Galton, who was a preeminent scholar in the field of . . ." He cocked his eyebrows at Taylor.

"Dactyloscopy?"

". . . the field of heredity, established that all fingerprints are different, and they never change throughout one's life. The British government appointed Edward Richard Henry to a commission to consider using fingerprints to identify criminals. Around the turn of the century, Henry had created the basic classification system they use in most countries, except for Latin America. His system is called, coincidentally, the Henry system. Over here, New York was the first state to start fingerprinting all prisoners. Around 1902."

When he came up for air, she asked, "If one were going to look for fingerprints, how would one do it?"

"One?" he asked coyly. *"One?* Well, it depends on the surface. You, excuse me, *one* should wear cloth gloves—not latex. If the surface is light-colored, you use a carbon-based dark powder. On dark, one would use an aluminum and chalk mixture. It's light gray. One would dust on the powder with a very soft, long-bristle brush. Then one removes the excess—"

"How?"

"Flip a coin," the detective said.

"One blows it off?"

"A lot of rookies think that. You spit and ruin the whole print. Use a brush. Now, powders only work on smooth surfaces. If you've got to take a print from paper, there are different techniques. If the print's oily, maybe it will show up in iodine vapor. The problem is that you have to expose it in an enclosed cabinet and take a picture of the print very quickly because the vapors evaporate right away. Sometimes latents come out with a nitrate solution or ninhydrin.

"Once you've got the print, you've got to capture it. That's where a lot of people screw up. You lift it off the surface with special tape, or else take a picture of it. Remember: Fingerprints are *evidence.* They have to get into the courtroom and in front of an expert witness."

John Silbert Hemming paused, then frowned and said, "when you say fingerprints, do you mean *fingerprints?*"

"I believe that's what I mean," Taylor said.

"Not genetic marker testing?"

"I think I mean fingerprints."

"Wonderful." He seemed pleased.

"Could someone like me take fingerprints?"

"If you practiced. But could you *testify* that prints A and B were the same? No way. Could you even *tell* if they were? Not easy, mama, not at all. They squoosh out, they move, they splot. They look different when they're the same, they're identical except for some little difference you miss. . . . No, it isn't easy. Fingerprinting is an art."

"Can you use a machine, or something? A computer?"

"Sure. It's all becoming automated now. The buzzword is AFIS—Automated Fingerprint Identification System. We're looking into one here. A laser scans fingerprints and stores the data digitally. The advantage is not only speed, but also accuracy. When you look at fingerprints, you'll see maybe seventy-five different minutia points—that's where the ridges branch off. You have to identify those points clearly to make an ID. The scanners can do it much better than rolled inkprints."

"I don't suppose I could rent one of those?"

"They cost a few million. But maybe if you told me exactly what your problem is, I could offer some solutions."

"It's somewhat sensitive."

"It always is. That's why companies like us exist."

"I do have one question."

The hand in which a basketball would look so at home rose. "Allow me to deduce. The inquiry is: Where you can get a Dick Tracy fingerprint kit?" Before she answered, he was writing an address on the back of his business card. "It's a police equipment supply house. You can buy anything but weapons and shields there."

"Thanks." She stood, looked at a glass case containing a collection of blackjacks and saps.

"Oh, and Miss Lockwood? Taylor?"

"Yes?"

"Before you leave, I was just wondering: Would you like to hear the lecture I give to our new employees on the laws against breaking and entering, and invading privacy?"

Taylor said, "No, I think I'd rather not hear that."

"What hurt the most, isn't this absurd, but what hurt the most were the portraits."

Donald Burdick knotted the silk tie carefully with his long fingers. He liked the feel of good cloth, the way it yielded yet was tough. Tonight the smooth texture gave him little pleasure.

"The portraits?" Vera Burdick sat at her dressing table in the bedroom of their Bronxville home, rubbing prescription retin-A cream on her neck. She wore a red and black silk dress, which revealed pale freckled skin along the unzipped V in the back. She was leaning forward studiously, watching the cream disappear. A handsome woman, in her early sixties, she had battled age by making tactical concessions. She gave up tanning fifteen years ago, and carefully gained weight, refusing to diet with the obsession of many of her friends, who were now knobby scarecrows. She let her hair go white, but she kept it shiny with Italian conditioner and wore it pulled back in the same style as her granddaughter. She allowed herself one face-lift.

(Just one year ago she had been propositioned for an afternoon quickie by one of her husband's clients. True, he was a man of seventy-four, but his sly wink and disappointment at her refusal thrilled her— more than the act ever could.)

Vera Burdick was now as she had always been: attractive, reserve, stubborn, quiet. She was pictured best in khaki, standing next to her husband on one of his beloved wildlife safaris, reloading the second Nikon for him.

Burdick sat on the bed. His wife offered her back, and he carefully zipped up the dress and hooked the top eyelet.

"You were saying, the portraits, dear?"

"At the meeting, when the firm voted to start formal merger negotiations with Perelli, they also voted to move the portraits of the partners downstairs into one of the conference rooms."

"Wendall Clayton's idea?"

Burdick laughed. "No. He's not completely evil. Joe Hanson— he's head of the decor committee—suggested it, and everybody agreed."

"Darling, what difference does it make?"

"No difference at all. It means nothing. I'm just telling you what was the most galling part of the meeting. It was my idea to put the portraits in the front corridor twenty years ago."

She took his hand. "Don . . ."

"Let's not have the discussion again." They never fought, and he said the words softly, chiding.

"You'll be retiring in four or five years anyway."

"Are we having the discussion again?"

"Yes," Vera said, "we are."

He walked to the dressing room telephone and called the maid, asked her to bring two scotches upstairs.

Vera said, "There's a time when you have to let go."

He sat with his hands clasped before him, head bowed. "Conceded."

"You're still working ten-hour days. You don't give enough work to associates—"

"I like what I do."

"—and you're no longer thirty-five."

"Also conceded."

"So what difference does it make? We can travel more. You've put off Tibet for five years now. You've been afraid to go someplace that doesn't have a telephone."

The maid brought the drinks. Burdick rose and took his. He walked to the window, looking out on the windswept grounds. Leaves had been raked that afternoon, but the grass was littered again with speckled brown and yellow curls.

"I've spent my whole life there, my whole professional life."

"You sound like an addict."

Burdick said, "Well, I *am* addicted, I suppose. You give so much to something. You create it, then someone wants to take it away from you. . . ."

"Well, if you ask me, you're more excited about the fight than anything else."

He looked at her for a moment, then smiled in a coy, hand-in-the-cookie-jar way. "I like a good fight, yes, I do. But I don't want this one. There will be a time to leave. Soon, maybe. I've thought a lot about retiring, you know that."

"I have the feeling if Wendall stopped the merger talks, you'd say fine, and the next day announce your retirement."

Outside the handyman padlocked the doors of the Tudor work-shed and yanked hard on the lock to test it. Burdick turned from the window. "No one is going to force me out of my own firm. Certainly not Wendall Clayton."

"Wendall's a good lawyer, he'd die for his clients. You've said that yourself."

"Let him be a good lawyer someplace else. He's crude, he fights dirty. He has affairs."

"That's—what do you lawyers say?—not relevant." She began on her makeup, glancing at him as he spoke.

"But Vera, it *is* relevant. I'm talking about the survival of the firm. Wendall does not have vision. He does not understand what Hubbard, White is, what it should be."

"And how do you define *should be?*"

Touché. She had him. Vera always had him. He grinned involuntarily. "All right, what *I've* made it. Bill Stanley and the others and I. Wendall wants to turn the firm into a mill. Into a big merger and acquisition house."

"Every generation has its own specialties."

"If Clayton has his way, the firm'll be going head-on against some of the biggest, toughest firms in the city. Firms three or four times larger. We'll put two partners and two associates on the deal, they'll put six partners and twenty associates to work. Hubbard, White has defended *one* hostile takeover. And it was the Justice Department that saved us, not any fancy lawyering on our part. What if Skadden, Arps is on the other side? They'll hoist us by our own petard."

"Are you sure you're not just looking at it from the nineteenth century?"

"Yes. Yes, I *am* sure."

Vera finished her makeup and brushed her hair, glancing at her husband in the three-paneled mirror. She set her hairbrush down. "I don't think I've ever seen you this riled, dear."

"The man's trying to kill my child. I'm not going to let him."

Vera took a sip of scotch and set the crystal glass down on the table. Burdick's eyes were distant, but hers were coalesced into dark dots. "Then you have to stop him." She rose and took the coat brush, ran it evenly over the built-up shoulders of his suit jacket. "The only thing is, dear . . . if your mind is made up, so be it. But let me offer an observation. If I were you, I wouldn't be too"—she paused, considering her euphemisms—"hesitant."

"Hesitant?"

She said, "With a man like Wendall, you have to hit him hard the first time. You won't have a second chance."

The doorbell rang.

"Oh, no," she said. "They're on time. And I have to see what Margaret's done to the pheasant." She kissed his cheek and whispered to him, "Hard, very hard."

Donald Burdick finished his scotch and listened to her footsteps recede down the stairs. She would run interference, he knew, give him a chance to brush his hair, to relax, to think up a few jokes, to compose himself and assume his most charming persona.

The guests were, after all, clients.

eight

Taylor Lockwood, undertaker's daughter, walked through breezy evening city streets whose curbs were banked with trash, and remembered a funeral several months earlier.

She'd sat in the front pew of the church, a woody and stone building funded, someone behind her had whispered, by old tycoon money. Although Taylor was in black, that color did not seem to be requisite at funerals any longer; any somber shade was acceptable—purple, forest green, even dusk-brown tapestry. She sat in this hard pew, and watched the family members in their unambiguous, unself-conscious rituals of grief, tears running in halting streams, hands shielding eyes, hands squeezing hands, fingers rubbing obsessively against fingers.

The minister had spoken with cribbed familiarity. He knew the parents better than Linda, that was clear, but he was eulogizing well. The rhetoric of kindness and hope. She saw the father, legs apart, hands together, head tilted down, eyes fixed on the communion kneeling stoop.

Not everyone had cried; suicide makes for an encumbered mourning.

There'd been a singer, an opera student. "Ave Maria." Taylor had resented the choice. The piece would be spoiled for her for years.

The minister had closed the service with one of Linda's poems, one published in her college literary magazine.

As he'd read, and he read very well, images of Linda had returned, and the tears that Taylor Lockwood had told herself not to cry appeared fast, stinging the corners of her eyes and running with maddening tickles down her cheeks. Then the organ had played a solemn cue, and the mourners had filed outside for the drive to the interment. Taylor had waited until the pain in her chest diminished, her breathing calmed, then wiped her face and worked away the smeared makeup.

Outside, she stood for a moment, looking at the clear September sky, the leaves not yet colorful but stripped of the rich gloss of high-summer green, surrounded by the prim, moneyed rurality of southern Connecticut. Then, all at once engines had started up, car lights clicked on, and drivers edged forward in anticipation of the sleek hearse.

Forget about Linda, Reece had implicitly said. *Too much of a long shot.* Yet Taylor could not. She wondered why. Perhaps because she sensed this was advice he himself would not have taken. He would not have held back. He would have followed every lead. Taylor wanted to be like this.

Tonight, making her way through the scrubby East Village, a shrill wind caught her, flipping dust into her face. She blinked. In thinking about Linda, she had missed the address she was seeking and had to double back to the scabby tenement. In the foul entry foyer, the intercom had been ripped out, but the front door was open, swinging in the breeze like a batwing door in a ghost town saloon. She started up the filthy steps.

"Sure, but the bank owns most of it," Sean Lillick said. He was sitting on the floor, looking for a clean sock. Taylor Lockwood, catching her breath from the climb up, was surveying a wall of keyboards, wires, boxes, a battered computer terminal, speakers.

A lot of wires. She could see mostly wires.

Lillick—a thin, dark-haired young man of about twenty-four— was smelling socks, discarding them. He was in black jeans, a sleeveless

T-shirt. His boots sat in front of him. The only clue as to his day job were two suits and three white shirts, in various stages of recycling, hanging on nails pounded crookedly into the wall. He studied her for a moment. "You look impressed or confused. I can't tell."

"Your place is a little more alternative than I expected." The apartment was a patchwork. Someone had nailed pieces of plywood, plastic, sheet metal over cracks and holes. Joints didn't meet, plaster was rotting, floorboards were cracked or missing. In the living room: one hanging bare bulb, one floor lamp, one daybed, one desk. And a ton of wires.

Lillick found a sock that passed the test and pulled it on.

"Have a seat."

She looked helplessly about her.

"Oh. Well, try the daybed."

"Daybed?" she asked. It was a mattress on top of plastic milk crates. She sat on the sagging platform.

"Hey, Taylor, listen to this. I just thought it up. I'm going to use it in one of my performance pieces: You know what a preppie is?"

"I give up."

"A yuppie with papers."

She smiled politely. He didn't seem concerned about the tepid response and wrote the line down in a notebook. Taylor walked over to a music keyboard.

Lillick said, "You're thinking organ, I know. But—"

"I'm thinking Yamaha DX-7 synthesizer with a digital sampler, MIDI and a Linn sequencer that should store about a hundred sequences in RAM."

"Glad you don't play pool. What are you, a musician or something?"

"You mind?"

He waved his hand. She sat on a broken stool and clicked on the Yamaha. She ran through *Ain't Misbehavin'*.

Lillick said, "This machine cannot deal with music like that. I think it's having a breakdown."

"What do you play?" she asked him.

"Postmodern, post-New Wave. What I do is integrate music and my show. I call myself a sound painter. Is that obnoxious?" She thought it was but didn't answer and read through some of his lead sheets. In addition to standard musical notation, they included drawings of pans and hammers, light bulbs, bells, a pistol.

"When I started composing, I was a Serialist and then I moved to Minimalism. Now I'm exploring nonmusical elements, like choreography and performance art. Some sculpture, too. I love what Philip Glass does, only I'm less thematic. Laurie Anderson, that sort of thing. I believe there's a lot of randomness in art. You ever done any chance composing?"

"You're talking to Ms. Mainstream, Sean." Taylor shut off the system. There was a satisfying pop from the speakers.

She asked, "Got a beer?"

"Oh. Sure. Help yourself. I'll take one, too, you're at it."

She popped them and handed him one. He asked, "You perform?"

"You wouldn't approve. Piano bars."

"That serves a valuable function."

Taylor said, "Are you being condescending?"

"No. I mean it. I just do something different, that's all. What's important to me is to rearrange perceptions. I want people to walk out of one of my performances saying, 'Holy shit.' But I like tunes, too." Lillick was up, enthusiastic, hobbling on one boot. "Charlie Parker. I got every Bird record ever made. Here, listen." He put on the disk, scratching and pure-sounding, authentic, even though CD's were a hundred times cleaner.

"Man, that was the life," Lillick said, "You get up late, practice a bit, hang out, play sax till three, watch the sunrise with your buddies. That's the life."

Taylor was lost in a solo. Finally, she said, "Man died young."

"Thirty-five."

"World lost a lot of music."

"Maybe it wouldn't have been so, you know, deep, so righteous."

Taylor said, "Maybe just the opposite. Hooked on smack's gotta affect you."

"Speaking of which . . ." Lillick retrieved a fat joint and lit it up. He passed it to Taylor. She took a hit and handed it back, then, bent like an old pensioner, she edged along his huge record collection. "Oh, you like Django? You know he was burned when he was young, he played all those licks with just a couple fingers on his left hand? I know guitarists could use ten fingers and not come close to him."

Lillick took off the Parker record and put on a Django Reinhart album. *Minor Swing* came into the room, tinny and rougher than the Bird. Like the sound track to a 1950s *film noir* classic.

"There is nothing in the world like vinyl," Lillick proclaimed.

Taylor asked, "What're you doing at a law firm, you're so into artsy-fartsy?"

"My relation with law firms is purely one of survival. I work because this place costs me seven-fifty a month. Because I like to eat food that doesn't come in a can, because I may be crazy, but I'm not stupid *and* crazy. I've applied for every grant I can think of. But you know who they give money to? Associate professors at Midwest schools who're synthesizing John Cage with Greek modal scales. It's bullshit. The way I look at it, Hubbard, White & Willis is supporting the arts. They don't know it, but they are." He offered her the joint again; she shook her head.

He suddenly pulled out a pad of music staff paper and a pencil. "Keep talking. I work best when I'm only using half my mind."

"What I came to ask you about . . . What do you know about Linda Davidoff?"

Lillick looked off in space for a moment and wrote a measure of music. He wrote from his head, without playing the notes on the synthesizer. After a moment, he looked up. "Sorry . . . Linda? Well, we went out a few times. I thought she was more interesting than most of the prep princesses you see around the firm. She wanted to be a writer. It didn't go very far between us. She was very independent. Temperamental. Sort of a gypsy, you know. Too much for little old *moi* to handle."

"Why did she stop working on the Hanover & Stiver case?"

He hesitated. "I'm not sure. She was sick, I know. She asked me about claims forms."

"Claims forms?"

"Medical insurance. At work."

"Do you know why she killed herself?" Taylor asked.

"No, but I'll tell you I wasn't wildly amazed she did. Linda was too sensitive. She took things too much to heart. I got this feeling like it wouldn't take a whole hell of a lot to send her over the edge."

"Did you work with her?"

Lillick erased and rewrote a line. He hummed it. "Give me a B-flat diminished."

Taylor turned on the DX-7 and hit the chord.

"Work with her? Only a couple days when I took over on the Hanover case. She didn't look good. You know how people look when they're sick—puffy and emaciated at the same time? That was Linda. In fact, she called in sick for a whole week."

"Did she live at home?"

"No, she had a roommate, another writer. He's moved, I heard, but you want, I can find out where he is."

"Could you?"

"What's up? Why're you so interested in Linda?"

"Reece has got a problem with one of the bills for Banque Genève. He wants me to check into the hours. . . . When you took over, did she say anything about the case?"

"What about it?"

"Anything at all, anything that seemed odd, unusual?"

Lillick shook his head.

Taylor asked, "Are you still working on the case?"

"Not much. Mitchell's doing most of it himself."

"Were you in the firm on Saturday?"

"Last Saturday? Nope." His eyes narrowed, and she sensed she was pushing too hard. She asked quickly, "When're you performing next? I'd like to hear."

"How's tonight?"

"Actually, not good. I need some sleep."

"Sleep?" Lillick laughed. "Listen, I'm going to meet a few people. We're going for roast goat up at this place on Fourteenth, I got to be there in fifteen minutes. You want to come? It's really a dive, filthy, a long wait, noisy."

Taylor yawned. "Sean, an offer like that is really hard to say no to, but I've got to rain-check it."

"Bummer. Best goat in the city."

"Kills me to say no, it really does."

He shrugged and began looking for a clean dirty shirt.

. . .

Hubbard, White & Willis is busy tonight.

It is nearly midnight, but for some reason the closing of a corporate merger that began at two that afternoon has run into difficulties and is not yet completed. There has been a delay in European regulatory approvals. Three of the firm's large conference rooms are filled with young men and women scurrying back and forth with huge stacks of papers. The impression is of ants carrying crumbs twice their size, though they all seem to be quite happy ants. The business executives—the clients who are merging their companies—on the other hand, are irritated that the law firms to which they are paying thousands of dollars an hour are dallying over technicalities. These men sit about, waiting impatiently to fulfill their sole task tonight—signing their names hundreds of times to documents the lawyers have prepared. They want to go home. Some partners are on a conference call to Los Angeles, and one is trying unsuccessfully to reach a firm in Berlin, which is handling the European matter. The time difference puts the hour near start of business in Germany, but there is no response, not even from an answering machine. Attorneys in other nations are often perplexed, and annoyed, at how hard their colleagues in America work.

Taylor Lockwood knows all these details about the closing because she is at this moment in a closed office right next to conference room 16-4, in which a series of unkind jokes about Germans are being told. She has her own frustrations at the moment. John Silbert Hemming had neglected to tell her that the powder does not come off.

She has just finished fingerprinting Reece's broken file cabinet and painstakingly transferred the sticky tape of the two dozen latents to cards. She thinks back to what Hemming told her. He had told her about the different kinds of powders. He had told her how to spread it around and how to brush the excess away. But he had not told her the stuff was like dry ink. Once you—once *one*—dusted it on, it didn't wipe off. The smear just got bigger. She is not concerned about the file cabinet. She is concerned about Mitchell Reece's coffee mug, emblazoned with "World's Greatest Lawyer," which she dusted to get samples of his prints to eliminate those from the ones she lifted off his cabinet. Fingerprinting powder coats the mug like Super Glue. She does her best to clean it, then examines herself. She pinches the midriff of her blouse between two fingers and fluffs the poor garment to see if that will dislodge the powder. This has no effect. She tries to blow it away, and accidentally spits into the smear, which immediately runs the powder into the cloth. Permanently, she suspects. Taylor sighs and pulls on her suit jacket to cover the smudges.

She hears more conference calls in the next room. There are laughter and shouts of excitement. The Germans are awake. The glitch has been solved, and the closing continues.

She takes this opportunity to sneak into the hall. She hurries down to Ralph Dudley's office, where she lifts samples of his prints, then continues to Thom Sebastian's, where she does the same.

Back in her cubicle in Halsted Street, she puts the fingerprint cards in an envelope and pulls her coat on. Just as she glances at the wall in front of her, seeing the stark words BANQUE INDUSTRIELLE DE GENÈVE v. HANOVER & STIVER in the hideous green court calendar that she'd pinned up, there is a huge explosion behind her.

Taylor spins around, inhaling a scream.

Her eyes meet those of a shocked young man in white shirtsleeves. He is standing half in the doorway, staring back at her. He holds a bottle of Veuve Cliquot champagne he has just opened. He apologizes for startling her. "We just closed," he said eagerly. "We got Deutschbank approval after all. Isn't that super?"

"I'm very pleased," she says, watching him open two more bottles and trot upstairs with them on a silver tray.

As Taylor Lockwood turns back to her cubicle and picks up her purse, her digital clock silently reaches midnight. At once, P.M. becomes A.M., Wednesday becomes Thursday, the twenty-seventh becomes the twenty-eighth, and the Hanover & Stiver case moves one day closer.

At three A.M., as Taylor Lockwood was in her apartment, dreaming of the lyrical topography of papillary ridges, and the lawyers from the Germanic closing were heading home to their beds, the drapery man stood in Taylor's cubicle in Halsted Street. Now, though, he was no longer dressed in a Triple A Drapery coveralls, but was wearing a bright-blue uniform with a badge on the pocket. He appeared to be a security guard.

He was preoccupied with his task: fitting a Japanese Akisha SR-10 transmitter into the fabric on the cubicle wall. The cardioid microphone was no bigger than a Susan B. Anthony dollar, though it was considerably more popular. The only problem was the range of transmission, which was only thirty yards because of the size of the battery. When he had pointed this out, his client had told him that such a range was fine; the girl's conversations would be broadcast to a receiver within the firm itself.

The drapery man finished the job, tested the microphone, and walked to the doorway, rocking on his feet over the hardwood floors to keep his rubber-soled shoes from slapping as he moved. He hesitated for just a moment, holding his breath and listening, then walked into the corridor. As he passed a lunchroom, he saw a half-empty bottle of champagne on the counter. It was dotted with moisture, and when he touched it with the back of his hand, he found it was still cold. He slipped on cotton gloves and poured himself a Dixie cup of the wine. He walked into the hall, lifted it, and drank down the champagne in one swallow. He crumpled the cup and put it in his pocket, then started down the hall to the exit door.

nine

Wendall Clayton believed that bringing one's first client into a law firm was the most significant milestone event in the career of a Wall Street lawyer. Unlike graduation from law school, unlike admittance to the bar, unlike being made partner—all of which are significant but abstract stages in a lawyer's life—the bringing into the fold of a money-paying client was what distinguished, in his metaphor, the nobility from the gentry.

Some years before, Clayton—a young, newly made partner at Hubbard, White & Willis—had finished the eighteenth hole at Meadowbrook Club on Long Island, when one of the foursome turned to him and said, "Say, Wendall, you interested in doing a little work for a hospital?"

That had been on Sunday, and by Tuesday, Clayton presented to the executive committee of the firm his first signed retainer agreement —with the huge St. Agnes Hospital complex in Manhattan. Other clients offered more interesting legal problems, and others paid more in fees, but being his first client, the hospital was special to him, and he made certain it had the best legal services he could provide, or exhort.

This Thursday morning, Wendall Clayton sat in his office, leaning back in his throne, chewing on his cigar, as he talked with two men. One was the chief executive officer of St. Agnes, a tall, mild-spoken veteran of hospital administration. The other was Mitchell Reece.

None of the men appeared pleased.

Reece, flanked by these two, was speaking calmly. "It's a long shot. What can I say? I'd give it forty–sixty in their favor."

Clayton was irritated by Reece's serenity. He wished the young man were not handling the case. Although St. Agnes was Clayton's client, he represented the hospital only in corporate matters. If the hospital was sued or wished to sue someone, the senior litigation partner, Lamar Fredericks, decided which litigator would try the case. At the time Benning *v.* St. Agnes Hospital et al. was filed, six months ago, Clayton had paid no attention to the selection of a trial lawyer. He let Fredericks give the case to whoever was available, and noted in passing only that Mitchell Reece had a good reputation and that he did a great deal of trial work for Donald Burdick's clients, which he found piquing but irrelevant.

Now, however, the merger discussions were proceeding at a breakneck pace, and Clayton could not afford to be embarrassed by careless representation of one of his clients. He would much rather have had the case tried by a partner and preferably someone senior like Lamar Fredericks himself, even though Fredericks was an ally of Donald Burdick and a feisty son of a bitch. Clayton did not want the case in the hands of a mere associate, especially this handsome, cocky young man, who sat calmly and refused to be aristocratized.

Certainly not a young man like this—one who was looking his, Wendall Clayton's own, client in the eye and telling him that the hospital had a good chance of losing a ten-million-dollar lawsuit. "They've got an expert. They've got pictures of the plaintiff just before he entered the hospital at a hundred fifty-eight pounds, and pictures when he was transferred to NYU at a hundred seventeen pounds. They've got the deposition of a St. Agnes nurse saying"—Reece quoted from memory—" 'I saw him after we'd treated him, and I thought, my God, we've gone and killed him. I was sure we'd killed him.' " Reece added, "She then said she went home and prayed for the plaintiff."

"Shit," the CEO said.

Clayton, who realized he had been squeezing his teeth together with fierce pressure, forcibly relaxed himself and said, "Well, Mitchell, perhaps it isn't as hopeless as you're painting it."

Reece shrugged. "I don't think it's hopeless. I never said it's hopeless."

Clayton said, "After all, we made the decision not to settle." The *we* was slightly emphasized, a reminder that Clayton had done what corporate attorneys always do—recommended settlement—while Reece had seemed confident that he could win the case, and the CEO had agreed to proceed to trial.

The CEO said, "Settlement. Maybe we should think about it now."

"Yes, how about that?" Clayton sensed he was looking too eagerly at Reece. He felt like a young woman being courted, hanging on Reece's words. He was not in control, and the sense of impotence infuriated him.

Reece shook his head. "We had a pretrial conference. The judge always brings up settlement, and the plaintiff refuses to consider it. They have confidence in their expert witness."

Clayton was impassive and traded glances with the CEO. Although he wanted to grab Reece by his lapels and scream that he was off the case and that Lamar Fredericks was taking over at this moment, he said simply, "Of course, you'll do everything you can."

Reece laughed at this statement of the apparent and said, "Considering that we're dealing with rampant malpractice here, I think we've got a fair shot."

The CEO shifted.

Clayton waited a moment for his anger to abate. It did not. In his calmest, most aristocratizing voice, he said, "I wouldn't say 'malpractice,' Mitchell."

"Well, of course it was malpractice."

"You're suggesting that St. Agnes—"

"—was guilty?" Reece seemed surprised Clayton was so naive. "Certainly."

Clayton considered for a moment. "Oh, I see, you're saying—what you're saying now—that's what the plaintiff is claiming."

"No," Reece said, tapping his chest. "*I* mean the hospital committed malpractice. Gross malpractice, in fact."

The CEO said icily, "If you think we're guilty, maybe there's no point in continuing representation with Hubbard, White—"

"No, no," Clayton said. "He doesn't mean that at all."

"No, actually, I do. Your hospital committed malpractice. Your doctor administered cortisone acetate along with indomethacin to an ulcer patient with arthritis and an adrenal problem. That's malpractice, pure and simple."

"Don't say that!" Clayton exploded.

The CEO looked from one to the other, appearing more frightened of Clayton's temper than Reece's words. Reece gazed back into the partner's eyes with tranquillity. "Wendall, the facts are the facts. We can't change them. Now if you'll excuse me . . . opening statement's in a half hour. You'll be in court?"

Clayton sensed his client's concern and knew he must now exude confidence. The matter was out of his control, though his anger was not. He smiled. "Of course. And good luck, Mitchell. I'm sure you'll do us proud."

If she hadn't been initiated, Taylor Lockwood would never have known she was watching a trial. She saw a bored judge rocking back in his chair, witnesses, lawyers, and clerks walking around casually, no one really concentrating on what was going on. No drama. Bored jurors. Few spectators. A half dozen or so retirees mostly, like the unshaven men who take trains out to Belmont or Aqueduct in the morning. They'd show up at nine-thirty for the 10 A.M. court sessions, trade gossip about what trials were going to be hot today, sip their coffee, and share their doughnuts. The legal reporters relied on them.

She sat forward on the hard oak pew. The door opened, in walked two men, one of whom she recognized: Wendall Clayton. She was wondering why the two were here, standing with arms crossed like surgeons observing a colleague perform a delicate procedure. She scanned Wendall Clayton's eyes, staring with intensity at Mitchell Reece, who sat at one of the counsel's tables in the front of the courtroom.

The judge said, "Mr. Reece, would you like to recess, or start your cross-examination?"

Mitchell Reece stood and—in smooth motions—buttoned his jacket, straightened his paisley tie. He glanced at the jury, dipping with camaraderie into the eyes of the six jurors, bored numb from an hour of medical testimony.

"Now, Your Honor."

Hunkered down behind two octogenarian trial buffs, Taylor could not be seen by Reece. Although he had mentioned he was on trial this morning, he had not invited her, and she wasn't eager for him to know she was here and not out tracking down suspects.

Reece walked to the witness stand and stood several feet from the handsome, gray-haired man in his midfifties. He gazed pleasantly out at the jury.

Reece said, "Now, sir, you've been called by the plaintiff in this case as an expert witness, isn't that right?"

"Yes, sir." Agreeable, understanding, humorous. You could see him in a commercial selling aspirin. *I give it to my children. Shouldn't you?* He'd be a tough one for Reece; experts like this were hired not for their medical credentials, but because they didn't get rattled under pressure.

"And you are getting paid how much for your testimony today?"

"The other lawyer asked me that—"

Mitchell Reece's voice cut him off. "I'm asking you now."

"Eight hundred dollars a day."

"Plus expenses?"

He said, still smiling, "Any time an expert is hired—"

"Doctor Morse, just answer the question."

"Plus expenses."

"I see your fee has gone up since last year. . . ." Reece turned to the jury, rolling his eyes. The jury smiled.

Morse said, "I assume your fees have, too, Mr. Reece. Probably much more than mine."

Some laughter. The judge told the jury to disregard the exchange.

"Very good, Doctor," Reece said. "Now, let me ask you, how often do you testify at medical malpractice cases like this one?"

"Just like this one?"

Reece was patient. "Let me just say, medical malpractice cases in general."

"Fairly often."

"Fairly often?" He asked it sarcastically. "That's a rather vague term. Twice a day?"

"Of course not."

"Four times a day?"

"Mr. Reece, please."

"Doctor, I asked you a simple question, you are giving me a vague answer."

Morse said, "About once a week."

"Thank you, Doctor. Yes, I would say that is fairly often. Now, in between your testifying against your fellow doctors, do you have any time for a medical practice on the side?"

"Objection."

Morse smiled and answered anyway. "In between helping people who are victimized by incompetents—"

"Strike both comments," the judge ordered. "Please just ask the question, Mr. Reece. And, Doctor Morse, please just answer it."

Reece said, "You do practice, don't you?"

"I practice, yes."

"You practice internal medicine, correct?"

"That is correct."

"You are Board-certified in internal medicine?"

"I am."

"And you have considerable occasion to administer various drugs?"

He said, "Well, I suppose that depends on what you mean by considerable."

Reece nodded broadly. "Ah, yes, Doctor, you're the one who has trouble with the concept of 'often,' I forgot. . . ."

Taylor could see that the jury was loving this. They'd brightened up. Something was happening. Reece's jacket, at some point, had become unbuttoned, and she noticed that in lifting his hand to straighten his hair, he'd mussed it. He looked boyish.

Reece said, "I apologize, Your Honor." He turned back to Morse. "In the course of your practice, you prescribe or administer drugs how often?"

"There's a distinction, counsel," the witness said. "Between prescribing and administering."

"Ah," Reece said, then: "How often do you administer drugs?"

"Several times a week."

"Now let us focus on the physicians at St. Agnes Hospital. . . ."

"Someone should," Dr. Morse said.

Reece grinned and ignored the comment. He continued, "Let's reiterate what happened here. In March of this year, a doctor at St. Agnes treated a patient—the plaintiff in this case—who has arthritis and adrenal insufficiency with seventy milligrams of cortisone acetate in conjunction with one hundred milligrams of indomethacin."

Morse shook his head. "I'm afraid he did."

Reece said, "You would not have done that?"

"Not with a patient who had a preexisting ulcerous condition, no. Absolutely not."

"Doctor Morse, there has been a lot of talk in this trial about what is an accepted level of medical treatment, has there not?"

Morse paused before answering, as if trying to figure out where Reece was going. He looked at his own lawyer, then answered, "Some, I suppose."

"Now if, as you say, you wouldn't have treated the patient with these medications, then I assume you feel that such treatment was below the standards of proper medical care?"

"Certainly."

Taylor found her palms sweating. She didn't understand Reece. All he was doing was having the witness repeat over and over again that the hospital had made a mistake, a message the jury would surely be remembering. She glanced at Clayton and saw him and the other man exchange troubled glances.

Reece walked to the blackboard and boldly drew a thick chalk line horizontally across it. "Doctor, let's say this is the standard-of-care line, all right?"

"If you will."

Reece drew a thin dotted line an inch below it, the chalk clicking in the hushed courtroom. "Would you say that the level of care St. Agnes provided was this far below the standard level of care? Just a little bit below?"

Morse looked at his own lawyer and was greeted with a shrug.

"No. It wasn't just a little bit below. They almost killed the man."

"Well," Reece drew another line, farther down. "This far?"

"I don't know."

Another line. "This far below?" Reece's voice had sharpened.

Morse said bitterly, "It was very far below."

Reece drew three more lines, rapidly, after each shouting, "This far? This far, Doctor? Can you tell us?"

Clayton shifted uncomfortably and actually stepped forward.

Reece threw the chalk across the courtroom. "You're not telling us anything! All right. I'll leave it up to you." He stormed up to the witness. "How would *you* characterize the treatment provided to the plaintiff? How? Give me a word, give me something tangible, will you?"

Morse shouted back, "Okay, it was malpractice! Blatant malpractice!"

Taylor was certain that in the minds of the dozen lawyers in the courtroom, hands were raising and silent motions to strike the testimony were being raised.

Yet Reece said nothing. He walked calmly back to the jury box. Softly he said, "Malpractice."

"Yes, malpractice."

The judge looked at Reece, opposing counsel looked at Reece. A murmur ran through the courtroom. Even Taylor recognized his mistake. An expert witness's job is to testify that a procedure was within the bounds of recognized medical treatment or below that level, and that's it. They themselves shouldn't use the word *malpractice* and prejudice the jury against the defendant. Taylor knew that Reece had, in this moment, lost the case.

Reece paced for a moment, looking confident. He asked, "Have you ever prescribed, or administered, any of the drugs I mentioned before?"

"Not exactly—"

Reece's voice shot out, "No? Yes?"

"No, but I have—"

Reece said, "Doctor, where are you licensed to practice?"

There was a moment's hesitation. "As I said before, California."

Reece walked toward the jury, smiled at one of them, put both his hands on the rail. Incredible. Not a single piece of paper, the questions were in his head. He moved the hair again from off his forehead, but it fell back with a flop.

Taylor stared at him; she felt a rising urge, a hunger, low in her body. She shifted in her chair. Watching the boyish mess of hair, the smooth pacing, the comfortable theatrics of his hands and arms.

"Is that the only state you've ever been licensed to practice in?"

"I was licensed in New Jersey, but I moved to California."

"No other state?"

"No."

Reece glanced at the jury and then swung to look into Morse's eyes. "Any other country?"

Silence. The witness was looking at the floor.

Reece said sharply, "I asked if you are now or have ever been licensed to practice medicine in any other country."

"No." The man's voice was a whisper.

"Have you ever practiced medicine in another country?"

"I just said I wasn't licensed—"

"The word I used was *practiced*, Doctor, not *licensed*."

Morse was scared. "I've done some volunteer work—"

"Please answer the question yes or no. Have you ever practiced medicine in another country? And His Honor will remind you that you are under oath."

"Yes, I have. I did some volunteer—"

Reece sighed. "And would you be so kind as to tell us which country, if that isn't too much trouble, Doctor?"

"Mexico." His voice cracked.

"Mexico." Reece said. "What were you doing in Mexico?"

"I was getting a divorce. I liked the country, and I decided to stay for a while—"

"That was after you abandoned your wife and children in New Jersey?"

"Objection, Your Honor, irrelevant."

The judge said, "Mr. Reece, could you hone in a little?"

"And you practiced medicine in Mexico?"

Morse was looking completely miserable now. He was playing with his fingertips. "Yes, for a while. Before I moved back to California. I set up a practice in Los Angeles. I found Los Angeles to be—"

Reece waved his hand. "I'm much more interested in Mexico than Los Angeles, Doctor. Why did you leave that country?"

"I was about to tell you. I wanted to open a practice in California."

"Why didn't you want to stay in Mexico?"

"I got tired of it."

"Is that the only reason?"

The witness lost his composure for a moment, a time-lapse bloom of anger spread on his face, then he controlled it.

Reece said, "Did you run into some kind of trouble down in Mexico?"

"Trouble, like the food?" He tried to laugh. It didn't work, and he cleared his throat again, and swallowed.

"Doctor, what is Ketaject?"

Pause. Morse rubbed his eyes. "It is the brand name of a drug whose generic name I don't recall."

"Could it be the brand name for ketamine hydrochloride?"

Pause. The witness whispered, "Yes."

"And what does that do?"

"It is a general anesthetic." His eyes were joined to Reece's by a current full of fear and hate.

"Doctor, when you were in Mexico, did you have a patient, a Miss Adelita Corrones, a seventeen-year-old resident of Nogales?"

Silence.

"Doctor, shall I repeat the question?"

"I don't recall."

"Well, I'm sure she recalls you. Why don't you think back to the St. Teresa Clinic in Nogales. Think back seven years ago. And try to recall if you had such a patient. Did you?"

"How did you find out?" A whisper, but it could have been a shout. "How on earth?"

Taylor felt a flush of warmth and passion. Reece's tie was loosed, his face was ruddy with excitement, and even from the back of the courtroom she could see his eyes shining with a lust. She shifted in her seat. She pressed her purse into her lap and lifted her hips against it. Her breathing was heavy. She swallowed.

"And on September seventeenth of that year did you, pursuant to a procedure for the removal of a nevis—that is, a birthmark—from Ms. Corrones's leg, administer Ketaject, and when you perceived her to be unconscious, did you partially undress her, fondle her breasts and genitals, and masturbate until you reached a climax?"

"Objection!" The lawyer was on his feet.

The judge said, "Overruled."

Morse's head was in his hands. "That was a long time ago."

Reece glanced at the jury with a look of shocked disbelief, then spun to face Morse. He said calmly, "And you really feel you can say my client is guilty of malpractice, when you can't even knock out a patient well enough to rape her?"

The other lawyer was raising his hand lethargically to flag his objection.

Mitchell Reece said softly, "Withdrawn, Your Honor."

Taylor understood suddenly what he had done. She saw his brilliance. Oh, Reece's clients had probably been dead wrong in prescribing the drugs. They were guilty as hell, and Morse's opinion had been correct. But since Reece had forced him to say the magic word "malpractice," then revealed the incident in Mexico, the jury's sole impression was that the one witness who claimed the hospital was negligent was himself incompetent and criminal.

His strategy thrilled her and she sent him a silent message of adulation.

Reece turned to the jury, and from where Taylor sat it appeared that he looked at each one of them, his partners in uncovering this fraud. "No further questions."

Taylor saw a gleam in his face, a flushing of the cheeks, his fists balled up in excitement. Hers were, too.

Reece noticed Wendall Clayton in the back of the courtroom. The two men looked at each other. Neither smiled, but Clayton touched his forehead in a salute of respect, then turned and stepped out of the room, which was utterly silent. Except for the sobbing of the witness.

ten

Taylor Lockwood was ten feet away from Reece in the firm's glossy marble, brass, and oak library. After the trial recessed for the day, she had followed him back to the firm. He had dropped off his litigation bag in his office and come immediately here, where he pulled several volumes off the shelves and began researching. She had entered a judicious ten minutes later, and acted surprised to see him. He had acknowledged her with a brief smile and returned to a heavy book. She sat at a table half a room away, and for half an hour had studied him, unable to rid herself of the image of Reece standing in front of the jury box.

Taylor forced herself to think of the stolen note, think about fingerprints, about suspects, about the ticking bomb of the Hanover & Stiver case, about the sickly green court calendar memo pinned prominently in her cubicle. In just sixty seconds or so, however, she realized the case had vanished from her mind and she was instead imagining what it was like to make love with Mitchell Reece.

How would it be? Good? Bad? Kinky? Embarrassing?

She'd done it all. She'd had playful lovers, serious ones, men who pleased themselves and hoped she came along for the ride. Men who pleased her first, then timidly rolled on top of her. The closest she'd come to a pure, unqualified lover was an Iranian student who'd made love with her twice a day and still had energy (she found out later) for a big, dark Persian girl he was seeing on the side. Sitting in a majestic library that had never known any sound more sensual that the rare rustle of nylons as women attorneys crossed their legs, Taylor Lockwood smiled at the memory.

She had trouble picturing herself with Reece. She feigned a yawn and pressed her knuckles into her eye sockets, searching the mottled blackness, but she was unable to create the scene. All she knew was that she felt an indefinable urge for him, which would be manifest differently than the typical rituals—the explorations under cloth, against flesh, the pressures and hesitations that were so familiar and so alien. There was something she couldn't identify about him, something that even now was affecting her. Maybe it had to do with strength, assuredness, control. And when she thought that, she heard a warning bell. Through a good friend Taylor had gotten the benefit of vicarious analysis and had diagnosed herself as having suicidal tendencies toward men. (This supposedly had some roots in resentment at her father's career.) She was destined to fall for those who were bad for her.

At the moment, she chose not to consider these broad implications, and focused on a simpler question: What would this boy be like in bed?

Good? Bad? Consuming? Energetic? Bawdy? He seemed the sort who would possess a woman. But that was just an impression, and Taylor knew how dramatically the reality of sex differs from the promise.

Had Reece known many women? Maybe not; with the hours he worked, he didn't have much time for affairs.

Maybe . . .

She replayed images of the St. Agnes trial. His tousled hair, loose tie, the way he strode back and forth in front of the jury. She remembered sitting forward on the pew, studying his gestures, listening for every word, as she rocked back and forth. She wanted so badly to tell him that she'd seen him, to tell him what she thought of his performance. But as far as he knew, she had not been there, and this sealed her lips.

Taylor rose. She walked to a Lexis computer terminal and signed on. Even before she sensed his presence beside her, she smelled his after-shave—Oscar de la Renta, she recognized it from a former boy-friend. She saw his distorted reflection in the glass. She said, "How did the trial go?"

"I think I'll win."

"You think?"

"You never know. It was continued till next week." As at the trial his hair was not slicked back, but fell forward across his forehead. She studied it in the computer screen.

"Aren't you anxious?"

He shrugged. "You do your best, then you stop worrying about it."

Impulsively, she asked, "If you're free, how 'bout lunch?"

"Can't. I'm meeting a witness at the Athletic Club. We're having lunch and then I'll be prepping him all afternoon." He added, "How's it coming?"

She said, "I fingerprinted your cabinet."

He laughed. "You did what?"

"I got my Taylor Lockwood Private Eye kit and decoder ring. I dusted the scene of the crime."

"What did you come up with?"

"Twenty-five latents—that's prints, to you. Fifteen completely unrecognizable. Of the other ten, most are partials, but seven seem to be the same person, and I think that person is you. I dusted your coffee cup—I owe you a new one, by the way, the powder didn't come off too well—and three others. One print is mine. One is unidentified. And one is . . . Thom Sebastian's."

"Thom?" Reece frowned. "Son of a bitch."

"Is there any reason why he would have been going through your files?"

"I've done a couple trials for him, but not in the past year. Anyway, he'd have no business going through anybody's office without asking." Suddenly Reece laughed. "Fingerprints. What an idea." He squeezed her arm, and his hand lingered on the silk, as if he enjoyed the touch. His eyes drifted to hers. She smiled, then he looked away and straightened up so quickly she thought someone had noticed them together. But no—a casual glance showed that those few lawyers nearby were obliviously lost in books densely filled with big words printed in tiny letters. Reece hovered behind her. She asked, "This weekend, should we get together? I'll have more information then."

"I'm going to New Orleans for depositions on another case. I'll be there through Monday morning."

She nodded and punched down the pang of disappointment.

"Some other time," he said and started to walk away.

Impulsively, Taylor reached into her purse. "Oh, one thing." Reece paused. "You asked about that tape."

"The demo tape."

Thank God he remembered.

She handed a clear plastic cassette to him. "You don't like it, you don't have to—"

He flashed a smile. "It's going right into my Walkman."

She'll be moody today.

Ralph Dudley sat in his creaky office chair. The back of his head eased into the tall leather back and he stared at the thin slice of sky next to the brick wall outside his window.

This was a talent, this intuition. Whereas Donald Burdick, with whom he constantly compared himself, was brilliant, Dudley was intuitive. He had sense and feeling, while Burdick had reason and logic. For instance, he knew without a doubt that Junie would be moody, and she was. She walked into the office and said a curt hello to Frances, Dudley's veteran secretary, then stood in the doorway in a hip-cocked stance, unsmiling.

"Come on in, honey," Dudley said. "I'm almost finished."

She wore a jumper, white blouse, and white knee socks. A large blue bow was in her hair. She gave him a formal kiss on the cheek and plopped into one of his visitor's chairs, swinging her legs over the side.

"Sit like a lady, now."

She waited a defiant minute, then slipped on her headset and swiveled slowly in the chair, planting her feet on the lime-green–carpeted floor.

Dudley laughed. He picked up the handle of his dictating machine. "I've got one, too, a recorder." He held it up. She looked perplexed, and he realized she couldn't hear what he was saying. He had learned not to be hurt at this behavior and unemotionally proceeded to dictate a memo that gave the gist of some rules of law he believed he remembered. At the end of the tape, he included instructions to an associate at the firm, who would rewrite the memo and look up the law Dudley hoped existed to support his points.

Ralph Dudley knew they sometimes laughed at him, the associates. He never raised his voice, he never criticized, he was solicitous toward them. He supposed the young men (Dudley had never quite come to terms with the idea of women lawyers) held him in all the more contempt for this obsequiousness. There were a few loyal boys, but on the whole, no one had much time for Old Man Dudley. Grandpa, he'd heard they called him. Partners, too, though somewhat more delicately, joined in the derision. Yet though this spoiled Hubbard, White & Willis for him and obliterated whatever loyalty he at one time felt, he was not overly troubled. His relation with the firm became just what his marriage to Emma had been: one of respectful acknowledgment. He was able to keep his bitterness contained.

Junie's eyes were closed, her patent-leather shoes swaying in time to the music. My God, she was growing up. Fifteen. It gave him a pang of sorrow. At times he had flashes—poses she struck, the way the light might catch her—that revealed her as a woman in her twenties. He knew that she, more than other girls, carried the seeds of adulthood with her. There would be turmoil inside her. She hadn't asked him any questions, and he prayed she wouldn't. He tried to imagine what Emma would have said to her. But there was no Emma, gone twelve years. There was only Dudley and a girl growing up fast, too fast for him.

When he was finished dictating, he handed the tape to Frances and said, "Junie and I are going out. Don't tell anyone, we've got a little shopping to do."

The stocky woman stood in the doorway. "Is it your birthday, honey?"

Junie slipped off the headset. "What?"

"Is it your birthday?"

"No."

"We're just going to get some clothes."

Frances said, "You've got, don't forget, that two-thirty with the people from Fallon."

"We'll be back by then. We're just going up to Lord & Taylor, then have a bite."

They were at the elevator when a voice said, "Ralph, excuse me, you have a minute?"

He recognized her, but couldn't recall a name. It stung him slightly that she had the effrontery to call him by his first name, but because he was a gentlemen, he did nothing other than smile and nod. "Yes, you're . . ."

"Taylor Lockwood."

"Sure, of course. This is my granddaughter, Junie. Junie, say hello to Miss Taylor. She's a lawyer here."

"Paralegal, actually."

"Ah, yes, that's right." Had he given her some work? An assignment?

"I'd like to ask you something. Would you have a little time?"

"About what?"

"You went to the University of Michigan Law School. I'm thinking of applying there."

Junie was getting restive. Dudley smiled. "I went there a long time before you were born. I don't think anything I'd have to tell you would be much help."

"Well, somebody here said you helped them decide to go to law school. You were very helpful. I was sort of hoping you could give me the same talk. Maybe tomorrow night? Could I buy you dinner?" The elevator came. He hesitated and she added, "Unless you have plans."

"I have plans for later tomorrow evening, but nothing for dinner. Yes, I'd enjoy that. Why don't you come to my club?"

Junie said, "Like, you told me they didn't allow girls in there."

Dudley said to her, "That's only as members, honey." To Taylor he said, "Come by tomorrow at six, we'll take a cab uptown. . . ." Then, calculating the fare, he added, "No, actually a subway would be better. That time of day, traffic is terrible."

Mitchell Reece had lied to her.

Taylor Lockwood, wearing her teal-green raincoat, was walking back to the office from Burger King when she saw Reece in the street. She was a half block away, and he didn't see her.

She quickened her pace to catch up with him, but then noticed something odd. He was walking *away* from the Downtown Athletic Club, where he'd said he was going to meet his witness for lunch. She slowed, stung at first (her heart pounded at this dishonesty), then thinking, *no, he probably meant another athletic club.* Sure, the New York Athletic Club, on Central Park South.

Only, if so, why was he disappearing into the Lexington Avenue subway stop? The train went uptown, but there were no stops anywhere near the NYAC. And why was he taking a train in the first place? The rule in Wall Street was that if you went anywhere on firm business, you always took a limo; subways were only for personal errands.

He *wouldn't* have lied to her, he couldn't have. Of course not. Plans had changed, and he'd come by her cubicle to ask her to lunch after all, but she was out buying a goddamn Whopper. . . . And now, disappointed he hadn't found her, he was on his way to Tripler's to pick up a couple of new shirts. That was all.

Chill out, honey. This is nothing. No. Big. Deal.

She stopped and turned toward the firm. Then she pulled a token out of her purse and hurried down the subway stairs.

This is pretty low, girl. Spying on a lover is bad enough; spying on a guy who's never even asked you out—that's pathetic. Anyway, it was purely innocent, his plans had changed. Give the guy a break. He'll get off the train at Fifty-ninth Street, he'll meet the witness for lunch, they'll walk over to the Athletic Club. . . .

Reece got off at Grand Central.

Taylor followed, climbing up the stairs, then skirting a small colony of homeless. She watched Reece buy a train ticket and walk toward the gates. She stopped.

Squinting though the misty afternoon light that spilled across the huge cavern of the terminal, she caught a glimpse of him standing at a vending cart in front of a gate. A crowd of passengers walked between them, obscuring him. Taylor stepped through them and after a moment finally spotted him again. She was sorry she had. What she was watching was Mitchell Reece buying a dozen roses at one of the vending carts in front of the gate, then hurrying to make his train.

· · ·

Smiles everywhere.

Gracious, curious, patronizing, insulting smiles, some perhaps even genuine—smiles hanging on the faces of a hundred spiffy people milling around the Temple of Dendur in the Metropolitan Museum of Art. Egyptian motifs no longer seemed to be as popular as they once had been in Manhattan decor, but the fund-raiser was for a good cause, and—more important—supposedly present were a Watergate conspirator, two ambassadors, a former mayor, and assorted movie-of-the-week actors and actresses.

Tuxedos and black dresses circulated in the exotic, ancient-scented, humid room, speaking chaste words of business and travels and families, words that echoed off the gray blocks of the temple of the fertility goddess who was both wife and sister of the same god.

"And you are . . . ?" Ralph Dudley tipped his head slightly as he asked the question to a woman in her midfifties. Her face was long and handsome, with a straight nose. A black dress covered her trim figure. The gown was gathered at the waist and had a sensuously scooped neck. She wore several rings and a simple diamond necklace.

"Amanda."

"Ralph Dudley."

He had (by intuition) a pretty good idea of who she was. Dudley had watched which hands gripped her arm and how her eyes aimed possessively at one of the executives from Amtrol, Incorporated, a corporate sponsor of the event. Amtrol was a *Fortune* One Hundred company that had just fired its law firm and was supposedly in the market for a new one. Donald Burdick had suggested that Dudley take a sudden interest in the Kipp's Bay homeless relief fund-raiser cocktail party.

He took her long, soft hand and believed he felt a vibration from her five-carat diamond and yellow-topaz cocktail ring.

Dudley figured that she would be the wife of the head of a major Amtrol division. Maybe the man in charge of European operations. The way she stood (with a tempered Gallic authority) and spoke (a vestigial accent), the way she was at ease with the waiters (not too familiar, not too condescending) all suggested to Dudley that she had experience with servants and chauffeurs, and that she had lived overseas. The rings and necklace, of course, explained that her husband did quite well—

there was so little inherited money any more. But the man she continually eyed was too young to be the CEO or president of Amtrol.

Dudley glanced at the huge gray structure of the temple, massive as Stonehenge. "I've never been to Egypt. I thought it would be great fun until I found they don't have elevators in the pyramids."

"I've been," Amanda said. "I got quite ill. I was careful to drink only bottled water and so on, but do you know what happened? My sandal laces often came untied and dragged on the ground. When I tied them, I got bacteria on my hands. I must have picked up some food with my fingers. . . . Cholera. It was extremely unpleasant."

They talked about traveling for a few minutes, and Dudley predicted exactly the moment she would ask the question that New Yorkers must ask one another at some point in the conversation: "What do you do?"

"I'm a lawyer," he said, his card appearing with surprising speed. (He avoided, however, the reciprocal inquiry, saving her the embarrassment—and him the tedium—of her defensive explanation of gardening and housewivery and the Armory antiques show.) He said, "Let me tell you a little about Hubbard, White & Willis. I'll try not to be a bore."

He gave her more information than usual and actually stepped over the line of discretion dictated by security-sensitive Manhattan business. He spent much time talking about the merger of Hubbard, White and the Perelli firm, which had not yet made the press but which was the talk of Wall Street. He explained it in simple terms, and he felt pleased that she seemed to understand. Ralph Dudley kept talking, enchanted by her deep blue eyes, which danced across his face with curiosity. He told her about cases the firm was working on, clients they had almost, but not quite, won. The personalities—some charming, some vicious, some voracious—of the partners. The antics of associates. She seemed fascinated, and they lost themselves in conversation, he sipping his Manhattan, she her kir.

Amanda was reticent. She nodded often and responded with effervescence, yet spoke little about herself. She was a trained hostess. Dudley did an impersonation of Frederick Phyle Hubbard—she laughed until tears dotted the corners of her sleek eyes. Then the husband swung by, slipped his arm around her, and nodded at Dudley. The men shook hands.

"Bill Schiavone."

"Ralph Dudley. And you're with Amtrol?"

The man said, "I'm CFO."

Dudley smiled. Chief financial officers often are the corporate executives in charge of hiring law firms. He said, "I must apologize for boring your charming wife with my long-winded talk about the law, of all silly things. . . ."

The man blinked. "Oh, Amanda's not my wife."

"Oh, I thought—"

Her smile ran full ahead toward Ralph Dudley. She said, "I'm with Sherman, Murdoch & Hannon. My last name is Wilcox."

The horror at the thought of the firm secrets he had just given away to her, and at his own foolishness, began like a volcanic eruption somewhere in the cavity of Dudley's stomach, then it miraculously became a loud laugh. "You're an attorney."

"I'm a partner at Sherman. In the corporate department."

"Oh, my."

Schiavone said to her, "I'm having that deal letter sent to you on Monday. We'll need the documents by Thursday, and we have to close within the month."

"Then that's when we'll close," she said with assurance.

Schiavone continued, "If we like your work, there'll be more where that came from." He kissed her cheek and walked away.

Dudley's eyes closed briefly, then opened and could not look at her. "I do have to apologize. . . ."

Amanda Wilcox considered him with a cocked head. "Not at all. *I* got the client, and you didn't. But now that we've got some ground rules established, why don't you get me another drink? We can exchange war stories."

Dudley's kindled face slowly turned to her. He said, "Yes, I think I'd like that very much."

As he stood at the bar, Dudley recognized Todd Stanton, a young associate from Hubbard, White & Willis who did much of Dudley's work. The boy was scanning the crowd, frowning. Dudley held up a hand to the associate, who noticed the movement and walked quickly to the partner.

"Enjoying yourself, Todd?"

"I sure am, Ralph," he answered, swallowing the sentence, as he always did when using the first name of someone nearly fifty years older than he. A quiet debate raged then was decided. "Ralph, there's something I think I should tell you."

"What?"

"I didn't want to tell you at first. I didn't want to get anybody in trouble. But it's been bothering me and I decided to say something to you."

"What on earth are you talking about?"

"It may be nothing, but the other day I found someone in your office. Taylor Lockwood? Do you know her?"

Dudley said, "What about her?"

"Well, it's probably silly. I hate to make a big deal out of nothing, but—"

"No," Dudley said, the smile gone, "tell me. Tell me everything."

eleven

"Never take a job," Sean Lillick said pensively, "that requires you to hold things in your teeth." He smiled with hopeful anticipation.

Carrie Mason, standing in the door, blinked. He wondered if this was at his solemnly delivered aphorism or at his total lack of interior design. She slowly walked into his apartment.

She was not his type. Although on the whole Lillick preferred women to men, the type of woman he preferred was willowy, had a boyish figure and passed steely-eyed, moody judgment, reasonable or not, on anything that took her attention. Ideally, Sean Lillick's perfect woman would have a former female lover in the woodpile. Carrie did not meet his specifications. For one thing, she was fat. Well, okay, not fat, but round—round in a way that needed pleated skirts and billowy blouses to make her look good. For another, she was quiet and polite and laughed a lot, which was evidence that she would rarely pass moody judgments on anything at all. Lillick also suspected she blushed frequently.

"Never what?" she asked.

"That's a line in the performance piece I'm working on right now.

It's a segment about careers. The piece is called *As Long as There's a Granite Springs.* It's spoken over music."

"Never take a job that . . . I don't think I get it."

For another, she doesn't get it. . . .

"There's nothing to get really. It's more of a statement than a joke. It's about careers and what people expect from other people."

"A statement."

Lillick took her coat. "You want a beer?"

She was looking with reverence at the keyboards and computers. Lillick had to repeat the question. She said, "Sure." Then ran her hand over the tie-dye bedspread and glanced at her fingers to make sure it didn't come off. She sat down. He opened a Pabst and handed it to her, thinking only after he did that he probably should have poured it into a glass. To take it back and find a mug would now seem stupid.

"I was surprised when you asked me out, Sean."

"Yeah?" Was she? She'd been hanging around him enough. Dropping off little presents of liver wrapped in bacon from cocktail parties upstairs in the firm dining room. Asking about his music, commenting on articles about his performances in the *East Village Examiner,* when he suspected that the only mags she subscribed to were *Self* and *Town & Country.* "It was kind of short notice." Lillick punched on a Meredith Monk tape. "I was just hanging around and thought you might like to get a bite."

"You want me to—" Carrie began.

"Huh?"

"Well, I was going to say, you want me to iron your shirt, I'm good at that sort of thing." It was an off-white shirt printed with tiny brown scenes of European landmarks.

He laughed. "You iron this poor thing, I'd have to have it committed."

Carrie said, "I like ironing. It's therapeutic. Like washing dishes."

"Yeah, I do that sometimes, too."

Outside a man's scream cut through the night. Then another, and a long moan. She looked up, alarmed. Lillick laughed. "It's the hooker. There's a guy turns tricks across the airshaft. He's a howler." He pointed to a machine. "That's a digital sampler. It's a computer that records a sound and lets you play it back through your synthesizer on any note you want." Carrie looked uneasily at the machine. "I recorded him screaming one night. It was totally the best. I did a piece from the Well-Tempered Clavier that's made up of a gay hooker shouting, "Deeper, deeper!"

She looked out the window toward the diminishing wails. "I don't get downtown very much. It's . . . colorful."

"Where do you live?"

"East Eighty-fourth."

Lillick pulled his jacket off a hook and started to dig papers out of his pocket—scraps, matchbooks, napkins. They all had writing on them. Some he read and stuffed into a notebook. Others he threw out. Carrie studied this ritual. "Friday night," she said, "I'm going up to our place in the country for the weekend. It's in like Bedford? A lot of people show up. If you'd like to come . . ."

"Like to, yeah, but I've got a meeting with Wendall Clayton. I've got a project going for him."

"Friday night?"

"And probably the weekend, too. He's a workaholic."

"He's also a dirty old man. He touched my, you know, boobs, once. Accidentally, he made it look like, but I could tell."

Lillick laughed. "Yeah, he's that way sometimes. . . . So, then, how's Mexican? There's a place near here, I call it the Hacienda del Hole."

"Sure, whatever." She was looking at him, sipping her beer. She didn't get up.

Lillick found one glove and began looking for the mate. He glanced up at her as if he'd just thought of something, and said casually, "Hey, Carrie, do me a favor. You're in charge of all disbursement billing, aren't you?"

"Yeah, they said it was a promotion when they gave me that job. That was a joke. It's like a royal pain."

"Well, see, what it is, last Saturday I was in the firm late."

She was looking at him blankly.

He glanced at her, then back into his drawer. "Damn gloves. How can you lose *one?* Anyway, I was doing some personal stuff. I made some copies."

"Of what?"

He paused. "Nothing. Just some of my music. I used my copier card in the Xerox machine."

"So?"

"Well, it was personal," he said. He shrugged and looked as contrite as a caught felon.

She laughed in surprise. "Everybody copies personal things."

"I'd just as soon nobody knew I was in the firm that night."

"Sean, nobody cares about the copiers. And anyway, you had to use your computer key to get into the firm, so they could find out. . . ."

He said, "Actually, I didn't. Somebody let me in."

Carrie was examining the wires, tracing one from the synthesizer to the sampler and back. She swallowed and didn't say anything. Lillick asked quickly, "Could you erase my number from the copier files?"

She swallowed again. Her gaze didn't move from the thin gray wire. "I don't know. . . ."

"Burdick's really cracking down on unnecessary expenses. I heard that some people were going to be fired. . . . Could you just erase that one file?"

"I didn't hear that about Mr. Burdick."

"I'll give you my computer card number and you erase all the copies made from that card on Saturday. No harm done."

"But why, Sean?"

"I can't afford to lose my job, Carrie."

"Mr. Burdick wouldn't fire you."

He looked into Carrie's eyes, which were not moodily judgmental or artistic or capricious, but were simply an exquisite blue-green, and he said, "What's the talk?"

"The what?"

"What is the only thing that everybody's talking about?"

"The merger. Is that what you mean?"

"Everybody's going over the firm with a magnifying glass. They're looking at every dollar. Even petty cash . . ." Lillick's voice faded. He turned back to his search and found his glove, held it up, and grinned. "Victory." After a moment he said, "No, you're right. Forget about it. I'm just being paranoid."

Silence flowed between them. Wendall Clayton had told him once that a negotiator should never fear silence. It should be used as a weapon. Now, Lillick slapped his glove into his palm several times and did not say a word.

Finally, to break the intolerable quiet, Carrie rubbed her palms on her knees and said, "I guess I could just call up the files and purge them for that date. I don't know how to do just your number, but I can purge them all."

"Thanks. I really appreciate it." An instant later he said, "It's just that things haven't been real good for me lately. . . ."

What am I doing? Why am I explaining myself to her? She's already agreed. Wendall had said to him once: "As soon as your opponent agrees with you, *shut the fuck up.*"

"Look, I don't want you to get in trouble," Lillick said, shocked to hear himself further weakening.

"If it's really that important"—Carrie lay back on the daybed— "I'll do it."

Lillick didn't move for a moment. The guilt he had felt suddenly vanished, his thin arms quivered with his victory, and, astonished, he considered how skillfully he had manipulated her. He quickly walked over to his Yamaha and turned it on. The amps sent a moan of anticipation through the warm air. "You want to hear something I just wrote?"

She slipped off her white plastic headband. "Sure." She shifted on the bed and ran her hand over the middle part of the mattress. "What's this?"

"What?"

"This lump?"

"I don't know. A shoe maybe."

He played an arpeggio; the music combined with his conquest elated him. But Carrie was frowning. "No, it's like weird. You better check it out."

What was she talking about? A totally gross daybed? All he wanted to do was play.

"Here," she said.

He stood up and sat on the bed next to her, and moved toward the lump, which only then did he remember was a Kostabi T-shirt he'd lost two days ago. His hand never reached it, though. What he was touching instead were her fingers—chubby and manicured, not artistic and temperamental—which gripped his hand firmly and led it to her breast. With her other hand she reached up and turned off the skewed floor lamp. The only illumination in the room was from the display lights on the synthesizer.

She pulled off her jeans and sweater. Lillick stared through the gloom at her huge breasts defined by the netlike cloth of the bra, nipples clear dark circles. The only thought on his mind was that he didn't want this. He had had only one goal in asking her here tonight, and that tactical objective had been attained. A goal that had nothing to do with the teal eyes, with the soft fingers firmly cradling his penis, with the swell of her belly, with the surprisingly sparse hair where her legs met. Nothing to do with her legs, which were round and smoother than any flesh he'd ever touched. Nothing at all.

He kissed her for a full minute.

Lillick noticed that he had not shut off the digital sampler, and it occurred to him that the machine was about to record and store the sounds of their lovemaking. He hesitated, but decided not to shut it off. You never knew when you might need good sound effects.

What he saw himself as was a juggler.

This was the image Thom Sebastian meditated upon.

The show had been Off-Broadway, years ago. But he remembered it perfectly. A variety show with a lot of hokey flower-child stuff and hippie humor like on the old *Laugh-In* TV show, psychedelic imagery. One performer Sebastian remembered above all the others: the juggler. He hadn't used balls or Indian clubs, but a hatchet, a lit blowtorch, a crystal vase, a full bottle of wine, and a wineglass.

From time to time, Sebastian thought of that show, of the tension that wound your guts up, taut, as the man would add a new object, send it sailing up in an arc, a smile on his face, eyes at the apogee (that was the juggler's trick that Sebastian loved; looking but not looking). The incredible tension, the penultimate skill. Everyone waited for the metal to cut, the torch to burn, the glass to shatter. But nope, the man's no-sweat smile silently said to the audience: So far, so good.

Sebastian, sitting in his office on Friday morning, feeling wholly depleted, now told himself the same. He knew that juggling seemed like magic and yet was nothing more than coordination of muscles and the absence of concentration. This might have been Zen. He wasn't sure. Sebastian knew nothing of religion or spiritual matters. But he liked the image of the juggler, and he saw in his own life this same orbit of many things. Some as fragile as glass, some as dangerous as gassy fire.

When he had learned that Hubbard, White & Willis had chosen not to make him a partner, Thom Sebastian had held a conference with himself, and decided after considerable negotiation to cut back on his working hours; he was going to relax.

Yet he found this to be one of the few bargains in his life he was unable to keep. Clients still came to him for help. They were often greedy, they were occasionally bastards, but a lot of times they were neither. And whether they were or not was irrelevant; they were his clients and they deserved the best legal work he could give them.

Sebastian found to his great surprise that he was physically incapable of slowing down. He continued at a frantic pace, his hours completely absorbed by two refinancings, a leveraged buy-out, a revolving credit agreement.

By own real-estate transactions, by his special project with Bosk, by his girlfriends, by Magaly his beautiful dealer, his family, his pro bono clients, his hunt for a new job. All in motion, all spinning, all just barely in control.

Thom Sebastian was at a low point. He felt buffeted and sensed that the airfoil of his life was fatiguing. As if brittle crystals were forming in structural members, and at any moment, the parts were going to crack. Bang! Into molecules. Yet he often felt this way. This was one interesting lesson he had learned about life; it was *not* like an airplane wing. The forces involved were infinitely complicated and not governed by the either/or principle. You flew sometimes, you crawled, you slept. But the motor kept going. It wouldn't come apart by itself— no such luck. (*You* had to make that decision—whether to go for the Big Dive, as Linda Davidoff had.) You pared and whittled and rigged and patched. And kept going.

So far. . . .

He desperately wanted sleep, and that thought momentarily brought to mind another: the brown glass vial still hidden in his briefcase. But it was no more than that, a passing image. Sebastian did not even consider slipping into the men's room. The concept of doing drugs within the walls of Hubbard, White & Willis itself was, to him, an obscenity.

. . . so good.

His phone rang.

"Sly Stallone, please?"

Sebastian's scalp bristled as he recognized Taylor Lockwood's voice.

He said, "Yo, youse speaking to da contendah. Dat you, Taylor?"

"I got stood up again this weekend. Only I suppose it's not being stood up, if I got advanced warning."

"You can do much better in the boyfriend department, Taylor, believe me."

"Anyway, I got a free pass to a jazz club in the Village. I was just wondering. . . . Is this forward of me?"

"Yes, but that part is fine. The bad part is it's also inopportune. I'm going to the Hamptons this Saturday. Don't you remember? Bosk? The mad dude you met at the club?"

"I didn't remember."

"Hey, let us not panic. You like touch football, walks on freezing cold beaches, a bunch of immature, spoiled preppies who drink until they barf?"

She was hesitating, and he was astonished when she said, "No, but if that's a gracious invite, I graciously accept."

"Everybody else is staying Friday through Sunday. I'm going out Saturday, coming back Sunday."

"Sure, I'd like to, you don't mind me inviting myself along."

"Not at all. I'll even do you another favor."

"What's that?"

"I'll kill your boyfriend for you. He deserves it."

"Maybe you could just maim him a little."

"Avec plaisir."

Sebastian set down the receiver and closed his eyes. He breathed deeply. Then lit a cigarette. He relaxed.

The motion of his imaginary juggler slowed. Unnecessary thoughts fell away. Projects that weren't immediate dissolved. The image of the Chinese-American girl he'd picked up last night and would be meeting at the Space tonight vanished. His job search fell away, as did a nasty, dark portrait of Wendall Clayton. Finally Sebastian was left with two thoughts, tossing them around slowly. One was the loan agreement he was working on, spread out on his desk before him.

The other was Taylor Lockwood.

He pulled the agreement toward him and looked at the words with a grave intensity. But ten minutes passed before he started to read them.

The Client is terrified.

"... We examined the fiscals ..." He shakes his head and starts again, correcting himself. "We examined the *financials* going back ten years. They were not audited. ..."

Beneath his suit of fine pink-and-gray plaid, the white shirt will be blotched with sweat. The Client's arm is extended and he works his right eyebrow between his thumb and forefinger, plucking away some hairs; that brow is much thinner than the left. Since Mitchell Reece has know him, the man has always been gaunt, but Reece believes he has lost even more weight in the past month, as they have prepared for the Hanover & Stiver trial.

"Some water?" Reece asks.

The Client shakes his head and plucks out another eyebrow hair. "... they were not audited because of a fire in the principal place of business some two years ago. However, I chose—it was my decision to proceed with the loan anyway."

They are sitting in Reece's office, on Friday afternoon. The man, the U.S. manager of Banque Industrielle de Genève, is sitting exactly one foot from the file cabinet that used to contain the note evidencing the money that his bank loaned to Hanover & Stiver. The Client does not, of course, know the note is missing. He is terrified enough even without that knowledge because it was he who authorized the loan to Lloyd Hanover—a man who has been revealed as not only offensive, which the Client deduced early in the negotiations, but also totally corrupt, a quality to which the Client was—or chose to be—oblivious.

The Client is terrified because he is in bad trouble. He is an American grudgingly hired by a bank of French Swiss who at best dislike Americans. The loan that he approved has already cost the bank several hundred thousand dollars in legal fees. If Reece loses the trial and fails to collect the principal, the U.S. branch of Banque Genève will probably close, and he will certainly lose his job. And in the tiny world of international commercial banking, a man who makes such a large, even though innocent, miscalculation can count on being out of work for a long, long time. The Client has a wife, two children attending Ivy League schools, and another son about to start college next year. He provides most of his mother's support. His job is his life, and it is the fuel on which the lives of these other people run.

Although the trial is still ten days away, Reece has agreed to help prep the Client today. He had called at midnight last night, and begged to get some pointers on his testimony so that he might rehearse for his court appearance. Reece now regrets his acquiescence. He must leave for New Orleans in an hour, and he wants to turn his attention to preparing deposition questions for that trip. Reece practices the art of compartmentalizing his life; he is irritated when, as now, he is forced to focus on something before its assigned time and place.

Still, he appreciates the Client's fears, and offers him suggestions on how to testify. He wants to reinforce the man's confidence. A week from Monday, when he takes the stand, he will be ridiculed and torn to pieces by Lloyd Hanover's lawyers. There will be little Reece can do to save him. He made a bad business decision, and in the financial world that is the least-pardonable sin, far worse than criminal activities.

Of course, the Client may not have to endure this treatment; Taylor Lockwood may not find the note, in which event the case will be dismissed within fifteen minutes.

A soft knock on the door, and Donald Burdick enters the room. He is radiating charm. The Client rises and shakes his hand with fawning excess and relief, as if Burdick were the governor on execution day. This puts off Reece somewhat, since it is he alone, not Burdick, who can save the man's ass now. Reece reflects, though, glancing at the gig in the file cabinet drawer, that it is also he alone who may have lost the man, and his expensive family, his income.

Burdick's mind is obviously elsewhere. He makes pleasantries, and does not ask about the substance of the case or how well the witness is preparing. The Client would like the partner to clap him on the shoulder and tell him everything will be all right, but this does not happen. Like Reece, even more so perhaps, Burdick has learned how to maintain priorities. Although he appears oblivious, Burdick is undoubtedly cognizant that the trial will begin in ten days and that this man's professional and personal life hangs on the outcome of that trial. He is aware, too, of how much money Banque Genève pays to both the firm and to Burdick himself. There will be time for concern, for great concern. But today, the partner has other matters on his mind. This is just a social call, to say hello to the Client.

After Burdick leaves, the Client says, "Mitchell?"

Reece focuses on him, on the thinning hair cut short, on the crease next to the eyebrow. "Yes?"

"I read the piece in the *Journal* today about the merger. You and the Perelli firm."

"Yes?"

"It said when mergers happen at firms, everything comes to a standstill. Somebody was quoted. I don't know who, but he said he'd lived through a merger, and it was like a shark frenzy."

Reece nods, surprised that Donald Burdick's public-relations man was able to get to the *Journal* so quickly. "Does it look like I'm standing still?" Reece waves his hand around his office at the piles of papers, some of which are four feet high.

"Donald seems distracted."

"He's a busy man. Besides, he's not a litigator. The details of the case don't mean much to him."

"I wish it weren't happening now."

"The suit?" Reece asks.

"The merger."

"If I can be completely honest," Reece says, "the merger should be the least of your worries. Now, go over your testimony about Hanover's defaults."

As the Client recites the endless orderly details, Reece nods encouragingly. But he finds that he is thinking of something unrelated to the Hanover & Stiver case. He recalls a closing statement from one of his recent criminal trials in which Reece's client, a young suspected murderer, was acquitted. Reece pictures himself pacing a gentle curve in front of the jury box and looking slowly into the eyes of each of the jurors as he spoke.

We are imposing upon you such a difficult burden, one you haven't asked for, one no reasonable person would want to take on. An appalling burden, a frightening one. And what's more, we're asking you to do more than simply shoulder this burden. We're asking you to seize it—and to do so with vigor, with diligence, with zeal. I am not seeking from you one hundred percent of your efforts on this case. . . . I am asking you for more than that. Much more. One hundred ten percent. One hundred fifty. All you are capable of, and then still more. . . .

Law is society's clearest eye and most just heart, and it is now in your hands, and yours alone, to attend to the burdens law requires. To see with that clear eye and to feel with that just heart. . . .

These are the words that loop through Mitchell Reece's mind, as he sends them silently, powerfully straight to Taylor Lockwood.

twelve

"Taxis."

The secretary who sat near Halsted Street looked up. "You want a taxi, Taylor?"

Taylor was pausing, staring down at the woman's neat desk, where a taxi voucher lay curled like a wood shaving. Another thought clicked. Taylor said, "And copiers."

The secretary said, "You want me to copy something?"

Taylor smiled with a look of triumph and walked down to the cost accounting department. She said to the computer operator, "I'm doing a bill for Mitchell Reece. Can you let me see the copier ledger and the taxi vouchers for last Saturday? November twenty-third."

"It's not the end of the month." The operator snapped her gum.

"Mitchell wants to give the client an estimate."

Snap. "An estimate of disbursements? It couldn't be more than a couple hundred dollars—"

"Could I just see the ledger?" Taylor said with a smile. "Please."

Snap. "I guess." She hunched over the keys and typed several lines. "There."

Taylor bent over the computer screen. The dull-white letters seemed to pulse. Four people had taken cabs from the firm on Saturday.

But all of them had left before Mitchell; none of them would have been in the firm when the note disappeared.

Taylor said, "How about the copiers? Can you tell me who made copies that Saturday?"

The fingernails tapped. The operator squinted, tapped some more, and stared at the screen. "Well, this's pretty funny." Taylor looked for the joke on the blank screen.

"Nobody made any copies on Saturday."

"Nobody at all?"

Snap. "That can't be right. There're always people in on Saturday, and they always use the copiers."

Taylor said, "Maybe they haven't been entered yet."

"Naw, the numbers go in automatically whenever you make a copy, it records the attorney number. Maybe the system was down on Saturday. Or maybe somebody erased the files accidentally."

Taylor asked, "Does that ever happen?"

"Not that I ever heard of."

"Thanks," she said.

"Like, no problem, Taylor."

Snap.

· · ·

My dearest Ms. Lockwood: We cannot thank you enough for the opportunity to review your demo tape. It so captivated the initial screener that he sent it to our A&R department, where it made the rounds in record (forgive the pun) time. Your masterly reinterpretations of the old standards in juxtaposition with your own works (masterpieces in fusion) make the tape itself worthy of production, but we would propose a three-record project of primarily original material. Enclosed you will find our standard recording contract, already executed by our senior vice president and, as an advance, a check in the amount of fifty thousand dollars. A limousine will be calling for you. . . .

Taylor Lockwood stood in her apartment building mailroom. She was simultaneously ripping open envelopes from three record companies. The yellow envelopes, all self-addressed in her handwriting, were wedged brutally into her mailbox by an angry mailman. The tops of the envelopes lay curled like flat yellow worms at her feet as she read the three form rejection letters. The one she decided said the most about the music business began with the salutation "Dear Submitter:"

She stepped into the elevator.

The elevator made its slow, grinding way up to the fourth floor. "They're all turds," she whispered, but it was, to her surprise, a cheerful whisper.

Inside her apartment, she saw a blinking light on her answering machine, and pushed the replay button as she stripped off her coat and kicked her shoes in an arc toward the closet.

Eeep.

"Taylor. Thom Sebastian here. Did you hear the one about the rabbi, the priest, and the cocker spaniel? Call me for the punch line and details about this weekend. *Ciao, bambino. . . .*"

Eeep.

"Hey, Taylor, this is Sean. If I don't sound too straight it's because I'm not. God, I hope you're not dating a guy from the DEA, who's maybe over there now and you're screening calls. All right, I confess. My name is Sean Smith. From Poughkeepsie. Anyway, I've talked to Linda's roommate. He's coming to my show tonight at the Plastic Respect. Avenue C. Bring your fingers, we can do a duet. Show time's at one. . . ."

One A.M. Brother.

Eeep.

"Taylor." It was Reece's voice, and she felt her temple skin bristle when she heard it. "It's Mitchell. I'm in N'awlins. Forgot to ask. . . . Come over for dinner Monday night? Notice that I'm not telling you where I am, so you can't say no."

Eeep.

The elation lasted for only five seconds—long enough for her to reset the machine and dance into the bedroom. Then the thought hit her: Was he alone in New Orleans? Sure, he was probably working, but was his Westchester girlfriend with him? She felt ill. He wouldn't have invited her, no. He'd be too busy. That's good.

No, that's bad. Maybe *because* he was so busy, he had consolidated business with a pleasure trip.

She thought of him walking through the humid French Quarter

with a young blonde on his arm. Taylor caught a glance of her face in the mirror, at the three-furrow frown.

Come on, girl, forget about it. He isn't with anyone, and even if he is, what business is it of yours?

She manhandled the thought away and walked into the bedroom as she pulled off her skirt and blouse and stood in front of her closet, debating. She pulled a dress off a hanger and began to slip it on. . . .

Ha, she thought triumphantly, he *is* alone in New Orleans. Reece bought the poor thing flowers because he *wasn't* going to take her with him. Men. Guilt. Bribes. Taylor Lockwood knew all about that.

She relaxed and looked at herself in the mirror, at first with approval, then with shock. *No, no, no.* She found she was wearing a Betsey Johnson that had a skin-to-cloth ratio of about three to one, and the former included plenty of chest and thigh. She pulled it off and found a longer, high-necked department-store dress.

If she was going to be spying on a man who was her grandfather's age, it was going to be as Kim Philby, not Mata Hari.

This is his club?

Cozy, monied, good-old-buddy. Taylor had expected that. But just thought it should have been more, well, spiffy. More of a power, platinum-card corporate watering hole and less of a college lounge. Well, maybe academia was allowed a little shabbiness. In any case, Taylor Lockwood looked at the fiercely bright lighting in the dining hall, the dusty moosehead sprouting from the wall, the threadbare school banners and uncarpeted floor, and asked herself again, *This is his club?*

But Ralph Dudley was excited. He was at home and seemed to be feeling the buoyancy of showing off his nest to a stranger. "Have the steak, Taylor. They have chicken, too, but order the steak. Rare, like mine." The old partner's excitement was infectious, eyes gleaming as if he were back in the arms of his alma mater—the pastoral of Quadrangle, the neo-Gothic collegiate architecture.

They ordered, and Dudley began telling Taylor more than she would ever want to know about the law school, even if she had actually been considering attending. It seemed an endless tumble of hard work, collegiate pranks, Whiffenpoof singers, respectable young gentlemen in suits and ties, and tearfully inspiring professors. All very Mr. Chipps, and forty years out of date.

She nodded, smiled till she felt jowls, and said, "Uh-huh" every sixty seconds.

The waiter brought the steaks, charred and fatty. They smelled and tasted sumptuous. The plates were skillet hot. Dudley had ordered a St. Emillion. "I think you'll approve of this," he said, proud, a natural host. The fragrant wine overwhelmed her with its richness. They ate in silence. Dudley, precise with his implements, sitting rock upright, could have been a model for a Normal Rockwell painting.

She looked at her watch. "You said you had some plans tonight. I don't want to interfere with them. I hope you're not working late?"

He gave her a charming smile. "Just meeting some friends. I gave up working evenings when I made partner."

Taylor took a sip of the heavy wine. "I hate working late. And working weekends. But I thought I saw you, didn't I? Last Saturday?"

A flicker of surprise? She couldn't tell. Then Dudley was shaking his head in amusement and took an elaborate sip of wine, which ended with another examination of the bottle. "Saturday? I don't think so."

Yep, a lie. The pulse of his eyes confirmed it.

"Maybe it was Donald Burdick." He talked quickly and seemed to feel a need to explain. "Yes, that was probably it. I'm told we look alike. No, I haven't worked on a weekend since, let's see, '79 or '80. That was a case involving the seizure of foreign assets. Iranian, I think. Yes, it was. Let me tell you about it. Fascinating case."

Which was a matter of opinion. It was an hour later when Dudley glanced at his watch and said he ought to be leaving. He signed the bill, and they wandered out of the club into the cold, damp ozone of a New York evening on the shag end of November.

Taylor hoped the cool air would wake her, but it had no effect. The narcotics of red wine and heavy food numbed her. She groggily followed Dudley to the front doors, wishing she had some of Thom Sebastian's Mr. Wizard wake-up powder.

He said, "You all right, Taylor?"

"Fine, just a little tired."

"Tired?" Dudley said, as if he had never heard of the word, and started down the steps in long, enthusiastic but gentlemanly strides.

• • •

"Wait."

Sean Lillick's voice was sufficiently urgent that Wendall Clayton stopped walking down the lobby stairs that led to the club's private rooms on the second and third floors.

"What is it?"

"There, didn't you see them? It was Ralph Dudley and Taylor Lockwood."

Clayton frowned. He resumed walking. "So?"

"What are they doing here?"

"Fucking?" Clayton suggested.

"They weren't upstairs. They came out of the dining room, it looked like."

"Maybe he bought her dinner and now he's going to fuck her. I wonder if he can still get it up." Clayton said it with what sounded like genuine curiosity.

"I don't want them to see us," Lillick said.

"Why not?"

"I just don't."

Clayton shrugged. He looked at his watch. "Randy's a little late tonight."

Lillick said, "I've got to leave about midnight, Wendall. If it's okay." His suit didn't fit well, and he looked like a college boy out to dinner with Dad.

"Midnight?"

"It's important."

"I suppose it's all right. What's up?" Clayton smiled. "Do you have a date?" He dragged the last word out teasingly.

"Just seeing some friends."

Clayton looked impatiently at his watch.

Lillick was wondering if Taylor had seen him. He doubted it. She would have signaled or said something, confirmed that she'd be at his show later that night. Several partners were members of this club, and she wouldn't at first think it was unusual for him to be here with Wendall Clayton. But then she'd notice they were coming down the stairs from the private bedrooms.

Clayton lifted his head and gave a reserved smile to a young man just entering the club. He had a long, rectangular face divided by thin tortoiseshell glasses. One of Clayton's protégés. Randy was, Lillick had been told, a lawyer whose mind dug to the core of a problem like an auger (Clayton's imagery). He also was, Lillick had observed, an absolute, vaporous cipher.

The three shook hands. Lillick's eyes kept straying to the door.

Randy said, "I saw Ralph Dudley outside."

"If he's a member," Clayton said slowly, "I should tender my resignation. . . . Sean and I have been upstairs for a while. I think we'll have something to eat, then the three of us can resume. You haven't eaten?"

Randy said, "No, I haven't." He was six-feet-three, thin and solid. Ralph Lauren might have designed a line of Connecticut sportswear around him. A mother and her two teenage daughters entered the lobby. All three eyed him with varying degrees of desire. He glanced through them, then back to Clayton, who was saying, "You brought the goodies?"

Randy blinked. "The goodies?"

Clayton nodded at the briefcase.

"Oh, yeah. I've got what you asked for."

The partner walked toward the dining room. "I'm starving. We should eat well. It's going to be a long night."

At the corner, Taylor and Dudley paused and shook hands. He inclined his head toward her in a Victorian way she found quaint, and said, "You going where? Uptown?"

"I'll walk down Fifth."

"I'll cab it, I suppose. Good luck to you. Let me know how you fare."

Taylor had thought she would have to do a private-eye number: *Hey, follow that cab; there's a fiver in it for you.* But no: Dudley was on foot, going to meet the mysterious *W.S.,* whom he had visited the night the note was stolen.

When he was a half block away, Taylor followed. Moving west through the glossy wetness of the streets and storefront windows, all lit for security. Still plenty of traffic, some theaters letting out now, people coming back from dinner, going to exotic glowing, low-lit, humming evening spots. Taylor felt the luminous energy of the city, she saw a million lights stronger and more varied than stars, people rushed along, driven and volatile, and she found that she had sped up to keep pace with the city and had nearly overtaken Dudley. She slowed, and let him regain a long lead.

Then they were into Times Square. The partner walked quickly, and several times looked at his watch. Taylor studied his old gray slope-shouldered coat and brown wingtips, worn at the heels.

Out of the brilliant, cold fake daylight of the Square, and moving west. Only now did Taylor feel the first lump of fear as she crossed an invisible barrier, into pimp city. The PR firms hired by New York developers called this area Clinton; most everyone else knew it by its historical name—the more picturesque Hell's Kitchen.

Taylor continued even when Dudley hit Twelfth Avenue, near the river, and turned south, where the streetlights grew sparser, the neighborhood was deserted, and there were no more lean girls and transvestites standing in the chill asking men, "How 'bout a date, honey?"

Then Dudley stopped so suddenly, catching Taylor in midthought, that she had to jump into a doorway to avoid being seen. The concrete reeked of sour urine. Hugging the shadows, she felt nauseous. When she looked again, Dudley was gone. Taylor waited for five minutes, not hearing a footstep or a voice, and she breathed shallow gasps of cold air, listening to the sticky rush of traffic on the West Side Highway. Then she walked toward the spot where Dudley had disappeared: the doorway of a small two-story building. There were no lights in any of the windows, though she saw they were painted over. An old sign, faded, read, *West Side Art and Photography Club.*

W.S. on his calendar. So, a place, not a person. He'd come here sometime the night the note disappeared. But what was here? A witness, a conspirator? Someone he'd sold the twenty-five-million-dollar note to?

She cocked her head and listened. She thought she heard something. Wait, wait. Taylor tried to block out the rush of the cars and trucks and believed she heard music, something syrupy, full of strings, like Mantovani.

She stood in a doorway, leaned against the stone, and watched a cluster of intrepid rats browse through a garbage pile across the street. *He goes in, he's got to come out.*

An hour later he did.

The door swung wide. Taylor caught an image of pink and lavender. Soft music and softer light spilled out into the street. A radio cab pulled up. Dudley appeared then vanished immediately into the car, which sped away.

The question was, what would Mitchell do?

No, that wasn't the question at all. She knew what he would do. The question really was, did she have the guts to do the same thing?

The grapevine says you've got balls.

Yeah, well. . . . Taylor turned and walked away from the club, toward one of the avenues where she saw a few cabs banging uptown along the uneven asphalt. When she got to the corner, she raised her hand to flag one down. She saw one up the street. Out loud she muttered, "Uck." She lowered her hand, then trudged back to the Art Club.

Oh, son of a bitch.

She pressed the buzzer.

A handsome black man, large and trapezoidal, opened the door. "Yes?" he asked, poised and polite.

Taylor said, "Um, I'm here. . . ." Her voice clogged.

"Yes, you are."

"I'm here because a customer—"

"A member."

"A member told me about your place. He said I might have a good time." Taylor swallowed.

The bouncer looked past her and then opened the door. Taylor stepped inside.

It was like the lobby of an exclusive hotel (the interior designer could have been the same one who dolled up Hubbard, White & Willis). Smoky pastels, brushed copper, leather furniture, a teak bar. Three Japanese men, all in dark suits, sat on a plush couch, smoking furiously. They looked at Taylor briefly—hopefully—then, when she met their gaze with restrained hostility, looked away.

A woman in her forties, wearing a conservative navy suit and white blouse, walked silently up to her. "How may I help you?"

Taylor said the first thing, the only thing, that came into her mind. "You probably don't get many women in here."

The hostess frowned with curiosity. "Why would you think that?"

"Uh . . ."

"The West Side Art and Photography Club is one of the oldest art appreciation clubs in the city. Here's some literature." She handed Taylor a glossy brochure. There were programs of music, art shows, classes. Oh, no. Oh, hell, she had it all wrong. She felt her face turn crimson. "You *are* an art club."

The hostess lifted her palms with polite surprise. "As the name suggests."

"Oh."

After a moment's pause, the hostess said, "How did you hear about us?"

"Ralph Dudley."

"Ralph?" the woman said quickly. "Oh, you just missed him. You should have said so." She took back the brochure and tossed it in a drawer. "Now, let's get down to business. Our membership fee is five hundred, and the hourly fee is two-fifty for one model, four hundred for two. I assume you want a man; he'll have to wear a condom. Oral sex is completely up to the individual model; most do, some don't. Tipping is not expected. The fee includes any standard toys, but if you want something special, it can probably be arranged. Oh, and you're right."

Taylor blinked.

The woman said, "We *don't* get many women in here. Will that be cash or charge?"

"Uh, American Express?"

"One hour?"

"One hour, sure."

The woman took the card and asked, "Do you have any special requests?"

Taylor said, "Actually, I was thinking about something a little unusual. Could I have the, uh, model that Ralph Dudley sees."

The hostess, trained to be unflappable, did not look up from the charge voucher. "You're sure?"

Thinking she'd never been less sure about anything in her life, Taylor Lockwood gave a slight smile and said, "Yes."

"There's a premium."

"No problem." Smiling, Taylor took the credit card slip and a pen. *I do this every day. See the steadiness of my hand as I sign.*

The hostess disappeared into the back room. Muzak played quietly, a guitar rendition of "Pearly Shells." She returned a moment later with a key. "I've talked to her. She hasn't been with too many women, so I haven't charged the premium this time. But I think you'll find her quite nice. Up the stairs, last room on the right. You want a drink, or anything? Drinks are free. Coke we can give you at cost."

"No, thank you." Taylor started up the stairs.

"Oh, one thing."

Taylor turned.

The hostess said, "Naturally, oral sex would be okay this case."

"Naturally," Taylor said and disappeared into the cool, dark hall. She was doing the math in her head. Thinking of how often she'd seen the W.S. in Dudley's calendar. Times two-fifty. An expensive habit. Five, six hundred a week—that could certainly drive you to theft.

She knocked on the door. A voice called, "Come on in."

Taylor took a deep breath, exhaled, and stepped into the room. She stopped, stared, shock in her eyes—an expression that perfectly matched the one on the face of the girl who stood, topless, in the center of the room.

The garter belt in Junie's hand fell to the floor with a dull clink as the girl said, "Oh, shit, it's you."

thirteen

"Y ou gotta close the door," the little girl said. "It's a like a rule. Johnny, he's the bouncer, comes around and gets pissed, you don't."

Taylor stepped into the room.

Junie said, "Like, Ralph isn't going to be so happy this happened, you know."

Taylor whispered, "You're his granddaughter?"

The girl was heavily made up, with dark streaks of brown and blue that made her face sleek and serpentine. Her small breasts were high, pointed outward. She retrieved the garter and began untangling it. "Like, what it is, he's one of my oldest customers." She laughed. "I mean one of the dudes I've been seeing for the longest time. But, you know, he's one of the oldest, too."

Taylor looked at a plush armchair. "You mind if I sit down?"

"It's your hour. Have a drink, you want."

Taylor poured chilled Taitinger into a crystal champagne glass. "You want any?"

"Me? I don't drink. I'm like underage, you know?"

Taylor said, "You mind?" as she eased her shoes off. A swell of pain went through her feet, then slowly vanished.

"Usually, people take off a lot more than their shoes."

"So tell me about you and Ralph."

"I guess I oughta ask why."

"I'll pay you."

"I guess I oughta see the duckets."

"The what?"

The girl held her palm out.

Taylor opened her purse. She hadn't brought much of Reece's bribe money. She wadded together about ninety dollars, keeping twenty for herself.

"I get that as a tip for a blowjob," Junie said.

Taylor handed her more money. "That's all I have."

Junie shrugged and put the money in a dresser drawer. She pulled out a T-shirt and worked it over her head.

"So, Poppie—that's what I call him—he likes girls my age. He came to the house a few years ago and we had a date. He kept coming back. It was like totally bizotic but I had a good time with him. We started meeting a few times outside the house. They get really dissed they find out, but we did. He brought me some totally def clothes. Nice shit, you know. From the good stores. Anyway, we did some weird things, like, he took me to this art museum, which was a real bore. But then we went to the zoo. . . . Like, I've never been to the zoo, that was wild. Animals are very, like, bizarre, you know. We just kept hanging out more and more. He's lonely. His wife died, and his daughter is a total bowhead. All she cares about is herself."

"Junie . . . is that really your name?"

"June. I like June."

"June, last Saturday night, was Ralph here?"

"Yeah."

"When?"

"Around midnight, I guess."

"Do you know where he was before that?"

"We had dinner, then we went to the company."

"What company?"

"You know, your law company."

"What time?"

"Can I take the stockings off? They're kind of itchy."

"Go ahead. When were you in the firm on Saturday?"

"I guess it was about nine or ten. Then we came back here for his regular appointment. He's real careful about it. We fuck at his place a lot, but because I, you know, work here, he comes over a couple times a week, so they don't guess nothing. If they found out I was seeing somebody private, they'd fuck me over like totally."

"What was he doing at the firm?"

Junie's eyes swept around the room. "Uh, you know, I'm telling you these things. Maybe you should tell me why."

"How about another hundred dollars?"

"I thought you don't have any more money."

"I can give you a check."

"A check?" Junie laughed.

"I promise it won't bounce."

"That was, what, five hundred you said?"

Taylor hesitated, then smiled. "You have a good memory."

She wrote it out and handed it to her. *Mitchell, you're going to see a very odd expense account for this project. . . .*

Junie slipped the check into her drawer. "Okay, I'm not exactly sure what he was doing. Looking through all these file cabinets and things, reading shit, I don't know. Then he left me alone for about an hour. I got bored and wandered around. You dudes got a great lunchroom at that place. You know that machine with the candy that's on this spiral thing, you put the money in and it turns and drops the stuff right into the tray below? I bought like ten packs of gum just to watch it."

Taylor asked, "Has he ever mentioned a company called Hanover & Stiver?"

"Naw, but he don't talk about his business too much. He like tried for a while, but it's mundo-boring, so whenever he starts up, I'm like, 'Come on, Poppie, *donnez-moi un* break.' So he gave up."

"Did you see anyone else in the firm that night?"

"Sure, that's why Poppie had the fight."

"Fight?"

"There was this megadweeb in the company. This guy, he was pretty old, maybe forty-five. Wearing these green pants and a yellow shirt, like, seeing those colors, you want to boot your lunch all over the floor."

"What did they fight about?"

"Well, me, sort of. Like I was telling you, I got bored and was walking around the halls. I saw this room filled with some totally excellent food. Bagels and cream cheese, doughnuts. So I sat down and started to eat. I mean, big fucking deal, nobody else was there. Then this dexter I was telling you about comes in and starts screaming at me. Poppie heard and he came in and he's like: 'What's going on here?' And this guy goes, 'This is a private conference room, what the fuck is she doing in here?' He and Poppie really started screaming at each other, and this guy says get the hell out or he'll make sure Poppie's kicked out of the office like he should have been a long time ago. . . . I've got a can of Mace in my purse, and I wanted to get him in the face, then wail the shit out of him. I mean, I don't let nobody fucking diss me like that. Nobody. But Poppie was freaked, so we just left."

"What was this guy doing?"

Junie shrugged. "You ask me, he was getting over with this kid who was there."

"Getting over?"

"You know, fucking."

"In the firm?"

"Hey, I'm like guessing. All I know is he was with this kid who you ask me was a stud-muffin, you know?"

"A—"

"Like he was too fresh to believe?"

"Try again," Taylor said.

Junie frowned and tried to translate. "He was like too cool for himself. Black shirt, baggy pants, an earring. He didn't look like the rest of the dudes I've seen at the place."

"Did you hear any names?"

"Yeah, the dexter, the guy in the green pants—I had me a pimp one time wore suits that color—was . . . it was a weird name. Wenton, I don't know. Some fag name."

"Wendall? Wendall Clayton?"

"Yeah, Wendall." Junie mocked a North Shore lockjaw accent: "He sounded like this. . . ."

From somewhere came a rhythmic squealing. *That'stheway, that'stheway, yeah, that'stheway.* . . .

Taylor said, "Did Ralph bring anything with him that night? Did he hide anything?"

Junie looked calmly at Taylor and said in a very adult voice, "I think you got enough for your money."

Taylor said, "I can write you another check."

Junie shook her head. "That's about all I want to tell you."

Taylor stood slowly, slipped her swollen feet back into her shoes. She walked painfully to the door.

"Hey, wait a second." Junie looked her over and grinned. "You still got some time. Why don't you stay? I was thinking, I've never got over with an older lady. How 'bout it?"

"Some other time."

"Hey wake up! Come on, I'm talking to you. . . ."

The cab driver was reaching through the smeared Plexiglas divider, shaking her by the shoulder and shouting. From his agitation and the occasional lapse into his native Israeli, Taylor guessed he'd been at it for a while.

"What time is it," she asked groggily.

"One-thirty."

"In the morning?"

"Come on. Fare is eleven twenty-five. Come on."

She paid. "Is this where I want to go?"

"This is where you *asked* to go. Where you *want* to go, hey, only you know that one, honey."

The storefront had been encrusted with tiles, pictures, bits of mirror, plastic toys, lacquered magazine covers. In handprinted letters above the door: *Plastic Respect.* The bouncer looked at her black leather pumps like a scientist observing a microbe and reluctantly nodded her inside.

The room was painted flat black. Along one wall was a warped bar. The floor was half-filled with people sitting around tiny, listing tables. Taylor saw straight couples, lesbians, gay men, a few singles. Black leather, baggy slacks, boots, and T-shirts were the uniform. A table of women with cropped hair studied Taylor's navy-blue polka-dotted Saks Fifth Avenue dress with sublime curiosity, then resumed their solemn vigil of the stage, where a funeral was in progress.

The object of their mourning was Sean Lillick.

His thin body lay in a cheap wooden coffin, out of which flowed a dozen wires. He was deathly with white makeup. His eyes were closed, but his fingers moved along a keyboard that rested on his chest. From the speakers came notes made up of human voices, recorded by the digital sampler and played back through the synthesizer. Ocean noises sounded in the background.

Another character walked onstage, and Taylor felt her heart give a fibrillating thump. It was a woman who looked very much like her. Same height and build, with the same tangle of dark hair. Her face was ashen with the same makeup Lillick wore, and she wore a sheet like a winding shroud. Over her left breast was a bloodstain. Taylor swallowed and watched the woman walk slowly, keeping the beat of the slow music, to the coffin, take a dried rose from it. She pivoted, then scanned the audience. Taylor wanted to hide from the woman's dark, searing eyes. But she could not. As the gaze passed over her without focussing, Taylor stood frozen. Finally, the actress turned and faded into the shadows behind the stage.

A relentless paralysis held Taylor for a vast moment, then her heart calmed and she walked straight to the bar. She asked for a brandy, a drink that no one had apparently ever ordered here before. The bartender didn't know how much to charge. Taylor put five on the bar, told her to keep the change. She drank half of the glass, and turned back to the stage, where the music was fading and the lights dimming to black. There was shuffling around the coffin, and the houselights came on. The applause was enthusiastic. Lillick came out from behind the curtain, bowed dramatically and bounded to the bar, waving at people in the audience. He hugged Taylor and sat beside her. He was pure vigor, gesturing and rocking back and forth. At first she thought it was coke, but then realized it was a performance high. She'd felt it herself, like no feeling in the world.

"That's a world premiere."

"I loved it. Really." She was not exactly lying. Taylor could honestly say she respected what he was doing. She did, however, generally prefer art you could enjoy, like ice cream, to art that you could only respect.

"But did you have to use a ghost that looked like me?" she asked.

Lillick frowned, then laughed. "God, I never thought about it. She does. Why, you feel something walk over your grave?"

"As a matter of fact, yeah."

Lillick was scanning the audience. "There's supposedly a reviewer here from the *East Village Informer*. Did I ever show you? I got a mention in the *Voice*. It said, 'Beware of Sean Lillick.' Can you believe it? The *Voice* was telling people to beware of me. Put me in heaven for a week." He gazed out over the diminishing audience. "Reviewers look just like everybody else, though. That's the problem. God, I hope there're people left for the three-o'clock show. That's when I really start cooking."

"Hello, Sean."

Lillick and Taylor turned to see a thin young man with crew-cut brown hair and mustache. He and Lillick shook hands. "Danny, this is Taylor Lockwood, she wanted to talk to you about Linda, remember? Taylor, Danny Stuart."

They smiled and nodded.

Danny laughed. He said to Taylor, "I love Sean's shows. He'll be the next Laurie Anderson."

"Do you perform?" she asked.

"No musical talent whatsoever. I'm an editor. A literary magazine. A computer programmer by trade."

Lillick said, "I think there's a fan that's dying to meet me." He walked off to a table in the corner at which sat a gangling solemn young woman with bright-orange hair.

Danny ordered an Amstel, then asked, "So, you knew Linda?"

"We worked together."

"Ah, you're at Hubbard, White? Are you a lawyer?"

"Paralegal."

He nodded. "Linda and I roomed together for, I guess, about nine or ten months. Until she died."

"Did you know her well?"

"She contributed to the magazine and wrote reviews for us. She was going to join the staff this fall. We were pretty close."

"How did it happen, the suicide?"

"She was up at her parents' summer house. The back deck was above this big gorge. One night, she jumped."

Taylor closed her eyes and shook her head. "It wasn't an accident?"

"She left a note."

"What did it say?"

"Well, it wasn't really a note. It was one of her poems. When Sean told me you were interested, I thought you'd like to see it. I made you a copy. It's dated the day before she died. It talks about leaving life behind her, all the cares. . . . I was going to publish it in my magazine, but I haven't had the heart."

He handed her the Xerox copy. Taylor read the title: *When I Leave, I'll Travel Light.* She put it in her purse.

She looked at Danny and said, "I hope I can ask you something in confidence. Something that won't go farther."

"Sure."

"Do you think Linda killed herself because of something that happened at work?"

"No."

"You sound pretty certain."

"I am. I know exactly why she killed herself."

"I thought no one knew."

"Well, I did. She was pregnant."

"Pregnant?"

"I don't think anybody knew except me. She got an EPT kit? It was just a couple of weeks before she died. I saw the kit in the bathroom and asked her about it. You know, we were like girlfriends. She confided in me."

"But why would she kill herself?"

"I think the father dumped her. But that's just a guess."

"Who was the father?"

"I don't know. She was seeing somebody, but never talked about him or brought him around the loft. I have no idea who it was."

"You break up with somebody, it doesn't seem like reason to kill yourself."

He looked at her, and Taylor thought, *poet's eyes,* and wondered in what metaphors he thought of Linda. As if Danny Stuart understood this, he said, "You're always surprised when someone kills themself, but what happened with Linda didn't shock me at all. She was very sensitive. Her face had this beautiful vulnerability about it. Diane Arbus would have photographed her."

"She never mentioned a problem at work, anyone approaching her about doing something illegal?"

"Nope. Not a word."

Danny said he had to be getting home. Taylor thanked him and watched him leave. She was discouraged. *So, you were right, Mitchell. Linda's death had nothing to do with the stolen note at all. Remember the murdered hobos. . . .* Taylor laughed, thinking the worst part of this particular venture tonight was that she could be home getting some sleep right now.

Lillick was suddenly standing next to her. He said a sorrowful "Strike three."

Taylor watched the young girl he'd been talking to stand up, flick her orange hair over her shoulder, and join a group of woman at another table.

"Was he helpful?" Lillick said.

"Yeah," Taylor said noncommittally.

Lillick was examining her. "You look a little tired."

"Long day."

He said casually, "You eat already?"

She was about to lie and tell him that she'd been at the firm all night, but Lillick could very well have been there and would know she was lying. She said, "I had something earlier."

"He took you out someplace fancy, huh?"

She didn't speak for a minute. "Who?"

"Your date." Lillick nodded at her dress. "You're all dressed up."

"Uh, no. I was out with a girlfriend."

Lillick looked at her, nodding. "Girlfriend."

For a moment, as often happened when she lied, Taylor had this thought that he knew the truth, as if he were psychic and knew that she'd had dinner with Dudley. But then he was looking away, checking out the audience, which was now filling up again to his delight. She decided she was being paranoid.

Taylor yawned and stretched. A joint popped. The walls were badly painted, swirls of dark paint (black? purple?) that didn't cover the lighter enamel underneath. The floor felt spongy under the chairs. Cigarette smoke and alcohol spills from the heavy, shallow glasses had pickled the wood. There was a postpunk, postmodern, postnew wave facade that didn't fool Taylor for a minute. This was pure Beat. Only the set designs had changed. The key was the jukebox. Dave Brubeck and Bob Dylan were one column away from the popular teenage groups racing for obscurity.

Lillick said, "You'll stay for the next show?"

She shook her head. "I need some sleep. I'm not an after-hours person. I'm a during-hours person."

Lillick was talking to her, but she did not hear a word of what he said. She had glanced into the corner of the club, where her look-alike sat, the ghost in the bloody robe. The actress absently ran a hand through her wild hair, and she was aiming her death-shaded eyes directly at Taylor Lockwood.

fourteen

"Why does it take a woman so long to have an orgasm?" Thom Sebastian asked Taylor Lockwood.

"Thom . . ."

They were in the backseat of a limo racing along the Long Island Expressway on Saturday morning. The driver's eyes flicked to the radar detector needle as often as they glanced at the highway.

"Come on, why does it take—"

"Okay, I give up. Why?"

"Who cares?" He rocked back and roared in laughter. He opened a beer and offered it to her. She declined.

"This is going to be a very weird day," he announced. "You know anything about Bosk?"

"I know his parents are serving time if they named him that."

"His real name's Albert. Albert L. Peterson. I believe he's the third. Or fourth. Boskie baby. See, that's a generational difference. If he had been born in the '30s or '40s, they'd call him Alp, or Alpie. See, A.L.P. But we live in the era of the figurative, so the man's name became Bosk. His father and mother have been separated practically since he was born. She has a house in Boston, and his father has an apartment on the Upper East Side. They kept the summer place in the

Hamptons, *quo vadis,* and have it on alternative weeks. They—that's the parents—can't talk to each other without bloodshed, so they have their lawyers set up the times when the house is free."

"Are we the father's or mother's?"

"The mother's."

"Sounds like it's going to be a bucket of kicks and giggles. What is she? Like an old crone?"

"All I'll say is she's stranger than his father."

"What does he do?"

"Dad? What he does is he's rich. He's a senior partner at Ludlum Morgan, the investment bank."

"Is Bosk—I feel like I want to give him a Milk-Bone when I say that—working there, too?"

"He will be. He serves his time at Richards, Levitt, then waltzes over to Ludlum at a neat two-fifty a year plus bonus."

"Life is hard."

"Give the guy a break. He's not young. He's twenty-eight."

Taylor changed her mind. "A beer, *s'il vous plaît?*"

He popped one, handed it to her.

"The mother?"

"Ada travels, entertains, does what any fifty-five-year-old sorority sister does: manages her portfolio. It's about sixty million." Sebastian finished the beer and squeezed her knee. "Ho, boy, Taylor. This's gonna be primo. We're gonna get stoned and lit and have orgies in the hot tub . . ."

"Thom." She lifted his pudgy hand off her skirt.

". . . and read from the Book of Common Prayer and watch the missus put up preserves." He opened another beer. "Mah, mah, what a glorious diversion we have ahead of us."

The family manse was a three-story Gothic Victorian house, painted white with dark blue trim. Two towers rose to widow's walks, which overlooked three connected outbuildings. The house itself was covered with skeletons of vines and wisteria. A spiked, wrought-iron fence surrounded a labyrinth of grounds. Much of the property had been reclaimed by tangles of forsythia with sparse tags of brown and yellow leaves.

"Addams Family," Taylor said.

The circular driveway was full of cars. The limo paused and they got out. "God, more German cars than in Brazil," Sebastian said. The driver took their suitcases to the front door.

"Porches. I love porches," Taylor said. She sat on a wooden swing and rocked back and forth. "It should be thirty degrees warmer."

He slung his bag over his shoulder and picked up her suitcase. "I'll take these up to our room."

Taylor said, "Plural."

Sebastian said, "I'll take them up to our plural."

He rang the bell. A woman in her late fifties came to the door. Her dry, blond hair swept sideways Jackie Kennedy style and was sprayed firmly into place. She wore a lime-green silk dress woven with pink and black triangles that pointed feverishly in all directions. Over one shoulder was a busy triangular black and white scarf. Her face swept downward. It was long and glossy, the high bones holding the skin like a taut sail. Her eyes seemed young and eerie. They focused, then looked away often. Her jewelry was large. A blue topaz on her tanned, wrinkled finger was easily fifty carats. It was set in thick platinum.

"Thomas." They pressed cheeks, Taylor was introduced to Ada Peterson—introduced, then promptly examined: the dynamics of the eyes, the contour of skin. The mouth especially. Taylor understood. Bosk's little girlfriends—age twenty-three or twenty-four—could be forgiven their youth. Taylor had probably broken the three-oh barrier, and yet had hardly a crow's foot or defining jowl.

Competition. *She's jealous of me.*

Yet the older woman's smile and charm did not waver; she had been brought up right. "Call me Ada, please. I don't know where Albert is. The others are playing football on the side lawn. If you brought a wet suit, you might try the ocean."

"No physical effort, Ada. I'm here to veg."

"Well, that's wonderful, Thomas. Good for you. Go on upstairs now. I don't think anyone's left to arrive, so whatever rooms are there are yours. Albert is social director. But I'm in charge of dinner. That will be at eight. You needn't dress."

Then she was gone.

From halfway up the stairs, a bellowing voice: "Sea Bass, Sea Bass!"

Sebastian turned and grunted. "Bosk-*meister!* Yo!"

Their host was in filthy chinos, muddy and torn. His shoes were Top-Siders. He wore a green sweatshirt. His hands and face were red, his eyes watering from the cold. The men howled, and circled their fists above their heads.

Bosk leaned forward, his arm on Sebastian's shoulders. "Jennie's here and she brought Billy-boy, you can believe it."

"No way can I fucking believe it. What is he, like zoned-out permanent?"

Bosk's eyes danced to Taylor.

" 'Lo. You're . . . ?"

"Taylor Lockwood."

"Right, you're the one who won't marry me."

"You bet. You have a nice place here."

"Thanks. I'll show you around later. It's fourth and goal, but I had to take a whiz. Pick a room, Mr. T, and wear something I can knock your ass in the mud in." He trotted outside.

Upstairs, Sebastian stepped into a small, dark-wallpapered room and tossed his bag onto a four-poster. "Oh, look, a double bed."

"I'm sure you'll be very comfortable in it, Thom. Plenty of room to thrash about in your sleep."

"Alone?"

"No, you and your sweet dreams."

"You're cruel, Taylor. Damn cruel."

She found an empty room next to his. It was bright. The walls were covered in pink Laura Ashley paper. The lace-curtained windows overlooked the beach. Sebastian would have known the house well, and Taylor figured that, showing his chivalry, he had taken the smaller, darker room for himself. Then she noticed that the room he had left for her did not have a door lock. In the corner of the room, she found a chair that would fit snugly under the knob at night.

As she was unpacking, Sebastian appeared in the doorway, wearing chinos, a maroon and yellow rugby shirt bulging with belly, green wool socks, and New Balance running shoes. "Come on, final quarter. They need us, Taylor. The team needs us."

"I didn't know we'd be rolling around in the mud. I didn't bring that kind of casual."

"You don't have to roll in the mud. That's optional."

In the backyard, Bosk introduced her to the crowd of people in their twenties. Names went past—Rob and Mindy and Gay-Gay and Trevor and Windham and MacKenzie (the latter both female), clusters of contemporary phonemes more distinct than the faces of the handsome men and pretty women they identified. Taylor smiled and waved and forgot the names instantly. They were friendly and cautious and Taylor wondered what they were thinking of her—a woman half wop, half mick, with a mass of kinky black hair, not a pert ponytail, and wearing a long paisley skirt and a black blouse. *(My God, there she was in Southhampton, I couldn't believe it, and she was looking like something from, I mean really, SoHo or something.)*

That was the message from the women. From the men there was something more. Something between casual flirtation and the blatant, European, knee-jerk invitation to hop in the sack. At halftime, Taylor figured there would be a lot of female arms twining through the belt loops of their men.

The air was cold and wet. Taylor could hear the ocean from some ambiguous, changing direction.

"Hey, Taylor, play the feetsball! Play the feetsball!" Bosk was motioning her onto the grass.

"No, go ahead. I'll be the cheerleader."

"Oh, boo!" he shouted.

Sebastian chugged a beer and ran onto the field. The game resumed. Bosk crouched behind the center, a petite blonde. He patted her butt. She turned and swatted his hand, then giggled and kissed him on the mouth.

Standing still, Taylor felt the cold. The wind was from the sea and lay on her skin like wet cloth. Her feet were aching. She walked along the sideline, past the spectators of green beer bottles, thinking that if there was one word to summarize what she was doing here, that word was: absurd.

Dinner was Ada's jurisdiction.

She presided with the quiet authority of someone for whom social propriety is statutory. Crystal and china were in exact placement. Somewhere, in a three-decades-old volume of Emily Post, this very layout of Waterford, Gorham, and Limoges was represented. Though the clothing was supposed to be casual, Ada's appearance in a rustling silk dress, black-velvet headband, and necklace with a lemon-colored stone the size of a fat thumb made it clear that, whatever happened in the frat dining halls or eating clubs these youngsters were accustomed to, a dinner in this particular house would be governed by a respectable modicum of formality.

Taylor tried a vain end run around the seating ("Oh, I'm sorry, was I supposed to sit there?"); Ada smilingly steered her away from Bosk's girlfriend (a potential source of information about Sebastian's project), scolding, "Boy, girl, boy, girl . . ."

Lobster bisque, a pear and Camembert salad, tiny veal chops surrounded by a yin-yang swirl of puréed peas and carrots, a green salad. A real butler served. No one—other than Taylor—seemed particularly impressed with the food.

Between polite words with the young man on her right, Taylor tried to overhear the conversation between Bosk and Sebastian, but Ada's voice was loud—a tight, drawling caricature of Long Island money that Junie had hit right on when she was mimicking Wendall Clayton. Ada touched the men's arms with her dark, bony fingers and flirted fiercely. Yet their hostess knew this game as well as she knew the proper wording for bread-and-butter notes. She would never risk a direct overture—not even if she found herself alone on the patio with young Tad or Robert or Sherwood. Rejection could be too devastating. Besides, she would want the event only on rare occasions, prepared with as much care as the dinner party: low-lit, completely private, not a bedroom, but someplace what would allow her, when she rose up off her knees, to hike her skirt up and turn her back to the eager, befuddled boy.

Sex was a strong undercurrent of the meal, and bawdy jokes flew back and forth. (The upper class, Taylor remembered, had by and large not been Puritans.) Sebastian became solemn. He was drunk on good wine. "You know something I've been thinking about? It's really troubling me?"

The crew turned their attention to him, waiting for an issue of world events.

"I'm curious how pillows get stains on them. I mean mattresses I can see. But pillows?"

"Gross! Disgusting!" The girls howled. Ada looked happily scandalized.

"Sea Bass, you is demented. . . . But you find a girl with stained pillows, give me her number, will you?"

Halfway through the profiteroles and espresso with anisette, the doorbell rang. Bosk looked at his watch and, rising to answer the door, caught Sebastian's eye. Five minutes later he returned with a man of about forty-five. Taylor disliked him at once.

She was not sure why. What she might in fairness read as groomed, discerning, and charming, she believed was vain (spun, sprayed hair combed forward, a close-fitting suit with shot cuffs, gold bracelet), pompous (a disdaining look at the children around him), and dishonest (a broad smile he could not have felt).

And insulting; he ignored her, while studying the bloused or sweatered breasts of every woman younger than herself. *Fucko son of a bitch!*

Ada seemed relieved another generation was now represented and had a chair brought around for him. His name was Dennis Callaghan, and when Bosk announced that the two of them, and Sebastian, were involved in a business deal together, Taylor put aside her prejudice and paid more attention. The conversation remained social, though. Callaghan's vacation house was not far away, and they talked about problems in finding groundskeepers, and the advantages and risks of helicoptering into Manhattan.

At ten, Bosk got a call from his office and disappeared upstairs. The servants cleared away the plates, and the party broke up. Ada took Callaghan away to show him some photographs of a château in Switzerland she was thinking of buying. Sebastian vanished into the recreation room downstairs, and a few minutes later Bosk joined him.

Taylor Lockwood tore herself away from a chipper young blonde who was giving her a thrilling account of the foreign exchange department at Shearson, and wandered into the dark, Gothic hallways of the house.

The closest she could get was outside.

Only one stairway went down to the basement, and though she

could hear Bosk and Sebastian racking up pool balls and the crack of the break, she could not hear what they said.

She took her leather jacket from the closet and walked out the front door, then strolled around the house until she spotted a four-foot-deep window well. She climbed down into it. A piece of glass was loose, and she worked it free. She could not see the men, but their words, carried on the warm air, streamed up to her, with the awkward-sounding hesitancies of conversations overheard but not witnessed.

". . . do you think they're bugged?"

Sebastian said, "Not necessarily. I'm just worried about it in general. I can't run downstairs to make a call from a pay phone every time I want to talk to you. Somebody sees me doing that twice, and we're fucked."

"What we should do is come up with a code."

Sebastian said, "No, they'd find a link between us, and a link between you and Dennis."

"What we could do . . . hey, what we could do is get an answering service. You call and leave messages, I'll call on a separate line and pick them up. We'll have a second answering service going the other way."

Maybe, Taylor Lockwood thought, what you should do is wear gloves next time you go through somebody's file cabinet so you don't leave fingerprints.

"They could still put us together." Sebastian's voice was soft. "Who's going to—"

Bosk's laugh was flinty. "You're a fucking thief, what do you want? A guarantee? You want to get walkie-talkies and scramblers? Disguises?"

Sebastian didn't answer.

They played for five minutes, during which Taylor's shoulders and neck began vibrating in the cold, and her feet grew numb. Finally, she heard footsteps on the stairs.

"So this is our inside man," Callaghan said. "Pleased to meet you at last, Thom. Here, got a present."

"Ah, nectar of the gods," Sebastian said.

"Sure," Bosk said. A long pause.

Coke? Grass?

Taylor was having trouble concentrating. It was odd what the cold did; she was addled. Her vision was fuzzy. The pool balls cracked. Taylor heard all three of the men sniffing and wheezing.

"Hot damn," said Bosk.

Callaghan said, "So how'd you do?"

"It went okay. I've got it."

"You bring it with you?"

"No."

A pause. She felt tension between the men.

"Any reason why not?"

Bosk began in a defensive tone. "Denny, the thing is, we've got a couple—"

Sebastian said, "Six, corner." *Crack.* "First, money. We've never got the terms worked out. Second, protection. I need to know how you're going to keep my ass out of this. Seven, side."

"Corner's a safer shot," Callaghan offered.

"Side," said Sebastian. *Crack.*

Callaghan said, "Money? The deal is a guarantee of a million for each of you. Against ten percent of proceeds."

Bosk said, "Seven, side. Up front. The money."

Sebastian sniffed. "Up front."

Crack.

Callaghan laughed indulgently. "I can't front two million. I can go seven hundred fifty, split between you, however you want. That's it."

Sebastian said, "Seven, corner. Five hundred each. *That's* it."

Crack.

"Okay. On transfer, when you give me the goods. But tell me why you're nervous. Nobody's on to you, are they?"

Sebastian said, "Just make it foolproof. Then you'll get delivery. Eight, side."

Crack.

"This is grand larceny," Bosk said. "Nothing's foolproof."

Sebastian, irritated that Bosk was supporting Callaghan, said, "I didn't say *genius*proof, I said *fool*proof. You don't get it until I'm convinced I've got a reasonably good chance of escaping with my ass intact."

Callaghan said, "Now you've got me nervous. You don't think they suspect you, do you?"

"No. . . . But I've got to tell you—there was a fuckup. The night I did it, I came in through one of the fire doors in the back of the firm, okay? I'd taped the latch open on Friday."

"And?"

"This old asshole of a partner, it turns out, uses my fucking entry key that same night. So suddenly there's a record that I'm in the firm."

"That doesn't sound so serious to me," Callaghan said.

"It's not *your* name is on the front-door log."

Taylor heard racking balls.

"I'll think about something, some kind of protection for you. Give me a few days. Here, I've got plenty more at home." *Callaghan handing over a vial of coke?* "Bosk, your mother's a charming woman."

"Yeah, I guess."

Callaghan's footsteps sounded up the stairs.

"What are you, a wuss?" Bosk asked.

"I just want some protection is all."

"You don't like him?"

"He's a scumbag."

"He's going to pay you a lot of money."

"I don't have to like him. A lot of people pay me money I don't like."

"You're really pissed at the world, aren't you?"

"I don't get mad, I get even."

The wind diced her face and ears. She closed her eyes against the cold. Her legs and thighs, the last stronghold of heat, were going. She touched the glass that separated her from a room that was fifty degrees warmer, where she heard the sounds of two chubby spoiled boys playing pool and sniffing the residue of cocaine from their nostrils. Her hands clenched and she began to cry silently from the pain. She rose slowly; then, when she heard voices again, she paused and sank down.

Bosk said, "What're you going to do with your million?"

"Get married, open a homestead somewhere."

"Eight ball, side. . . ." *Crack.* Bosk said, "Shit. . . . So what's with this Taylor? She put out?"

"Fuck you," Sebastian said unemotionally.

"That's what I'm asking."

"You've got gonads for brains, Bosk. Is that all you think about? Sex?"

"Money, too. I think a lot about money, but mostly sex."

"She's a nice girl," Sebastian said.

"Does she have a big clit?"

"How'd you like it, somebody sees you on the street and says, 'Hey, there's Bosk. He have a big dick, I wonder?' "

He considered. "I'd like it."

"Fuck you."

Bosk said, "She seems older than you. . . ."

"Eight ball. Corner."

". . . but maybe it's just maturity."

Taylor left them to their banter and walked inside, as unsteady as a hip replacement patient. She stood in front of the black and red ember glow of the fireplace until the sting of cold became a fierce itch and finally died away. Then she said good night to Ada and the children.

Upstairs, she crawled into the deep bed and fell asleep immediately, only to be wakened at one A.M. Sebastian was trying a halfhearted assault, standing outside her door, singing the Ohio State victory song. He didn't, however, test the door (just as well, because she had forgotten to wedge the chair under the knob). Eventually he headed off to bed, and she stayed up for an hour, listening to him snore in contented sleep.

It is dawn, Sunday morning. The drapery man walks through Greenwich Village under huge trapezoids of bruise-purple clouds. They probably hold rain or snow, but what comes to mind isn't the weather. Rather, he thinks of hunting.

When the drapery man was young, he would hunt with his father. Both would dress in brown, humming corduroy, and go walking through scarred November fields. They walked through stalks of corn, low and fibrous and pale, contrasting with the blood-black dirt. A pheasant or grouse or wild turkey would lift off in fluttering alarm, and he'd give it a sporting flight, then feel the kick of the Remington over-under, hearing the explosion that always seemed twenty feet in front of him. And in the distant sky: a flak burst of feathers, and the bird would tumble to the ground.

The drapery man continues down the street. Suddenly, a small bird flies past. The drapery man squints, leads, and tenses his muscles against the recoil.

In his mind, the bird dies.

In his mind, it cartwheels to the ground.

He looks at the buildings and realizes that he has arrived at what he seeks.

At the service entrance, he inserts his lock gun and flicks the trigger a dozen times until the teeth are aligned. The door opens easily. He climbs to the fourth floor and picks another set of locks.

Inside the apartment, he finds: A bag of needlepoint (one is a Christmas scene that will not be finished in time for the holiday). A box of Weight Watchers apple snacks. A garter belt in its original gift box (the drapery man has only seen the girl once, but he can picture her in the garter, and he likes the image). Cartons of musty sheet music. An elaborate, expensive-looking reel-to-reel tape recorder. Dozens of tape cassettes with the same title: *The Heat of Midnight. Songs by Taylor Lockwood.*

He locates and reads her address book, her calendar, and her phone bills. He listens to all her answering machine tapes. His client had hoped that she would have a diary, but as the drapery man told the client, very few people keep diaries anymore. Taylor Lockwood is no exception. He can find nothing that reveals how much she knows or what she is thinking.

He walks slowly through the apartment, taking his time. The drapery man knows his client will grill him at length about what he found in her apartment, and he wants to make sure he overlooks nothing. Although the rooms are small, walking through them reminds him again of walking through cornfields, hunting with his father. He remembers one day, staring at a bird lying where it had tumbled in the curled yellow glove of a pumpkin leaf, its body hardly bloodied by the fine birdshot. He had bent down and studied it, fascinated. He watched it until he heard the ruffle of feathers in speed, and the blasts of his father's shotgun, followed by his whoop of joy at a double kill.

Taylor and Sebastian left on Sunday afternoon. He was moody, and dozed in the back of the limo with the Jets game on the small Sony. She wondered if it was the meeting with Callaghan or her resistance to his overtures that had depressed him.

As the sandy, flat South Shore of Long Island sped past, she reviewed her suspects. Sebastian was now the front runner. Callaghan, she decided, was playing the role of a broker or middleman. Perhaps he was a colleague of Lloyd Hanover. She couldn't understand Bosk's involvement. Taylor was troubled by Sebastian's apparent guilt. He may have been boisterous, he may have been greedy, but his boyish charm was infectious, and she had trouble disliking him.

She was hardly positive that he was the one, of course. Wendall Clayton had been in the firm the night the note disappeared, too, along with his earringed boyfriend. Neither had shown up on the key entry list, and that meant that each might have wanted their presence in the firm to be unnoticed.

Then there was Ralph Dudley, too, with his expensive little habit.

She had more questions than answers. Her dinner with Mitchell was tomorrow night, when he returned from New Orleans. She wanted to tell him something specific. And there was nothing. She felt panic rise. The trial was a week from tomorrow. She closed her eyes and tried to put the thoughts out of her mind. She kept seeing images of Reece, up in front of the jury box, explaining to them about a missing note. Finally she dozed and had a brief dream in which she found the note. Reece hugged her, and she felt the heat of his gratitude pour over her. The next thing she knew, the limo was exiting the tunnel, and Sebastian was rocking her awake with a chaste hand on her shoulder.

"Where to, m'lady? Your apartment or my hot tub?"

She stretched and felt the disappointment at waking from the false dream stab at her, then said, "Neither. The firm."

"I thought you were going home?"

"Some things I thought of to do."

Sebastian gave the driver instructions, and the car sped downtown to a deserted and subdued Wall Street. When they arrived outside the firm, Sebastian's spirits had improved. He flung his arms around her and turned what started out as a brotherly cheek kiss into a serious mouth-to-mouth. Taylor tolerated the embrace for a moment, then pushed him away with a playful squeal. "Thom!" She laughed in a way that the rules of the game required, and slipped out of the long Lincoln, escaping into the firm.

fifteen

It was a dusky seven P.M. The firm was in its Sunday evening quiet —the day-end, low-blood-sugar slump. A dozen or so lawyers still working (the practice was, if you were working a six-day week, Saturday was the one you took off). They wore their favorite blue jeans with tieless dress shirts or blouses.

Taylor wrote out a thank-you note to Thom Sebastian and took it to his office, where she propped it on his chair and proceeded to search the room like an eager rookie cop. In his desk she found: condoms, Bamboo paper, an unopened bottle of Chivas Regal, matches from the Harvard Club and the Palace Hotel and assorted late-night clubs around town, approximately twenty-five take-out menus from down-town restaurants (in descending order of popularity—Szechuan, Can-tonese, deli, Japanese, and steak), chatty letters from his brother and father and mother (all neatly organized, some with margin notes for when he responded), brokerage house statements, checkbooks *(son of a bitch, where'd he get all this money?),* some popular spy and military paperbacks, a coffee-stained copy of the *Lawyer's Code of Professional Responsibility,* assorted photographs from vacations, newspaper articles on bond issues and stock offerings, *Pennystock News,* candy bars, crumbs, and paper clips.

What do you want, Ms. Detective? Pictures of Reece's office with a big black X over the file cabinet? A mask and a sap, maybe?

On Sebastian's bookshelves were hundreds of bound volumes, in navy and burgundy and deep green, hunter green. They contained copies of all the documents in transactions that Sebastian had worked on. They would be great places to hide promissory notes for twenty-five million or other incriminating evidence. If she had a week, maybe, she might find something in them. The thick spines of the books bulged; Sebastian's name in embossed gold aimed right at her. Must have been a hundred thousand pages, a hundred fifty. Her heart spiraled downward. The note could be anywhere. Maybe hidden under a loose tile in the men's room, in the stuffing in his couch.

Maybe it was in his apartment. She could think of only one way to get in there, and she was not yet desperate enough for that.

Downstairs, she walked into the empty file room, a large, dingy space filled with row upon row of file cabinets. The smell reminded her of her father's mortuary, and she breathed very shallowly.

She opened the "C" drawer and found Wendall Clayton's recent time sheets, little blue carbon slips of paper filled with his imperial scrawl, describing every minute he spent on firm business. She read the one for November 23, the day the note vanished, then the time sheets for the Friday and Sunday before and after that day. She replaced them, and did the same in the "D" drawer and "S."

Taylor started to leave, then paused at the "R" cabinet. She rested her hand on the pull, and felt it grow heavy in her hand as the drawer opened. She stared in astonishment at the booklets. There were hundreds of them, all revealing what Mitchell Reece had done every working day for the past six years. Christ Almighty. Half again as many books as anyone else's. Maybe twice as many. Reece had nearly the whole drawer to himself. She pulled one out at random—May—and thumbed through it.

A typical day in the life of Mitchell Reece: New Client relations —1/2 hour. Banque Industrielle de Genève *v.* Hanover & Stiver, Inc.— 4 1/2 hours (depositions). Westron Electronic et al. *v.* Larson Associates —3 1/4 hours (motion to quash subpoena, J. Brietell). State of New York *v.* Kowalski—1/2 hour (conference with D.A.'s office; pro bono). In Re Summers Publishing—2 1/2 hours (research, briefing Chapter 7 bankruptcy issue). . . . Lasky *v.* Allied Products. . . . Mutual Indemnity of New Jersey *v.* Banque Industrielle de Genève . . . office general—1 1/4 hours. . . .

That day, he'd taken a half hour for lunch. He was still at the firm at midnight. The next day's time sheets picked up where the previous one's left off. Every day was the same. *Arguing motion, arguing motion, on trial, writing brief, on trial, on trial, settlement conference, arguing motion, on trial. On trial. On trial.*

She paused.

Don't do it, girl.

She replaced the books and closed the drawer.

Don't . . .

She opened it.

. . . do it.

Taylor lifted out the booklet containing the most recent of his sheets. She flipped through them until she found the day that she had followed him to Grand Central Station.

Damn. She stared at the sheet. For the three hours he was out of the office until the time he returned, he had marked the time Code 03.

Which meant personal time.

The time you spend at the dentist's office.

The time you spend at PTA conferences.

The time you spend in Westchester, lying in bed with your girlfriend, next to a bouquet of fresh roses.

She riffled the pages of his time sheets and felt a stale breeze cross her face.

Ah, well, what's the problem? That he lied to you, or that he's got a girlfriend?

All of the above.

Taylor felt her skin crackling as she flipped through other lunch hours. In the past month, he'd gone once a week—the same entry. Three hours for personal time in the middle of a workday. Mitchell Reece taking time off for a tryst. . . .

She put the time sheets back and closed the drawer.

He hired you for your mind, for your chutzpah. For your balls. That's all he's in it for. And he's treating you better than a lot of men have. Keep it professional, darling.

Taylor glanced into the hall, saw that no one was watching her, then hurried down to Halsted Street, where she pulled her coat on, then left the firm and decided to walk home through the cold night air. She slipped her headset on, then her earmuffs, and began to walk briskly, though she didn't begin to feel better until the tape began to hiss and Miles Davis started into "Seven Steps to Heaven."

One week from the day that Mitchell Reece would do battle against Hanover & Stiver, Taylor Lockwood stood in the doorway of his loft and found he had a talent she had not known about, and would not have guessed about him.

He could have been a professional interior designer.

Taylor would have thought he'd have no time for decor. So when he opened his door and ushered her into the huge loft, she exhaled a sharp, surprised laugh. She was looking at a single room, probably twenty-five hundred square feet. There was a separate elevated sleeping area with a brass railing around it, containing an oak armoire and a matching dresser.

And a bed, which caught her attention immediately. It was dark mahogany, with a massive headboard that would have dwarfed any smaller space. The headboard was carved in a Gothic style—the characters cut into the wood were cracked and worn. She couldn't tell exactly what they were—perhaps knights and gargoyles and hunted animals.

On the wall above it hung Victorian mirrors (in whose tarnished, obscured surface she now saw herself, and restrained a hand that began to lift automatically to her mussed hair).

Around the room she saw plants, sculpture, antiques, tall bookshelves, tapestries. Pin spotlights shot focused streams of light onto small statues and paintings, many of which looked ugly enough to be very valuable. The walls were brick and plaster that was painted with mottled white and gray and pink. The floors were bleached oak, stained white, and covered with satin polyurethane.

This boy cooks, I'm marrying him.

"You did this just to impress me, I know."

"Let me take your coat." Reece wore baggy pants and a blousy white shirt. Sockless oriental shoes, soft. His hair was still damp from a shower.

Taylor had chosen noncommittal vamp. Black stockings but low heels. A black Carolina Herrera dress, tight but high-necked. *(Cleav-*

age? a roommate had once bluntly assessed. *Forget about it, Taylor, don't wear low-cut. But the rest of your bod—it's the best. Short and tight, remember that. Short and tight.)*

Taylor noted with wild pleasure the sweep of Reece's eyes all along her body. He was subtle, but not subtle enough; she caught him in reflection in one of the mirrors above the King Arthur bed.

Okay, Westchester, can you get into a dress like this? Can you?

She followed him across an oriental rug that was thick and solid. The dinner table was near a huge window. It had feet, and on the side, carved faces of the sun. They were solemn.

"Your table looks unhappy."

"He gets bored. There's not much company here. He'll be happy tonight."

As Reece took the wine she'd brought, she looked at him carefully and decided he wasn't very happy either. His eyes were bloodshot and he seemed to be forcing himself to relax, to push the distractions of the office away.

"How was New Orleans?" she asked.

"Will you hate me if I say hot and sunny?"

"Probably."

He walked into the kitchen area and put the wine into what looked like a refrigerator. She looked inside; it contained nothing but bottles. "You should try groceries sometime," she said. "Lettuce, pizza. You can even get chickens all cut up and ready to cook."

"That's my wine cellar," Reece said, and opened a bottle of Pouligny-Montrachet. "Fridge is over there." He pointed to a tall Sub-Zero, then took two crystal goblets between his fingers and carried the wine and a ceramic cooler out into the living area.

He's real slick at this. He must have a lot of practice.

He poured and they touched glasses. "To winning."

Taylor held his eye for a moment and repeated the toast. The wine was rich and sour-sweet. More like a food than a drink. The goblet was heavy in her hand. A medieval vessel.

What's so far on the list? The to-get-before-Mitchell-comes-to-dinner list? Throw out the A&P glasses, the Conran's plates. Then a new tablecloth, furniture, paint, carpeting . . .

"Have you ever lost a trial?" she asked.

He smiled and, as if it were a simple fact, said, "I always seem to win."

"Is that your motto, or something?"

"Maybe I should get a crest. I wonder what that would be in Latin." He asked her, "Where do you live?"

"Fifth Avenue and Ninth Street."

"Nice."

"Okay. Small. It's a little schizophrenic. For a while I was 1930s Nick-and-Nora Deco, then I got into '50s Greenwich Village. Now my decor is pretty much in between eras."

"I'd like to see it sometime."

Oh, don't you worry about that, buddy boy. . . .

Taylor walked toward a long rosewood shelf. "My mother," she said, "would call this a knickknack shelf. I used to think knickknack was French for small, ugly ceramic poodle."

She was looking at an army of metal soldiers.

"I collect them," Reece said. "Winston Churchill probably had the biggest collection in the world, and Malcolm Forbes' wasn't too shabby either. I've only been going at it for twenty years or so."

"What are they, tin?"

"Lead."

Taylor said, "My brother used to get these big bags of plastic soldiers. One birthday that was all he got. I used to play with them as much as he did. Between the two of us, we must've had the entire Normandy invasion in green plastic. One year my parents finally broke the gender barrier and gave me a B-29. I nuked most of his army. You have other things, too? Like cannons and catapults?"

"Soldiers, horses, cannon, and caissons . . ."

She sipped the wine and was thinking, *Sometimes in life, this craziness falls right on top of you, and you find yourself floating up and away from your body like gurus probably do, looking down, and all you can say is, shit a brick, this is so weird: standing with a handsome man wearing a sexy shirt and slippers, drinking wine must've cost thirty dollars a bottle, talking toy soldiers.*

Taylor laughed and told herself not, under any circumstances, to get drunk.

He played with some of the figures. "I have a British Square. I made it when I was sixteen."

"Like a park? Like Trafalgar Square?" This seemed a little more conversational—at least a step away from combat troops, about which she didn't have a whole lot to contribute.

Reece was laughing. "Taylor, British Square? A fighting formation? You know, Gunga Din."

"Kipling," she said, raising her eyebrows.

"The ranks divided into two lines. One stood and reloaded, the other knelt and fired. The fuzzy-wuzzies were the only warriors to break through the square."

"The, uh . . ."

"Zulus. African tribal warriors."

"Ah. Boer War."

"That was twenty years later. I'm talking the 1870s."

"Ah," Taylor said. "Of course."

"You're laughing at me, aren't you?"

"Yes," she said.

He hit her playfully on the arm and let his hand pause on the thin cotton for just a moment. She leaned toward him, smiling, head cocked, then broke away and walked to the end of the shelf.

"The better ones I keep at my father's. These aren't quite as valuable. They've been around. Somebody's played with them, they weren't sitting under a glass case or on somebody's"—he laughed— "knickknack shelf."

"Which one's Wellington?" Taylor asked.

"In the officer's mess right at the moment. The marquis of Chumley has a great Waterloo. He's got twenty thousand in his collection. His cannon are firing. He uses wool from Scotch sheep for the smoke. Oh, and his kaiser has a withered hand."

She nodded toward a half-dozen photos in pewter frames. She looked at them closely.

"Father," he pointed from one to the next. "Father and Mother. Grandmother. Stepmother." The pause required a response. Reece said, "My mother died. Eighteen years ago."

She said, "Sorry. A tough age for that to happen."

He shrugged. "Life goes on. Say, what does your father do? You never told me what his small business was."

The grin came up involuntarily. "Uh, my father?" She paused, wondering how many times this very same question had immobilized conversations like this one. "Well, the truth is . . . he's an undertaker. Excuse me, funeral director. We were always supposed to say funeral director."

"Don't look so defensive. I won't joke."

Taylor recited, "Stiff competition in the business, dig up some new clients, the profit picture is grave. . . ."

"You were tormented a lot in school."

"Yep. The St. Louis burbs are a breeding ground for liberals. If I'd been a black or Hispanic, no problem. But undertakers' children aren't a constitutionally protected group. I guess there are some advantages. It saved me from getting felt up in high school."

"No aspiration to follow the family business? It's supposed to be very profitable. Lowest failure rate of any small business in America."

"I want to open a franchise: Taylor Lockwood, mortician and CPA. Get it? Keep both markets covered."

He'd never heard the joke, and laughed hard. Then he said, "Oh," pointing to his stereo, "I listened to your tape on the plane back from New Orleans. I've got to tell you that I expected okay, but you are really good. You blew me away."

A fiery blush. "Well, if I had real sidemen and a producer—"

"No, it was wonderful. Gershwin right next to Thelonious Monk. And your own pieces . . . Really, I loved it. I think you're going places. You'll leave us all in the dust, Taylor. You'll forget all about your friends at Hubbard, White & Willis."

"The responses ain't been jim-dandy."

"It only takes one record company."

Eight-thirty. She could smell nothing simmering. Were they going out to eat? *Well, scratch one: He can't cook. Still Reece'd make an okay catch. Do you promise to love, honor, obey* . . .

The doorbuzzer sounded.

"Excuse me."

He let a tuxedoed young man into the loft. The young man nodded politely to Taylor and, from a large shopping bag, took plates wrapped in stippled foil. Reece set the table with bone china plates, silver, and a candlestick.

The young man said, "Would you like me to pour the wine, Mr. Reece?"

"No, thank you anyway, Robert." Reece signed the offered slip of paper. A bill changed hands.

"Then good night, sir."

. . . and in health for so long as you both shall live?

Reece said, "I hope you don't mind. I don't have much time to cook. And going out, well, it's not quite as"—he looked for a word and found one that she approved of—"intimate."

Taylor Lockwood held her glass up and thought, *I do.*

sixteen

Dinner: blini with beluga caviar and sour cream, veal medallions with slivers of fresh truffles in a marsala sauce, braised endive, and cold marinated green beans.

They talked about the firm, partners, affairs, who was gay, who was on partnership track, who was not. She supplied most of the information, and was surprised he knew so little about the gossipy side of the firm and its politics, and Taylor reflected that it was curious that those who leaned toward litigation, like combat a communal endeavor, also inclined toward isolation.

It was more astonishing to her that he knew so little about the merger. Although the lawyers and staffers of Hubbard, White spent more hours debating the merger than billing time for clients, Reece seemed oblivious. She mentioned the rumor that Clayton had a German lawyer inquire about accounts Burdick may have opened in Switzerland. "He's trying to get something on the old guy."

"Really?" Reece asked with what seemed unsophisticated surprise.

"Aren't you worried about it," Taylor asked, "about what will happen if Wendall wins?"

"No. As long as I can try cases, good cases, that's all I care about. Whether it's Donald in charge or John Perelli, I don't much care."

When they had finished eating, he rose to take the plates away. She started to help him.

"No, leave it, please. . . . The family rule was the first three times, you're a guest. After that, you help out."

"So, I'll help out now and save my guest passes."

"Okay, but when I'm over at your place, the same rule applies." She stood up quickly and began to help him.

"Coffee? Dessert?" Reece said, though without encouragement. She was disappointed; she had wanted to prolong the social aspect of the evening.

"Couldn't possibly."

This was the right answer, because he was already on his way into the living area, saying, "Tell me what you've found."

They both sat in a leather sofa that protested against their weight with a low hiss. Reece looked eager and nervous, and she understood that she had been watching this uneasiness all evening. She understood too that it was not the residue of a long business trip or the lack of sleep, but was the very thing that had brought them together: the theft of the note. Any thought of the ambiguous messages before dinner vanished, as did the dark presence of the Girlfriend in Westchester. Between them, all that was left was business, and Taylor Lockwood felt her stomach fall and her thoughts tumble like an unprepared student's. Reece would want from her what he gave: coherence, order, concise conclusions. She felt her mouth dry with anxiety, and she swallowed before she spoke. "I haven't really got anything. Not definite." She watched his impassive face for clues to his reaction. She saw nothing, except perhaps a slight degree of desperation. "Thom Sebastian is number one. I told you about his fingerprints. He denied he was in the firm that night, but I know he was. He snuck in through the emergency door in the back of the sixteenth floor." Briefly, she explained about Bosk and Dennis Callaghan. Reece seemed impressed with her deep-freeze espionage. She asked him, "You ever hear the name Callaghan in connection with the Hanover & Stiver case?"

Reece shook his head. "But what about Sebastian's motive, though? He's risking prison just to get even with the firm?"

"What would *you* do if they passed you over for partner?"

"I've worked hard enough to make sure they don't."

"Well, I think Thom sees the money he'll make as something the firm owes him. Remember, he's been trained by the firm for six or seven years to look only at the bottom line. He got shortchanged and he wants revenge."

She continued, "Remember I mentioned Dudley? Well, are you ready for this?" She told him about Junie.

"Oh, my God," Reece blurted. "He's insane! They'll put him away forever. Statutory rape, soliciting, contributing to the delinquency—"

"He's paying a thousand dollars a week for her."

Reece muttered, "Supply and demand."

"You told me he's got money problems. And he lied about being in the firm that Saturday. I know he was in—Junie said he was pawing through file cabinets that night. And what on earth would Ralph Dudley be doing in the firm on Saturday night? I checked his time sheets and he didn't bill any client time that Saturday. So whatever he was doing in there was personal. . . ."

"Did you find his prints?"

"No. But there were some that I couldn't identify."

Reece shook his head and rubbed his eyes with his knuckles. "It doesn't sound—"

"There's one more. Wendall Clayton."

"Wendall?" Surprised blossomed in his face.

"Junie told me that on that Saturday night she got into a fight with Clayton. He was pissed she was in his conference room. He was with somebody she didn't recognize. A young man. She said he looked gay."

"But you said Wendall wasn't on the key entry sheet."

"Not completely true. He wasn't on *Saturday's* report. But he was on *Friday's*. He had some hot case that started Friday night."

"Sure, the TRO case. I heard about that. In fact, it's funny now I think about it, he called me on Friday night to see if I'd be able to help him out."

"He did?" Taylor asked.

"I told him I had two trials on and couldn't handle it. In fact, I remember, he asked me specifically if I'd be around Saturday night. That's interesting. . . ."

"Junie said he was holed up in a little conference room, I think that one near the library. He stayed until three A.M. on Sunday. He never left the firm on Saturday, so he never used his key. I cross-checked against his diaries, and he billed eighteen hours on Saturday. That leaves six hours for sleep. Or for looking through your file cabinets."

"Fingerprints?"

"Not conclusive."

"But Wendall? Impossible." Reece seemed irritated at the frivolousness of the suggestion. "Why would he do it? What possible motive would he have? He's rich. He doesn't need the money. He—"

Taylor said calmly, "Banque Genève is whose client?"

"I told you. Donald Burdick's. One of his oldest, and biggest."

"And what happens if we lose the case because the note's missing?"

"What happens? A—Banque Genève fires us. B—They sue the firm and me personally for malpractice."

"How about an A and a half? Banque Genève takes their business elsewhere, and Donald loses, what?, five million in billing?"

"Close to seven this year."

Taylor said, "And Clayton points to him and says, 'This is the sort of lawyer who's opposing the merger. We need new blood. Put me in charge, and I'll straighten up the firm.' "

Reece looked skeptical at first, then he sat upright, wholly alert. "But there's something else. The partners' voting power is based on their clients' billing."

Taylor said, "So if Burdick loses Banque Genève, he probably loses a big chunk of his ability to vote down the merger."

Reece smiled and said slowly, *"That* is a motive."

He stood, walked into the kitchen, and returned with two glasses of cognac. He handed one to Taylor, the liqueur leaving thin, syrupy waves on the glass. He kicked his slippers off and sat down next to her. "Tomorrow, Wendall's having a party at his Connecticut place. Why don't you come along? You might be able to find something."

"Oh, I couldn't go. I'm just a paralegal."

"It's a firm function; they just have it at his house. It's held for the new associates, an annual thing. Nobody'll pay any attention to you."

"We shouldn't be seen together."

"True. We'll split up once we get inside. We'll get there late and just slip in."

"I guess, sure. Oh." She blinked in surprise, looking at her empty glass. "I suppose I should have been sipping. I got carried away."

"Have some more. The bottle's in the closet next to the stove." She walked into the kitchen.

Reece shouted, "So how come you don't have a boyfriend?"

"Don't ask me," she called back. "Ask them."

"You ever been married?"

"Nope. Not even close."

Taylor squatted down in front of the cabinet and located the liqueur. When she stood up, her dress was hiked high around her thighs. She giggled—the fuzz from the wine and the electricity from the brandy were clashing with hilarity. She wiggled her hips as she pulled her hem down.

"What's the joke?"

"I don't know. . . . Hey, do you ski?"

"I've never been."

"And I know why," Taylor said. "You hear rumors all the time that you can get very seriously killed skiing. A true possibility, but only if you haven't had proper instruction. That's why you're so lucky. I'm going to teach you to ski."

God, I'm not saying this. I'm drunk. I can't be drunk. He's going to think I'm a complete idiot. Did I really say that? Please let me not have said it. . . .

Reece just laughed. "Skiing? That's with snow, and everything?"

His mood had changed for the better as soon as she had told him her suspicions of Clayton, and she felt ecstatic. She poured a couple of fingers of liqueur into her glass. "Snow is a definite plus when you're skiing. In fact, that was going to be my first lesson. You're catching on already."

Girl, I got to tell you again . . .

"Hit me, too," he said, holding the glass up, slouching back into the leather. He played with the top button of his shirt. His hair was mussed, fallen toward one eye. He tried to brush it back, but the thick comma stayed put.

"Know what?"

Taylor walking over to him with the uncorked bottle, said, "What's that?"

"I'm glad."

"About what?" Taylor felt it then, sensing—what was it, intuition maybe, experience?—sensing what was unfolding. Was it going to be good or bad? It was coming soon, quick as a wet-leaf skid. Okay? Decide, good or bad? *Decide fast, honey, you got about three minutes.*

"I'm glad we haven't caught our thief yet. I like working with you." His voice was husky, though he spoke softly.

Reece held his glass up.

Come on, Lockwood, this is the moment. Now. You going, or staying? You've still got the power. It hasn't tipped yet. You can do it easy, diffuse the whole thing. Thank him for dinner. That's all it would take. But now is the time. One way or another, decide: Would it be good or bad?

She poured a little of the liqueur into the glass. An ounce, no more than that, but he twisted his wrist, and a splash of the cognac hit the side of the glass and spilled onto the front of his shirt.

"Oh, sorry," she said.

Come on, good or bad? Make it your *decision. Choose. . . .*

"Here, let me clean it up," she said. Or perhaps she didn't. Afterward, she couldn't remember. What she did remember was looking at his face, the faint smile on it, the lids lowering slightly. And she remembered watching his hands—they were large and strong—and seeing them cover her breasts, feeling the strength in his fingers as they then slid around behind the dress, probing for fasteners. All of those she remembered.

Those and the long, satisfying sound of the zipper.

And Taylor remembered something else. She remembered thinking, *Yeah, it would be good.*

John Perelli shrugged and pushed the memo, stamped CONFIDENTIAL, away from him.

Wendall Clayton responded with an unemotional quirk of an eyebrow.

Clayton savored times like this: being in his office late on a weekday night. This feeling of almost manic joy came from some very pleasant memories—liaisons on his couch at around this time of night, and from negotiating or closing international business deals. These were the two passions in his life, and Clayton thought it was appropriate that a large number of each had occurred in this room.

He sat on his throne, Perelli across from it. They had just finished reviewing audited financial statements of the two firms. On the couch, four other attorneys—two from each firm—were poring over other documents that tracked the health of the firms like hospital monitors. Occasionally one would mutter something about "bad debt reserve" or "pension overfunding" and jot a note on a piece of foolscap or accounting ledger paper.

Clayton wasn't much interested in their opinions. Men who aristocratize for a living should not be overly concerned with nits. At the moment, he was taking John Perelli's pulse, and the result did, however, concern him.

Clayton asked, "Are you troubled?"

Perelli did not speak for a moment. During this silence, Clayton noticed more associates than usual strolling past his open door. He assumed word had gone around that Perelli was in the firm, and the children were eager to get a glimpse of their potential stepfather. He rose and swung the door shut.

"It's a gut feeling, Wendall. I see the numbers. They're okay. They're not bad. They can be made a hell of a lot better, but"—he held up a hand to arrest the protest an impassive Clayton did not make— "but I think we can bring them under control."

"You know we can," Clayton said with a patrician nonchalance.

"I know it. Yes."

"Well?"

Perelli said, "I've got a friend at Chase."

"Yes."

"Did you know Donald's talked to them about taking on long-term debt?"

Son of a bitch. Goddamn that man! He had not known. Yet Clayton's anger was primarily with himself. He should have considered it. A classic takeover defense, and he had not expected it. The only evidence of Clayton's fury was a gathering of muscles at the corner of his mouth, and he spoke calmly. "The executive committee can take on up to thirty million in debt without firm approval."

"That much?" Perelli barked. "Jesus Christ, don't you guys have any controls here?"

Clayton didn't answer, and Perelli continued, "That'd skew your balance sheet too much for us. I'll tell you right now I'll never get my people to merge with a firm that owed that much money. I guarantee that they'll walk away."

Clayton had calmed completely. "How far along are the discussions at Chase?"

"My man said he doesn't think they'll cut a check even to Hubbard, White without a full chain of approval. But you know Burdick. If there are strings to be pulled, he knows how to yank 'em. I'd guess two weeks at the latest."

Clayton stood up and paced. He ended up at the window. He looked out over the shimmering lights of Brooklyn, which, as they extended east, merged into a mottled plane of dusty luminescence, then faded to darkness. Without turning around, he said, "What's the tally?"

One of the lawyers on the couch responded immediately. "As of this moment?" Clayton didn't answer the foolish question, and the lawyer quickly continued, "We're right on the borderline, Wendall. Depending on who's at the meeting, who—"

"Borderline?"

Clayton was furious at the imprecision of the answer. Yet he knew the associate would not have risked such a sloppy response if he had not researched the question thoroughly. He turned to Perelli. "Right now, based on those figures, and assuming we lose only a few clients as a result of the merger, will Perelli & Sullivan approve the consolidation?"

Perelli scowled. "*If* the firm doesn't take on any more debt, and *if* you keep the clients that are cash cows, and—"

"Who's on that list?"

"Obviously, MacMillan Holdings, SBI, Crocker, Sung-Dai, the University, St. Agnes."

"Okay," Clayton said. "On those two conditions?"

"*And* if you reconsider your pogrom to oust half of your own firm, then I can guarantee you'll have my firm's approval."

Silently, to himself, Wendall Clayton considered a number of matters, then said to the senior associate who was still watching him attentively, "Send out a meeting notice over my signature. I want the merger vote this week."

"This week, Wendall?" the associate asked, his voice rising high in surprise.

Clayton gave him a suitably aristocratizing glance, then stood up. "If you'll excuse me for a moment, gentlemen."

Downstairs, in Halsted Street, he found the two of them. The pretty boy and the cow of a girl. Clayton did not understand what Lillick saw in the chubby paralegal. She was shy, she was unassertive. She seemed to have no mind of her own. To Wendall Clayton, she was a ridiculously easy fuck, and the sort who were far more trouble than they were worth —a clinger.

When they saw him coming, they stepped apart, and Clayton noticed, though he pretended not to, that Lillick had a hard-on. Making out in the paralegal pens. He thought it was charmingly juvenile.

"Hello, Sean. Carrie."

"Hi, Mr. Clayton," the girl said nervously.

"I hope I'm not interrupting anything?" *Other than two little puppies in heat humping away.*

"No."

Carrie said, "We were just talking."

Clayton looked into the girl's face. It was actually pretty, and she had amazing green eyes. He pictured her face on the pillow, pictured himself above her, licking her closed eyelids. He found he, too, had an erection. He said to her, "If you'll excuse us, Carrie. Sean and I have some business."

Neither of them moved. Lillick looked at the floor. Carrie cleared her throat and said, "We've been working all night. We were going out to get something to eat."

Clayton didn't say anything.

Lillick said to her, "Why don't you meet me there?" He turned to Clayton. "This won't, you know, take long, will it?"

"No."

Carrie hesitated and looked away from Clayton's scrutiny. She picked up her coat and purse, saying to Lillick, "Don't be long." She hiked off down the corridor.

Why should he hurry? You'll wait till he gets there, Clayton thought. *You'll wait forever.*

Clayton's gaze followed her, as he leaned against a desk, then he turned to Lillick with a cruel, silent grin. The boy's eyes fished away, and involuntarily he too grinned, though in angry embarrassment.

When the door clicked shut behind her, Clayton said, "Sean, you recall our recent discussions." He then noticed, with some anger himself, Lillick's earring. Although they had fought about it in the past, and Lillick had agreed not to wear it in the firm, Clayton tonight let the matter pass. He continued, "You've been helpful. But I need you to be a little more helpful."

"Helpful," the boy sighed.

"You're very well liked at the firm, Sean."

Lillick grunted.

"You're well liked," Clayton repeated. After a moment, he whispered, "I need some gossip. About Burdick. Do you know something about him?"

"No."

"I need votes, Sean. And I need them at once. It's crucial."

"Wendall, I don't like this. I've already done enough." Lillick spoke defiantly, yet in the time it took the words to leave the resolute mouth, Clayton knew the boy would capitulate. The partner said, "I'm not asking you to do anything illegal." He gave a reassuring taunt. "Nobody will know where I got the information."

"No. I just don't want to, Wendall."

Clayton said, "Consider the education you're getting from the firm, from me. When you go to law school, it will be extremely valuable."

"I *think* I want to go to law school. I've never said for sure."

"Of course you want to go. You'll do well. You'll be a brilliant lawyer."

"Well, I don't want to do any more of this. I'll do your regular paralegal work, but I'm not going to do anything else. I'll—"

"Sean."

"Forget about it!" Lillick barked.

Clayton's voice hissed, "What did you say? 'Forget about it!'?"
Lillick turned away.

Clayton calmed and touched Lillick's shoulder. "If I had a son who said that to me, do you know what I'd do to him? I'd pull his pants down and take a cane to him." Clayton paused. "I wish you were a student of mine, so I could do that to you."

Lillick looked back passively. Clayton thought the boy would appear outraged, but no, he looked back, scared and almost curious. Clayton's comment seemed oddly appropriate. Life was very English boys' school at Hubbard, White & Willis. It seemed perfectly normal that he should take Lillick to the gymnasium, pull his shorts down . . .

Clayton said nothing further, but just leveled his eyes at the boy. After thirty seconds Lillick said slowly, "There is something."

"Yes?"

"It might be kind of helpful."

"It has to be *very* helpful," Clayton said. "I don't have time left for subtleties."

Taylor sat in Mitchell Reece's loft, at his big antique desk. It was three-thirty in the morning. She had awakened a half hour before, suddenly. A dream had done it, a dream whose image vanished as swiftly as her ability to fall back asleep. She lay awake for fifteen minutes, then slipped out of bed and into the kitchen. (Warm milk helped her sleep, but she settled for it cold, intimidated by the huge professional stove.) Then she wandered around the apartment, lit by uneven streetlight. She'd paused at his desk and sipped the milk while she read the front page of the prior day's *Times*.

Taylor stretched back in the swivel leather chair. She was wearing one of his dress shirts, which he had tossed onto a varnished old-fashioned wooden trunk.

How many times have you borrowed men's shirts on Sunday morning, buttoned them over your dark dresses so passersby and doormen would not think you'd spent the night with a man?

Not too many, but enough.

She counted her marriage proposals (six), the live-in boyfriends (three), the men she'd slept with (twelve; ah, make that thirteen). She thought of the men she couldn't stand who had loved her. The ones she had lusted or pined for who didn't care she existed.

Mitchell, who is she? Who is the Westchester Girlfriend?

Now, it's a fair question.

Now, now, I have the right to ask.

She turned to watch his form, lying heavy in sleep. He head was sunk deep into the solid down pillow, and he seemed lost in intense contentment.

I have the right. . . .

Taylor sipped the milk.

Or do I?

Oh, be careful, girl. Remember Thom Sebastian's myth of the beautiful woman? Well, beware the myth of the absolute moment—when we lie together, muscles ticking, limbs at their most relaxed, bathed in the uncaution and certainty of love. The absolute moment, when we forget that love is not forever, that words are not steadfast, that we are never safe from the comic and aching differences that we ignore so desperately and oh so well.

Taylor Lockwood thought about catered dinners, recipes she might make for him, about his family. She wondered when he had last shared his medieval bed with the other woman. (What thoughts had leapt into his mind while he pulsed on top of her?)

Yes, yes, yes! I have the right to ask. . . .

Though she knew that she would not. You must be ready for any answer when you risk asking questions like those. And Taylor Lockwood was not.

She turned to the bed and with her eyes followed his outline under the sheets. Would she end up wounded? Would he joke about her with his friends? *I've gone to bed with many a beautiful woman, and wakened with many an ugly one. . . .* No, he wouldn't think about her that way. She wouldn't be conquest fodder, the way she'd be for Sebastian or Bosk.

Of course not.

This would be different from the others.

Yes, of course it will. Of course.

seventeen

E very color clashed.
    Taylor Lockwood looked over the apparel of the crowd milling in the living room of Wendall Clayton's country home in Redding, Connecticut. She saw plaid. She saw lemon yellow with orange. She saw lime green with red.

She saw madras! Her mother had told her about madras; in the *ancien régime* of the sixties, star-burst tie-dye marked the hippies; madras flagged the nerds.

To be fair, the collision of hues was almost exclusively on the frames of the older lawyers. The younger crowd of associates were in chinos and blazers or skirts and sweaters. A lot of pearls, a lot of blond hair, a lot of pretty faces. The rooms were filled with perhaps seventy-five, eighty people, standing in awkward thickets—hands in pockets, hands holding drinks, hands holding cigarettes.

It was Tuesday night. Reece and Taylor had cruise-controlled up the wide parkway in the rental car, then turned east and immediately lost themselves in the charming, dark roads of North Salem and Ridgefield.

They had found Clayton's place after asking directions twice, and walked into the house without knocking. They stood, unnoticed, in the entrance foyer.

"We're overdressed."

Reece pulled his tie off and stuffed it in his pocket. "How do I look?"

"Like an overdressed lawyer without a tie."

He said, "I'll take the first floor. You take the second."

"Okay," she said quickly, then hesitated.

"What's wrong?" Reece asked.

"We're kind of like burglars, aren't we?"

He recited quickly, "Burglary is entering a dwelling without permission with the intention of committing a felony." He gave her a fast smile. "We've got permission. Therefore, it's not burglary."

She nodded, then found the bar. The bartender was doing a big business with false-bottomed mugs of sweet, mint-laced Southsiders. Taylor shook her head at the offered drink and got a glass of Stag's Leap Chardonnay. Before the first sip, Thom Sebastian cornered her.

"No, it's true, Taylor," Sebastian was lecturing through the haze of a half-dozen beers. "A man doesn't have sex with a beautiful woman once every couple of days, the problems he can get—I'm talking prostate, I'm talking kidneys, I'm talking serious!"

"Thom"—she patted his smooth cheek with her palm—"I have to run."

"Aw, Taylor, come on. . . ."

She ducked away from his sloppy bear hug and fled into the living room, where she circulated for fifteen minutes, slowly working her way to the stairs, listening to snatches of conversation.

. . . *He's going to do it. For sure. Next month, we're going to be Hubbard, White, Willis, Perelli & Sullivan.* . . .

. . . *You're out to lunch, dude. No way'll Burdick let it happen.* . . .

Do you realize the vote is Thursday? That's two days from now.

. . . *You hear about the detective that was going through Burdick's Swiss accounts?* . . .

. . . *You hear Burdick had somebody check Clayton's law review article to see if he plagiarized.* . . .

. . . *That's bullshit.* . . .

You want to talk bullshit, this merger is bullshit. Nobody's getting any work done. . . .

As she made her way into the hallway, she noticed an older woman scrutinizing her carefully, with a look of almost amused curiosity. Taylor tried to avoid her, but once their eyes met and held, she felt the power of a silent summons and walked to the woman. She was about the same age as Ada, Bosk's mother, and dressed similarly, in a conservative *haute couture* red silk gown.

"You're Taylor Lockwood," the woman said.

"Yes."

"I'm Vera Burdick, Donald's wife."

"Nice to see you," Taylor said. They shook hands. The woman must have seen the surprise in Taylor's face—surprise that the Burdick camp would be represented in enemy territory. She said, "Donald had business tonight. He asked me to come in his stead."

"I'm surprised you remembered me. I think we only met once, several years ago."

Vera didn't answer. She smiled and looked placidly into Taylor's eyes.

"It's a nice party," Taylor said.

"Yes, Wendall is kind enough to donate his house for the evening. He does the same for the summer associates in July. It's a sort of fresh-air outing for lawyers."

They exchanged glances pleasantly, two people at a party who have nothing to say to each other.

Taylor broke the stalemate with "Well, I think I'll mingle a little."

Vera Burdick nodded, as if her examinations of Taylor had produced satisfactory results. "A pleasure seeing you again, dear."

Taylor watched the partner's wife join a cluster of associates nearby. As the woman's voice rose in laughter, Taylor started again for the stairs. She got halfway across the hall when she heard another voice —a man's voice, soft, almost faint, directed at her. "And who are you, again?" Her neck hair bristled.

Taylor turned to look into the face of Wendall Clayton. She was, at first, surprised that he was only a couple of inches taller than she. Then she noticed that he was much more handsome than she'd realized.

And then her mind went blank. For three or four seconds, she was utterly without a conscious thought. Clayton's eyes were the reason. They were the eyes of a man who knew how to control people, a man to whom it would be excruciating to say no, even if he made his demands with silence.

"Pardon?" Taylor asked.

He smiled. "I asked who you were again?"

The same person I've always been. No "again" about it, hotshot. Then he dipped into her eyes, and the motion of the room faded, and she forgot her snappy comeback. She said, "Taylor Lockwood."

I will not call him Mister. Lord, seal my lips.

"I'm Wendall Clayton."

She said, "Yes, I know. I'd thank you for inviting me, Wendall, but I'm afraid I crashed. Are you going to kick me out?" She found a smile somewhere and slipped it on.

"On the contrary, you're probably the only person in this crew worth talking to."

"I don't think I'd go that far."

He took her arm. She had never been touched in this way. A firm grip, not a disciplinarian's, or a friend's, or a lover's. In the contraction of the muscles was a pressure of authority. Then it relaxed. It left an unclear message of urgency. Clayton said, "Would you like a tour of the house? It's an authentic 1780s. I—"

"Taylor! You're here!" A young woman associate trotted between them. She, too, was overdressed, wearing a bulky houndstooth suit. She was thin and wore glasses and no makeup. Her hair was short and curly. She stuck her hand out. "Mr. Clayton, I'm Martha Owen. B.U. I just joined the firm."

"Welcome, Martha." Clayton took her hard-pumping hand.

"A real pleasure to meet you, Mr. Clayton. I read the deal binder on the HGA International refinancings. I mean, you did some incredibly fascinating things with the cross-collateralization."

"Yes," he said. "Well, thank you."

"I hope to work with you someday. I really hope I can." She shoved her glasses up high on the bridge of her nose. "Isn't this good wine?"

"Martha," Taylor said, "Wendall was just going to give me a tour of his house. Why don't you join us?"

"Oh, I'd love to."

"Wonderful," he said, and Taylor believed she heard a hum of anger.

Clayton moved them quickly through the old place like a tour guide goosed by a tight schedule. It was a rambling house—big, though the rooms themselves were small and cockeyed. Beams were uneven, floorboards sprung. Much of the furniture was painted in drab Colonial colors. The gewgaws were of hammered tin and wicker and carved wood. The wall paint looked unfinished, as if the workers had primed and sanded, then quit. "Pickling," Clayton ran his hand along it. "An eighteenth-century painting technique. I found a local crafts-man who could do it."

He led them upstairs. Taylor pretended to be studying portraits of horses, Shaker furniture, and armoires, while she looked for places where the note might be hidden. She glanced into a small room that seemed to be an office and saw a desk. She didn't notice that the other two had walked ahead.

"Are you with us, Taylor?" Clayton asked, and she hurried to join them. He continued the tour. ". . . Mark Twain's house, the house he died in, isn't far from here."

"Are you a son of the American Revolution?" Martha asked.

Clayton spoke with a feigned indignity that rested on real pride. "The Revolutionaries? Why, a gaggle of newcomers. My family was one of the original settlers of Nieuw Nederlandt. We came over in 1628."

"Are you Dutch?"

"No. My ancestors were Huguenots."

Taylor said, "I always got those mixed up in school—the Hugue-nots and the Hottentots."

Clayton smiled coldly.

Oooo, doesn't like potshots into the family tree.

"The Huguenots were French Protestants," he explained. "They were badly persecuted. In the 1620s Cardinal Richelieu ordered a siege of La Rochelle, a large Huguenot town. My family escaped and settled here. New Rochelle, New York, by the way, is named after La Rochelle."

Martha seemed thrilled. "What did your ancestors do when they got here?"

"There was considerable prejudice against the Huguenots, even here. We were barred from many businesses. My family became arti-sans. Silversmiths mostly. Paul Revere was one of us. But my family were always better merchants than craftsmen. . . . We moved into manufacturing and then finance, though that field had largely been preempted by . . . other groups." For a moment he looked wily, and Taylor suspected he was suppressing an opinion about early Jewish settlers.

Martha was eager to keep *The New Colossus* lecture rolling. "So what happened? Your family stayed, or pushed west?"

"My family was strictly Upper East Side. Always has been. I was born within a five-block radius of my father and grandfather's birthplaces."

That touched Taylor. "You don't see that much anymore. Today, everybody's spread all over the world."

"You shouldn't let it happen," Clayton said sincerely. "Your family history is all you have. You should keep your ancestry and be proud of it. This year, I'm steward of the French Society. . . ."

Martha, of the front row in law school, blinked. "Oh, I've heard of that. Sure."

Clayton said to Taylor, "After the Holland Society, it's the most prestigious of the hereditary societies in New York."

Martha was impressed, but another need intruded. "Say, Mr. Clayton, where's the little girls' room?"

Oh, honey, don't fail me now. . . .

He smiled. "We've been having problems with the one up here. Why don't you go downstairs? We'll meet you there in a moment." Martha trotted off, and it was then that Taylor realized they had ended the tour in Clayton's bedroom.

He smiled at her and Taylor asked, "Isn't your wife here?"

"No, she's in Manhattan. She doesn't get out here very often. She doesn't like the country. That's a mystery to me."

The bedroom was dramatic, Ralph Lauren dark, filled with rust and red florals. English hunt green and brass. This was the room of a nobleman, a man who would ruthlessly bed milkmaids and domestic help.

Clayton closed the door. "You're very attractive."

Taylor avoided his eyes. "I should be getting downstairs."

He took her hand. To her astonishment, she let him, and the next thing she knew some undefinable pressure overwhelmed her and she found herself sitting on the bed next to him.

"Wendall. . . ."

"Look at me."

Taylor did, and she felt a growing power, like a supermagnet drawing, tugging at her soul and at the soul of everything around her. It seemed to Taylor that her hair actually stirred in this invisible wind.

"Wendall—"

"I want to tell you one thing," he said calmly, "this has to be completely clear. Whatever happens—or doesn't happen—has no affect on your career at Hubbard, White. Is that understood?"

She pulled her arm away. "I don't even know you. I've never even spoken to you before." She was shocked to hear that her words seemed weak, as if she were wavering.

He shrugged. "Spoken to me? I don't want to have a discussion. I want to make love to you."

There was no physical impediment to her leaving. He was not even standing in her way. One foot before the other, and she could troop right out the door. Yet she didn't.

Clayton crossed his legs, knocked the tassel of his hair off his forehead.

"I have commitments," she explained.

No, no, no . . . Don't say that. You're meeting his argument. Tell him to fuck off. Forget who he is. Forget the case. Just say it now: Fuck off. Fuck. Off. Say it!

"Dear Taylor, we all have commitments."

She felt her throat thicken.

Don't swallow. It's a weakness. Don't.

She swallowed. "We don't know each other."

Clayton smiled, shaking his head. "We're not communicating. I don't want to marry you. I want to make love to you. I'm telling you, you are an incredibly attractive woman."

"Thank you."

"It's not a compliment, it's an observation. I know how to make love to women. I do it with great regularity. I'm very good at it."

"You're married. . . ."

"Please, that's a whole different issue." He seemed confused. "Don't you find me attractive?"

"That's not the point—"

"So you do?" He smiled.

And she understood now that she was no match for him, not this way. He would best her at this match of persuasion. She felt the concessions piling up, felt herself falling toward him, toward the ultimate concession. She was dazed. Did she feel arousal? She couldn't tell. Perhaps she did. Or was it a different response to a different kind of potency? She shifted and looked at the door, and did not stand up.

He stroked the bed, in what seemed to her a very feminine gesture. "I want to sleep with you."

Taylor smiled. "You don't want to sleep with me at all. You want to fuck me."

"No!" he whispered harshly, then smiled. "I want us to fuck together."

Mistake, girl. He likes dirty talk.

"Look." He waved his hand in front of his crotch like a magician. He was erect.

Careful, careful. . . .

She found herself leaning back, first her palms on the rich bed-spread, then her elbows.

"Do you know the first thing I noticed about you?" Clayton whispered, touching a renegade strand of her hair. "Your eyes. Even from across the room."

She rolled onto her side. She glanced down between his legs and said, "You're a pretty gifted man, Wendall. I would have thought that with all the excitement at the firm, you'd be somewhat distracted."

He hesitated then said, "Excitement?"

"The merger."

He didn't move for a moment. Just a second or two, but she saw she had thrown him off stride. He laughed seductively. "I think I'm remarkable. I have large appetites."

Taylor rose up on one elbow and scanned his face, which was no more than twelve inches from hers. "I read somewhere that hunters lust before the hunt," she said. "Sex is supposed to steady the hand." She shook her head. "Me, I think it's dissipating."

"Ah, dissipate me, dissipate me. . . ." But the words fell short of their intended playfulness, and he sounded like a college boy making an inappropriate joke.

He whispered, "Lie down, put your head on the pillow." He spoke in a mesmerizing voice, and Taylor was suddenly aware of his penis pressing through two layers of cloth against her leg. She sensed how much he desired her; her thoughts were muddled.

Clayton caressed the pillow, as he had done the bedspread, and said, "I have some toys."

"Do you?"

"I can make you feel very, very good. Like you've never felt before."

"Never?"

He laughed, "Almost never."

Taylor Lockwood asked, "Why do you hate Donald Burdick?"

"I'm not interested in talking about him. Or about the merger."

"Why not?"

"I'd rather make love to you."

"The merger is all everybody's talking about."

"Are you worried about your job? You won't have to be. I promise you that," he said, as if promising her eternal comfort.

"I haven't worried about a job for years. I'm mostly just curious why you dislike Donald Burdick so much."

Clayton seemed befuddled. The evidence of his passion hadn't diminished, but he was following her lead and rising up on one elbow. He seemed uncertain, as if he had met and overcome all types of reluctance in seducing women over the years, yet had now run into a new situation—his prey didn't seem to want to escape, yet was more interested in peppering him with difficult questions than in fucking. He said, "I don't dislike Donald personally. He's one of the most charming men I know. Socially, I admire him. He's a fine representative of old money."

"The rumor is that you want to destroy him."

Clayton considered his answer. "I hear lots of rumors at the firm. I suspect those that I hear are no more accurate than the ones you hear. The merger is solely business. Destroying people is far too time-consuming. . . ." He squinted for a moment, as if trying to find his place again. In his seductive tone, he asked, "How would you like to come to Florida with me tomorrow? Or perhaps Aruba after the merger vote?"

He lay back down and smiled.

But it was too late. The spell had been broken.

Taylor Lockwood easily sat up and ran her fingers through her hair. "You should go downstairs. You are the host, after all."

Clayton was mystified. "But . . ." His hand strayed across the bulging front of his slacks.

Taylor said, "It's the best compliment I've had in a month of Sundays, Wendall. Does a girl's heart good. Now, if you'll excuse me."

Taylor hid out in the upstairs bathroom (which, she noticed, seemed to be in perfect working order). After Clayton, sullen and mystified, had walked downstairs, she slipped into the office.

Inside, in addition to the desk, were an armchair, a Victorian tea serving table, several floor lamps, two large armoires; there were no closets. She turned on one lamp and pushed the door partially closed.

The desk was unlocked. Its cubbyholes were filled with hundreds of slips of paper. Bank statements, canceled checks, memos, notes, personal bills, receipts. Taylor sighed, then sat in the red-leather chair and started going through them one by one. She had been doing so for fifteen minutes when she heard a voice in the doorway say, "Ah, here you are. . . ."

It was Wendall Clayton's.

eighteen

As she spun around and stood up, a stack of papers slipped to the floor and spread like spilled water.

Clayton was outside the door, talking to someone else; she was just out of his line of sight. She reached toward the papers, then heard Clayton say, "Let's go inside here for a minute, shall we?"

Taylor reached for the light. *No, leave it! He's seen it on.* She kicked the papers under the desk; they all disappeared except for the corner of one letter. She reached down for it, but the door was swinging open. Taylor leapt behind an armoire. She pressed herself flat against the wall, her head pressing painfully into the hard, cold plaster.

Another voice spoke. A man's voice. One she recognized, said, "What is it exactly you wanted to see me about, Wendall?"

The door closed. "Have a seat, Ralph."

"Is something wrong?" Dudley asked Clayton. "If it's about last Saturday night—"

Clayton's voice was curious. "I don't remember the light being on." Then he said, "No, Ralph, nothing about that at all. I lost my temper. Please accept my apologies. You and your granddaughter."

"Of course."

Silence. What were they doing? Could they see the tips of her shoes, the corner of the paper under the desk? Was the chair she'd sat in still warm, still at 98.6 degrees or 97 or 96? Were they staring at her shadow on the wall?

Clayton said, "Ralph, you're part of, I guess I'd call it, the old guard, the old-boy network at the firm."

"I go back a ways, that's true."

"You and Donald started at about the same time, didn't you?"

"Bill Stanley, too. And Lamar Fredericks."

"I see you at the DAC with Joe Wilkins and Porter quite a bit, don't I?"

"Yes, we go there often. What exactly—"

"Enjoying yourself tonight, are you?"

"Quite, Wendall."

Silence. Feet shifting.

Clayton spoke, "Young people here tonight. Lots of young people. It's funny, isn't it, Ralph? When I was their age I was making fifty, seventy-five dollars a week? These youngsters make ninety thousand dollars a year. Amazing."

"Wendall, is there something you want?"

"Ralph, I want you to vote in favor of the merger on Thursday. That's what I want."

"I can't, Wendall. You know that. If the merger goes through, I lose my job, Donald loses his, a lot of people do."

"You'll be well provided for, Ralph. A good severance. We can put it in writing if you like."

"I can't. I can't afford it. I've got seven years before retirement. I'd need a present-cash-value payment of over a million."

"We'll be generous. We can't be Santa Claus."

"I'm sorry, Wendall."

"I am too, Ralph." Clayton's voice was cheerful.

Silence again, but a different kind—a thicker silence. Taylor imagined Dudley's thoughts grinding to catch up with Clayton's. Taylor's had already arrived, and her heart went out to the old partner.

"You don't mind blunt talk?" Clayton asked. "On things as important as this, nuance is bullshit. Let's get it right on the table: If you don't vote for me . . . I should say, vote in favor of the merger, I will make public what I know about your little girlfriend."

The choked laugh didn't mask the despair. "What are you talking about?"

"Ralph, I respect your intelligence, I hope you'll respect mine. The little whore, the one you dress up and parade around as your granddaughter, which makes it all the more disgusting—"

The slap of a blow, a laugh of surprise from Clayton, feet dancing in the awkward shuffle of wrestling. Finally: a sad, desperate groan from Dudley—a sound filled with pain, struggle, hate.

Clayton laughed again. "Really, Ralph. . . . Are you all right? There, sit down now. Are you hurt?"

"Don't touch me." The sounds of the older man's sobbing echoed softly in the room.

Clayton said patiently, "Let's not be emotional. There's no reason for me to tell anyone. I meant it when I said you'd be well taken care of. And you bring me some more votes, and you'd be surprised how generous we can be."

"But—"

"Well, why don't you think about it." Clayton's was the voice of luxurious moderation. "Just think about it. It's your decision. Come on, go downstairs, have a drink. Relax."

"If you only understood—"

Clayton's voice cut like a searing burn. "Oh, but that's the point, Ralph. I *can't* understand. And no one else will either."

The door opened. Two pairs of feet receded. Both slowly. One pair in triumph, one in despair, and the sound they made was the same.

In the angry quiet of the den, Taylor was concentrating on a single noise.

She had remained completely still for ten minutes. Though she knew Clayton was no longer in the room, she was worried that he might be lingering in the corridor. At first the only sound she sensed was the crowd noise and music wafting up the stairs. But she now heard something else.

A whisper, the hint of a squeak.

She couldn't place it at first. It was very familiar, but she associated it with an entirely different frame of reference.

Rhythmic and soft.

No, couldn't be. . . .

She cocked her head to the wall. It was coming from the next room. Clayton's room.

It couldn't be. . . .

Taylor stepped out of the corner and over to door that led into Clayton's bedroom. She pressed her ear against the oak.

She heard Martha's high voice say, "That's it, I'm almost there, that's it, fuck me!"

Yeah, guess it is. . . .

Martha may have finished quickly, but it took Clayton considerably longer. Long enough for Taylor to go through the desk slowly. She found one thing that interested her. She looked at the invoice for a long time, deciding whether to steal it. What would her detective friend John Silbert Hemming do? The most ethical thing, which was also probably the least incriminating: She carefully copied all the information on it and put the invoice back.

Fingerprints!

Did she have to worry about them?

Taylor paused, then wiped the pen, the chair, and the drawer pulls with a Kleenex. She closed the desk, shut the light off, and winked a farewell to the lovers in the next room.

It was eleven o'clock. Taylor walked casually down the stairs. The crowd had dwindled. She noticed that Vera Burdick had left, as had Thom Sebastian. She stood before the long table where the caviar, the roast beef, the steak tartare, and the sesame chicken had been, and where all that now remained was broccoli.

Taylor Lockwood hated broccoli.

At midnight, as Reece was accelerating south onto the highway, Taylor stretched out in the reclining seat of the Lincoln, listening to the moan of the transmission. The flabby suspension swayed her nearly to sleep.

"Security Services?" Reece asked. "Euphemism for industrial espionage."

"It was an invoice for unspecified services. Seventeen hundred dollars—not a bad line of work."

"Maybe coincidence. Who knows? Maybe he just wanted somebody to install an alarm in the house."

"Or maybe," she said, yawning, "he wanted somebody to break into your office and steal a note. One odd thing about it: The invoice was addressed to Wendall Clayton at home. But there was no return address."

Reece said, "I know that a lot of security companies give invoices for tax purposes, but get paid in cash, in person. They don't like to leave a paper trail."

"Did you hear the talk at the party? My God, these are first-year associates, and all they were talking about was the merger. Wendall's out on a limb. If he doesn't get the merger through, he's lost a lot of credibility. . . ."

Reece laughed. "Ha, he doesn't get the merger through, he's lost his job. . . ." He looked over and caught her in the midst of a huge yawn. "You okay?"

She said, "I think I remember a time when I used to sleep. You should try it sometime."

"I did once. It wears off."

He reached over and began massaging her neck.

"Oh, that's nice. . . ." She closed her eyes. "You ever made love in a car?"

"Never have."

"I never have either. I've never even been to a drive-in movie."

Reece said, "One time when I was in high school, I—Jesus!"

A huge jolt. Taylor's eyes snapped open. The road was gone, she was staring at a blur of trees and plants racing at them at seventy miles an hour. The undercarriage scraping and groaning, thin metal and plastic ducts and supports popping apart. Then brush and reeds were flashing past the car's windows. A terrible pain shot through Taylor's back as Reece shouted, "That car, that car! He ran us off the road! He ran us—"

He was braking, trying to grip the wheel as it spun furiously back and forth, the front tires buffeted by rocks and branches. The car slowed as it chewed through the underbrush, the buff-colored rushes and weeds whipping into the windshield.

Taylor's head slammed against the window; she was stunned. She felt nausea and fear and a huge pain in her spine.

Then they were slowing fast, the car skewing but the wheels starting to track, coming under control. . . . She heard him say reverently, "Son of a bitch," and saw him smile as the car started a slow final skid on the slippery vegetation down a hill. Thirty miles an hour, twenty-five. . . .

"Okay, okay . . ." Reece muttered to himself. He was a master, steering carefully into the skids, breaking lightly, regaining control, losing it, then regaining it. "Okay, come on. . . ." he whispered to the huge Lincoln.

The car slowed to ten miles an hour. Taylor took his arm and whispered, "Mitch. Oh, Mitchell." They smiled at each other, giddy with relief.

As she looked at his face, his smile vanished.

"God!" He shoved his foot onto the brake with all his weight. Taylor's head spun forward, and she saw the brush disappear as they broke out of the foliage and slipped down a steep incline toward the huge lake, a half mile across, its surface broken with choppy waves. The locked wheels slid without resistance along the frost and dewy leaves.

"Taylor!" he called.

With a last huge rocking jolt, the scenery and the distant gray horizon disappeared. A wave of black oily water crashed into the windshield and started coming into the car from a dozen places at once.

At nine-thirty the next morning, Wendall Clayton walked into his office. He didn't pause—slipping off his coat and hat, hanging them behind the door, taking the coffee his secretary had placed on the corner of his desk exactly where he had taught her to put it. He pried the lid off and looked across the desk at Donald Burdick.

"Morning, Donald. Missed you in Connecticut last night."

"I sent Vera to make an appearance."

"She's a charming woman." Clayton spent a moment assessing his opponent. Donald Burdick looked like hell. The gray suit he wore was wrinkled—Clayton had never once seen the elder partner in an unpressed suit—and his wet eyes seemed deeply withdrawn into their sockets. He lifted his palms. "And what brings you here so bright and early?"

Clayton in fact knew exactly why Burdick was here. His only surprise was that it had taken him so long to do so. A king should meet his enemy straight on. Burdick was, unlike Dudley, a worthy adversary. Clayton believed he and Burdick were a lot alike. What he'd told Taylor Lockwood was correct. He respected Burdick, whose fault was not a fault at all, but an anachronism. Burdick came of age in practice at a time when you could be unimaginative. Clayton felt pity for Burdick and thought it was a shame Burdick had to be removed, when he would much rather ruin a man who was objectionable, like Bill Stanley, or weak, like Ralph Dudley.

"May we talk for a few minutes, Wendall?"

"Certainly."

"I see, of course," Burdick said, "you've called a meeting for tomorrow. I assume the merger is on the agenda?"

Clayton nodded. "I'm having the agenda sent around presently. In accordance with the bylaws." *Ah, your posture, Donald. Exquisite. In older people it becomes vital. See how he sits, straighter even than a military man taught under a sergeant-major's baton.*

"I spoke with Ralph Dudley this morning."

"He's up early for a change."

"How did you do it, Wendall?"

Clayton decided he may not have been completely accurate in his discussion with Taylor Lockwood. He found himself now caressing Burdick's agony, and he enjoyed the sensation erotically. *Perhaps it is personal, Donald.* "Do what?"

"They're now in favor of the merger. What did you do, what did you offer them?"

"What did he tell you?"

Burdick said, "Nonsense is what he told me. I want to know what you said."

The speed with which the news had traveled heartened Clayton immeasurably. It meant Burdick was taking the pulse of his patient frequently, like a deathbed nurse.

"I can't speak for him, Donald."

Burdick was silent for a moment. He let the quiet reign, then said, "You know, Wendall, you're a young man. I remember when we hired you. Perhaps it's the perspective of age, but you don't seem to have gotten any older since then."

Clayton smiled impassively.

"You're a good lawyer. You're born to do the kind of work you love. But if you want my opinion, you're doing this wrong. You're trying to make Hubbard, White into your image. I'm not saying it can't be done, but is it something that makes sense?"

"You think it does not."

"You'll have a Pyrrhic victory. Why carry around the baggage of an old firm?"

"Donald. You're here to give me your proposal. Why don't you?"

Burdick's eyes focused away as he swiftly discarded the arguments he now saw to be futile. "Wendall, I will pay you one million dollars as seed money for your own firm. You can take your clients with you, if they choose to go. I suspect there'll be more than a few partners who want to join you. If it's a significant number, we can work out something with the word processors and secretaries. . . ."

"No."

"Wendall—"

"I've considered starting my own firm. You call me a young man, but that's not how I feel. I've practiced law for over twenty years. There is, in everyone's life, an opportunity. You had yours. This is mine." He smiled, yet in the crescent of his lips there was neither victory nor pride.

Burdick's hands gripped the curled arms of the leather chairs. "I am not accustomed to imploring. I have worked all my professional life to make this firm what it is today. You may not think much of that result, but our clients do. The associates here do. . . ."

"You have my answer."

"A million five."

"Donald. Don't demean yourself."

Burdick sat back in his chair, then rose. "Thank you for your time, Wendall."

Water flowing over her, water so cold it scraped with pain. Then a duller pain, in her chest, a pull against what would not yield, sucking for air when there was only water. Turning in a slow spiral. Where was the surface? Where? She only had minutes to find it. No, seconds. . . .

There, a slight discoloration in the murky water! Yes, a light. That was it. The surface! Her feet found a grip and pushed toward it.

A stunning pain as her head collided with the windshield and she sank back down into the dark, flecked water.

Swallowing water, breathing it, eating the dark, thick paste of water. . . .

Taylor Lockwood screamed.

Mitchell Reece took her by the arm, shook her awake.

The room light went on. "Taylor."

Her eyes opened wide with fear. Sweat coated her face, her heart slugged away in her chest. "Oh, Mitchell." She held him.

The motel room where the state police had taken them was battered, done up in sixties porn decor—turquoise walls, Formica furniture, orange and brown shag carpet. Magic Fingers under the mattress. It was little place off one of the Westchester County parkways, making most of its revenue from bleak weekday affairs and emergencies like this. There wasn't much other reason to stay in the Valhalla Starbright Auto Lodge.

"It was a dream," she announced as if she were reassuring him.

"It's okay now."

She laughed. Just the way she'd laughed last night after the car had plowed into the water and rocked to a stop in the reservoir. They'd waited, frozen in terror in their seats, listening to the comic noises of the car settling, air bubbling and spurting, the engine's groan and tap against the frigid water. Waiting for the Lincoln to twist front-end down and slip under the waves.

Nothing had happened. The car sank into some ooze, a foot or two. That was all.

They'd laughed. After fifteen minutes it wasn't so funny; they couldn't open the doors, and the electric windows wouldn't work. The police cruiser found them an hour later, and the trooper used a crowbar to shatter the side windows to get them out.

He had taken them to the motel. Reece called the rental car company and broke the news to them. The toll-free operator sounded as though it happened every day. They could have another car waiting in

North White Plains if they wished. They debated, then chose to spend the night and take a commuter train into the city in the morning.

Taylor's nightmare woke her at nine-thirty. She looked at the milky white autumn light coming through the orange drapes. She turned and pressed her head against Reece's chest.

Compounding the alarm of the accident, Taylor felt another sudden shock. She realized where they were—in Westchester. Possibly somewhere near Reece's girlfriend. She lay tensely in bed, hugging him hard, half-wanting to put an ultimatum to him right here and now. When he suddenly turned to her and said, "That's it. It's over with," she felt a moment of horror, thinking that, as if he had read her mind, he was tired of her clinging to him and was now telling her that their affair was over.

But he didn't mean that at all. He continued, "I'm going to Burdick, to the police. I'm going to tell them everything that's happened."

Her hands shook in relief, then realized what he had said. "Why? We're so close."

"Last night wasn't an accident. The car that ran us off the road had been behind me for miles, from the time we left Wendall's. As soon as we got to the reservoir he came right over the line at me."

"God—"

"Who was there last night? Wendall, Ralph Dudley."

"Thom Sebastian was there. But so was a quarter of the firm. I saw Sean Lillick and Carrie Mason and all of Clayton's little clones."

Reece said, "We should go to the cops."

"No."

"We have to, Taylor—"

"We do that, and word gets out about the theft of the note. You'll be fired."

"A job is one thing. Lives are something else. I'd never forgive myself if anything happened to you."

"Mitchell, we're almost there. I can feel it. The trial is Monday. Let's hold out until then." She took his head in both her hands. "Just until then?"

"No."

But he was weakening. She repeated, "Just until then," though when she said the words this time, they were not spoken as a question, but as a command. He opened his mouth to protest, but she shook her head and touched his lips with her finger. He seemed powerless before this intensity. After a moment, he nodded. She gripped his hair and her lips took the place of where her finger had pressed against his mouth. She kissed him hard, and he kissed back. They tumbled out of bed and rolled onto the ugly shag carpet.

nineteen

"Donald, you're white as snow. Damn it, man, you've got to get more fresh air. Brought your racket, I hope?"

Burdick leaned against the railing of the penthouse suite in the Fleetwood Hotel in Miami Beach and looked at the cool disk of sun. "More business than pleasure today, I'm afraid, Steve."

Immediately after leaving Wendall Clayton's office, Burdick had taken a limousine from the firm to the Marine Air Terminal at LaGuardia, where the Canadair 600 jet was waiting, engines already warmed up, to fly him to Florida. He had arrived exhausted, but had ordered the car service to bring him directly here before checking in to a room. He hoped he could be on his way back to New York within an hour.

Steve Nordstrom, shaking martinis like a bartender, was the president of MacMillan Holdings. Thick and square, with gray hair trimmed so impeccably it might have been injection molded in the company's Teterboro plant. He wore tennis whites and sandals.

Burdick did not want alcohol. He preferred not to drink during the day, but he knew he would take the offered glass from Nordstrom, a man of 50, whose central face was already in bloom.

"How's the board meeting going?" Burdick asked.

Nordstrom licked martini off his finger. He grinned happily. "We're cutting a melon this year, Donald. Three sixty-three a share."

"Ah," Burdick said approvingly.

"You read the *Journal,* you read the *Times,* everybody's cratering but us. Who can explain it?" He shrugged and looked at Burdick as if he were expecting an answer.

"What about those Icahn rumors?"

Nordstrom said, "Pissing in the wind. He hoovered up that two percent, then just went away. The whole thing crashed and burned. I thought he'd make me a millionaire, but no such luck. Tomorrow we're meeting on the new industry association. You want to sit in?"

"Can't. But tell your people to watch what they say. I told you that Justice is heating up again, and Antitrust is looking at price-fixing. Don't even mention dollars. No numbers at all. Remember what happened in seventy-two."

"Always looking out for your client, Donald?" Nordstrom's question contained the silent modifiers *biggest* and *most lucrative.*

They sat down at a table. The bellboy, who had been waiting patiently, brought out lobster salads in half pineapples and set them on the balcony table. The men ate the salad and raisin rolls while they talked about vacations and family and house prices and the administration in Washington.

When they were finished eating, Burdick accepted another martini and pushed away from the table. "Which of our boys is down here helping you, Steve?"

"From Hubbard, White? Stan Johannsen is here, and there's Thom Sebastian covering the front in New York. I understand he didn't make partner. What happened? He's a good man."

Burdick looked out over the flat scenery at a line of cars shooting flashes of glare from the expressway. After a moment he realized he had been asked a question and said, "I don't remember exactly about Thom," and didn't explain further. He wished Bill Stanley were with him. Or Vera. He wanted allies nearby. Already he missed New York, even with its winter slush.

Nordstrom frowned. "But that's not what you're here for, is it? About the board meeting."

"No, Steve, it's not. . . ." Burdick stood and paced, hands

clasped behind his back. "Hubbard, White has been doing your legal work for, let's see, thirty-five years?"

"About that. Before my time."

"Steve, I'd ask you to keep what I'm going to tell you between you and me and Ed Gliddick. For the time being, at least."

"You betcha, Donald. What's up? You look upset."

"I am upset. It's not easy to ask your favorite client if they'd consider looking for a new law firm."

"What?"

"Do you know about the merger?"

"Of course."

"Well, there's more to it than meets the eye." Burdick explained to him about Clayton and his planned massacre after the merger was completed.

Nordstrom said, "So you'd be out? That's bullshit. You've made the firm what it is. You *are* Hubbard, White."

Burdick laughed sadly. "Let me tell you why I'm here, Steve. I want you to agree that if the merger goes through, you'll pull your business out of Hubbard, White."

"Poison pill, huh? Perelli may get the firm, but the biggest money-maker is gone, right?"

"I'll announce it as soon as I get back, and hope they'll call off the talks."

Nordstrom picked up a fat piece of lobster and sucked it clean of dressing, then chewed and swallowed it slowly. He said with grave sincerity, "Don, of course I'll recommend it."

Although Nordstrom's hedge was as smooth as a bullfighter's veronica, Burdick heard it at once. *Recommend.* He set his glass on the table and folded his arms.

Nordstrom probed for more lobster. He settled for raisins. "If I had the final say, I'd agree in a minute. I'd do anything to help you out. But Ed's the chairman. He's got to make the final decision. It probably ought to go to the board—"

"No, under your bylaws either the president or the chairman can make the decision. You alone can do it, Steve."

"I *can,* yes." Nordstrom laughed. "And Ed *can* fire me, too. I've got a golden parachute, not a titanium one. But not to worry. Ed's a reasonable man. He likes you."

"But he came in from the outside. He's only been there three years. He doesn't have the rapport you and I do."

"I'll put in a good word for you, Don. But Ed's got to have the final say."

"Is he in this hotel?"

"He is, yes, but he's got a tennis date now. He'll be back for tonight's session. You can steal his ear then. Have a drink, relax."

"I think I'll go for a swim."

"Nice shot, you son of a bitch," Ed Gliddick said to Wendall Clayton.

Gliddick stooped to retrieve the fluorescent tennis ball, which shone in the pale Florida sun. He liked the ball's radiant green color. He liked the trim grass surface. He liked small details. He was chairman of a company whose primary line of manufacture was small plastic parts that disappeared into other products and served a number of rarely seen but critical functions. One of which was to catapult Gliddick's net worth to about twenty-five million dollars.

Gliddick was sixty-five. He was stooped and paunchy amidships; when his shirt flew up, you could see where his boxer shorts left a mottled band like a pink belt around his squooshy waist. His ruddy skin was wrinkled from years of sun on golf courses and tennis courts around the world. Sparse gray hair, a hook of a nose. He hated to lose, and especially hated to lose to men who were handsome and younger than he was, but he never let that prejudice interfere with what might be a good business decision.

So he said to Clayton, "Keep talking. Oh, and if you rush the net, I may make you eat that fucking ball."

Clayton served. "What I was saying was, I can save you over a million a year in operating expense. And I can save your job."

They volleyed. Finally, Clayton had a chance to miss a tough shot and give Gliddick the serve. Clayton danced forward, swung a vicious overhand, and blasted the ball into the corner of Gliddick's court. Clayton smiled at his victory.

"That was not a nice shot," Gliddick said, grumbling. "It was a cheap shot. You're still a son of a bitch, but tell me about my P&L. And tell me about saving my ass, too."

"Upstairs, in my suite," Clayton said. "The grass has ears."

They showered, and walked into the penthouse of a hotel just three blocks from the Fleetwood, where at that moment Donald Burdick was completing his third lap of the pool. Clayton mixed whiskey sours.

Gliddick said, "I have the board meeting soon."

"This won't take much time."

The chairman sipped the sweet drink. "You know Donald Burdick was supposed to be flying in to talk to Steve Nordstrom about something."

"I know. You and I are going to be discussing the same thing, more or less. You know about the merger? Hubbard, White and the Perelli firm."

"In general terms. The *Journal* piece."

"What I want is your commitment to stay with us afterward."

"Why would we go anywhere? Donald's been with us for must be thirty years. . . ."

"Donald won't be there after the merger."

Gliddick nodded. "I see."

"It's not revenge," Clayton explained. "There are reasons I don't want him at the firm any longer."

"That's your business."

"As a matter of fact, part of it is your business. I've gone over your billings, Ed. I'm not saying Donald's robbing you. But your costs are out of control. You're paying a hundred sixty bucks an hour for first-year associates who know shit. You're paying for limo deliveries when messengers can take public transportation, you're paying premiums on routine legal work. You stay with us, I can pare that down by an easy million a year. And if the merger goes through, we'll be able to do your labor and real-estate work at reduced rates. Perelli's got one of the best labor departments in town. They'll positively fuck your unions."

"Donald's been a linchpin. He's nothing to me personally. But he and Steve Nordstrom have been tight for years. Hell, he was on our board for I don't know how long. There are a lot of people won't take it kindly that we've sold him out."

"Kindly?" Clayton said the word like a priest attempting an obscenity. "Under your bylaws, *you* can hire any law firm as long as the rates are reasonable. I'm giving you a bargain. Your audit committee will think they died and went to heaven."

Gliddick said, "You mentioned my job?"

Clayton said, "At next week's security analysts meeting down at the Vista, MacMillan is going to be mentioned as one of the more attractive takeovers—"

"Ah, we always are. Icahn—"

"—GCI from Toronto has already been contacting your institutional investors."

"They have? How did you know that?"

Clayton continued, "I put it six months till a tender offer. If you want, you can go to Skadden or Wachtel. Or you can come to us. We'll handle it for two-fifty, tops. That's a guaranteed cap."

Gliddick finished his drink. Clayton poured another.

"Wendall, I don't know. I can't argue with what you're saying, with the numbers. It's a moral decision. I don't like moral decisions."

There was a knock on the door. A young woman. Blond, about five-two, wearing a short leather miniskirt and tight white blouse walked into the suite.

"Oh, Mr. Clayton. Sorry. I didn't know you were in a meeting."

"That's okay, Jean, come on in. Meet Mr. Gliddick. He's one of the firm's biggest clients."

They shook hands. Gliddick's eyes skimmed the white silk.

"Jean is one of my assistants." Clayton glanced at his watch, then turned to him. "Ed, I'm going to have to be rude. I have a meeting downstairs. Would you excuse me for about an hour?"

Gliddick frowned. "What am I going to do with myself for an hour?"

Clayton looked troubled for a moment, then brightened. "Say, Jean, maybe you could keep Mr. Gliddick company."

"Oh, I'd be happy to."

Clayton walked to the door. "Ed, you want anything to eat or drink, just call room service. It's on the firm."

By the time Gliddick said he would and turned back, Jean's blouse was already off, and when she undid her bra, she pulled the elastic a little farther than she needed to so that when she let go, it popped. That was something she'd learned they always loved.

· · ·

John Silbert Hemming may have kept mineral water in his desk, but he was not averse to beer. He finished his sixth mug of dark ale at McSorley's and called for three more. "They're small."

True, though Taylor was having trouble with her second.

She told him about the Supreme Court case that required the pub to allow women in.

"Some achievement." He scowled, looking at the carved-up bare wood tables, and wishbone collection growing a dark fur of dust, and crowds of young frat boys shouting and hooting. He glowered at a drunk, beer-spilling student stumbling toward them. The boy caught his gaze and changed direction quickly. The detective asked Taylor, "Are we having a date?"

"I don't think so."

"Ah," he said and nodded. "How did the fingerprints work out?"

"Not bad. I'll send you a postcard of them."

"If you want, I'll show you how to do plantars."

"Vegetable prints?"

"Feet, Ms. Lockwood."

"Taylor."

"Feet."

Taylor handed him a piece of paper with the information from the invoice she'd found in Wendall Clayton's desk. "John, have you ever heard of this company?"

He read, "Triple A Security? They're not around New York. But we can assume it's a sleaze outfit."

"Why's that?"

"It's an old trick to get in the front of the phone book—to have your listing first. Name your company with a lot of A's. You want me to check it out?"

"Can you?"

"Sure." A waiter carrying fifteen mugs in one hand swooped past and dropped two more, unasked-for.

"Would somebody from a security service—say, this disreputable Triple A outfit—commit a crime?"

"Jaywalking?"

"Worse."

"Stealing apples?"

"That category. More valuable than fruit."

He sat up and towered over her for an instant, then crouched forward again. "At the big security firms, like our place, absolutely not. You commit a crime, you lose your license, and your surety bond's invalidated. But these small outfits"—he tapped the paper—"there's a fine line between the good guys and the bad guys. I mean, somebody's got to plant the bugs that my company finds, right? And planting bugs is illegal."

"Any funny stuff?"

"That's not a term of art in my profession."

"Say, hypothetically, trying to run somebody off the road."

"Run somebody off . . ."

Taylor whispered, "The road."

Hemming hesitated a moment and said, "This Triple A Security, you could possibly find somebody there who might be willing to do what you're talking about. Possibly. It's been known to happen."

Taylor finished the bitter dark ale. She opened her purse, pulled out a twenty, and signaled the waiter.

John Silbert Hemming said, "How about dinner?"

"Can't."

"I was going to let you take me out, so you could deduct it."

She said, "I've got plans."

"Plans are what contractors and shipbuilders use."

"Some other time?" she asked.

"Sure," Hemming said. Then, as she started to stand, he held up a finger. "One thing . . . there's this friend I have. He wears a badge and works at a place called One Police Plaza, and I was thinking you . . ."

She was shaking her head.

". . . might be interested in talking to him?"

Taylor said, "No."

At ten P.M. that night, in Miami, the phone in Donald Burdick's hotel room rang.

He had been lying on his bed, lulled to sleep by reading through the day's *Wall Street Journal* for the third time. He glanced at the phone, then sat up, dizzy. His head ached.

"Donald? Ed Gliddick here."

"Ed, how've you been? I was hoping to catch you before the meeting." Burdick fumbled the clock radio, trying to turn it to see the hour. It fell to the floor.

"Sorry, I got tied up and just made it back for the evening session. We just adjourned."

"Ed, could we meet in the lounge for a drink? There's something I've got to talk to you about."

Hesitation. "Actually, Donald, I talked to Steve after the meeting. He told me what you proposed. I've thought about it. I'll have to say no."

The words hit Burdick like a gunshot. He felt pain coursing through his chest. He couldn't speak for a moment. Finally he said, "How's that again?"

"Sorry, Don. I understand the predicament you're in, but we're a very visible company. *Fortune*'s featuring us next month. We can't very well switch law firms for what amount to personal grudges."

"But Ed, do you know what kind of service you'll get from Wendall Clayton?"

Burdick thought he heard laughter coming from the other end of the line. "Yes, Donald, I think I do. I'm sorry. Merger or no merger, my choice is to stay with Hubbard, White. Listen, my friend, you up for some tennis tomorrow morning?"

"No, I'm flying back tonight."

"Well, you all have a pleasant flight, you hear?"

The next morning, sitting in the big conference room at Hubbard, White & Willis, Donald Burdick had a grisly thought: If this room cratered—say, a 747 plows through the window, or the FALN wanted to make a statement—how much money would be lost? He figured about fifty million dollars a year in collective income. Over ten years, plus bonuses and inflation, that would be an easy two billion dollars. In this room alone. Sitting here right in front of him.

Burdick considered this. A grotesque image, certainly, but it seemed natural for him to contemplate extremes.

What would the repercussions be? Aside from despondent trust officers and brokers?

Not much, he decided. The tiny vacuum created by the event would be filled in a blink.

Perpetual motion does exist; it is called business, and the fuel driving it is ambition.

The partners entered with uncertainty. They lingered at the door, pretending to leave messages with the conference room secretary, pretending to wait for comrades so they might enter with human shields. As always, few of the younger partners looked at Burdick, but this morning he felt it was not a distance in social station that kept his fellow partners' eyes averted, but hostility and shame.

The danish on the Limoges china, the coffee in the sterling urn were practically untouched. Burdick, looking down, reviewed a loan document that did not need reviewing. He heard conversations about the Jets and Giants, about concerts, about vacations, about closings, about the *faux pas* of opposing counsel, about the Supreme Court's latest excursions to Olympus, about rumors of other law firms breaking up.

Finally, eleven o'clock. Burdick glanced up, and was about to call the meeting to order, when he noticed that Clayton was not in his usual place. Instead, he had yielded his seat to a younger partner, and picked a seat at the far end of the U, in a darkened corner of the table, the area usually reserved for newcomers. He sat there with a faint smile on his face and looked infinitely benign.

Nothing in his professional life had ever disturbed Burdick so deeply as seeing Clayton sitting there so calmly—on the hillside, watching his phalanxes stream forth. Utterly at peace. Burdick immediately understood the implication. He understood that if Clayton won the vote today, the seizing of Rome would be swift, the retribution harsh and absolute. Seeing the murky apparition of his opponent far across the room, Burdick understood finally that, with the merger complete, Clayton would destroy him. There was no hope for a truce; Burdick would be ousted immediately. His hands were cold, and he felt his breath rush in, bringing air to his fearful heart.

When he realized everyone was looking at him and there was silence in the room, he cleared his throat.

"Meeting's called to order. Quorum's present, it appears. We'll dispense with the reading of the last minutes. There's only one item on the agenda for this morning. That is the merger, of course. You've all had an opportunity to review the proposal. Obviously, if we decide to go ahead, there will be a number of specifics to work out. Today we'll vote whether to approve the merger in principle. If so, we'll elect a committee to prepare a letter of agreement and execute it with the Perelli firm. Any questions? I suggest we get on with the polling. It's going to take a bit of time."

He turned to Bill Stanley, who began barking out the names of the partners, and noting their responses with his battered old mechanical pencil.

twenty

*L*ook, *I'm in kind of a jam. Maybe you can help me. . . .*

The going rate for access to a Manhattan apartment was apparently five hundred dollars.

I feel so stupid, I promised my uncle I'd come by and do some laundry for him today, and I left his keys at my apartment. . . . He told you I was coming, didn't he?

The fee might have been less, Taylor Lockwood reflected. In the shabby lobby of the Upper East Side building, when the doorman had smiled knowingly and greedily at her attempted bluff, she had shown him the five carefully fanned hundred-dollar bills. There was no negotiation; he pocketed the money, slipped her a spare key, and turned back to a tiny black and white television.

"I'll just be an hour or so."

He had not responded.

As she walked into the apartment, she recalled, too, that Ralph Dudley had cost her the most of any of the suspects. Over a thousand in bribes so far. She decided John Silbert Hemming must handle business differently; a private eye who operated the way she did would be broke in a month or two.

Dudley's apartment was much smaller than she expected. Although she knew about his financial problems, she had assumed that an elderly Wall Street law firm partner like Dudley would be living in elegance, jaded though it may be. In fact, the four rooms in the pre-war building did not have much more square footage than hers. The walls were covered with cheap paint, which blotched where it was thin and peeled where the painters had bothered to apply several coats. She gave a cursory once-over to the living room, which was filled with old furniture, whose tattered, cracked arms and legs were tied together neatly with twine. She saw chipped vases, lace that had been torn and carelessly sewn, books, afghans, walking sticks, a collection of dented silver cigarette cases. Walls were covered with old framed pictures of relatives, including several of Dudley as a young man with a large, unfriendly-looking woman. He was handsome but very thin, and he stared at the camera with solemn introspection.

In his bedroom, beside a neatly made bed, she found what looked like a wooden torso with one of Dudley's suit jackets hanging on the shoulders. A clothes brush rested on a small rack on the torso's chest, and on the floor in front of it was a pair of carefully polished shoes with well-worn heels.

His fussiness made her job easy. Each of the pigeonholes in his oak rolltop desk contained only one category of documents. Con Ed bills, phone bills, letters from his daughter (the least-filled compartment), business correspondence, warranty cards from household appliances, letters from his alumni organization, receipts. He had separated opera programs from concert programs. In the last compartment was a *To Whom It May Concern* letter, which gave instructions about his death—where his will was located, where he wished to be buried and in what suit. Taylor finished the desk in ten minutes but could find nothing linking Dudley to the note or to Hanover & Stiver.

She opened the door of the room's closet and was met by a heavy smell of camphor. Apart from clothes, there were some boxes of photographs (all of which had been taken in the fifties or sixties) and carefully arranged boxes of home health items like hot water bottles, ice packs, and heating pads.

Taylor spent an hour looking through the rest of the apartment. She found nothing. Discouraged and feeling hot and filthy from the search, she walked into the kitchen, illuminated with pallid light from the courtyard that the room's one small window looked out on. She drank some water from the tap, using her cupped hands, then dried them on a paper towel, which she put into her jacket pocket.

Taylor leaned against the sink. In front of her was Dudley's small kitchen table, on either side of which were two mahogany chairs. One side of the table was empty. On the other was a faded place mat on which sat an expensive, nicked porcelain plate, a setting of heavy silverware, a wineglass—all arranged for his solitary dinner that evening. A starched white napkin, rolled and held by a bright red napkin ring, rested in the center of the plate. The gaudy ring was the one item glaringly out of place. Taylor picked up the cheap plastic—the kind sold at the bargain stores in Times Square, where tourists buy personalized souvenirs—cups, dishes, tiny license plates.

She turned it over; the name sloppily embossed in the plastic was *Poppy.*

One hundred twenty.

Donald Burdick stood at his window, wondering how many degrees of vista his corner office let him see.

One twenty, one twenty-five, he guessed. From the Trade Towers to maybe a thousand yards off the Verrazano Bridge. Watching the gray light, he considered how the landscape had changed in his days at the firm. The same way that the style of Wall Street was changing—showing its cuffs more. Life here was no longer what it used to be—dark and somber, Morgan and Vanderbilt somber, bearing up under the terrible, crushing burdens of wealth out of control. The newer buildings in the vista before him had imagination. They showed a smarter kind of power, more educated, more subtle. Expansive, glassy, pastel, textured, marbleized.

Just like Hubbard, White & Willis itself.

All the changes—he'd watched them from vantage points just like this one throughout his career. Burdick always said he approved of change. Out with the old, make room for the new.

Unless you were the old. The one having to vacate.

The members of the firm vote, fifty-eight to twenty-four, two absent, to enter an agreement of merger with the law firm of Sullivan & Perelli, Wendall Clayton to chair the merger committee.

That was it. Next point of business. Scented soap in the men's rooms, new computers for the steno pool.

Burdick rocked back in his massive chair. It no longer smelled of leather. Was it just the age of the hide? Or was it his own age, his senses going dull? Getting weak?

Well, he had given it his best shot. And, *Gott in Himmel,* it had been easier pulling off that Appellate Court appointment than getting those last few votes to say no.

The son of a bitch.

He pictured the four-day weeks, then the three. Watching his beloved clients being stripped away while Clayton and the younger men moved in—salesmen and marketers and public-relations experts as much as lawyers. His clients calling other men at the firm for advice. He saw the hours stretching before him, hours dull as time spent in a small-town museum on a summer afternoon. Pathological hours. Hospital hours. He feared those blocks of time as much as he dreaded the days if Vera were to die before he did. Suddenly he was struck by a sensation he had not felt since the death of one of his sons years before: He wanted to cry.

Donald Burdick clenched his fist tightly. He coughed and cleared his throat. He stood up and walked out into the corridor.

Bill Stanley looked up at Burdick and waved him into his Williamsburg-green office. He was smiling, a hollow twist of his mouth. "Well, Don, didn't quite make it, did we?"

"Not too early, is it?" Burdick walked to Stanley's rolltop desk, opened it, and poured two brandies.

"Didn't really think we would, did you?" Stanley asked with uncharacteristic cheer, taking the snifter from him.

"I wasn't sure."

Stanley said, "At least we know who our true friends are. And enemies."

Burdick warmed the liquor between his palms. "No, not enemies. Clayton has them running scared. If I were thirty-three, I'd have voted the same way."

"Ha! When you were thirty-three, you did." Stanley rocked back in his chair. "And so did I."

"There will be quite a migration in a couple of months, Bill. You, me, Lamar, Ralph Dudley, the rest of the old guard. He's going to move fast, you know. Like lightning.''

"Blitzkrieg.''

Stanley was looking toward the harbor, where the Statue of Liberty stood pale and diminutive. "An agreement in principle. There's still a ways to go before it's over: He can still stumble, don't you think?''

"You're asking me? I voted for Dewey. Look at everybody he's gotten in his camp.'' Burdick's hand rose, then fell, palm down on his knee, "They're all in agreement—I'm a has-been, on my way out. Me, a lame-duck partner nobody needs.''

Stanley laughed harshly. "Don't be so dramatic, Don.''

Burdick didn't answer. He swirled the liquid in his glass absently, compulsively. "Bill, remember when all we had to do was practice law?''

"No," Stanley said, grumbling. "That must have been before my time.''

There were doormen with principles after all.

No amount of money was going to buy her access to Thom Sebastian's building, which was much more upscale than Dudley's. She tried five hundred, then seven, then a thousand, and each time she was greeted with a shocked shake of the head. When she started to walk away in exasperation, the heavy-set East European redeemed himself, however, by adding slyly, "But sweets, maybe you pay me a hundred, I forget you asked.''

"Asked what?''

"Asked to bribe me, you know.''

"You're a creep, you know that?''

"A hundred?'' He smiled.

She peeled off the bill, wadded it up, and threw it at him.

"Thanks, sweets.''

Outside, walking to the subway along upper Lexington Avenue, Taylor Lockwood considered the alternative means of assaulting Sebastian's apartment, one that she had been aware of all along and yet refused to pursue even though it was the simplest approach, guaranteed to get her inside for as long as she wished.

It was Thursday; the trial was in four days.

Should she, should she not? Taylor knew that if she debated the matter, her nerve would fail. Impulsively, she stopped at a pay phone, dropped a quarter in, and dialed the number before she weakened.

At eight P.M., Thom Sebastian arrived at the restaurant, Les Trois Moutons on Fifty-fourth, chugging up to Taylor quickly, his huge attaché case thudding against his solid leg. He was agitated and manic. He rambled without looking her in the eye. "Sorry, darling. They went on and on, pompous bastards. Indemnification, they made the indemnification into Custer's Last Stand. Tedious little fucks, pardon my *français.* Anyway, the deal is almost done, and boy oh boy was I glad when you called. I need a break."

Taylor had already checked her coat, and Sebastian stopped talking long enough to eye her low-cut Betsey Johnson. Tonight, she was Mata Hari.

"Let's go inside," he said abruptly.

The maître d', whose miraculous facade could whipsaw from hostilely perplexed to supercilious in milliseconds, greeted Sebastian warmly, and spirited them past the ornery, impatient crowd at the bar into a quiet, pastel room that hummed with the motion of the helps' salmon-colored jackets.

Sebastian remained nervous. "Kir royales," he ordered, with a perfunctory glance toward her. "Easy on the cassis." Then the waiter was gone. "Bigwigs here and there," Sebastian was saying to her before she understood the words. He pointed out a Paley, a Zeckendorf, a Rockefeller, some Rothschild-related money. He launched into a humorless story about his negotiations that day, which Taylor did not listen to.

Other thoughts occupied her mind.

The captain, whom Sebastian knew by name, hovered nearby as if he were bound to the table by fishing line. Specials were recited with an accent that was a bastard of Hungarian and French. Sebastian ordered for both of them. "Fresh foie gras to start, extra toast, arugula with cilantro, free-ranging chicken with lingonberries. A bottle of Bin 56, the Bordeaux? And start a couple of Grand Marnier soufflés. Is that okay, Taylor?"

"Well, uh, sure."

"You're not allergic to chicken, or anything?"

"Sounds fine, Thom."

The words fluttered out. The deal he was working on with Bill Stanley, football, a couple of job interviews that seemed promising. He did not mention Bosk or Callaghan.

Taylor Lockwood sipped the blushing champagne, cocked her head, and wondered if she was looking at someone who had tried to kill her.

She thought not. Not because she wanted to believe he was innocent, but because she believed he was not a strong enough person to be dining with someone he had tried to drive off the road into a reservoir. Wendall Clayton was surely a person like that. Ralph Dudley, too; a man who could keep a secret like Junie would have the desperate edge about him that Sebastian did not. Or did not *seem* to have. That, of course, was the problem. Taylor Lockwood simply could not tell. Why couldn't she have Mitchell's brilliance? His powers of observation and deduction? It was as if she could see no farther into Sebastian than the makeup and padding that her father did for the deceased, which told nothing of the person they had really been. Was Thom acting? Why was he so agitated? Taylor examined every laugh, every glance, every pudgy finger dancing in the air, every word whispered or exclaimed, and she could see nothing beneath them.

His words streamed by, propelled by the energy of his nerves, perhaps supercharged by several inhalations of a felony-possession controlled substance. "Lake Forest . . . fucking Great Lakes . . . undergraduate . . . PiEpsilonAlphaSigma . . . law school, a bear . . ."

Taylor ate the buttery liver and watched Sebastian, who waved to adjoining tables and commanded the waiters with slick overbearing— like a poor boy turned rich, an ugly boy married beauty. She listened and observed, yet always the same debate raged: She knew the magic words to unlock the door to Sebastian's apartment, and those words were simple: *I want you, take me . . .* This was not, of course, a question of love. What was love in this age of definition by convenience? The real question was: Could she sleep with Sebastian for Mitchell?

". . . I see these guys in Litchfield, Newport. . . . My dad sold computer typesetters . . . suburbs . . . sister's married, a nurse, scared of the city. . . . Can you believe that, Taylor?"

She offered a general-purpose "That's wild." And he nodded in agreement.

The assault would come. He'd threatened often enough. The playfulness would be shelved, and he'd go for the goodies. He'd be a tough adversary—he was born to negotiate. On the other hand, he was cute and boyish and malleable and probably, like most people with a taste for food and drink, would make good, uninhibited love.

But could she do it? Would Mitchell expect it?

No, he wouldn't. But still she was addled. The orders were vague. *Find the note. Do everything you can to get me the note. . . .*

". . . first day in the city . . . Turtle Bay, but that was, you know . . . All-nighters, Stanley and Burdick . . . Nothing like it at all . . . My parents freaked . . . My dad looks at the right side of the menu and goes . . ."

And what if she found it?

What a triumph that would be! She pictured the note fluttering down on Reece's desk. She'd play it up real nice. *Oh, Mitchell, lose this?* Taylor Lockwood looked at the boyish man across the table from her, holding the heavy silver expertly, she looked at his face, which was clearly burdened by things he wasn't saying and yet remained relentlessly boisterous and charming and coy.

Oh, Mitchell, what do I do?

They finished dinner at nine. Her palms were wet; she dropped her pocketbook and two busboys collided gently, stooping to retrieve it. Sebastian left no tip on the Amex voucher; on the way to the French-curtained outer door, he doled out crisp rectangles of folded bills.

This is it, girl. . . .

Except that it wasn't. Not yet. Sebastian took her arm and directed away from the door. "Hey, want to see something really primo? Follow me."

He walked to an elevator in the lobby of the restaurant and pushed the up button.

"There's a private room upstairs. They rent it out. Let me show it to you."

They rode to the top of the building. The elevator doors hissed opened to reveal a large, dark room. Sebastian stepped out. Taylor, her heart pounding with uncertainty, held back. He looked at her and held his hand out. She hesitated, then took it. He led her to the top of a sensuously curved brass stairway where there was a small sitting area in front of a balcony that overlooked the East River. The lights of Queens and Brooklyn pulsed like a spray of stars, and even the workhorse lighters and barges and tugs that churned along the river beneath them seemed magical in the camouflage of night. As she knew it would be, the door to the balcony was unlocked. He pushed it open.

"Come on outside."

"It's cold." Her voice shivered.

He said softly, "I'll keep you warm."

She hesitated at the doorway, feeling the rush of wind two hundred feet above the sidewalk.

"No."

Sebastian said, "Come here. It's nice out."

She stepped out, but stopped short of the railing.

He turned away from her and leaned against the brass, looking out over Brooklyn, his hair mussed in the breeze. His arm rose and slipped around her shoulders. She noticed his hands were shaking.

She sensed he was debating something furiously, almost muttering to himself. "Taylor, there's something . . ."

His arm tightened on her neck, and, terrified, Taylor suddenly began to step away. Before she could turn and run, he spun around and gripped her shoulders.

Then she saw a look of terror on his face that matched her own, and in his gaze she had a clear picture of herself—tumbling over and over slowly to the cold, rigid ground below. . . . Abruptly, he released her, shaking his head. He leaned against the railing. She stepped quickly back to the doorway, breath coming in gasps.

"I'm sorry," he whispered.

For what, Thom? What are you going to confess?

"I get carried away," he muttered.

Taylor nodded, feeling the terror give way to relief—both at her immediate rescue and at the decision that had been made for her; whatever had just happened, whether he had tried to kill her or not, Taylor Lockwood knew that she would not now spend the night with Thom Sebastian.

"Are you all right?"

He did not answer.

"You want to call it a night?" she asked.

He nodded again and hesitated. "It was a really long day."

"Is there something you want to say to me?"

He paused. She heard him inhale a deep breath, then exhale slowly.

Something you want to confess? Let me absolve you. . . .

He laughed briefly. "No, not really." The coy smile returned, and the real Thom Sebastian vanished. "Hey, yours truly managed to wheedle some tickets to the Blue Devil on Saturday."

"The jazz club? You got tickets?"

"Would you like to go with me?"

It would be in public, it would be safe, and she might just get him to confess. "I'd love to, Thom. But why don't we call it quits for tonight. You look like you've got a lot on your mind."

He said, "You don't know the half of it, Taylor."

twenty-one

At six A.M. on Friday, Taylor awoke in Mitchell Reece's loft to find him sitting at his dinner table poring over a law book and jotting notes on a yellow pad.

She sat up, pulling a robe on, and walked to him. The floor of the loft was ice cold, and her bare feet began to cramp before she was halfway there. She detoured to the carpet and circled around him. He may have been aware of her, but he didn't look up.

She stood above him for a moment, then pulled out a chair opposite and sat down. He looked up suddenly, startled, and she realized he had been oblivious to her approach.

His eyes were watery and darkened by shadows. His hair was a mess. His skin looked gray. Taylor reached over and turned on a floor lamp he seemed to have forgotten was next to his chair.

"Thanks." He looked back at the book, then up awkwardly, as if not sure what to say to her.

"How's it going?"

He shrugged. "I'm trying to put together an argument for the judge so we can proceed with the suit without the note."

"Can it be done?"

"I doubt he'll buy it. But I've got to go through the motions."

She said, "I haven't exactly saved the day, have I?"

"It was a long shot. We knew it. Anyway, the game's not over with yet. You've still got three days."

"I didn't sleep much last night. I was thinking. What I'm going to do today—"

But he was holding up one of his hands, and reaching for hers with his other. She saw a well of disappointment and despair in his face. He said, "Do what you can, Taylor. Whatever you want. I have to concentrate on this now. It's going to take all weekend."

She nodded and squeezed his hand. "I'm sorry, Mitchell."

He smiled and touched her face with the back of his hand. It was a poignant gesture. Almost a farewell. She felt a chill. Looking at his grim face, his pale coloring, she had a flashback to Lillick's club—the ghost girl who resembled her. Only it wasn't Taylor who was the victim, but Mitchell Reece.

He kissed her hand, and lowered his eyes to the book. She stayed seated for a moment, and when he didn't move or say anything further, she stood and walked into the kitchen.

At nine she left the loft, leaving Reece still hunched over his books.

Taylor hurried to a local business school library, where she remained for most of the day.

It was time well spent; she learned that Dennis Callaghan was a crook.

Well, perhaps not technically. He had been indicted, though not convicted, of stock fraud and insider trading. He had owned at least three companies that had gone bankrupt and had come under SEC investigation for giving preferential treatment to officers and stockholders just before going under. Looking for a connection between Lloyd Hanover and Callaghan, she examined sheet after sheet of microfiche containing magazine articles on illegal business activities. Nothing linked the two men, though both were frequently mentioned. Even *People* magazine had included a blurb on Callaghan. She learned that he had homes in Palm Springs, Los Angeles, and the Hamptons. His wife was wealthy, and his mistress was beautiful. The magazine included a photo of Callaghan at South Street Seaport last year. He was laughing and talking to an unidentified young blond man who was turned from the camera. Taylor Lockwood couldn't be sure, but it seemed to her that she was looking at the back of Thom Sebastian's head.

She returned to the loft late, at eight. She ate dinner, took a bath, and fell asleep at nine-thirty. She awakened briefly at midnight, when Reece came home, dropping his massive litigation bag on the floor and falling into bed, still wearing his shirt and socks. She finished undressing him, and helped him under the blankets. He mumbled something. She listened, and believed that he said something about *love.* She bent down and kissed him, and he kissed her back. She stood up and slipped off the T-shirt she wore to bed. By the time she lay down, cradling his head with her breast, Reece was asleep.

At about dawn on Saturday, Taylor believed she had a dream: Reece sitting above her, talking to her. Although she could not hear him, she thought he was talking about finding the note, pleading with her to do so. When she opened her eyes, she realized she had not been dreaming; he was indeed sitting beside her, stroking her hair, though he was not speaking. He appeared grim and somber. She muttered, "Mitchell." And he blinked, perhaps surprised to have been caught at this sentiment.

His lips brushed her forehead, and he told her to go back to sleep.

Taylor complied, and when she woke up at nine-thirty, he was gone. A note neatly written on a square of yellow lined paper said he would be at Banque Genève all day, preparing witnesses. With growing panic and frustration, she spent Saturday at the firm. Her mood, and her strategies, whipsawed, and she recognized the first signs of panic. At first, she wondered if maybe the Banque Genève note hadn't been stolen at all, but that Reece had merely misplaced it. She went through his cabinet, file by file. Then she looked under and beside it. Then she thought that perhaps the note had been shredded, and she went to the mail room, which was filled with two weeks' worth of compressed cubes of shredded paper. She took one look at the hundred or so bales and walked out. She skipped lunch, and spent the rest of the day going through the file room, and the offices of Ralph Dudley and Thom Sebastian one more time. She made several attempts to strafe Wendall Clayton's office, but he, John Perelli, and a half dozen other lawyers were ensconced there. They remained there all day.

In anger, she stalked out of the firm and took a subway back to her apartment. She changed clothes and called Reece. There was no answer, and she panicked that he was in Westchester, visiting whoever the hell she was. That possibility wiped out her appetite completely; it actually made her nauseous. She found she was staring at the phone long after the beep had announced she was supposed to leave a message. She couldn't think of anything to say. She hung up, and lay down on the bed to take a brief nap before meeting Sebastian at his jazz club.

Junie was wearing a plaid skirt and a white blouse. She wore no makeup, and her hair was tied in pigtails, bound with pink elastic bands. She wore white knee socks and black patent leather shoes. She sat on her bed in the West Side Art and Photography Club, swinging her legs back and forth. She looked flirtatiously at the man who was sitting down next to her.

Ralph Dudley reached a fluttering hand out and touched her hair. He rubbed it between his fingers, lifted it to his nose and smelled the shampoo. He released the blond strands and stood up quickly. He grabbed his coat.

Junie sighed. "You like going to do this again? You gonna stay or you gonna go?"

Dudley looked at her. He walked back and sat down, laying his coat carefully on a chair. His eyes scanned her body and settled on her thin knees. He reached down and rubbed the back of his hand across the joint. Dudley turned his palm over and caressed her thin legs.

He whispered, "You are so beautiful."

She reached for his crotch, but he stopped her hand. "I just want to look at you."

"You always say that, but then you want to do it."

"No, I just want to look at you."

"Yeah, right," Junie said in a bored voice.

Dudley's breathing grew deeper, and he reached his hand for her breasts. Then he stroked the curve of the cloth, leaning toward her, his hand moving faster, his breath matching the speed of his fingers.

Suddenly he froze and pulled his hand away. He stood.

Junie said, "Poppie, this is like getting to be too much. Are we gonna fuck or aren't we?"

He paced slowly. "I should go."

"You're acting really zoned out lately, you know."

He turned and looked at her again. She lay back on the bed. The short skirt was high on her thighs. She grinned playfully, maliciously, and said, "The boys at school touch me."

"No, don't say that."

"You know where they touch me? They take me to the girls' room, and they touch me. They like touch me here." She rubbed her hand across her chest. "Sometimes it kind of tingles, you know. It feels good."

"Junie, not today. I've changed my mind." But he didn't leave. He watched the girl slip her hand into her panties.

"This is where it feels the best," she said, tensing her buttocks and lifting her hips high.

"No," Dudley whispered. Sweating, breathing heavily, he studied her small fingers.

She undid the buttons of her blouse.

"Please, stop," Dudley whispered, his hand pressing into his lap.

But she didn't stop. She closed her eyes and began moaning softly.

"Do you want me to take off my panties?" When he didn't answer, she challenged him, her eyes gleaming: "Well, do you?"

"Yes," he whispered.

Dudley leaned against the wall. He slowly unzipped his pants.

She pulled her skirt high and ran her hand around over the mound of her lemon-yellow panties. Then she slipped them off.

Slowly Dudley's hand reached out, aiming for her breasts. Junie moved closer to him, but he withdrew his hand and continued to touch himself, stroking faster and faster.

"Oh, Lord, you're beautiful," he said with a moan.

Junie pressed her fingers against herself and closed her eyes.

"Kleenex," Dudley said in a whisper. "You have a Kleenex?"

"Just come," Junie said. "Like don't worry about it."

"Kleenex . . ." Dudley said again, moaning.

Junie shrugged. "The top drawer."

Dudley stepped quickly to the dresser, opened it up, looked in. "Junie . . ."

She sat up, frowning at the look of shock on his face. "Poppie, what is it? Are you okay?"

"Junie." Ralph Dudley lifted Taylor Lockwood's check out of the dresser. He leaned against the wood and stared at the wrinkled piece of paper.

"Hey, Poppie, it's . . ."

But her voice faded as he swung around to look at her. She swallowed. She saw in his face sorrow and anger, but she saw something else, something scary. She'd seen it only once before—the look on the face of a pimp just before he'd lifted a pearl-handled straight razor out of his boot and slashed the lips of one of the girls who'd been cheating him.

Thom Sebastian sat at the bar of the Blue Devil on West Fifty-seventh. A trim place, with a mostly black audience, dressed super-sharp. He was working on a vodka gimlet and thought, *It's going to be okay.*

After three hours' sleep and some hot food, he was feeling better. His equilibrium was not restored, but it was under control. He'd gotten the loan agreement finished. He'd started networking and calling on headhunters, who'd assured him that with his credentials, he should soon be able to find a job in the low six figures.

Tonight, he found himself coolly considering partnership at Hubbard, White & Willis, and he remembered—almost with amusement —that he'd always considered it a matter of life and death.

After Wendall Clayton had called him into his office and told him in that soft, even voice of his that the firm had regretfully concluded they would be unable to extend the offer to him, Sebastian had sat, shoulders curved downward, for three, four, five minutes, smiling. It was a rictus gaze, what to Clayton must have been a grin of madness, teeth bared, eyes crinkled. The partner spoke, his words carefully measured and delivered, telling Sebastian how the firm appreciated Thom's efforts and would not hesitate to provide him with a good recommendation. It was simply that certain economies had to be effected.

Effecting economies. That term inflamed him like acid. He was out of a job because of effecting economies.

The grin . . . The hyena's smile Sebastian had pulled into the smooth skin of his face finally faded, as Clayton's words overran him like commandos. He had lowered his head and had seen an object on

Clayton's desk. An inlaid dish of Arabic design. Sebastian's eyes had clung to that dish like a life preserver, as though if he stared hard enough he could encapsulate the terrible reality in the cloisonné and escape, leaving it trapped behind him.

Tonight, he smiled as he remembered how he'd considered suicide, and had done so in a way that was fitting for his organized, Ivy League-trained mind. Checking out if his insurance policy had an suicide exclusion (it didn't), revising his will (he used another lawyer, a specialist in trusts and estates work), reading up on what would be the most painless, efficient, and tidiest (despite the risk of troublesome regurgitation, the answer was an overdose).

He thought of Linda Davidoff. Recalling how he asked her out brashly and eagerly, how—horrified—she said no. Recalling how she blushed and smiled painfully when he made his crude jokes in front of her. What a child she was.

That had been just two weeks before she died.

Life and death.

But now, finally, his life was back on track. A few minor problems —he was still waiting for the details from Callaghan on their scam. And there was still the difficulty about Taylor Lockwood. This troubled him more than anything at the moment because the only solution he could think of was totally unpleasant and completely alien to his personality. But he couldn't falter now. He remembered his juggler, the spinning cleaver, the blowtorch, the wine glass. . . . He had to survive. So far, so good.

"Huh?" the bartender asked. And Sebastian realized he'd spoken out loud. He looked at his Rolex. "Got to meet somebody. Back in five."

The man in the Dodge wouldn't have bragged that he knew it all. There was a lot he couldn't understand or couldn't do even if he did understand it.

Only one thing he was sure of: It shouldn't be handled this way. Not in Midtown, not in front of all these witnesses.

He'd have to ditch the car, the shotgun, the gloves, his hat and overcoat. For at least half an hour, he'd be the hottest suspect in the city of *Nuevo York.*

He waited on the corner in the old car. Watched a few people ambling into the club. Funny nightclubs in this town. But this one looked okay. It was too bad he didn't get to see the inside. He'd seen some bea-u-ti-ful ladies. Man, some of them six feet tall, dressed in really classy coats. Light-skinned, cream-in-coffee color. Tell 'em to dump the short coons they're with, guys making thirty a year and dropping twenty-nine on clothes, and go out with a spender, man, a real spender.

The door opened and the man in the Dodge tensed. He saw the pudgy blond lawyer, the one the vic would be meeting in just about a minute. Here he comes strolling out the door like nobody's business. The man in the Dodge looked around for the woman. He'd memorized her photo. She was pretty. He wondered: Did it bother him? Killing a woman? A pretty woman?

He thought about it, then decided that not only did it not bother him, it was kinky.

The lawyer was leaning against a concrete stairway that led to a Cadillac dealership. He looked at his watch, then put his hands in his pockets. Suddenly he straightened up and waved to her.

Instinctively, the man in the Dodge reached over to the passenger seat and felt the breakdown—a Remington automatic 12-gauge. Six in the extended magazine. Six more shells wedged into the seat, business end down.

Oh, boy, señorita, there you are. You so pretty, you so sexy, you gonna . . .

Walking up the street, wearing a conservative overcoat, even high heels.

. . . be so dead.

The man in the Dodge checked for blue-and-whites, then eased the car forward. He pulled up as the lawyer was reaching out to shake her hand. *Come on,* señor, *you safe. Don't worry. Just move your fat* culo!

The lawyer stepped aside.

In a single smooth motion, the man in the Dodge swept up the shotgun, aimed over the bead sight, and pulled the trigger. The huge recoil stunned his shoulder. He had a fast image of the lawyer leaping to the ground, rolling away and away from her, as the woman took one load in the face, a glancing hit. He fired two more toward her back, but the way she fell, it seemed that only one caught her, and even that wasn't a square hit.

Human screams and horns wailed, and cars screeched to a halt in panic and to avoid the pedestrians who dived into the street. The man in the Dodge eased the car forward, drove to the intersection, and, signaling properly, made a careful turn into downtown traffic.

Mitchell Reece was exhausted, but not so much so that he failed to make one observation about Hubbard, White & Willis, which was: Although the merger had been approved only two days ago, a shift of power had already occurred.

He noted this as he climbed what the associates dubbed the Stairway to Heaven—the marble staircase that led from the sixteenth floor up to the seventeenth, where the senior partners' offices were. He paused at the top of the stairway to catch his breath—he was winded from no sleep and little food—and noticed that lights were on in two offices on this floor: at the end of the hall to Reece's right, which was Donald Burdick's, and at the opposite end to his left, which was Wendall Clayton's.

Reece could see the elder partner sitting at his desk, alone, reading a thick document. From an expensive CD player came the staccato notes of a Bach two-part invention. Outside of Clayton's office, a secretary and a messenger were camped out. Inside the office, a half-dozen attorneys in shirtsleeves paced or sat, gesturing with their arms, arguing, shouting, laughing. If he had not known the firm, and had been asked which office was that of the chief partner, Reece would have answered "Wendall Clayton" without hesitation.

He reflected, walking toward Burdick's office, that that response was now the correct one.

"Mitchell, come in," Burdick called.

Reece took a seat across from the partner, who added, "I've gone over the Banque Genève *v.* Hanover & Stiver file. It seems to me you're as prepared as ever."

Reece had never seen Burdick looking this gaunt. *Like Death warmed over,* a favorite expression of a partner he had once worked with. "Preparation is what wins trials," he said. Reece felt heartsick. He believed he now understood why Burdick had asked him stop by. He dreaded what he was about to hear.

"Mitchell, can I say something to you off the record?"

"Of course."

"I suppose it's no mystery to you that I'm part of the plunder."

"Plunder?"

"The deal Wendall is so hard at work on at the moment with *Il Duce* Perelli down at the end of the hall. He's trying to get me out with as much fuss as possible."

"I didn't know that for a fact, Donald, but most of us assumed that was the way it would go. I'm sorry."

Burdick rocked in his huge chair, flipping the pages of a document back and forth. He said, "I have been in discussions with Fabrienne Garre and Charles Lecroix at Banque Genève."

No, no, no! Why this, why now? Reece kept his face emotionless.

"They're expanding in a big way after the first of the year, and they'll need a chief general counsel. They've asked me to join them."

This was worse than Reece had thought. "Congratulations," he said evenly.

"It's not my first choice, but it's a good group of men. The hours are reasonable, and I think it would stave off boredom in my golden years." Burdick chuckled sadly and then shoved sentiment aside. "I suppose you know what I'm saying to you. And I suppose, too, it doesn't need saying. Not to a litigator with a record like yours. But it is very, very important to me that Banque Genève wins that trial on Monday. I know this is introducing a personal element into firm business, but, well, Wendall has made this whole merger personal."

Reece said a calm, "I'm confident that we'll win, Donald."

"Now, get on home, get some rest."

"I won't be much longer. Just a few odds and ends."

They said good night, and Reece was in the hall before Burdick called to him. "Mitchell . . ."

He turned and raised an eyebrow at the partner.

"You're the best we have," Burdick said solemnly. "I've got every confidence in the world in you."

twenty-two

"Thom Sebastian had stopped crying by the time they got him to the precinct house, though everybody was still staring at him, the cops, the hookers, a lawyer or two. It was the blood mostly. Nobody could figure out how somebody could be this bloody and not have a six-inch stab wound.

He slumped on a bench waiting for the booking officer to get around to him, staring at his brown wingtips. A girl sat next to him, a tall black girl with a tank top and hot pants under her fake fur coat. She looked at the blood, then shook her head quickly, a shiver. Her stiff hair vibrated.

Sebastian felt a shadow over him, someone walking close. He looked up, eyes red, face moist and puffy.

Taylor Lockwood said, "You look awful."

Sebastian was completely quiet, paralyzed. He just closed his eyes and lowered his head again slowly, resisting his encompassing pain.

The desk sergeant said to her, "Want something?"

Taylor said, "What happened?"

"You just a friend, you're not supposed to be here. This isn't a social event."

How much did she remember? How many depositions and court calendar calls had she made?

She turned to him with a glare. "I'm his lawyer, and just for the record, you have anything else funny to say?"

His face reddened. "I'm not trying to be—"

She barked, "What's he been booked on?"

"Nothing yet. The arresting's on the phone to the medical examiner." He turned gruffly back to a mass of papers.

A uniformed officer came up, a thin man, slicked-back hair, gray at the temples. He looked over Taylor and was not pleased. His was a joint prejudice: against defense lawyers in general (who spent hours torturing cops on the witness stand and reducing them to little piles of incompetence) and women defense lawyers in particular (who had to prove they could torment more gleefully than their male counterparts).

Taylor Lockwood cocked her head and tried to look like a ballbuster.

"I'm Mr. Sebastian's lawyer. My client was out on the street, waiting to meet me, as a matter of fact. And when I get there, there's blood all over the goddamn place, and they say he's been busted. What's going on?"

A roar of a voice from across the station house. "Hey, Taylor!"

It had to happen—one of those moments when the gods get bored and decide to skewer you just for the fun of it. Taylor gave an inaudible sigh and turned toward the voice, now booming again, "Taylor Lockwood, right?"

A huge cop, a faceful of burst vessels, tan from a vacation in Vegas or the Bahamas, stalked across the room. He was off-duty, wearing designer jeans and a windbreaker. Thirty pounds overweight. Trim, razor-cut blond hair. A boyish face. Early forties.

Taylor glanced at Sebastian for help. He was visiting oblivion, and she looked back at the cop.

"Hey, Taylor, it's me. Tommy Blond. Don'tcha remember? Tommy Bianca, from the Pogiolli case."

"Sure, Tommy. How you doing?" She took his massive, calloused hand.

The man was looking down at Sebastian. "He okay?"

"Nosebleed is all," the arresting said. "We thought he'd taken one, too. EMS looked him over, said he'll be okay, he keeps an eye on his nostrils."

Tommy Blond looked at the arresting and the desk sergeant. "Hey, treat this lady right. She's okay. She was working with the lawyer got off Joey, youse know, Joey Pogiolli from the Sixth? Got him off last year some asshole says Joey worked him over on a bust. . . . Hey, Taylor, you was a paralegal then. What, you go to law school?"

"Nights," Taylor said, grinning and wondering if the sweat that had gathered on her forehead would start running.

"That's great. My kid's applying to Brooklyn. Wants to be FBI. I told him they don't need law degrees anymore, but he wants to do it right. Maybe sometime he could talk to you about school? Got a card?"

She patted her hips. "None with me. Sorry."

Sebastian stared at the floor.

Tommy Blond said, "Whatsa story, Frank?"

The arresting said, "Some slash took a couple rounds of double-ought. Name of Magaly Sanchez. We think they were using him"—he nodded toward Sebastian—"to ID the hit. She was his regular dealer. Had about five grams on her, all packaged and ready for delivery. Maybe she'd ripped off the supplier and they wanted to ice her in front of a customer, you know, to get the message across. Uh, Mr. Sebastian had on him a quarter gram. . . ."

Taylor rolled her eyes. "A quarter gram? Come on, you guys."

"Taylor, I know what you're asking. . . ." Tommy Blond said, then: "That's a lot of blood. You're sure it's just a nosebleed?"

She remembered a buzzword. "What was your probable cause for search?"

"Probable cause?" The arresting blinked in surprise. "He was shaking hands with a known drug dealer got whacked right in front of him? That's not probable cause, that's for-damn-fucking-sure cause."

"Let's talk." She walked over to the bulletin board. The cops looked at each other, then followed. She stood with her head down. *Think, girl, what've you seen, what've you heard?* "Look. He's never been arrested. A quarter gram—you and I both know a collar like that's optional. Give him back to me and if the judge seals his testimony, I'll guarantee he tells you everything you want to know about Miss Sanchez."

"I don't know. . . ."

"Look, he works for the same firm got your buddy Joey off."

Joey, Taylor remembered, was the patrolman who maybe did get a little carried away with his nightstick on that black kid who maybe lifted a wallet but maybe didn't. And who maybe reached for that tire iron, even though, funny thing, it was found twenty feet away from the scuffle. Took the ER fifty-eight stitches to repair Officer Joey's handiwork on the kid's face.

"Come on, boys, give the guy a break. . . ."

Tommy Blond looked at the arresting, who said, "We haven't wrote it up yet."

The cops exchanged a look that's shorthand in law enforcement; it translates, *I don't need this shit.*

The arresting said, "Get him out of here. Oh, and tell him to clean up his act. I mean, like really. Next time they won't leave nobody around."

Taylor said, "Thanks, gentlemen."

She walked back to Sebastian, who had been slumped in his seat, out of earshot of the bargaining. Okay, she asked herself, how would Reece handle it?

She knelt down next to him. Took a tissue out of her purse, wiped blood from his lip. "Thom, I've got to ask you something. I need an honest answer. . . . Look at me."

Boy's eyes. Indignant, hurt, scared boy's eyes, round and three-dimensional with the refraction of tears.

"You went through Mitchell Reece's file cabinet sometime recently. Why?"

A furrow ran through his bloody forehead as he frowned. He sniffed. "What are you talking about?"

Taylor said, "Damn it, Thom, I can get you out of here, or I can leave you, and that'll be the end of your career. It's your call."

"What the fuck is this? You some kind of—"

"What were you doing in the firm?" Her voice was low and fierce.

He reached down, to his slacks, and touched the speckle of the dealer's blood, like a black constellation. "Looking for things."

"Thom."

He whispered pathetically, "Taylor, please, get me out of here."

"What things?"

His eyes fell to the grubby linoleum. She touched his arm. He pulled it away. "I was getting information on all the firm's escrow accounts."

"The client accounts? Why?"

He swallowed. "Bosk and Callaghan and I have this idea. We're going to transfer money out of the accounts."

"To steal it?"

"No, no, just borrow it. Callaghan was going to buy futures. Short-term. When we sold, we'd replace what we'd borrowed and split the profit."

"That's what you've been doing with Bosk?"

"We haven't done it yet. I haven't decided. But what business is it of yours?"

"Thom, look at me. What about the Hanover & Stiver case?"

"The what?" He was truly puzzled. "I don't know what you mean."

Taylor stood up. She seemed to tower over him as she studied his huddled form. "One more thing, Thom. The night of Clayton's party. In Connecticut. How did you get home? Did you have a car?"

"Why are you—"

"Tell me!"

"A train," he spat out. "A bunch of us took the train from Westport. You can fucking ask the guys I was with."

"Okay."

"Are you going to . . ." His lips quivered. He swallowed.

An odd feeling swept through her. Her legs were suddenly weak. Her face burned. She understood. She'd done what Reece would have. She'd been strong and tough. She'd been brutal. She'd won.

Power.

That was what she sensed. Sebastian, defeated in front of her, bloody and fearful as a child, was hers. The cops were hers.

"It's okay," she said. "They're letting you go." Sebastian rose to his feet slowly, and she took his arm to steady him.

Taylor said, "I was interested in something else. You answered my question, Thom. Let's get you home."

The hooker watched them leave and said, "My, my, this be some court system we got ourselves. Anybody gotta ciggie?"

· · ·

Fatigue had settled on Wendall Clayton like a wet coat.

Unlike John Perelli, who sat across the table from him, Clayton had not loosened his tie or rolled up the sleeves of his white, Sea Island cotton shirt. He sat the way he had been sitting for the past ten hours, upright, only occasionally dipping his face forward to rub his bloodshot eyes. From this position he could call up the expressions in his personal arsenal. A smile (perplexed or humoring), a frown (confused, condescending, impatient), a mask (impenetrable).

What he really was thinking no one could tell.

Beside him sat two of his young partners. They were on the executive committee of Hubbard, White. Burdick had rallied hard to keep them off the committee, but Clayton had maneuvered their elections through. The men across from them were counterparts—John Perelli, a junior partner, and a senior associate. Before them were drafts of a document, spread out like a patient under a surgeon's scanning eyes.

Clayton glanced outside the door at a young woman, a secretary from a free-lance legal services staffing firm. The woman knew every major word processing system in the United States and could take dictation and type at eighty words a minute. These skills were fetching her thirty-two dollars an hour, though at the moment she was being paid that fee solely to sip coffee and read a battered paperback called *Surrender, My Love.*

The room was cold. The radiators were off, and a quartz room heater pulsed out its burning orange glow. The overhead lights were off —everyone had complained about stinging eyes and headaches from the twelve-hour workday—and illumination was provided by Clayton's desk and floor lamps. Skin and hair were greasy, and the air was sour with musky human scent, cigar fumes and the aftermath of a deli sandwich dinner.

Perelli wore half-rim glasses. These were low on his nose. He looked up and stared into Clayton's eyes. "Wendall, we're down to this last point. I know we talked about it, but I've got to draw the line here. We've given in on all major financial issues. This I can't agree to."

"I understand your hesitation, John, but it's in everybody's interest."

Perelli's young associate looked at the agreement. Clayton liked him. He was brash, almost obnoxious, though he tempered it with humor. He knew how to aristocratize, but he also knew his place. That tightrope was a tough one to walk, and Clayton would keep his eye on the boy. He would be partner within two years and would have to be made to feel dependent on Clayton.

The young man looked up. "I'll tell you my problem. The firings are not strictly for economic reasons, and few job performances have been questioned. Of the eighty people you're proposing to fire, Wendall, more than half are in EEOC-protected classes. Of course, not many women or minorities," he said dryly, and everyone in the room smiled. "But age is going to be a problem. People over forty. We're looking at a half dozen, at the minimum, suits. Donald Burdick could sue us, and given his present attitude about this whole thing, I suspect he will."

"It's a risk," Clayton said.

Perelli smiled. "And one we just can't buy into. Some of the recent EEOC damage awards. . . . I can't recommend we go forward unless you agree to gradual cutbacks, over, say, two years."

"No." Clayton shook his head.

"Wendall, come on, we've come so far. We're almost there. I can't believe this is so important to you." Perelli sat back in the chair and lit another cigarette.

One of his partners spoke. "Wendall, what we could do—"

Clayton waved his hand to shut him off and said, "Here's my final proposal. We'll shift two hundred fifty thousand from the Hubbard, White bad debt reserve into a special EEOC defense fund . . ."

"That's not going to be enough—"

He held up his hand. ". . . and I will personally match, dollar for dollar, that fund up to the half million. Over that, the firm takes the hit."

"Your own money—not your partnership share?"

"My own cash. We'll escrow it. Provided I get interest at prime."

Perelli was impressed, though he concealed it under a yawn. He hesitated for a long moment. "I'll agree to it on one condition: Everyone else can go, but we'll have to keep Donald Burdick with the firm for a year."

The regal head was shaking before the sentence was finished.

"No. Absolutely not."

"Wendall, my partners and I have talked about this at great

length. It's in all our best interest to avoid as much disruption as possible. Strip Burdick of his power, take him off the executive committee, give him Tinkertoy clients. Make him resign. But it's going to look very bad for you and for us if you oust him."

"No . . . and I think it's unconscionable that this comes up at the eleventh hour. We discussed this at our breakfast meeting two weeks ago."

Perelli began, "I thought—"

Clayton motioned his hand at his senior associate, who leaned close. Clayton whispered something in his ear. They both looked grave. The associate whispered back, and Clayton nodded, smiling slightly. Perelli watched this uncomfortably, then continued, "I thought we could talk reasonably. Apparently I was wrong. Whether the subject came up before or not is irrelevant. The point is, we don't do the deal unless Burdick stays for at least twelve months. If he chooses to quit, fine. But we can't afford a suit from him, and we won't jeopardize bad press and risk losing clients because of that."

The silence was that preceding the seventh card in high-stakes poker.

Clayton's associate jotted a note on a piece of yellow paper—the noise seemed like rubbing sandpaper in the stillness of the room. Clayton looked at the scrawl and didn't respond.

Perelli said, "Wendall, you'd risk cratering a multimillion-dollar deal because of one man?"

Clayton lifted an imperial hand. "I'd ask you the same."

Perelli asked, "Shall we adjourn, and resume our discussion next week?"

Clayton said, "I assume if Burdick did something wrong—say, was guilty of some moral turpitude, was arrested, or was found to breach a fiduciary duty—you would have no objection to firing him."

"Of course not. I simply don't want him purged."

Neither moved or shifted his gaze. Finally Clayton said to the partner at his side, "Get her started." He nodded toward the secretary.

The young man stared for a moment, perhaps surprised that Clayton had given in so quickly. Yet he had been taught well and would never have thought about questioning a decision of Clayton's in front of anyone. He walked into the hall to summon the woman.

The tension in the room flooded out with the man's receding steps.

Perelli and Clayton shook hands with finality.

Clayton reflected contently that the outcome of the final show-down was almost exactly as he had predicted. In fact, it was somewhat better. He'd thought that Perelli would insist on keeping Burdick for eighteen months. He looked glum, and he felt ecstatic.

Perelli stood and stretched. He poured coffee. "You going to use a special pen to sign, Wendall? Like the president does?" And he was surprised at the intensity of Clayton's laughter. "No, John, no. I'll just use this old thing."

He uncapped a battered old Parker fountain pen, one he had used for years. Not long after Clayton had started at Hubbard, White, he found himself at a closing without a pen. Donald Burdick had shot him a gruff glance and slid this pen to him. "You should always be prepared for anything, Wendall. Keep that one as a reminder."

Wendall Clayton set the pen in front of him and took the coffee John Perelli offered him.

twenty-three

Taylor Lockwood had spent the night at her own apartment after dropping Thom Sebastian at his place. Sleeping alone for the first time in several days was disorienting, and she had been awakened three or four times by nightmares. It was not, however, the dream scenes that troubled her upon waking. Rather, two images kept returning to her thoughts as she lay among the wadded blankets and tried to get back to sleep: One was the slow procession of the bloody ghost woman in Lillick's performance. The other was the pale green managing attorney's memo printed with the stark words "Banque Industrielle de Genève *v.* Hanover & Stiver, Inc. December 9." She lay awake until four A.M., then fell asleep. She awoke groggy and disoriented at nine-thirty.

Now, feeling better after a shower and breakfast, she dropped a Melita filter full of coffee grounds into the garbage can and drank half a cup of French roast before she continued packing. At Reece's loft were two blouses, a nightgown, a pair of Reeboks. Her toothbrush was here, her diaphragm was there. Underwear? Both places. She'd forgotten how these periods of transition in relationships took a lot of planning. Love is great, only where do you keep the clothes?

Taylor walked along Fifth Avenue, north, toward Chelsea, past several of the Village's massive Protestant churches, crowded now with late-morning parishioners. North of Fourteenth Street, the broad side-walks were sparser. She zigged around patches of ice, remembering how her music teacher taught her to think of footsteps as musical beats. As she walked she'd break the spaces between the tap of the steps into half notes, quarter notes, eighths, triplets, dotted quarters, and eighths, whispering the rhythms.

One two and uh three four . . .

Taylor maneuvered through the empty sidewalks of Chelsea, near Sixth Avenue. The professional photographers, who had once shared the area only with printers and warehouses and Korean importers, were now situated around residential lofts and cavernous restaurants with a life expectancy of about six months. It was a gloomy, dark, functional territory.

One, two, three . . . One, two, three . . . One—

The scenery vanished as the arm went around her face.

The man wasn't strong, but she was so completely surprised that she went over on her side without a fight, tripping on some cable and boxes in the alley. She threw her hands over her face, unable to scream, the breath knocked out of her. Taylor twisted away, smelling rotting bean sprouts and chicken bones and garlic from restaurant trash. Fists pounded down on her.

She was going to die, she was going to die! *Mitchell!*

But the hands pummeled her without skill. With passion and fury, but without focus.

Then they stopped, and Taylor heard crying. It wasn't her own. A man's raspy voice wheezed between the sobs. "I hate you, I hate you. . . ."

Hands gripped her lapels. She pushed them away and staggered to her feet.

"Ralph!"

Dudley glared at her in raw hatred, then slowly sat on an over-turned trash drum, gasping for breath. "Why did you do it?"

"Are you mad?" She stepped to the wall of the building, began brushing her coat off, rubbing at the oil and grease stains. "Look at this? Are you crazy?" She picked up her bag.

He eased a Foster's can back and forth with his foot. He stared blankly at the motion it made. "I've been waiting for you since nine. At first I wanted to kill you. I . . . The thought actually went through my head. I wanted to kill you."

"What are you talking about?"

"You went through my desk. Todd Stanton told me. And you followed me. You bribed Junie to find out about me."

Taylor was silent for a long moment. "You lied to me, Ralph. You lied about being in the firm that Saturday night."

He started to speak several times, but couldn't. He stood up and paced beside a disintegrating garbage bag. "How can I make you understand?"

"Ralph—"

"I'm not a bad person. You may not believe me, but I was good for as long as my wife was alive. I never saw anyone else. No affairs. No, you know, prostitutes."

Taylor's fear had changed into pity and embarrassment. The desires to flee, to slap him, to put her hand on his shoulder were all in balance.

He lifted his head; his mussed hair and narrow face made him look like a madman. He started to speak, then lowered his face into his hands. A dozen cars crashed over a pothole in the street next to them before he spoke. He said in a whisper, "Have you ever felt real passion? I mean, this incredible hunger for something? Do you know how rare that is? Do you know how incredibly rare passion is?"

"Ralph, I don't want to hear these things. You don't want to say them to me."

"Oh, but I do, yes I do. You have to understand." His wet, crazed eyes pled with her, and Taylor was silent. Dudley cleared his throat and then played with a thread dangling from his worn, unraveling gloves. "Everybody needs passion for something. Some people, I suppose, find it with their husband or wife for a while at least. Or with their lovers. They're lucky if they can be passionate about, you know, normal things. My passion? Well, I don't have to tell you. . . . It's a disgrace.

"Maybe I should have gone to see somebody about it. A psychiatrist. Maybe they could have helped me, I don't know. Anyway, I thought I could control it. And I did for years. But . . ." He looked up at her. "You're young—you wouldn't know about this, but . . . desire doesn't recede when you get older. For me it was just the opposite. I began obsessing."

"Ralph, you just assaulted me. I don't think—"

"Please hear me out! Please!" He wiped his face, which was bright red from the cold and his tears. Taylor stood awkwardly, hands at her side. "Do you know what I'd do? I would walk past schoolyards, I'd buy copies of teenage magazines. I bought some tapes once—somebody on the street saw me looking at the schoolgirls. But they turned out to be of boys. I threw them out. I'm not that way." He paused, to be absolutely certain he was conveying the exact nature of his lust.

"I was sure I was going to do something awful. I knew I was. That was when I heard about the art club. I met Junie and I fell in love. I really am. She's not a child. She may be fifteen, but mentally she's twenty or thirty. It's not like some little girl at the zoo or at school. I really do love her." Her face must have revealed no recognition of his words. He asked her suddenly, "Why did you do it?"

"Do what, Ralph?"

"Bribe her? Tell Clayton about us?"

"I didn't tell Clayton anything. I talked to Junie, but I didn't tell Clayton."

"Somebody . . . somebody did."

"That law firm is like Borgia's villa. Everybody's got their spies. You wrote your appointments down in your diary and left it on your desk. It wouldn't have been that hard to find out."

"But why did you go to the club? Why did you follow me?"

"There are problems at the firm. I needed to know where some people were at a certain time. You lied to me about being in the firm that Saturday."

His eyes blazed. "All right, you want to know what I was doing there? You want to know?" He opened his briefcase and pulled out sheets of paper, threw them into her hands.

She fumbled them, then read quickly. She looked up.

Dudley leaned forward and said viciously, "I'm trying to *adopt* her. That's all I was doing—drawing up the petition, researching the law." His voice cracked and tears slipped from his ruddy eyes. He repeated, "I'm trying to adopt her."

"But why?" Taylor whispered.

"I *love* her!" he shouted, eyes wide, filled with contempt. "I want to raise her, get her out of that house. I want to send her to school. I want to stop . . ." His jaw was quivering. His voice was hoarse. "Do you understand?"

"Ralph—"

He continued, speaking to the ground, "If she's my daughter, I won't touch her any more. I wouldn't dare. I couldn't. It's the only way for me to stop." He took back the papers and ordered them carefully, neatly aligning corners.

"Why don't you go home?" She spoke softly, as if she were speaking to her own grandfather. "Let's both just forget what happened."

He did not answer.

She walked to the front of the alley and looked back. He was sitting on the trash can in a wash of dull, elusive light, most of it reflected from the low buildings around them. His breath popped out in small, disappearing puffs. He didn't move, he stared at the papers, sitting completely still, as Taylor turned the corner and walked out of sight.

The loft door was open. She paused in the hallway, seeing the trapezoid of ashen light fall into the corridor. Taylor felt a jab of panic. In a burst of frightening memory she remembered the car accident, and she thought for an instant that the driver of the car had come back and killed Mitchell. She ran to the door.

He was lying on the couch, wearing blue jeans and a wrinkled dress shirt. His hair was mussed and his arms lolled at his sides. His eyes stared unmoving at the ceiling.

"Mitchell!" she cried.

He turned on his side slowly and looked at her.

Taylor stopped, halfway to him, and pressed a hand against her mouth. She continued walking and crouched next to him and took his hand. "I thought . . . you were hurt or something."

She felt the slight pressure of his hand on hers, but no other response. His eyes returned to the squares of the tin ceiling.

"I've been figuring something," he said.

"Are you all right?"

"Do you know how many hours I've practiced law?" His voice was groggy, and Taylor looked around casually for a bottle of liquor. She didn't see one, though she did notice that the loft was in total disarray: Hundreds of law books, sheets of yellow paper, Xerox copies of cases, charts and diagrams for the jury, thick wads of transcripts were scattered throughout the rooms.

"Mitchell—"

"You can figure it out, you know. In fact, you don't even have to do any of the work yourself. The billing system at work has it all on computer. You just punch in your number, and out comes the total. Last night, after I had a meeting with Donald, I did that."

"You had a meeting with Burdick?"

Reece looked at her but did not answer. She ran her fingers through his hair, affectionately, yet also trying to smooth it so he didn't look so crazed. "Do you know how many hours I've billed for Hubbard, White? Eighteen thousand three hundred and forty-two." He turned to her, and she saw a redness in his eyes. She thought of Ralph Dudley—a man with eyes like these, desperate eyes, tragic eyes, yet she was so drawn into Reece's that she completely forgot about the old partner. He continued, smiling in despairing humor, "Of course, that's not counting the past two days. You'll have to add another thirty hours or so onto that."

"Mitchell, you need some sleep."

"When I graduated from law school, I had a chance to become a corporate lawyer. The money was better, the firm was just as prestigious as Hubbard, White. You know about corporate lawyers—they speak the voice of moderation, they negotiate, they compromise. They bring people together. And do you know something else about them, Taylor? They never lose. Because there's nothing *for* them to lose. They put together a deal, then go on their way. No risk. It's all win-win. But I couldn't do that. I had to be a trial lawyer." The pressure on her hand grew until it was painful. A second before she shifted, he released it. He continued, "It was perfect. The ultimate validation of my life—I could justify myself every day, over and over again, by winning my cases. The danger never occurred to me, the risk—that if I lost, I was nothing."

"Mitchell, how can you say that?"

"Tomorrow morning, I'm going to lose a case. I'm going to lose it for a reason that's totally disgraceful. Because I was careless. I'm going to do my best, but I'm going to lose, and when I do, I'm walking into Donald Burdick's office and resigning."

"It isn't—"

"I don't blame you, Taylor," he said with such intense sincerity that she believed him. "Not at all. You got farther than anybody could have. I almost got you killed." The pressure returned to her fingers, but now she felt the insistence of gratitude in his closing hand. She rose and sat on the couch next to him. She took his shoulders in both hands and lifted him to a sitting position. He looked at her curiously.

She said, "It was Wendall."

He did not say a word.

"I've eliminated Thom and Ralph. It has to be Wendall." She explained about the shooting and about Dudley's assault on her. "And I talked to my private detective. He said there is a Triple A Security—the receipt I found in Wendall's desk—and he checked the grapevine. It's in Florida. He said they're a firm that has a reputation for doing labor work. Which he tells me is a euphemism for rough stuff, like stealing documents and bugging offices and even beating up people."

"But the merger's over with," Reece said. "Wendall won. He doesn't need to disgrace Burdick. . . . Wait." Reece sat up. "Wait. Last night Donald told me that there's still some question about keeping him with the firm for a while. Perelli doesn't want him to go right away. If we lose the case, Clayton will have a better argument for firing Donald outright."

His eyes were alive again. They danced across the carpet. She wondered where his mind was going, and what it was analyzing—this mind that had billed over eighteen thousand hours. Mostly she was enraptured that she alone had changed his mood so completely.

But then he frowned. "But you still don't know where the note is, do you?"

"No. I have no idea, Mitchell. That's as far as I could get." She wanted to say that she wasn't like him—it wasn't that she couldn't give the extra effort, she just didn't know how. She wasn't brilliant. Her thoughts ran into the wall of her limitations. "I just can't figure it out. It could be in his apartment. In his house in Connecticut. He could have given it to somebody at Hanover & Stiver. . . . He could—"

He ran his hands through his hair and stood up. He turned to her suddenly, and now *his* hands clasped her shoulders. His face moved close to hers. "Where do you feel that it is?"

"I . . . I don't know. I just can't figure it out, Mitch."

He repeated deliberately, "Where do you *feel* it is?"

"I—"

He looked past her, and she felt the pressure slacken. Was he disappointed in her? Was she losing him because she couldn't reason the way he needed her to? Impulsively, she said, "It's in his office."

"His office?" he asked abruptly. His voice was harsh and disbelieving. "Why do you say that?"

Her hands shook, and she was thankful she'd never been cross-examined by Mitchell Reece on the witness stand. "Because we looked in his house in Connecticut, and—"

"There were a million places we didn't look."

She thought for a moment, then said, "Okay, he wouldn't have had the party at his house if it was hidden there. For the same reason it wouldn't be in his apartment—if he did happen to get caught, it would be harder to explain how it got into one of his private homes. If it was in his office, he could claim it was put there by mistake—that maybe you or some paralegal just lost it."

"Good," Reece said with satisfaction. "Very good." Then he stopped smiling and asked sharply, "But why not give it to Lloyd Hanover, let him take the risk of getting caught?"

She hadn't had an answer for that, but from nowhere the thought came to her: "Because Wendall would have to get it to him somehow, and he'd have to risk being seen with Hanover."

Reece nodded. Then he said, "But why are you certain it's in his office, and not someplace else in the firm?"

Taylor Lockwood felt eyes upon her, and she looked to her side. The carved sun faces on Reece's table were gazing at her solemnly. She turned back and said, "I'm not certain at all. I've looked through a lot of the firm, and I've done everything else I can think of, and now we're out of time. The only thing I can think of is go through his office tonight. If it's not there . . ." She shrugged. "All I can say is, I'm sorry."

He stood up and walked to her. He touched her cheek. She felt electricity in his fingers. "You don't even have to say that."

She sensed a churning power coming from him, sexual, basic, necessary. Where had she felt it before? Why, Clayton, that's where it was. His eyes, those light eyes that drew her in, the current streaming around her.

From Reece she felt the same vortex. "I want you," he whispered.

The room vanished into motion: His arms around her, under her legs, sweeping her up, nearly over his shoulder as she rolled onto the sun-carved table, books falling, papers sailing off onto the floor. He eased her down on the tabletop, her blouse and skirt spiraling off and away, his own clothes flying in a wider trajectory. He was already hard. He pressed his mouth down on hers, their teeth met, and he worked down her neck, biting. Pulling hard on her nipples, her stomach, her thighs. She tried to press up toward him, but he held her captive, her butt and leg cut by the sharp corners of a law book. The pain added to the hunger.

Have you ever known real passion?

He was on her, his full weight on her chest, as his hands curled around the small of her back and gripped. She was completely immobile, her breath forced out by his demanding strokes. Still she felt a similar hunger, and rather than push against him, she dug her nails into his solid back, her own teeth clenched in a salivating lust for the pain it was causing. His fingers probed down her back, farther, farther, around her tailbone, pressing inward. Slowly, unstoppably.

She screamed as she shuddered, her toes curling downward, her muscles in their tiny spasms. He finished a moment later.

Taylor lifted her hands. Two nails were bloody. She shoved the law book out from underneath her; it fell with a resonant thud. She closed her eyes, she slept.

When she woke, the sun was down. She dressed. Reece was at his desk, scribbling notes frantically, reading cases. He wore tortoise-framed glasses. She'd never before seen him wear them. She stared at his back, walked closer, then hesitated. Taylor looked over the dozens of beige law books, thousands of sheets of typewritten paper and foolscap, the blowups of exhibits on tripods. She sat down beside him, and surprised herself by asking, "Who are you seeing?"

The Cross pen paused in Reece's hand and he set it down on the yellow pad, exactly perpendicular to the precise lines of his writing. He took off his glasses and squeezed the bridge of his nose, then carefully stacked some papers. "You know?" he asked.

"I saw you in Grand Central. You said you were going to be prepping a witness. You went to visit her."

He was nodding. He turned and sat on the table, hands together in front of him. He shook the mop of hair out of his face and said, "It was a woman I'd been going with for a while."

Taylor was listening to verb tenses—an important indicator when a man tells you about his girlfriends.

Reece continued, "We were serious for a time. Earlier in the year. But things just didn't work out. Not romantically."

"Are you still seeing her?"

"We're just friends now, Taylor."

"Then why didn't you tell me about her? If you were just friends, I wouldn't have minded."

"Sure you would have." He smiled wanly. "You would have felt just the way you feel now, and the way I'd feel if you told me you and an old boyfriend were just friends. And I didn't want to lose you."

"You lied to me."

"You're important enough to me that I was willing to do that. I'm not proud of it. But it *is* over. Completely."

"You bought her flowers." Tears filled her eyes.

"I buy my stepmother flowers, too."

"This woman—what's her name?"

"Does it matter?"

"I guess not. Do you love her?"

"No. We're still close, but I can't be intimate with her anymore."

"Did you want to marry her?"

He said, "We talked about it. Things didn't work out."

"Will you keep seeing her?"

"Do you want me to stop?"

Why do they always ask that? Throw it back on us?

Taylor Lockwood said, "Yes."

Reece said, "Then I will."

Taylor blinked. "Just like that?"

"Just like that."

•   •   •

At six P.M., wearing her cat burglar outfit of Levi's and a black blouse, Taylor Lockwood walked into Hubbard, White & Willis. Her black Sportsac contained a pair of kidskin gloves, a thermos of coffee, a tuna salad sandwich, a screwdriver, and a pair of pliers. Wendall Clayton and two of his junior partners were still in his office. They were speaking in quiet words, his Upper East Side drawl occasionally stopping the discussion with jokes and querulous commands.

Taylor slipped into a small utility room opposite the partner's office and left the door ajar. She sat down on the carpet, drank a cup of coffee, and waited for them to leave. For an hour she read parts of the *Times*. Then she stretched out on her side and continued to read, and also studied the pattern the carpet made on the skin of her elbow. At nine, anxious with boredom, she heard bustling and sat up hopefully. But Clayton and his entourage were still at work; they had simply made journeys to the men's room. They returned five minutes later. Taylor's heart sank as she heard them order dinner to be delivered.

They all ate together—Clayton and his lieutenants and Taylor Lockwood, though the men didn't know they had company; she was thirty feet away eating a soggy sandwich while they slowly worked through crab cocktails, steak, baked potatoes, and, for dessert, strawberries and cream. Cigars were lit, and the pungent aroma drifted out to her destroying what little of her appetite remained.

Finally, at eleven, Taylor heard Clayton say he wanted to be home by one or one-thirty, and there was general agreement that this would be fine with the others.

Thank you, Lord, Taylor Lockwood thought. That would give her five full hours to comb the room. She knew just where to start, what to look for. John Silbert Hemming had told her all the classic hiding places in offices.

Suddenly she felt oppressively sleepy, and that alarmed her.

Come on, honey. Almost there. Wake up, wake up! No rest for the devious. . . .

Taylor poured the last of the coffee into the red plastic thermos lid and gulped down the lukewarm liquid. She stood and rolled her head from side to side, then went through a few half-hearted calisthenics— the closest she'd ever come to aerobic exercises. She sat down—if not refreshed, at least uncomfortably energized enough to ward off sleep.

Taylor Lockwood crossed her arms and pulled her knees up under her chin, the way she would sit by herself as an outcast schoolgirl and watch the cluster of other children playing on the seesaws and jungle gyms. She sighed. She closed her eyes.

Then the next thing she was aware of was the sound of Wendall Clayton saying a cheerful good morning to his secretary. Dizzy and nauseous, Taylor jumped to her feet. She stared at her watch.

It was nine-thirty on Monday morning.

twenty-four

He did not truly live anywhere but here.

In the murky, echoing rotunda.

In the eroded marble corridors, lit by glare filtering through grimy windows.

In courtrooms like the one in which he now sat.

Mitchell Reece studied the structure of the room, where the opening volley in Banque Industrielle de Genève *v.* Hanover & Stiver, Inc. would be fired in about thirty minutes. He studied the vaulted ceilings, the sternness of the jury box and judge's bench (as aloof and solid as a conning tower), the dusty flag, the pictures of stern nineteenth-century judges. The room was unlit at the moment. He smelled lemon-scented ammonia and paper and dry heat from the radiators. There was a scuffed, well-worn aspect to the room; it reminded him of old subway cars. After all, Reece reminded himself, justice was just another utility of society, like public transportation and trash collection.

He sat for a few minutes, but was restless; he stood suddenly and began to pace. He paused at the window. Outside, through the soiled window, he watched pellets of wet snow falling on men and women hurrying along Centre Street: attorneys and judges and clients arriving.

The distinction was easy. Lawyers carried big litigation bags, clients carried briefcases, and the judges held nothing. Some of the lawyers looked very young.

When he first began trying cases, Reece would stay at the firm until the last possible moment, sitting in front of a Lexis or Westlaw computer screen to find last-minute cases he might recite dramatically to the judge. This practice rarely yielded epiphanies, though, and Reece finally concluded that although the law requires obsession, this was unproductive obsession and should therefore cease. Litigation requires technology, but technology is not what wins cases. The revelation occurred to him early in his career—he was representing a young boy blinded in one eye when a lawnmower fired a rock out of the grass chute and into the child's face. The father had unscrewed the grass-catching bag and had never replaced it, despite a warning molded into the metal not to operate the mower without the bag in place. Reece sued the manufacturer, claiming it was defective despite the warning.

It was understood by everyone that—because there was a warning and because the father had acted stupidly—Reece had no chance of winning. The bored judge knew this; the hawkish opposing counsel did, too. Even Reece knew it. Six people who did not know, however, were the jury, who awarded the snotty, self-pitying little kid one point seven million bucks.

Theater.

That was the key to litigation: no logic, a little law, a lot of personality, and considerable theater.

The hope from last night had faded, and later turned to alarm when Taylor Lockwood had not returned from the firm, had not even phoned. He had called her apartment several times during the night and heard only her machine. He went so far as to call Wendall Clayton's office, at least to find out if the partner were present. There was no answer, and Reece refused to consider his darkest fear—that Clayton had caught her trying to break in.

Reece had fallen asleep at four and awakened at seven. He took the subway to the firm and met his witnesses. On the pretense of seeing if Burdick was in, he had walked up to the seventeenth floor, straying past Clayton's office. The door was open, but the room was dark. There was no sign of Taylor.

Finally, his stomach in a clench, he had given up hope. He

assembled the executives from Banque Genève, took a limo to the courthouse, and left them in the cavernous domed cathedral of New York State Supreme Court while he slipped into the courtroom by himself.

He now reflected that the matter was wholly out of his hands. He had prepared for the case as best he could, and if the note did not appear, then he would still fight bitterly. He would lacerate Lloyd Hanover and his underlings. He would glorify his own client and show their generosity in making the loan to save Hanover & Stiver during a period of economic difficulties. He would show what the loss of this twenty-five million would mean to a small European bank that had courageously decided to invest in an American company, creating jobs and infusing money into the recessed Northeast. . . .

He would fight hard. And he would lose.

Mitchell Reece had not prayed for perhaps thirty years, but today he addressed a short message to a vague deity, which he pictured looking somewhat like blind Justice, and asked that she keep Taylor Lockwood safe and please, please, let her find the note.

You've done so much, Taylor, just a little more. For both of us. . . .

Reece took his seat again. The chairs were less comfortable than in federal court, but he thought that these were more appropriate—oak, collegiate, solid, scarred. He liked to have an edge before he went into trial. He liked to be hungry, he liked to be a little cold. He could be comfortable later. Reece closed his eyes and lost himself in some sweeping, inarticulate meditation.

She stood at a window overlooking a sooty air shaft. New York Harbor was beyond, obscured by a slow, damp snow. She stood with her hip cocked and the angle of her shoulder steep. Her arms were crossed. Staring, but she wasn't looking at the gravelly wall ten feet away or at the distant murky plain of the harbor; she was gazing at the panorama of her failure.

She reached forward and touched the chill glass; her silver-pink nails tapped against the pane like small switches.

Taylor Lockwood had played music in front of many people, she had impressed many lawyers as she helped them prepare cases. She had done well. A good musician, a good paralegal. But now she had ruined it all. Who the hell did she think she was? She was no cop, no detective, no John Silbert Hemming, no feisty lawyer examining till-dipping employees. She was simply a failure at this business. Pure and simple. She had been on duty, and she'd fallen asleep.

Ah, Mitchell, you should've picked different.

She stayed in the utility room for a moment. She waited. No movement. Then some activity. Was Clayton leaving? No. Sean Lillick was walking into the office.

She could hear their voices. Other lawyers were arriving. Clayton's secretary was sitting at her desk, already taking calls for her boss. Taylor heard the way she capitalized the *He* when she referred to him.

More footsteps up and down the hall. Soon the porters would arrive and start the old Mr. Coffee machine in the room where she was hiding.

Soon Mitchell Reece would be on trial. He would lose the case, and his career at Hubbard, White & Willis would be over.

Taylor Lockwood turned around and studied the small room. She opened the refrigerator, found a loaf of stale raisin bread on the bottom shelf. She took it out and set it on the counter, and debated with herself for only a few seconds before opening the package with nervous anticipation, thinking she was about to do something she'd always wanted to.

Sean Lillick's eyes were red. They stung from a vile combination of vodka, cigarette smoke, and an early wake-up call from the man he was now sitting across from.

He rubbed dried mucus from his eyes and drank the coffee that Clayton had bought for him. The partner had remembered he liked it with sugar.

Clayton looked at him for a minute, then pointed to his shoulder. "Your collar."

Lillick adjusted his suit jacket. He coughed.

"Are you all right?"

"Fine."

"You don't look fine."

"I didn't get much sleep last night." Lillick's voice didn't engage, the words were tenor and came out slippery. He cleared his throat, the grind of a car with a bum starter.

"I didn't either. I was here till two, then up at seven and back at nine-thirty."

Lillick didn't respond.

"Sean, I need that favor."

The young man sought refuge in the coffee, sipping it slowly.

"I want to explain exactly what's going on so that you understand it. I need something on Donald Burdick, something personal. Like what you gave me on Dudley. Does he fuck? If so, who? If not, what does he do with his money? Is one of his kids an addict?"

"No." Lillick put the coffee cup down. He swallowed. His hands were trembling.

Clayton did not seem to hear. A thought occurred to him. "Does his *wife* fuck anybody?" He nodded approvingly. "That's good. I don't trust Vera Burdick an inch. Why don't you—"

"No."

"What?"

"I said, 'No.' "

Clayton laughed. "Are we having another one of our attacks, Sean? You get ethics like asthma."

Lillick delivered the words mechanically, as if he had picked them out of bins, lined them up in their proper order, and pushed them toward Clayton. "I'm not going to help you anymore. Not this way."

"But why not?"

"I just don't want to."

"Tell me why."

"No. I'm not going to tell you why. When I tell you why, you have answers for it."

"I have answers because your feelings are not logical."

"No." Lillick reached for the coffee, then withdrew his hand.

"Sean, do you realize how important it is—"

"You've got your merger."

"*The* merger, not *my* merger, is progressing."

"Oh, come on, you make it sound like it's the will of the people—"

"Shut up!" Clayton's voice was so loud it stung. Spittle flew. "It *is* the will of the people. I created it, but the *firm* voted for it. The merger is what two thirds of Hubbard, White & Willis wanted. I don't have to remind you that you've been involved as deeply as I have. You can't simply decide you're not having fun anymore and skip off. I've paid you a lot of money. I don't have to remind you your father hasn't been quite as generous as me."

"No, Wendall. I'm tired of you controlling my life. *You* decided I'm going to law school, *you* decided I'm going to be your spy. *I* want to make some decisions."

The partner's words cut like bits of birdshot. "Why, you little shit, you think you're going to be a big musician? That trash you write is nothing but indulgent crap! I couldn't keep a straight face when you were playing it." Clayton's booming voice sent faint symmetrical rings of vibration across the pale surface of Lillick's coffee.

Lillick sat back. He was astonished that Clayton's control had slipped. He was afraid. An odd feeling was summoned out of his past—an after-school feeling. Physical fear of someone.

"There is no fucking way in the world you'd be working here if it wasn't for me. I'm the one who pays for your apartment, I'm the one who lets you buy those ridiculous organs and computers. I ask you to do me a couple of favors—nothing more than you owe me—and you say no. . . . I own you, son."

"Wendall"—Lillick slammed his hand down on the desk—"that's not fair. I've done—"

"I fucking *own* you!" The partner leapt to his feet and continued to shout at the boy, but Lillick could not hear him; the words were lost in another sound, one even louder than Clayton's unrestrained voice— the piercing electronic wail of the fire alarm that started low, then rose to an abrupt stop, and started all over again.

"Bench conference, Your Honor?" Mitchell Reece asks. He is standing in front of the plaintiff's table. The judge is surprised. The opening statements have just been made. Bench conferences never occur this early in a trial; nothing has happened that the two attorneys might argue about.

The judge lifts his eyebrows, and Hanover & Stiver's lawyer rises to his feet and walks slowly to the bench.

The courtroom is half empty. Reece is distressed to see some reporters present. He does not know why they are here; they never cover cases of this sort. He is also surprised—though relieved—to see that Donald Burdick is not present. At the defendant's table sits Lloyd Hanover, tanned and trim, his hair combed forward in fringe bangs, his face an expression of blasé confidence.

The two lawyers stand at the bench. Reece says, "Your Honor, we have a best-evidence situation. I'd like to move to introduce a copy of the note in question."

Hanover's lawyer turns his head slowly to look at Reece. But the judge is more astonished, and it is he who whispers, "You don't have the note itself?"

No one in the jury box or elsewhere in the courtroom can hear this exchange, but the surprise on the judge's face is evident. Several spectators look at each other. Reporters lean forward, smelling blood.

The Hanover lawyer says tersely, "No way. Not acceptable. I'll fight you on this all the way, Reece."

The judge says, "Was it a negotiable instrument?"

"Yes it was, Your Honor. But there is precedent—"

The Hanover lawyer: "A negotiable note is like cash. You prove to me it's destroyed, I mean, show me ashes, and then maybe, but you don't put the original into evidence, I'm moving for dismissal."

"What happened to the original?" the judge asks.

"We suspect it was stolen."

"Well, wouldn't that be convenient, to have the note disappear just now," the Hanover lawyer says, "especially if it turned out that it wasn't properly executed in the first place."

Reece turns on him. "Are you saying that Banque Genève forged a note, then lent your client twenty-five million dollars?"

The lawyer looks hurt. "Mr. Hanover's position is that the bank improperly declared default and is trying to get its money back because interest rates have turned and they can invest that money elsewhere for a higher profit."

"Gentlemen, a bench conference is not the place for the merits of the case. Mr. Reece, this is very unusual. A suit on a note, especially a negotiable note, requires the original document. Under the best-evidence rule, if you cannot explain the note's absence, you are precluded from entering a copy into evidence."

Opposing counsel: "Your Honor, I have to assume this is the end of plaintiff's case in chief."

The judge ignores him and says to Reece, "This is very serious."

Reece says calmly, "I would like to make a motion to submit other evidence of the existence of the note."

"Your Honor," opposing counsel says, "I would point out that it is Mr. Reece's client that sued on the note it alleges is properly executed. It is his responsibility to present that note. I've flown in witnesses from all over the country. I have experts costing me a thousand dollars a day."

Reece says, "Your Honor, it is very important that the administration of justice not get bogged down in technicalities. The note is merely evidence of the debt owed—and remaining unpaid, I should point out—by Hanover & Stiver. It is true that the best-evidence rule generally requires the original. But there are exceptions."

"With all due respect to Mr. Reece, I am reminded of a case once in which a similar claim of a missing note was made, and it turned out that the document in question had been sold by the bank to a third party. I would never suggest that Banque Genève was guilty of any such wrongdoing, but if Mr. Reece has no further evidence . . ."

Reece walks to the counsel table and picks up two copies of a memo backed in blue cardboard. As he returns to the bench, he sees the lawyer turn to Lloyd Hanover. Reece is not sure exactly what passed between them. He believes it is a wink. He ignores the communication and hands both the judge and the lawyer a copy of the memo. "I move to allow the introduction of secondary evidence of the note. I've briefed the issue in here. If you would like to recess for twenty-four hours to allow my opponent here to respond—"

The other lawyer shakes his head. "You lost the note, I'm ready for trial. Don't put it on my shoulders, counsel. Your Honor, I move for a directed verdict in my client's favor."

The judge flips through the brief that Reece has prepared, then looks out over the courtroom for a moment. "No, I will not grant a directed verdict. I will grant a motion to dismiss without prejudice. That will allow Mr. Reece to bring his case in the future. However, given the nature of defendant's financial condition, I doubt they'll have much money for your client to collect, Mr. Reece."

The opposing counsel begins the formalities: "Your Honor, I move for dismissal—"

"Mitchell!"

The judge looks up, glaring.

"That's my assistant," Reece says. "Perhaps she has some good news."

The judge waves Taylor Lockwood to the bench.

"I'm sorry, Your Honor," she says.

She hands Reece an envelope. Inside is the note—a single sheet of eight-and-a-half-by-eleven paper filled with one paragraph of dense writing and subscribed with several signatures. No embossing, no scrolls, no decorations. The document is impressive nonetheless; the first sentence contains the words, "The Principal Sum of Twenty-Five Million Dollars, plus interest as set forth below."

Reece exhales slowly, and must take three breaths before he is able to say, "Your Honor, I would like to introduce Plaintiff's Exhibit A." He hands it to the opposing counsel, who looks at Taylor with a gaze of distilled hate. "No objection." He returns the note to Reece's unsteady hands.

Taylor sits down at the counsel table.

Reece walks back to his favorite space, in front of the jury box. "Your Honor, before continuing with my case, I first must apologize to the jury for this inexcusable delay." He smiles contritely. The six men and women smile back and forgive him.

Taylor sat in the courtroom throughout the day and observed the rest of the trial, watching him marshal the case like an army general.

It was a short trial. The jury deliberated for two hours and at 7:10 P.M. found for Banque Genève. Taylor had been to hundreds of trials, and the verdict was as anticlimactic as they always were. The foreman read a statement. The judge said a few words, there were some scowls, a few smiles, the sound of pent-up throat clearings like during the pauses between concert movements.

In the courthouse rotunda, the three Banque Genève executives clustered together, giddy with relief. Taylor followed Reece to a small vestibule that contained public phones, which unlike most in the city, were in old-fashioned booths with closing doors. He pulled her inside one and kissed her hard. After a moment, he stepped back. His eyes danced with pleasure. "It was Clayton?"

She nodded. "It's a long story. Can you leave now?"

He shook his head. "I've got to baby-sit the client for a little while longer. Buy them dinner, do some brown-nosing, you know. Give me a minute."

She stepped out of the booth and leaned against a warm radiator while he made several calls, occasionally glancing at her through the glass and smiling. He stepped out a moment later. "Donald's out till tomorrow morning. I made an appointment to see him at nine. Both of us. I don't want to tell him over the phone. This is too serious." He added, "Maybe, just to be on the safe side, we ought to stay in a hotel tonight."

"You don't think Clayton would try anything, do you?"

"Remember the reservoir?"

She nodded.

"I'll be finished with the clients by eleven or twelve. Pick a hotel in Midtown. How about the Algonquin? Pay cash and register under a fake name."

"Mrs. Mitchell?" She blurted it and blushed instantly. "I mean—"

He laughed. "Too obvious, darling. How about Johnson?" He kissed her on the cheek. "I'll pick up toothbrushes and razors on my way. Anything else?"

"I can think of something," she said.

"What?"

"I'm embarrassed to say."

"Well, give me a clue."

"Men wear them, women don't. They're rubber."

"Got it. Athletic supporters. Why? Are we going to do aerobics?"

When he turned away, she swatted him discreetly on the butt.

"I think that's a first. No one has ever done that in the Supreme Court rotunda—at least not to me." He returned to the three clones of bankers.

• • •

Reece showed up at the hotel at eleven-thirty, still lugging his huge litigation bag and Redweld file folder. "God, clients. It's not enough I win their case. I had to buy them dinner at the Four Seasons. Of course, I'll mark it up a hundred percent and put it on their bill."

She had ordered champagne, but had refrained from drinking any until he arrived. Reece walked into the small room. The paint was peeling, and the screws were missing from the doorplates, which swung at lazy angles. "Midtown elegance?" He disappeared into the bathroom and took a long shower. When he came out, he poured the wine.

"So, how did you do it?" he asked.

"I'm guilty of a misdemeanor. I set fire to some raisin toast—it was easy, I've had a lot of practice—and then I hit the fire alarm. I've always wanted to do that. Everybody evacuated the building, and I went through Clayton's office. I found all of this hidden in a deal binder."

Reece took the sheets of paper that Taylor offered. Shaking his head, he looked at them closely. A copy of a letter to the *National Law Journal*. "Re: Careless Security Costs Firm Client." Dated tomorrow, the letter blamed Burdick and the executive committee. Also, a type-written list with the names of several other clients and cases.

"He was going to send it out after you lost the case. And look at the other clients. They're all Burdick's. Clayton was going to screw them up, too, somehow." From her purse, she took a small tape recorder attached to a radio. "This was behind the binder on his shelf." She rewound it and hit the play button. They heard Reece's voice, thick with static. She shut it off.

"Son of a bitch," Reece said. "He bugged my office. That's how he knew we were after him. He's known all along. He followed us after the party in Connecticut and tried to drive us off the road."

"Or had somebody from Triple A Security do it."

"Jesus," Reece whispered reverently. "I never guessed it was this serious."

"What do we do now?"

"Tell Donald the whole ball of wax. First thing tomorrow. It's going to be a nightmare. I don't see how to keep the police out of it. Grand larceny, attempted murder, assault, invasion of privacy, illegal wiretap. . . . Whoa, Clayton's gonna do time for this."

Taylor was giddy from the wine. With her stockinged foot she played with the towel around Reece's waist. She lay back. "Did you get everything you were supposed to get at the drugstore?"

He held up his purchases. "Sure did. Toothbrushes. Antiplaque toothpaste. Shave cream—lime-scented. Razors."

"Anything else?"

"Yep. Deodorant."

Taylor pouted. "That's all?"

"Well, one thing." He hid his hand behind his back.

"What? Let me see." She grabbed for it. He gave her a packet of dental floss. She frowned.

"Bag's empty." He showed it to her.

"You didn't get anything else?"

"I didn't say that. I said the bag's empty."

"Well, if it's not in the bag, where is it?"

Reece just grinned and snapped out the light.

Donald Burdick was as angry as Taylor had ever seen him. "You should have told me, Mitchell." He glanced at her, and she looked away from his towering fury.

They sat in Burdick's office early on Tuesday morning. Bill Stanley sat on Burdick's couch, a fat ankle resting on a fat knee, and read over the papers Taylor had found. "Wendall—what a stupid, stupid man."

Reece said to Burdick, "Maybe I should have. It was a judgment call. I made the decision."

"You almost lost the case, you almost got yourselves killed."

Reece seemed beyond contrition. "It never occurred to me that someone would act so crazy."

Burdick took the papers and the tape recorder from Stanley. "He wanted the merger so badly, he'd do this? He'd break the law?" Burdick's anger was giving away to astonishment.

Stanley said, "He'll have heard by now that you found him out."

Burdick said, "A tape recorder. Wiretapping in Hubbard, White & Willis. . . ." The partner put the papers, recorder, and transmitter into his desk and locked it. "What's the damage assessment?" he asked Stanley.

"Mitchell," the partner asked, grumbling, "did you or Taylor tell anyone about this? The police? Anyone?"

Reece said, "No. Obviously the last thing I'd want is to go public."

Taylor said, "When I found those things in his office, I took them right to Mitchell. Nobody else knows about what I was doing."

Stanley nodded and continued, "We have to cut him loose. It's going to look very bad for us, what with the merger letter signed and everything. But that's a risk we have to take. We've got to hit him with everything we can."

"I'm not so sure," Burdick said. "The publicity . . ."

Stanley barked, "Donald, you're thinking you want to negotiate the man out of here. Do you realize what he's guilty of? If we don't go directly to the attorney general and the Bar Commission, we'd be suborning felonies."

"I'll take responsibility for that."

Carol, Burdick's secretary, appeared at the door. She held an interoffice envelope marked with a bright red URGENT sticker. She said, "Mr. Burdick?"

Burdick glanced at her, then signaled for the envelope. He continued speaking as he opened it. "The point is that nothing tragic did in actuality happen. Mitchell and Taylor are safe. The case—" Burdick stopped speaking as he read the memo. His face registered shock. Calmly, he rose and walked out of his office. Stanley called, "Don, what is it?"

Two minutes later Burdick ran back into his office.

"What's wrong?" asked Reece. Stanley stood up.

But Burdick was ignoring them, snatching up the phone in his hand. He punched in three numbers. "An ambulance," he said. "You have to come at once." He gave the address of the firm.

Taylor and Reece glanced at each other, then ran into the corridor, toward Clayton's office. Stanley walked quickly behind them.

All three paused in the doorway.

Wendall Clayton sat in his throne of a chair, leaning back like a duke contemplating a matter of state or wondering whom to aristocratize. Eyes gazing up at the ceiling, focusing in the distance. He was completely still.

His arm stretched toward the floor, hand curled and finger extended like the hand of God in the Sistine Chapel, pointed down to where the gun lay. The gun that had left a surprisingly small purple dot in his temple, out of which ran a thin line of dark blood that had soiled his perfectly starched white collar.

twenty-five

Politics is the human will as applied science, and Taylor Lockwood had never appreciated the finesse with which it could be practiced until this moment. For hours she and Mitchell Reece had watched Donald Burdick at work with his quiet formulas and calculations—the police, City Hall, the medical examiner's office. Favors were called in, debts created, pressure brought to bear. And all the while, Burdick remained as he always was, or appeared to be: calm, charming, insistent, smooth.

"We're going to manage this crisis," he had told them.

And he was doing just that.

When he hung up the phone, at three on Tuesday afternoon, he said to them, "Do you have anything else that has to do with Wendall or the theft? Anything at all?"

Reece shook his head and looked at Taylor, who said only, "I didn't think this would happen."

Burdick looked at her blankly for a moment, then pulled his leather key container out of his coat pocket and unlocked his desk. Reece looked calm but pale. Taylor's heart was pounding, breath fast, head light. She felt a rush of tragedy and wondered if she was going to faint.

The partner pulled a piece of paper from his desk. "There was the suicide note on Wendall's desk. The police have that. It talked about being despondent, pressures of work. But he wrote another. That was what I received in the envelope when you were with me. I assume he put it in the interoffice mail to me just before he shot himself."

Taylor read:

"Donald, I'm sorry. To you. To Taylor, to Mitchell. Believe me, I never wanted to hurt anyone. But I know that they know everything now, that I stole the note, that I tried to drive them off the road. It is important now that you understand why, Donald. I did it for one reason only: I truly believed that the merger was for the good of the firm. That was my sole motive. All I will offer is this from Milton: Men of most renowned virtue have sometimes by transgressing most truly kept the law."

Burdick said, "Mitchell, I've decided not to show this to the police. Wendall stole that note to embarrass me, to get me out of the firm. This is Hubbard, White's dirty laundry, and no one else's. I can't see any purpose to be served by letting word out about the theft. Publicity would be bad for everyone. Bad for the firm, and bad for Clayton's widow."

Widow . . .

The word carried the stun of a nearby lightning strike.

"The newspapers will get a watered-down story," Burdick said. "I've called the public-relations company, and Bill Stanley's with them now. They're preparing a statement. If anybody asks, we'll refer questions to them." He lowered his head and looked into Reece's eyes, then Taylor's. She had the same sense as when she met Reece's gaze, or Clayton's. A pure confidence, strong as ringing bronze. Her mind went blank. She was for a moment completely his, lost in his power. Burdick asked, "Will you back me on this? If I thought there was anything to be gained by a full disclosure, I wouldn't hesitate to reveal everything. But I can't see any upside to it."

Men of most renowned virtue.

Reece said, "I won't lie, Donald. No matter who asks me. But I won't volunteer anything." He looked at Taylor. What were they asking her, these powerful men?

She nodded.

Men of most renowned virtue. The hairs on the back of her neck stirred.

Widow . . .

A man was dead, and someone just like her father was going to dress the body and lay him out, all false and pretty. . . .

The phone rang, and Burdick took the call. He mouthed something about the call being from someone at City Hall, but Taylor missed it. She was staring at the suicide note. The stark typeface of the words was chilling. She vaguely heard Burdick explain something in a low, reassuring tone. They were words that she could not comprehend.

She watched his long jowly face, expertly shaved, crowned with sparse gray hair in precise alignment.

And what the hell had she been doing all along? What did she think would happen when she fingered the thief? He'd lose his job, right? That was all. That was the procedure in the genteel world of Donald Burdick, the world of Victorian men of honor, Messrs. Hubbard, White & Willis. Expose the thief, let him go hence, never to return, slink off with his shame. Purge the traitor and get back to work. Right?

Renowned virtue.

Burdick up hung the receiver. "I think we'll get away with it."

A moment's pause. Taylor, trying to figure out what he meant. *Get away with it?*

"The M.E.'s office has ruled suicide. The A.G. agrees."

Reece blurted an astonished laugh. "Already?"

Burdick said, "I've been owed favors for a long, long time."

The partner took back the copy of the suicide note. Then looked at his watch. He held out his hand to Reece, then to Taylor, and they shook. Taylor first wanted to wipe her palm; it was damp. Burdick's was dry as ever.

"You two get some rest. You've been through a hellish several weeks. You want any time off, I'll arrange it."

"Thank you, Donald," Reece said and walked toward the door.

Taylor nodded, but she paused. She was waiting for something to arrive, some phrase summarizing and neat.

Nothing occurred; her thoughts had jammed.

She walked to the door.

Burdick said, "Oh, by the way, I do hope you'll both be joining us at the Snowflake Ball. It's on the twenty-second."

Reece said he had forgotten about it, but would keep the invitation in mind.

Snowflake Ball . . . Taylor thought the phrase sounded familiar. "The what?" she muttered.

"The firm dinner dance. It's in two weeks. I do so hope you'll be there, Taylor."

She looked back at Burdick, who sat so calmly and regally, so charmingly in his tall chair. She said, "I'll try, sir." And followed Reece into the corridor.

At dusk, sitting in her cubicle down in Halsted Street, she decided she had never been so tired in her life. Her face felt puffed up, her head sagged, her eyes stung.

After they had left Burdick's office, Reece had to make some urgent calls to New Orleans about the trial scheduled there for January. They had made plans to meet for dinner. But she called him at six. "Mitch, I'm sorry. Can I beg off? I want to go to bed early."

He hesitated, then asked, "Are you all right?"

"Yeah. I've got the fatigues is all. Bad."

"That's it?"

"Well, you know, with everything happening."

"You don't want to come by?"

"I'd somehow rather be by myself, if you don't mind."

Another pause. He would probably be thinking what she was really trying to say, when in fact her message was nothing other than *I've got the fatigues is all I want to be by myself nothing more nothing less.* She didn't care. She felt she'd earned some privacy.

"I'll call you?" He seemed to be asking permission.

"I hope so." She tried to sound encouraging.

He paused again. "Taylor, I know this's turned into a real mess, but what you did, it was good. More than I ever expected from anybody." He seemed more awkward than she'd ever heard him.

"What I'm trying to say is I'm sorry it worked out this way, but thanks."

"Sleep well, darling," she said, intending the endearment only half-jokingly.

At home, she took a long bath. She called her mother and talked about her Christmas trip home. She had planned to stay for four days. On impulse—she surprised herself—she said she would stay for seven. She put a frozen pouch of spaghetti into a pot of water. That and an apple were dinner. Then she lay on her couch, watching a *Cheers* rerun.

Taylor Lockwood, curled on the old, sprung sofa, thought about the times when, as a teenager, she would lure her Labrador retriever onto the bed next to her, then scoot him off the bed after ten minutes. She would lie still, waiting for sleep while she felt, in the warmth from the adjacent pillow, anticipation and comfort, and, though she didn't understand it at the time, felt also the evidence that the pain of solitude is a false pain.

Tonight, too, Taylor Lockwood finally slept.

She spent the next day, the day of Wendall Clayton's funeral, shopping.

Sean Lillick had asked her if she'd wanted to attend the service with him, and she had answered no in such a horrified way, as if the boy had spat out an obscenity, that he actually backed away with a frightened grin on his face. She apologized and claimed exhaustion. When Mitchell Reece extended the same invitation, she declined more gracefully, and headed into Midtown, armed with her credit cards.

She thought shopping would distract her, but the reality of Christmas shopping intruded. The jostling and chaos set her on edge. She shouted at an overly aggressive panhandler, and abandoned several purchases because the line at the register seemed hardly to move. Walking through the streets made her anxious, and she took cabs to and from Saks, though a subway would have been faster and cheaper. On the trip back the driver had to ask her twice where she wanted to go. She had mumbled the first time he had asked.

At one stoplight, Taylor saw a huge woman—maybe three, four hundred pounds—in a wheelchair. She wore a pink cap, the kind from the sixties, the Carnaby look. She carried a waxed paper cup and held it out lethargically toward people as they passed by. She caught Taylor's eye and started toward the cab, the chair's gray inflated wheels flattened against her weight.

Taylor sat back and stared at the stoplight. Out of the corner of her eye she could see the woman coming, closer, closer. Her arm outstretched, the coins in the cup jingling dully like stones.

"Leave me alone," she whispered. The driver looked into the rearview mirror. "Huh?"

"Why's this light so long?"

"It ain't that long."

The massive woman, sweating with effort, was ten feet away now. What did she want? What had she read in the glance Taylor had given her? The woman was grinning. Her teeth were crooked, and even in the December chill there was a slick of sweat on her forehead.

The dirty muzzle of the cup pointed at her.

The light changed.

"Go, go!" she shouted.

"You want to drive, maybe?" The cab shot away from the light and turned toward her apartment.

A self-addressed envelope sat in her mailbox. She opened it and slipped out the demo tape. This wasn't the last—there were still about a half dozen out at various companies—but it was the important one, the tape the A&R committee had been reviewing, the tape she carried around in her thoughts and pulled out occasionally for hope. There was no response letter; someone had simply jotted on her own cover note, "Thanks, but not for us."

She came close to shoving the tape into the fine white sand that filled the cigarette disposal stand beside the elevator. But she calmly slipped it into her pocket and took the elevator upstairs.

Inside her apartment, she dropped her bags on the couch and looked at the *Times,* sitting where she had left it in the center of the dinner table. She read the article again, for the fifth time.

Burdick had pulled it off. His artistry was astonishing. Not a word about the Hanover & Stiver case, nothing about the theft of the note. Nothing about her or Mitchell. *Wall Street Lawyer Suicide.* Burdick was quoted, calling the death a terrible tragedy and said that the profession had lost a brilliant attorney. The reporter also quoted several members of the firm discussing Clayton's huge work load and moodiness, and found that in the past year he had billed over twenty-six hundred hours. There was a sidebar on stress among overworked professionals. She sighed and threw the newspaper away, then washed the tainted ink off her hands.

The answering machine showed no messages. She felt a strong relief she couldn't easily identify, then poured a glass of wine and began to wrap packages.

At five-thirty the doorbell rang.

Who? Neighbors? Thom Sebastian assaulting her, pleading for a date? Ralph Dudley simply assaulting her?

She opened the door.

Mitchell Reece, wearing a windbreaker, walked inside and asked her if she had a cat.

"Mitchell!"

"A cat?" he repeated.

"A what?"

"Animal, four legs, often with a tail."

"No, why? Are you allergic? What are you doing here?"

"Or fish, or anything you have to feed regularly?"

"Just occasional boyfriends."

"Come on downstairs. Get your coat. Shut the lights out and lock the door."

"But—"

He held his finger to his lips, and she did as she'd been told. Downstairs a limo waited, a maroon Lincoln. He opened the door and pointed inside, where she saw three large boxes from Paragon Sporting Goods, and two sets of new Rossignol skis propped across the seats.

Taylor laughed. "Mitchell, what are you doing?"

"Time for my lesson. Don't you remember? You were going to teach me to ski."

"Where? Central Park?"

"You know of someplace called Cannon? It's in New Hampshire. I just called the weather number. Four inches of new powder. I don't know what that means, but even the recorded voice sounded excited, so I assume it's good."

"But when?"

"But now," he said.

"Just like that?"

"The firm jet's on the ramp at LaGuardia. And they bill us by the hour, so I suggest you hustle your butt."

"But I don't have anything. Let me pack. . . . This is crazy. What about work?"

"I've cleared it with Donald. It's his Christmas present to us."

"But clothes?"

"We'll buy whatever we need."

"My toothbrush."

"Okay, we'll cancel the trip because you don't have your toothbrush."

The smile of surprise became one of excitement. She dropped her head against his chest. They climbed in the car.

"I've bought everything we need, I think. They told me what to get. Skis, poles, black stretch pants, boots, bindings, sweaters, goggles. And . . ." He held up a box.

"What's that?" Taylor asked.

"That? The most important item of all."

She opened it. "A crash helmet?"

He shrugged. "Maybe you're a good teacher, and maybe you're not."

twenty-six

The helmet wasn't a bad idea. Reece had been on the bunny slope for only fifteen minutes when he fell and jammed his thumb. A local doctor, a cheerful Indian, had taped it.

"Is it broken?" Reece had asked.

"No, no fracture."

"Why does it hurt so much?"

"You fell on it," he said, beaming.

Afterward, they sat in the small lounge in the inn.

"Oh, Mitchell, I feel bad," she said. "But you did a very respectable first run."

"My thumb doesn't feel too respectable. Is it always this cold?"

"Cannon's got the coldest, windiest runs in New England, dear," she said, pulling his head against her neck. "People have frozen to death not far from here."

"That's good. We wouldn't want to have too much fun now, would we?"

He actually did not seem too upset about the accident or the weather. And she learned why: He preferred to sit out the day with what he had smuggled with him—files from his New Orleans case. Taylor did not mind. She was dying to get out onto the advanced trails, and didn't want to baby-sit him on the beginner slopes, or worry about him on the intermediates.

She kissed him. "Sit in the lodge and behave yourself."

As she crunched away toward the lifts, he called, "Good luck. I assume you don't say, 'Break a leg.' "

She smiled, stomped into her skis, and slid down the slight incline to the bottom of the lift.

At the top of the mountain, she slid off the chair and braked to a stop just past the lift house. She bent down and washed her goggles in snow. The White Mountains were son-of-a-bitch cold, and the cross-wind steadily scraped across her face. She pulled silk liners on and replaced her mittens, then poled her way into position and looked down the mountain. Her impression had always been that most runs never look as steep from the top as they do from the bottom, but as she gazed down toward the lodge, over a half mile straight below her, she saw a plunge, not a slope. Her pulse picked up, and in the moment she hesitated, she realized how right Mitchell had been to arrange the trip. This was no vacation for him at all. The poor boy, cooped up with his papers, surrounded by loud fun-lovers, totally out of his element. No, he had prescribed this all for her. He had understood what she needed. To get away from the city, to distance herself from Hubbard, White & Willis, from Wendall Clayton, from the jabbing finger pointed down to his own escaping blood.

A time of regrouping.

Or was it one of escape?

Wasn't she on the lam? After all, here she'd killed a man (not as the perpetrator, but an accessory, the D.A. would say), and she and Reece were now in hiding. Maybe she was feeling what criminals did— this brooding distraction, always mindful of the posses searching for them. Taylor had been keeping watch over her shoulder too, only not for the law, no, but for her own guilt.

She pushed off the crest of the mountain.

It was the best run of her life.

Immediately, Clayton vanished. Taylor kept in a low crouch, doing giant slaloms, then tucking her poles on the straight stretches, aiming downhill.

Speed, speed, speed . . .

This was all she wanted, speed. Her mouth was open slightly in the ellipse of fear or a sexual height. Her teeth dried and stung in the frigid slipstream, but the pain added to her surge of abandon. The goggles of the slower skiers followed her trajectory.

Taylor danced over moguls the way girls skip double-dutch jump rope on playgrounds. Once, her skis left the ground, and she landed as if the snow had risen timidly to stroke the bottom of the fiberglass. Trees, bushes, other skiers were a swift-ratcheting backdrop sweeping past, everyone hushed, it seemed, listening to the cutting hiss of her skis.

She was sure she hit sixty or seventy miles an hour. Her hair was whipping behind her. She wished she'd borrowed Reece's helmet—not for the safety, but to cut the wind resistance of the tangled mass of drag.

Then it was over. She brodied to a stop near the base of the run, her thighs in agony but her heart both astonished at her performance and filled with a glorious rush of fear and victory.

She did four runs this way, until on the last one, on a big mogul, she lost control and had to windmill her arms to regain her balance. It sobered her.

Okay, honey, one suicide a week is enough.

But when she had that thought, it was without a dash of guilt. She laughed as she slowed, then finished with a respectable series of giant slaloms.

A tall, thin man came up to her and said in a light Germanic accent, "Hey, those were some, you know, pretty snazzy runs. You feel maybe like another one?"

"Uh, no, not really."

"Well, how about a drink?"

"Sorry." She picked up her skis and walked toward the cabin. "I'm here with my boyfriend."

And she realized suddenly that, by God, she was.

In the mornings, she skied, he worked.

She'd come back to the find the room cluttered with papers and documents delivered by FedEx or DHL, and Reece on the phone to New Orleans or the New York office. She would sit opposite him, wincing as she pulled off her sweater and bra and stretch pants and began massaging her thighs and calves.

It was around that time that Reece usually hung up the phone or stacked files away in a corner.

After lunch, they'd go to antiques stores, which here weren't the precious collections of cheese dishes and brass surveying instruments you find in Connecticut or New York. These were barns of furniture. Rows of dusty chairs and muddy-finished tables and dressers and pickle jars and canopy beds and armoires. Very rustic and practical and well cared for. None of the shopkeepers seemed to expect them to buy anything, and they never did.

In the evenings, they would eat in one of the half-dozen interchangeable inns. The food: veal chop, steak, chicken, *canard à l'orange,* salmon almondine. Afterward they'd have a drink in the common room in front of a huge fireplace.

They sometimes made love, and sometimes did not, and when not they would lie under the garden patch quilt of a thousand hexagons of cotton and feel the pressure of each other's thighs and the smell of the cold as it streamed through the inch-open window and gathered on the floor. By morning it would have filled the room and overflowed onto the bed. They took turns leaping up to get the heater going. They waited impatiently for the *whump* of the gas flame, as they talked about what they would do that day.

Taylor Lockwood began to forget about Wendall Clayton.

Several hundred miles to the south, the life cycle of Hubbard, White & Willis continues, never pausing.

Donald Burdick views this motion in a simple metaphor: the mechanism of a clock, an interconnection of precisely milled alloys and pure metal, springs and shafts and levers in a complex relation. Unlike a clock, however, the movement is silent. He enjoys the cleverness of how it all fits together, parts complementing and meeting within delicate tolerances. Hubbard, White & Willis —*his* Hubbard, White & Willis—will tell time for another hundred years, or two or three.

He has moved quickly. Clayton's clients have been divvied up, and Burdick personally has taken over as the lawyer for one of the nation's largest soft-drink companies and for the trustee of a major utility in bankruptcy. He also triumphantly assumes the role as St. Agnes Hospital's lead attorney. These new clients boost his income by six hundred thousand dollars a year. The matter of the merger has been put on hold for a suitable period of mourning. Burdick has had only a brief conversation with John Perelli, though he knows a more substantial discussion will soon occur. The tough Italian litigator will be weighing his options, one of which will be to insist that the merger go through despite Clayton's death.

Tomorrow. There will be time for that then. For the moment, Donald Burdick must concentrate on his facade of mourning.

While her husband is busy retrenching, Vera Burdick appears at a gala social auction for the benefit of AIDS research—a charity she has no interest in whatsoever. She attends because it is the most visible of the season's gatherings and the press will be abundantly present, she attends because she will have a chance to publicly express shock and sorrow at the sudden death of Wendall Clayton. If he had only come to her husband and discussed his work load, Vera laments, something might have been worked out, the tragedy prevented. Donald Burdick, she tells a reporter, has in fact been looking into an employee assistance program to help the attorneys and staffers of Hubbard, White & Willis cope with such pressures. She herself urges all law firms to reassess the demands put on their lawyers, especially younger associates and partners.

The *Times*'s article covering the event includes what could only be described as a strikingly handsome picture of her. Minkie Bigelow, who organized the whole event, was neither pictured nor quoted.

Vera had attended Clayton's funeral with her husband, and out of respect to the dead did not cry false tears. Nor did she, however, gloat over the man's passing. Her sole emotional response to the incident occurs one night, when her husband has returned late from meeting with clients. She watches Burdick enter their den, regal in his dark smoking jacket, and walk jauntily through the room to the bar, with his ramrod-straight posture. As he pours them both a sherry, she walks to him and takes his arm, then kisses him on his cheek.

"Darling," she said.

He turns to her, confused at this unanticipated affection.

She shrugs as if to say that she does not understand this either, but says to him, "I feel that somehow you've been away, and now you're home again."

Although he does not usually have the time or inclination to look at his employer through figures of speech, Thom Sebastian nonetheless chooses his own metaphor for the firm: a race. A race that he has concluded is fixed. Once he looks at his situation that way, he feels remarkably better about not making partner.

In fact, he feels happy—very much that same kind of glowing happiness he felt when he woke up late in the frat house on a warm Saturday morning, popped a Bud, and wandered down in his pajama bottoms to read the sports section and think about his date for the game that afternoon. A category of happiness he had not felt since.

He is not sure why he should feel this way. He has considered his personality and can honestly say he is an extremely competitive person. Turbo. Type A. He hates to lose. He flies into a rage when his school's team loses, he has broken pencils when his clients stupidly give away negotiating points. Yet, Tom Sebastian is as close to content as he has been for years.

The failure of Hubbard, White & Willis to name him partner taught him about the quality of races, and he thinks (without admitting) that perhaps he made a mistake: A race with stacked odds is a race that he has no business competing in.

But justice has been served, of course. The man who was responsible for fixing that race is dead. When the memo went around about Clayton's funeral (which he did not attend), Sebastian wadded it up, threw it away, and tried hard to contain his smile.

There is only one person keeping him from being completely at ease. Taylor Lockwood still troubles him a great deal. She knows everything about his deal with Bosk. More than that, however, she has seen him vulnerable. This is one thing Thom Sebastian cannot stand. He has a plan for her, of course. As precisely organized as the closing list in a leveraged buyout. He knows exactly what he must do with her, and he knows that he will, in fact, do it. But his courage keeps breaking. It is like standing on the top of the high dive at the Piping

Rock pool, knowing he is going to leap but not yet feeling the consolidation of will that will let him do so.

He looks at an expensive antique globe in his office and thinks about countries that will take him outside the reach of the FBI and the police. Thom Sebastian listens to the odd hum of the firm—it is three A.M.—and for a moment allows himself one more poetic thought: He wonders if this hum is simply the heating system or is instead the troubled soul of Frederick Phyle Hubbard stalking the halls of his firm.

For Ralph Dudley, the cyclical motion of the firm—in fact, the firm itself—does not much enter his thoughts. Oh, initially he felt an incredible elation, the sort he had not felt since he squeaked out of law school with below-average marks. Everything has worked out: Clayton is dead, his secret is safe, the merger has fallen apart.

And Dudley has turned his full attention to the process of adopting Junie.

He has taught himself to read cases again (he had forgotten not long after law school graduation), and relearned the Byzantine formalities of the courts—the size of pleading paper, proper headings, dates and places of filings. He has practiced oral argument.

Like Thom Sebastian, he is troubled by what Taylor learned about him, and this occasionally interrupts his thoughts. Yet on the whole, making Junie his daughter occupies him full time.

He attends a benefit dinner party and manages to sit next to the wife of the CEO of a company that Burdick has been wooing for years. He is flattering and charming, and avoids looking at the scars from the inexpert tuck job. But he is careless in picking a postdessert humor-in-the-courtroom story. *I recall*—actually he read it somewhere—*a young female attorney who had to leave a cocktail party and rush to court to defend a temporary restraining order. She didn't have time to change into her business clothes and stood before the judge in her low-cut gown. She began her argument with the traditional formality, "May it please the court . . ." The judge looked down at her plunging neckline and said, "Oh, it does, counselor, very much, but perhaps in the future, something less revealing might be more appropriate."*

It is just the kind of risqué anecdote that passes muster on upper Fifth Avenue. But his target, the executive's wife, receives it with a chill smile, and does not speak to him for the rest of the evening. Dudley later learns she recently had a radical mastectomy. (He had even changed the story—from a miniskirt to a plunging neckline— because of the woman's varicose veins.)

He is troubled by this incident until he notices, at another table, Amanda Wilcox gazing at him. He excuses himself from the table and, carrying two glasses of Château d'Yqem, invites her into the library of the triplex apartment in which the dinner is being held. She, too, has been trying, with equal unsuccess, to snag this client. They agree to call a truce for the rest of the evening, and they spend the next two hours talking about former spouses, travels, life in law firms. They sit in front of a gas fire until he realizes it is nearly one A.M. and most of the other guests have left.

In the morning Ralph Dudley is at his desk at nine A.M., working on the adoption petition.

Sean Lillick is aware of a curious lull. A breath-holding. He slips into Wendall Clayton's office at dusk one day and stays for hours. The lights are out, the windows open, and the gray light enters hesitantly, re- flected off the dark mesh of sky.

Clayton's death has relieved Lillick, as it did so many people in the firm. But this pleasure soon becomes tarnished by a feeling of impending disaster—a sense he was not prepared for, one he has never before felt. He is not sure how this cataclysm will arrive or what its consequences might be, but he knows that it is simply a question of time until tragedy descends.

Sitting on Clayton's throne, he suddenly pulls out his pen and writes some lines that spring into his head:

> *For those who remain,*
> *a soul's departure brings about an alteration*
> *of the whole terrain.*

He decides this will be the core of an opera he is going to write, an opera in the style of Philip Glass. The subject: the sorrow of Wendall Clayton. It might very well be the last thing he writes before . . . before this disaster strikes, but he *will* write it. He thinks about nothing else, none of the other people or events that had occupied his life until this moment—his performances, his job, Taylor Lockwood, Carrie Mason, whom he has been dating regularly. Lillick must complete this work, and must do so soon.

He composes the first movement as he sits at the man's desk, feeling huge satisfaction as the pen presses into the thick blotter, filling sheet after sheet of improvised music ledger paper. He feels himself tipping toward the manic, but he does not slow. The room is cold; he does not turn on the heat. It is dark; he does not reach for Clayton's antique lamp. He writes his music, the notes tumbling down onto the paper. When, because of the darkness, he cannot see the notes any longer, he stops. Then he scrawls on the top of the yellow pages, *The King of Wall Street.* And Sean Lillick goes home to play the piece on his synthesizer.

And for everyone else at Hubbard, White & Willis—the attorneys and paralegals and secretaries and messengers and Xerox machine operators and librarians—the firm continues as it always has. A man has died, and that will be a subject of hushed gossip for years to come, but clients continue to bring their complex greeds and fears into these quiet halls, to receive erudite advice, and to pay oh-so-dearly for that wisdom.

A man has died, but the firm's silent, perpetual pulse does not slow at all.

Taylor Lockwood skied fast and recklessly through the gray afternoon. She smelled the clean electric moisture of snow, the biting perfume of fireplace smoke. Today, however, the speed had none of the cleansing effect as on her first day out. It made her scared and vulnerable. She felt lonely, abandoned.

After one run, she loaded her skis and boots into the rental car, drove back to the inn, and went into the bar, where she was to meet Mitchell Reece. She ordered a scotch, neat. Drank it fast, ordered another.

Where and for a first cause of action, Taylor Lockwood did willfully . . .

The bar door swung open. Taylor looked toward it and saw a couple disappear out into the snow.

. . . and with full knowledge of the consequences, did, without a warrant or other license enter the office of one Wendall Clayton, the decedent, and . . .

She was surprised and disappointed to find she'd finished the second scotch without getting drunk. She waved for another.

Where and for a first cause of action, Taylor Lockwood did willfully ascertain and make public certain facts about one Wendall Clayton, the decedent, that caused . . .

Taylor sipped the numbing liquor, staring in the mirror at the heavy oak door that led out into the lobby of the inn.

. . . that caused said decedent to blow his fucking brains out.

Mitchell Reece opened the door and walked up to her, kissed her on the mouth, and wrapped his arms around her.

"Started without me, huh?"

He had been outside. She could smell the cold, fresh-air scent about him. He stood back, maybe sensing the response somehow was off. She squeezed his arm as he slid onto the stool and ordered a beer. "How were the slopes?"

"Cold. It's bleak out."

He asked for a beer and winced as he picked up the glass.

"Thumb still hurt?" she asked.

"A bit. I tell you I'm no good at this sort of thing. . . . I'm much better with simpleminded, safe sports. . . ." He seemed to be groping for a joke, something cute, but he must have sensed that she was troubled. "What's up, Taylor?"

She shook her head.

"What is it?" he persisted.

"Mitchell, you know history?"

He motioned with an open palm for her to continue.

She asked, "You know what the Star Chamber was?"

"A medieval English court. Why?"

"We learned about it in my European history course in college. It came back to me last night. The Star Chamber was a court of the Royal Prerogative. Under the Tudors. When the king thought the regular court might decide against him, he'd bring a case in the Star Chamber. You got hauled up before these special judges—friends of the king.

They'd pretend to have a trial, but you know what happened. If the king wanted him guilty, he was guilty. Off with his head. Very fast justice, very efficient."

He looked at the beer, swirled it. He set it down without drinking any.

She blurted, "Christ, Mitchell, the man is dead."

He was frowning. "You don't think it's your fault?"

A spasm of anger passed over her. *Why can't he understand?* "I was so stupid."

They were silent for a moment. A boisterous crowd of college students entered, hooting and laughing. She glared at them. The noise was like arcing electricity on her skin.

"For God's sake, Taylor, he tried to kill us."

Taylor looked at him briefly, then away. Wondering how Clayton had felt lifting the gun. Had it been heavy? Had there been pain? How long had he lived after pulling the trigger? What had he seen? A burst of yellow light, a second of confusion, a wild eruption of thoughts, then nothing. That was what she imagined.

"Taylor," Reece said with measured words, "Clayton was crazy. No sane man would've stolen the note in the first place, and no sane man would've killed himself if he'd been caught. How could we guess he'd go to those extremes? How could we possibly guess he'd try to drive us off the road or bug my office?"

She gripped his arm firmly. "But that's the point, Mitchell. *You're* thinking the problem is that Wendall outflanked us—that our fault was we weren't clever enough. *I'm* saying we shouldn't have been involved in the first place."

On the TV screen above the bar, an acrobatic skier did a slow motion somersault off a ramp. Reece stared at it. "No, Taylor, I'm not as cold as you think," he said in a melancholy whisper, then turned to her. "I understand exactly what's happened—that you and I were responsible for a man's death. But if I don't lay part of the blame at Clayton's feet, it undermines all my beliefs as a lawyer." He touched his chest, empassioned. "It undermines all that I am. You know, this is something I'm going to have to live with too."

And Taylor believed she now saw another aspect of Mitchell Reece, not all powerful, not in control, not immune to pain. She saw a man whose eyes were filled with the same regret she felt, but who—

perhaps for her sake, perhaps for his own—was struggling hard to maintain a stone facade.

A facade that she had just cracked.

She lowered her head onto his arm. His hand twined through her hair. "I'm sorry, Mitchell. This is very odd to me. It's not the sort of thing *Ms.* or *Savvy* prepares the working girl for."

He rubbed her shoulders.

"Can I ask a favor?" she said.

"Sure."

"Can we go back?"

He was surprised. "You want to leave?"

"I've had a wonderful time. But I'm in such a funky mood. I don't want to spoil our time together, and I think that I'd be a drag to be with."

"But I haven't learned to ski yet."

"Are you kidding? You're a graduate of the Taylor Lockwood School of Skiing Injury. You can go out now and break arms and legs all by yourself. With that kind of education, there's no telling how far you can go."

"Let me see when I can get the jet."

She kissed him. "It has been a wonderful time. I'm sorry I'm so, I don't know, strange."

"I wouldn't want you any different."

twenty-seven

Exactly one week after Wendall Clayton's death, Taylor Lockwood stood in front the Metropolitan Museum of Art on Fifth Avenue, looking up at a brown brick apartment building across the street. She checked the address again and verified that she had found the right building. She was somewhat concerned because she didn't have the number of the apartment she sought, but when she walked into the lobby, she found the number was unnecessary.

"Sixth floor," the doorman told her.

"Which apartment?" she asked.

He looked confused for a moment, then said, "It's the whole floor."

"Oh."

She stepped into the private entryway where the leather-padded elevator had dropped her off. She smoothed her hair at a brass mirror, a huge thing. The foyer was in dark red, wallpapered and filled with Georgian yellow-and-white dovetail trim. The picture frames were gilded. The small couch was upholstered in tapestry, and everywhere were scrolls and angels and columns and gingerbread going in a thousand directions.

An ageless, unsmiling woman in a plain navy shift answered the door and asked her to wait, then disappeared down the hallway. Taylor glanced through the doorway. The rooms were larger versions of the foyer. She looked back into the mirror and stared at herself, at the person who was thinner than she'd expected. Thinner and . . . what else? More drawn, gaunter, grimmer? She smiled ferociously. It didn't take. Her mouth fell and she sighed, brushing her hair with her fingers.

I'm here to give you my deepest sympathy.

I'm here to say I worked with your husband.

I'm here to say that even though he's dead, don't feel too bad because he tried to fuck me.

I'm here because I helped kill your husband.

A shadow passed across her, light from the open door was cut off. Mrs. Wendall Clayton stood in the doorway. A woman in her late forties, wearing the stiff, straight-cut, big-patterned clothes that people who learned style in the sixties still sometimes favor. Her straight hair was pulled back in a ponytail. Her thin face was handsome, severe. The foundation makeup had been a long time in application, and still the dry blotches of skin were visible. On her narrow feet were black pump shoes. They shook hands, and Taylor followed her into the living room. *Why the hell am I doing this? What possible point could it have?*

Mrs. Clayton sat upright, in an uncomfortable satin wingback. The upholstery depicted birds flying over a sparse grass, hunters firing from below, in yellow and green. Would the widow glance at a hunter's gun, woven into the fabric, and start to sob?

What the hell am I doing here?

Men of most renowned virtue, remember?

Mrs. Clayton asked if she cared for tea or coffee. Taylor said no, and only then was she aware that the woman's dress was red and that this was not a household in mourning—the room was festooned with antique Christmas decorations, and there was a faint, rich scent of pine in the air. Taylor looked at the woman's cocked eyebrow and her expression, which wasn't one of bitterness or sorrow. It was closer to impatience.

"I worked with your husband, Mrs. Clayton."

"Yes."

"I just came to tell you how sorry I was. . . ."

And Taylor understood then, only at that moment, that uttering those words was all she could do. Watching this brittle, lone woman

(Taylor could not picture her as one half of *the Claytons*) light a cigarette, she understood that Donald Burdick and the firm rose like ghosts before her to lay cold, pinching fingers on her lips. She could not, even here, in Clayton's home, do what she desperately needed to do: explain. Explain that she'd been the one who'd uncovered the terrible secrets, that she was an aspect—the probable cause—of his death.

No, there'd be no confession. Taylor knew what bound her. For this joint venture, Hubbard, White & Willis had secured her soul. If Burdick said the man had killed himself because of some newsstand-magazine despondency, so be it. She understood how impotent she was against the firm, and against men like Mitchell and Burdick and Clayton.

"That's very kind of you." Delivered noncommittally. Saying really: *So get to the point.* After a pause, she decided to say, "Did I see you at the funeral? There were so many people."

"I wasn't there, no." Taylor sat back in the chair.

Now she looked around the room, aware of its size. The ceilings were twenty feet high. It reminded her of National Trust mansions and palaces in England. Taylor said, "He was an excellent lawyer. . . ."

Clayton's widow said, "I suppose." She was staring at a tabletop. It seemed to be a dust inspection. "But then we didn't talk much about his career."

Taylor was counting the squares in the carpet. Trying to figure the designs. Finally: Dogs sleeping before fireplaces in a medieval castle.

Mrs. Clayton gave a short laugh and said, "We didn't talk about much at all, now that I think about it."

Taylor focused on her.

"I'm sorry," the woman said. She paused. "The truth is I'm a little bewildered. I don't know you, Ms. Lockwood, though we may have met before. But you seem so upset by my husband's death. You are not like the little sycophants who have come by since he died. You could see in their eyes the amusement. You could see that they were glad he was dead. I know they'd chuckled about it over their beers when they were alone. Do you know why they were here?"

Taylor was silent.

"They came because they thought word would get back to the firm that they'd done their duty. They'd made an appearance that might earn them another point or two, get them a step closer to being partner." She pressed out her cigarette. "You see, Ms. Lockwood, I am skeptical of sympathy calls—that sounds so Victorian, doesn't it? Sympathy call. Well, I'm skeptical. They were here like little toadies. . . . And that is so ironic, of course, because they do not grasp the situation. They should be avoiding this house as if it were a leper colony. If word gets back to the firm that Randy and Frederick and Douglas were paying respects, then, my God, they're in Dutch. Because this is the house of the defeated. Donald Burdick won. There was no possibility he was going to let Wendall take over your firm. My husband was a bully. Brilliant and gorgeous, but a bully nonetheless. And the Donald Burdicks of the world always defeat bullies.

"So you see, Ms. Lockwood, I am a little perplexed by your visit. You aren't here to toady. You aren't here to gloat. You are genuinely upset. I can see that clearly. But, well, you may have worked with my husband, you may have thought he was a good lawyer. But I doubt very much if you respected him. And I know without a doubt that you didn't like him."

Taylor was silent, watching this shrewd, narrow person, hands red and bony, light another cigarette. She looked as if the smoke that floated out of her had taken with it her weight and softness.

When she didn't say anything, Mrs. Clayton laughed. "Well, whatever your reasons, I appreciate them. I mean that, my dear. I hope I haven't offended you. But don't feel sorry for me. Don't feel bad about his death. I certainly don't. I suppose what I will miss is a certain familiarity. But ours was not a marriage. It was a merger. His assets and mine. Love? Was there any love between Williams Computing and RFC Industries when they consolidated? To name just one of the deals that took so much of Wendall's time . . ."

She looked out over the park, spindly with branches, early-afternoon pale green and white, with the residue of snow faintly surviving in shadows. "Love . . . it's so ironic. Cold, scheming Wendall, power broker. And why did he kill himself? He killed himself for love."

"What do you mean?" Taylor heard herself ask.

"Why, love," she said. "That's the one thing Wendall didn't understand and couldn't control. Love. Oh, how he wanted it. His fatal flaw. Like Oedipus, like Medea. And like so many beautiful people, it was denied him. He was addicted to love. An alcoholic of love. He'd go off on his benders. With his chippies. His little tarts. A charming man, witty, rich, looking like a professor with that careless hair of his. He dyed it, did you know? He was prematurely gray. But he was the pretty boy of the firm. A movie star, no? All of the women thought so. A few of the men, too, I should tell you. How they all would want him!"

Taylor felt the passage of the woman's eyes over her face and body. She knew she was thinking that perhaps Wendall had taken her to his bed, too.

"He'd spirit them away on carriage rides, buy them a dozen roses, have a breakfast tray put together at Le Perigord and sent to their apartments. Wendall goes a'courting. He averaged about an affair or two a year. And they were all disasters. They never quite lived up to what he wanted. The older ones—they turned out to be every bit as superficial and material and cold"—she laughed again, dropping a worm of ash in the ashtray—"as cold as I was. Or he'd pick a young puppy, some ingenue, who'd cling to him desperately, rearrange her life around him. Then he'd feel the arms around his neck, dragging him down. Someone relying on him. My Lord, we couldn't have that, could we?"

This brought the only fragment of emotion so far, a flickering in the woman's eyes. She said, "Then he'd dump them. And back he'd come to me. Back into the fold, back to the country clubs, to our place here. Our marriage of inconvenience, which he couldn't stand but couldn't leave."

Her eyes glowed with a bitter, dark humor. "Could you see Wendall standing in line at the movies with some twenty-five-year-old, her hat pulled down over her ears, like a Barnard sophomore? Standing in line to see some rock-music movie? I did, once. I'd known for a long time about him. But I had never seen him, and I wondered what I'd feel if I ever saw him on the street with another woman. And there he was, standing right outside the 57th Street Playhouse with this girl. And do you know what my reaction was? I laughed out loud. I really did. Not a shred of jealousy, not an ounce. You see, I knew then that I had him. I had absolute control over him. I saw that he was nothing. Just a sad, pitiable man. The only question was did I want him in my life. And I decided that I did. For various reasons. There were accommodations we made, certain comforts. Familiarity. All of those little things."

She gazed out the window for a long moment. Taylor studied her profile for sorrow and found none. Mrs. Clayton continued, "You know what touched me the most? Wendall's note. His suicide note. He could have said what a bad relationship we had, he could have said a lot about me. But he didn't. That was kind. I knew he was hurting. I thought it was just preoccupation with this merger, or plans for the new firm—"

"What new firm?"

She looked at Taylor cautiously, then pushed out her cigarette. "I suppose it doesn't matter anymore. In case the merger didn't go through, he was going to leave Hubbard, White & Willis, take his boys and a couple dozen partners, and open his own firm. It was his alternative plan. I think he almost preferred that to the merger. Because of his name, you understand? Clayton, Jones & Smith, or whatever. He always insisted on top billing." She resumed her examination of Central Park flora.

Silence urged departure. Taylor stood up. "I should go," she said, "I've taken up enough of your time." Taylor extended her hand, and Mrs. Clayton clasped it briefly with her own dry, weak fingers, which hardly curled at all.

She rose and looked at her watch. "I would like to talk to you longer." She picked up her Dunhill cigarette case. "Only bridge club convenes in ten minutes."

Aristocratize.

Taylor Lockwood was sitting at Wendall Clayton's desk.

It was late afternoon, a yellow-gray light came in from outside. The office lights were out. The door was closed. The room was still, but she felt Wendall Clayton's overwhelming presence. His specter stood over her, but chose, for the moment, not to speak.

She looked at the jotting on a faded piece of foolscap.

Aristocratize. Was that a word? Taylor glanced at the brass, the carpets, the vases, the tile painting, the wall of the deal binders (the one that had held the note and hidden the tape recorder was slightly askew). The huge chair creaked as she moved.

Men of most renowned virtue . . .

She was still, technically, on vacation, courtesy of Donald Burdick. Taylor could leave at any time and go to Reece's loft. (It turned out that he could cook after all, and was at this moment making tortellini salad.) She wanted to lie in his huge bathtub, a wonderful bathtub that had claw feet, to lie in the water with a thin-stemmed glass of wine and smell him cooking whatever went into tortellini salad.

Instead, what Taylor Lockwood did was to slouch down in Clayton's chair and spin slowly in a circle, three hundred sixty degrees, once, twice, a final time. She let the motion of the smooth swivel dissipate.

Taylor opened the top drawer of Wendall Clayton's desk.

A half hour later, even though she was late for Mitchell's, Taylor Lockwood walked slowly downstairs to Halsted Street. She made certain that no one was in the cubicles surrounding hers, then sat down and spun her chair around so that she could look up the corridor to see if anyone approached. She wanted complete privacy for the phone call she was about to make. She looked through her address book and found John Silbert Hemming's number.

He felt a huge jolt as he saw her come out of Wendall Clayton's office.

Sean Lillick stopped abruptly and stepped into a darkened conference room, where Taylor Lockwood could not see him. It had scared the hell out of him, as he was walking toward the office, to see the sudden shadow appearing in Clayton's doorway. For a split second he had forgotten that Clayton was dead, and he expected to see the partner hurrying to a meeting, pulling on his jacket the way he did, the way Lillick knew so well, as if racing to an emergency. Then he remembered Clayton was dead, and he saw Taylor Lockwood leave the office.

He let his heart calm, and was so upset with himself for being spooked that it was several minutes before he began to wonder what she had been doing inside. It wouldn't have mattered if she'd come out with a file or a stack of papers, casually strolling as if she had an assignment for a partner who was picking up Clayton's work load. But the way she walked was odd: She had glanced about, like a spy, like someone who'd discovered something secret and was eager to escape.

Lillick waited until she'd gone downstairs; then he slipped into Clayton's office and locked the door behind him.

. . .

It was excellent tortellini salad—with pignolia nuts, olives, shallots, chanterelle mushrooms, nutmeg, celery, and sun-dried tomatoes. The bread (he'd baked it himself!) was lopsided but yeasty and moist. He'd dropped chunks of sweet butter onto the top, and the baking heat had melted it into a thick white and yellow liquid. He opened a Poully-Fuisse.

Mitch, I hear December weddings have become very popular lately. . . .

They ate for ten minutes, Taylor nodding as he told her about the impending New Orleans trial. Normally, she liked it when he talked about the law because, although she didn't always understand the nuances, the animation that lit up his face thrilled her. She tried to be a good audience, but tonight she was listless.

She set down her fork with a tap.

"Mitchell."

He refilled their glasses and cocked an eyebrow at her.

"There's something I have to tell you."

"Yes?" he asked cautiously, perhaps suspecting some personal confession.

"Wendall didn't kill himself."

Reece's wine glass slowed en route to his mouth.

Taylor picked a crumb off the table and dropped it on her plate. "He was murdered."

twenty-eight

Mitchell Reece smiled, and waited for the punch line. When she didn't say anything else, he asked her, "Are you serious?"

"I went to see his widow," Taylor said, then added quickly, "Oh, I wasn't going to tell her what happened. But . . ." She paused, embarrassed. "Well, I wasn't sure why I wanted to go, and I'm still not sure why I did. It was something I just had to do."

He said, "I hear she's a bitch."

Taylor shrugged. "She was civil enough to me. But you know what she told me? That if Wendall couldn't get his merger through, he was going to start his own firm. He had it all planned out. I went through his desk. I found business plans, bank loan applications. He even had the firm name selected. Clayton, Stone & Samuels. He had a sample letterhead printed up, and he'd been looking at space in the Equitable Building."

"What are you saying?"

"Think about it. If Wendall was ready to start his own firm, it makes no sense for him to risk his career just to create a scandal to discredit Donald. Stealing a note? He'd be disbarred, he'd probably be prosecuted. I mean, the man had an ego, but he wasn't crazy. No, what I think is, somebody else stole the note and planted it in Clayton's office. Then when we found it, he murdered Clayton and made it look like suicide."

Reece considered. "I can't buy it, Taylor. I've had plenty of murder cases. They don't work that way. What happens is somebody gets pissed at somebody else and pulls a knife and guts the guy. Or a wolf pack shoots somebody to steal his Guess? jacket or knuckle ring. What's the motive to kill Clayton? You don't murder somebody just because he's a pompous ass."

"You trying to tell me you're not interested?"

He grinned. "Let's say I'm skeptical. But fascinated. Keep making the case. I'm a jury. Convince me."

"At first, I wondered if his widow might have done it. I mean here she was hosting a bridge party a week after he died. She told me about all these girls Clayton had affairs with. So she certainly had a motive."

Reece nodded. "And she must have inherited some bucks from him."

"But if it *was* her, I figured she'd be more contrite. Anyway, the killer would need to know about the firm and have to be able to get in and out easily, without arousing suspicion. So that probably lets her out. Then I started tallying up suspects. It's gotta be a long list. He probably made plenty of bedroom promises he never kept. He had a lot of girlfriends. And some boyfriends, too."

"So he was bi, huh? That was always a rumor." Reece seemed captivated by what she told him, and Taylor felt a surge of excitement seeing his skepticism fade.

She said, "Think about Ralph Dudley. Clayton had found out about Junie and was blackmailing him."

"All right, now *there's* a motive. Agreed." Reece's eyes scanned the ceiling as he thought. "What about Thom Sebastian? Clayton was the main reason he didn't make partner."

"That occurred to me, too. . . . And one other possibility."

Reece frowned as Taylor's smile curved upward. "Think," she said. "Just think about it."

"My God . . ." Reece stared at her. "It can't be."

Taylor Lockwood nodded.

"Donald Burdick," he whispered. Then he began to shake his head. "Look, I know the motive's there. But Donald? I can't believe it.

He'd have to risk my career in the process and risk losing one of his own clients."

"People get crazy, Mitchell. He was losing his law firm. It was his baby. Sacrifices have to be made."

"Murder . . ." Reece swirled the wine. Taylor hadn't seen him this excited since the victory at the Hanover & Stiver trial. He said, "If it was true, I tell you, I'd love a piece of that case." In his eyes, he seemed to be planning his opening statement to the jury.

Taylor said, "Another thing. Think about the gun."

"The gun he used?"

"I called my detective, my private eye, and he talked to some buddies of his at the police department. The gun Clayton used was a .38 Smith & Wesson knockoff—that means imitation—made in Italy. No serial number. It's one of the most popular street guns there is. 'Like your McDonald's of firearms' is what he said. But if you're going to kill yourself, why buy an untraceable gun? You go to Redding Sporting Goods, show a driver's license, and buy a 12-gauge shotgun."

Reece nodded. "Look at how well Burdick covered it up! All the markers he called in. The medical examiner . . . nobody knows about the stolen note. I'm sure he's shredded everything by now. The suicide note, it's all gone. . . ." Then he shook his head. "No, we're getting ahead of ourselves. Let's think about it. Burdick doesn't have any idea you suspect, does he?"

"I haven't told anybody. I did go through Clayton's desk, but nobody saw me."

He stood up and paced, then lay down on the bed. She pushed away from the table and joined him. He rolled on his side and twined her hair around his fingers. In a soft voice he said, "This could be very, very dangerous."

"Should we go to the attorney general?"

Reece said, "I know a couple of prosecutors. . . . But think about it: Burdick's got friends all over the place. He's willing to kill, and he's willing to use his influence to cover it up."

"What can we do?" she asked.

"I've got to go to New Orleans tomorrow. I'll be back in two days. Don't do anything until I get back. Promise me."

"I just thought I'd poke around—"

"No, Taylor." He took her face in his hands. "I mean it. He's already killed once. Second and third killings aren't going to mean anything to him."

"I—"

"Promise me."

"I promise."

The computer room was busy, and the girls gave her a little trouble. She wasn't insistent and polite, the way Mitchell Reece might have been. She got snotty.

The supervisor arrived, a bouffanted, well-foundationed woman in her late thirties—she looked like a Bible slinger on Sunday morning TV. "What seems to be the problem?"

In a threatening monotone, Taylor said, "What I was explaining, what I explained *twice,* was that I need a computer key summary. Who was in the firm between nine P.M. on Monday, December ninth, and two A.M. the next morning. And I need to know now."

"Who exactly are you?"

"Taylor Lockwood. I'm a paralegal here—"

"A paralegal."

"*And* I'm on a special assignment for the executive committee. Because of the merger we're studying the efficiency of support services. Your department is the first."

In five minutes, a page of green-and-white striped paper was streaming out of a printer. One of the operators handed it to her and walked away. It was blank. Taylor said, "Hey, *no hablo.* Can you translate?"

The operator ignored her, and Taylor walked into the supervisor's office and dropped it on her desk. The woman said, "Looks like there's a problem."

"One possible interpretation," Taylor said. "You mean there's supposed to be something printed there?"

Which the supervisor took to be insulting, and maybe was, Taylor had to admit.

"The last time we had this trouble, there was a new operator who initiated the disk. That erases whatever's on it, initiating it accidentally."

"So we have no way of knowing who used computer keys in the office at those times?"

Exasperated, the supervisor held up the printout. "What does this tell you?"

"Not very much at all."

"Then I suppose that's your answer."

After Taylor had left, the supervisor called Donald Burdick's office. She said into the phone, "Is he there? I have a complaint about one of his paralegals." She cocked her head as she listened to the response, then said, "Well, I don't know if *he'd* think it's important or not. But I happen to feel that politeness is a matter of great importance."

At seven that evening, Taylor Lockwood was helping Sean Lillick assemble documents for a major corporate closing. On the way to the conference room in which the closing would be held tomorrow, they passed the firm's wood-paneled dining room. Donald and Vera Burdick stood before it in formal dress, hosting one of the firm's cocktail parties for clients. Taylor nodded cordially and did her best to look preoccupied, thinking they had absolutely no idea how much adrenaline the sight of them had just forced through her system. Suddenly Burdick stepped forward and exchanged greetings with the two paralegals. "You know my wife, Vera, I believe."

Vera shook their hands, and, as she clasped Taylor's firmly, held her gaze. Taylor had a momentary thought, before she looked away from the woman's piercing eyes, that she was shaking the hand of someone who was an equal to Donald Burdick and to Wendall Clayton.

"Yes," Vera said, "we know each other."

The partner and his wife turned to some arriving clients, and Lillick and Taylor continued on to the Xerox room to collect the final drafts of the documents, then began carrying the armsful of paper back to the conference room to lay them out for the signing the next morning.

They worked for two hours, making trips back and forth.

Walking back from the copier room with the last batch, both

slouched under the weight of the paper, Lillick said, "So you think I'm strong enough to be a lawyer?"

"They should pay us by the pound."

"I'm serious. You think I'd be a good lawyer?"

"No," she answered.

They arrived in the conference room and set down their burdens. Lillick pulled a battered yellow and green paperback out of his pocket. *The Complete Law School Companion.* "Wendall thought I'd be a good lawyer. So does Carrie. Her father's a biggie in the Harvard Law alumni association. She thinks he can help me get in."

"What about your music?"

"I don't see why I can't do both."

She laughed caustically. "Why not?"

Lillick's face brightened. "Look." He pointed to a paper plate of appetizers on the table.

"What's that?"

"Horsey dovers. That's what I called them when I was a kid. Horsey dovers. I guess from the cocktail party. Somebody must be thinking of the proles."

He held up another book—a study guide to the Law School Admissions Test. He began reading sample questions. "I'm taking the test in February."

Taylor quickly ate all the shrimp. Lillick scowled and grabbed the tiny quiches. "That's why we need law. Otherwise the piggies of the world get all the shrimp."

The time was close to midnight when she got back to Reece's loft, and the huge space seemed cold and unfriendly, as if it had reverted to its pre-chic, industrial state. The faces on the table seemed particularly morose. Taylor called Reece's hotel in New Orleans, and when the clerk said he had not returned called the firm where was working, half-expecting the janitor to say to her, *Sure, miss, they left about an hour ago, went up to Maude's, that topless place up the road a ways. . . .*

But the woman who answered told her with a crisp drawl, as if it were ten in the morning, "I'm sorry, Mr. Reece is still in conference. Is it important?"

"No. I'll phone him tomorrow."

She wished she had not called. That would be two messages she had left. The receptionist would tell him that a woman had called, and Reece would know it was Taylor. He'd think, *Ho, boy, another one getting misty-eyed and clingy. . . .*

She ate a few bites of supper, drank a large glass of wine, and while the bathwater ran, spent twenty minutes figuring out his stereo. She found a Kenny Burrell album and put it on. Soft, ringing electric guitar filled the room.

Taylor stripped off her clothes and sank into the luscious water. She submerged for a moment, then surfaced, and inventoried her body. Not bad for a thirty-year-old. A few creases, a few swells. Only her stomach bothered her. (Well, thighs, too—but what can you do about thighs?) She had a slight rounding of her abdomen. She'd first become concerned while lying with a boyfriend after they'd made love. He'd pressed his hand on her navel and told her that he got turned on thinking about sleeping with someone who was three, four months pregnant.

She'd gone on a diet the next day and had been wrestling with her belly ever since.

Mitchell doesn't seem to mind. He—

She sat up suddenly. A deep, churning pain struck her just below her breasts. Her face burst out in sweat.

"Oh . . ." She moaned, pressing the skin above the pang hard with both her hands. It ceased for a moment, then exploded in another eruption of agony.

Taylor stood up. Water cascaded onto the floor. She stepped out of the tub, tried to stand, then slipped and fell hard on one knee. She began to black out, and tried to control her fall to the tiles. She lay curled up, quivering in pain. Her eyes slowly opened.

Claws.

The claws of the tub were tearing at her. Inside, in her stomach, throat, the back of her mouth.

She moaned, a low, animal sound.

Sweat filled her eyes and ran down her nose. Her face enfolded with creases of pain. Taylor crawled to the toilet, opened the seat, and held herself on one arm while she vomited and retched for what seemed like hours.

The shrimp! The appetizers in the conference room . . .

The pain flared like fire in her gut. Searing. Her hands shook. She began to faint, and lowered her head. Consciousness returned, but the pain in her temples was so bad she blacked out anyway. She heard, from a different level of awareness, the sound of her head hitting the tile floor.

Pain, on a hair trigger, exploded with every breath and blink of her eyes and tremor of her arm.

She knew suddenly how Donald Burdick had found her out. Of course, she had been stupid again. She had called Hemming to ask about the gun. If Burdick had tapped Reece's phone, he would have tapped hers as well. And now he had poisoned her. She retched again, over and over, shouting to herself to stop, begging, praying. Slamming the toilet with her fist in fury, she realized she had no feeling in her hand. It was completely numb. Taylor Lockwood began to cry.

She crawled into the living room, toward the phone. Her toes were twitching, then they, too, grew numb. She shivered violently. The phone was on the desk. She tugged at the cord until it fell, striking her on the shoulder. She felt no pain. She started to punch in her gynecologist's number, then slammed her cold hand down on the button. *Don't be a fool. . . .*

She dialed 911.

Taylor heard, "Police and fire emergency."

Taylor couldn't speak. Her tongue had turned to wood. The air was becoming thinner and thinner, sucked from the room.

Her hands shook. She closed her eyes.

The voice said, "Is anyone there? Hello? *Hello? . . .*"

twenty-nine

They walked through Chinatown, south, through the cold, airy morning. The neighborhood was an Oz of food. Fish on blankets of ice. Complicated vegetables. Ruddy, glazed ducks hanging by their necks.

Junie loved the ducks.

She looked nice, Ralph Dudley thought. A simple dark pink dress, a navy straw hat, and a white sweater under a navy cashmere coat. Silk, Junie had said when she touched the coat for the first time. She thought all smooth cloth was silk. He'd bought her the clothes at Lord & Taylor. My God, the expense of children's clothing nowadays was ridiculous. And naturally Junie liked only designer fashions. Perry Ellis, Calvin Klein, Laura Ashley.

The night before they had been to see *A Christmas Carol* in a theater on West Forty-second Street. They watched a handsome, voice-projecting Cratchit perched on a stool, a hobbling Tiny Tim, a re-forming Scrooge, a joyous Christmas morning. All this, six blocks from where Junie had fucked hundreds of men. The play confused her. "Man, the dude that wrote that, he's like totally zoned out."

They continued south past the soiled, jaundiced Criminal Courts Building on to the Surrogate's Court, which was in Dudley's opinion the most beautiful and stately court in the state. He paused outside, and decided that there *was* something Dickensian about it, something old and English and . . . gentlemanly. He was pleased that he would be making his first court appearance ever in this edifice.

They were early, and they found a bench in one of the Gothic hallways that belonged more in a museum than a courthouse. Dudley took out his handkerchief and wiped a smudge off Junie's cheek, while she fidgeted against this attention and read a comic book, her lips moving. Dudley smoothed her hair, then leaned away from her slightly and studied her beautiful face, as he wondered how he could explain his burden to his late wife.

Not that he pictured himself sitting by the graveside and chatting with her like in some old frumpy Jimmy Stewart or Jack Lemmon movie, but Dudley sometimes imagined things being different, if, on one of those interchangeable evenings in which she sat knitting and he scanning the newspaper, he had turned to her and said, *Emma, I must talk to you. You see, I've got this problem.*

What would she have done?

He considered it honestly and decided that she would have done nothing.

Well, he believed she would have drunk more, that was one thing. As long as Emma didn't drink, she was a source of some strength. What did alcohol do to aggravate that massive, sucking, hurt ego? Whatever the process, it had a sick alchemical effect.

And he believed she would have instantly come to hate him, and not for his depravity. Oh, no, but because he had a secret passion and she did not. She was not furtive. Emma was a big-boned family woman, whose vice was simply a metastasizing love of herself; she understood it, and was at ease. Her husband's, on the other hand, was an addiction that could not be reconciled. It was by definition wholly without character, wholly unsympathetic *(Short eyes, short eyes!).* In the contest of evils, he would win hands down, and she would have held him in all the more contempt for that.

No, there would have been no help for him from Emma. No sympathy. Nothing of that roll-up-the-sleeves attitude of the Good Spouse. The sacrifice of St. Housewife. *We'll bring him through this one, don't you worry.*

Ralph Dudley survived a marriage, his duty done, his secret

intact, and here he sat, an old fool, in the beautiful rococo gaudiness of Surrogate's Court. A fool in spades, adopting a fifteen-year-old hooker. A girl who had more talent for taking men's cocks into her mouth than he had for the profession of law.

He touched Junie's hand. She tolerated it for a moment, then pulled it away to turn a page.

A voice startled him. "Ralph?"

He looked up and saw Amanda Wilcox standing over him. She wore a navy suit, black stockings, and navy pumps with a burgundy stripe down the side. He stood up at once and took her hand in both of his, considering for a millisecond whether to kiss her. She answered for him and bent forward in a chaste way. As their cheeks met, he smelled Chanel No. 5—straightforward and neutral, the Switzerland of perfumes.

Dudley had worn his one suit that had no shiny patches or escaping threads. He faced her full, and inclined his head slightly toward her. Amanda smiled at Junie, who gave her a fast grin, which disappeared instantly, and looked back at her comic book.

Dudley debated furiously. He chose not to introduce them.

"I didn't know you did surrogate's practice. You never mentioned it."

"I do an occasional adoption or guardianship. It's a fascinating area of law. I wish that I'd specialized in it when I was younger." He was speaking too quickly, feeling the urge to explain. He forced himself to relax.

"More satisfying than lending money or exchanging stock, if you ask me," Amanda said.

Dudley looked at his watch. "I'm sorry, but I have a calendar call now."

She put her hand on his arm. "I enjoyed dinner the other night, Ralph. I hope we can do it again."

"We shall." And he nodded in a suitably Victorian way, then watched her walk down the glossy hall.

As he turned back, he saw his reflection in the window of a door— an old, foolish, passionate lawyer—and turned quickly away. He took Junie's hand and they walked toward their assigned courtroom.

"You ever been in court before?" he asked.

She straightened the blue bow on her broad-brimmed straw hat and said proudly, "Yeah. Like once I knifed this chicken hawk."

"What?" Dudley asked in horror.

"Me and a this kid was on Forty-sixth Street, and this pimp comes up and starts dissing us, and my friend goes, 'Like fuck off.' And this guy starts pounding on him, no reason, and is like making him eat sidewalk, so I took this kung-fu knife and shoved it in his leg."

"My God, did you get arrested?"

"Sure, I was a Y.O."

"What's that?"

"A youthful offender." She rolled her eyes at his ignorance.

"But you have a record," Dudley said, wondering if the clerk at the hearing this morning might check her files.

"Naw, I told you," she answered impatiently, "I was a Y.O. You don't get no yellow sheet, you're a Y.O."

"Oh," Dudley said, then corrected her, "You don't get *a* yellow sheet."

The courtroom itself was gaudy, filled with abrupt turns of wood, scallops, pilasters, moldings. Antique portraits of solemn judges blended into the dark wood.

Junie didn't notice the architecture. "Hey, Poppie, this is like totally weird. Does this mean, like after you adopt me, we aren't going to fuck?"

"Shhh." Dudley looked around.

"Aren't you even going to watch me undress?"

"Be quiet, honey. . . . I love you. I want you to be like my real daughter. I can talk to you, we understand each other. I can give you a good home."

"If I have a boyfriend, will you get jealous?"

"Probably. Don't all fathers?"

"Like don't ask me. I don't know who mine was."

The surrogate entered the room. She was an attractive, heavy-set black woman.

"All rise."

They stood up. The clerk called the first case, and everyone sat. The procedure reminded Dudley of the liturgy at the Church of the Ascension.

"It'll be cheaper, won't it?"

"Shhh."

Junie said, "I mean, if you don't fuck me, you'll save a lot of money."

"Shhh."

"Could we take a trip together?"

"We can take a trip, of course. And I want to start a savings account for college."

She snorted a laugh.

The surrogate was bored and impatient as she ruled against the father in a child support case. The mother smiled gleefully and walked with her lawyer down the center aisle. She led her daughter, a cute Chinese girl of about ten, by the hand. Dudley's eyes followed her thin legs.

The clerk called out, "Matter of June R., an Infant."

"What the fuck is this infant stuff?" Junie whispered harshly. Heads turned.

Dudley said, "Shhh. The law says everybody under eighteen is an infant."

"Well, that sucks," the girl muttered.

He wiped his hands, slick with sweat, stood quickly, and took a deep breath. He said, "Petitioner ready, Your Honor."

The surrogate pulled the file toward her.

"And what do we have here, Mr. Dudley?"

"A petition for guardianship and adoption, Your Honor."

"Ah," the surrogate said and opened the file.

"What happened?" Sean Lillick asked.

The doctor was a woman in her midthirties. She had straight blond hair and wore no makeup except for bright blue eye shadow. Lillick couldn't look at her face without staring at the eye shadow. Her badge said *Dr. V. Sarravich,* and encased in plastic was a very bad picture of her.

Sarravich said, "Botulism."

"Botulism? Food poisoning?"

The doctor was a woman who did not comprehend delicacy, but

she understood how, like drugs, it should be administered. "I'm afraid she ate some severely tainted food."

"Is she going to be okay?"

"Botulism is much more serious than other types of food poisoning. She's unconscious, she's in shock. Severely dehydrated. The prognosis isn't good. We should get in touch with her parents."

"I don't know where they live. I'll give you the name of someone who can get in touch with them. Can I see her?"

"She's in the Critical Care Unit. You can't visit now," Dr. Sarravich said. Medical people were all so serious, as if the fight against the inevitable breakdown of the body stripped them of all humor.

Lillick asked, "Is it really bad?"

She hesitated—a concession to delicacy—and said, "I'm afraid it may be fatal."

A pen and paper appeared, and the doctor asked, "Now, whom should I contact?"

Lillick wrote a name and phone number. The doctor looked at the pad. "Donald Burdick. Who is he?"

"The head of the firm she works at. I'm sure he's very concerned about her condition."

Taylor's eyes opened slowly. Her skin burned from the sandblasting of fever. Her vision was blurred. Her head was in a vise of fiery pressure. Her legs and arms were useless, like blocks of wood grafted to her torso. The nausea and cramps were still twining through her abdomen, and her throat was dry as paper.

There was a young woman in a pale blue uniform making the bed next to hers.

Taylor had never been in such pain. Every breath brought pain. Every thought was a throb of pain. She assumed that the nerves in her hands and legs had died, and thought that was a blessing; If each finger and each toe hurt this much around its circumference, she would have to kill herself.

Taylor whispered.

No reaction from the young woman.

She screamed.

The attendant cocked her head.

She screamed again.

No reaction. Taylor closed her eyes and rested after the agonizing effort.

In several minutes, the bed was made. As the attendant walked toward the door, she glanced at Taylor.

Taylor screamed, "Poison!"

The girl leaned down. "Did you say something, honey?" Taylor smelled fruity gum on her breath and felt like gagging.

"Poison," she managed to say.

"Yes, food poisoning." The girl said and started to leave.

Taylor screamed, "I want Mitchell!"

The girl held up the watch on her pudgy wrist. "It's not midnight. It's eleven in the morning."

"I want Mitchell. Please . . ."

The girl left.

Taylor closed her eyes. She tried fiercely to hold on to consciousness, but it spilled away like a handful of sugar.

When she opened her eyes again, Sean Lillick was next to her.

She whispered something.

He leaned forward. "What?"

Her voice was clear for a moment. Awareness flooded back. "Where's Mitchell?

"I left a message on his machine if he calls in, but the firm in New Orleans said he's already on his way back. I've talked to Donald Burdick, too—"

Her reaction shocked him. Her eyes opened with fear. "No."

"What?"

"Don't tell. . . . He can't come."

"Why not? He said he wants to."

"Poison."

"It was food poisoning. Botulism."

"Not Donald . . ." Taylor tried to sit up with effort.

Lillick studied her face, then looked away. It was white, matte, taut against the bone.

"You didn't want me to tell Donald? Why not?"

"Keep him away. Stall."

"Okay, sure."

"And could you please . . ."

Lillick said, "What?"

She muttered something.

Lillick leaned forward and asked her to repeat it, but Taylor's head lolled to the side. Her eyes were unfocused. Sweat suddenly coated her face. In alarm, Lillick rose to get the nurse.

"Albert," the agent said to Bosk, "you can either wear a wire, or just carry the recorder with you. Which do you prefer?"

They were in the office of the New York State Bureau of Investigation high in Two World Trade Center, in one of several crowded rooms set aside for the Joint Federal–State Investigative Task Force on White-Collar Crime and Corrupt Practices. The great bustle of activity here suggested the organization had a lot to investigate.

The room looked like the digs of a low-class law firm or insurance company, and the agent he was now speaking to looked like Ward Cleaver on the old TV series.

"What's the difference?" Bosk asked miserably.

"Wires are more easily concealed, but you have to tape them on your body. The recorder is bulky, and you have to carry it in your pocket. Obviously, with a recorder it's easier to get caught."

"What's he going to do"—Bosk laughed nervously—"make me go sleep with the fishes?"

The agent didn't smile.

"A wire," Bosk said. "Make it a wire."

The agent handed the young man a card. "Come by this address tomorrow before you go to the meeting, we'll get you fitted. The technicians will tell you how it works."

"Works?" Bosk asked. "Do I have to do anything?"

"Where you should stand, away from certain types of electrical equipment. Don't worry, they'll tell you all about it."

"Don't worry," he whispered. "Sure."

After he left, a senior district attorney, a tall, balding man in a gray checked suit, came into the office. "Sit down, Albert. I've met with the U.S. attorney, and here's what we can agree to. You're facing two counts of wire fraud. If you can get us a conviction of these two men, we'll drop the criminal charges against you and go for a civil penalty. It'll mean treble damages; you'll probably have to pay back a couple hundred thousand. But you'll stay out of jail."

Bosk was thinking of the eating club at Princeton. God, was life simple then. Why couldn't college last forever?

He nodded and felt an urge to tell a joke, something stupid just to break the tension. Nothing funny occurred to him.

"We've gotten close to Dennis Callaghan before, but he's a smart SOB. I know he's done at least three insider trades, and there's one case of market manipulation I'm sure he's guilty of. This other guy, the one who's supplying the account information, he's a first offender, but we're going criminal against him, too. We started arresting people ten years ago, and still nobody pays any attention to us. We have to keep hitting them."

Bosk asked, "What's he going to get?"

"Who?"

"Sebastian."

The attorney consulted his notes. "Grand larceny, falsifying business records, in addition to the Code of Professional Responsibility violations. He'll be disbarred, and probably serve twenty-four months. A half-million-dollar fine. Should discourage him for a little while."

The attorney looked at Bosk's mournful face with what seemed to approach pity. "What is it, he a friend of yours?"

A sliver of a cold smile crossed Bosk's dry lips. He said, "Yeah, but what's a friend nowadays, right?"

At seven-thirty P.M., Donald Burdick's telephone rang. He was in his study. He heard his wife's footsteps complete a circuit that started from the kitchen. He followed her path with his eyes, so that when she knocked and opened the door, he was looking at her.

"Phone, Don," Vera said. "It's a doctor."

The Wall Street Journal crumpled in his hand. He picked up the den phone.

"Yes?"

"Mr. Burdick?" a woman's matter-of-fact voice asked. "This is

Doctor Vivian Sarravich. From Manhattan General Hospital? I spoke to you the other day. About Ms. Lockwood.''

Burdick sat forward. The paper avalanched to the floor. "Yes?''

"I'm afraid I have bad news, sir. Miss Taylor has slipped into a coma. We feel she won't be coming out of it.''

Burdick nodded Vera next to him and held the phone out so she, too, could hear. "But that can't kill you?'' he asked the doctor. "Food poisoning?''

"This is the most severe case of botulism I've ever seen. The infection was much greater than usual. She's had two respiratory failures.''

There was silence. Burdick stared at the desktop.

"Hello, Mr. Burdick?''

"Yes, I'm here.''

"I wanted to tell you, sir. We've already contacted the family.''

"Yes, well, thank you, Doctor. Do you know . . . do you have any idea what her chances are?''

There was a long pause. "We've talked about it at some length, a toxicologist and myself. I'm afraid we have to say the chances of her regaining consciousness are practically nil.''

"What a tragedy,'' Burdick said. Vera shook her head.

There was a knock on the door. Vera walked across the room and opened it. The maid said, "They're here, Mrs. Burdick.''

She nodded and returned to her husband, who said into the phone, "Well, thank you, Doctor.'' He hung up.

He looked at his wife and said, "She says, if it's any consolation, she isn't in pain any longer.''

"I suppose that's a blessing,'' Vera said matter-of-factly. "Now hurry and get dressed, Donald. Your friends are here, and dinner's almost ready.''

thirty

Donald Burdick poured port into Waterford glasses. His hands left fingerprints in a slight coating of dust on the bottle, which, he noticed, had been put up in 1963.

The year that a Democratic President had been killed.

The year he made his first million dollars.

It was a very good year for port.

He carried the glasses two at a time to the guests. Bill Stanley, Lamar Fredericks, Woody Crenshaw—all old fogies, his granddaughter would say, if kids still used that word, and they probably did not—and three other members of the executive committee. Young, anonymous men to whom Burdick was making a point of being kind and deferential. Three men who were living in absolute terror at the moment— because they had been picked and polished by Wendall Clayton, and then leveraged by him onto the executive committee.

The men were in Burdick's study. Outside, wet snow slapped on the leaded glass windows.

"To Hubbard, White & Willis," Burdick said. Glasses were raised, but not rung together.

The Reconstruction had began swiftly. Secessionists and collaborators were given the shaved-head treatment, then kicked onto the summer outing and hiring committees. But none of Clayton's coterie, the pretty young men and women associates, was asked to leave, the theory being they'd work even harder to rid themselves of the contamination.

These three Nameless were the last order of business in the Purge. One of them said, "Your wife, Donald, is a charming lady."

Burdick smiled. They had, of course, met Vera before this evening, though she had never served them dinner, never entertained them, never told them stories of her travels and anecdotes about her famous political friends; never, in short, captivated them (as all the while she sized up their loyalties and telegraphed her assessment to her husband with her cerulean eyes).

He set the assassination-year bottle in the middle of the tea table.

He said, "Bill knows this, but for the rest of you, I have some news. I'm meeting tomorrow with John Perelli. We have a problem, of course. We've signed a letter of agreement on the merger, and there's a good chance they'll hold us to it."

A Nameless spoke. "Donald, I know that letter very well." (This particular Nameless being one of the drafters of that letter, the one sitting on Clayton's right hand in the cold, sour-smelling conference room until 2 A.M. as they hammered it into shape with John Perelli.) "It's full of contingencies."

Impressed that the man returned his gaze, Burdick said, "But we agreed to negotiate in good faith. The firm has now decided that we do not want to go forward simply because we do not want to go forward. That is not good faith. We have a serious contract problem. Look at Texaco and Pennzoil."

Another Nameless: "I know the law, Don." This was a little brash, and he continued more contritely, "I agree they'd have an argument, but I think we hedged well enough so that with Wendall gone, the basic deal has changed."

"Was Clayton's presence a condition?"

"No."

Burdick, smiling, shrugged. "Then, I submit, we still have our problem."

The first Nameless said, "If they sue, how could they even prove damages?"

Bill Stanley said, "The point is, we don't want a suit."

Burdick said, "It's the last thing we want. Absolute last thing. A senior partner kills himself? Bad enough publicity, and we're going to lose clients because of that, my friend. Then a suit from Perelli? No, I want to preempt them."

Lamar Fredericks, round, bald, and roasted from two weeks of golf on Antigua, said, "Preempt? Bull, Don, you mean bribe. You want to pay them off. Cut the crap and tell us what it's going to cost."

Burdick looked at Stanley, who said to the group, "We'd pay five million. Up to, that is. Full release and agreement not to say anything to the press. If they do, liquidated damages of a double refund."

Crenshaw snorted. "What does that do to our partnership shares?"

Burdick was petulant. "It'll be a cut out of operating profits. Take a calculator and figure it out yourself."

"Will they buy into it?"

Burdick said, "I'll be as persuasive as I can. The reason you're all here is that it would be an expenditure out of the ordinary course. I don't want to present it to the firm. So to authorize it, we need a unanimous vote of the executive committee."

None of them had suspected that this was solely a social dinner, of course, but it was not until this moment that they understood the total implications of the invitation. They were the swing votes, and were being tested; Burdick had to know where they stood.

"So," Burdick said cheerfully, "are we all in agreement?"

This was the final exorcism of Wendall Clayton. In these three trim, handsome, brilliant lawyers resided what was left of his ambitious spirit. Was his legacy as powerful as the man?

Gazes met. No one swallowed or shuffled. When Burdick called for the vote, they each said, "In favor."

Burdick smiled at them and, when he poured more port, gripped one of them on the shoulder. Then Burdick sat down in his glossy leather wingback chair and reflected on how much he despised them for not having the metal to take Clayton's fallen standard and shove it up his ass.

Burdick then grew somber. "Oh, just so you know: We have another problem, I'm afraid. There's probably going to be more press."

"Press? What do you mean?" Stanley's voice was a harsh whine.

"One of the paralegals is in the hospital. They don't expect her to live."

"Who?"

"Taylor Lockwood."

One of the Nameless said, "Taylor? Oh, no, that's terrible. What happened?"

"Botulism. Nobody knows exactly how she got it."

Stanley was shaking his head. "God, I hope it wasn't anything we catered."

The first thing Thom Sebastian noticed: the size of the office.

He guessed they could multiply his own office times five and drop it in here and there'd still be room for the Erte bronzes and the rowing machine and stair-climber.

The second thing he noticed: Dennis Callaghan—whose huge office this was—was wearing his hair combed forward, Roman-emperor style, over his bald spot. He had never before seen this aspect of vanity in Callaghan, and it troubled him to have missed a fault of this sort, which Sebastian always looked for in business associates.

"Yo, Sea-bass!"

"Bosk-*meister!*"

Bosk, sunk into a sofa of black leather supple as silk, gave him a five-high slap and winked. Above the couch was a ten-by-twenty canvas encrusted with slabs of paint. The walls were gray, the carpet salmon.

"Well, Thom, come on in, have a seat." Callaghan strolled past him (a vain walk) and closed the door. He did not return to the chair behind his desk, but sat instead next to Sebastian. He crossed his legs casually, revealing light-gray socks.

"Coffee?" Callaghan.

"Nothing, thanks."

"How's tricks at Hubbard, White & Willis? Didn't you have an . . . incident there?"

"A partner killed himself."

"Ah, a tragedy. Personal problems?"

"I think that was it, yes."

"There's a lot of pressure in the business, I'm sure. I thought of law school myself," Callaghan said. "But all the hard work. . . . It was really too much for me. I'm impatient, not a detail man. I have great respect for lawyers, though. You probably take a lot of digs."

"Some," Sebastian said, "but the thing is, anybody insults me, I can always sue their ugly ass."

Bosk laughed. "Usually, though, Thom just tells bad jokes, and the other side caves."

Callaghan said, "I'm on my way to the islands tomorrow. You boys ever been to the Caribbean?"

They looked at each other. "Club Med," they answered in unison. Sebastian said, "I don't think we'd be welcome back."

"We did some totally aggressive partying," Bosk said.

Sebastian said, "Among other things."

Callaghan was not much interested in their stories. He didn't particularly care about either Bosk or Sebastian and certainly did not want to have them as drinking buddies or hear about their childish exploits. But Dennis Callaghan was a man who had made millions and millions of dollars by knowing when to laugh and how loud, so he chuckled and shook his head before saying, "Well, Thom, let's talk some business. You've got the account information, and we're ready to roll. You've agreed to the dollars. Let me tell you what I propose about protecting you and—"

"There's a little problem," Sebastian said.

"Problem?"

"I changed my mind."

Bosk closed his eyes.

The smile in Callaghan's round face did not deflate. "Cold feet?"

Sebastian took a breath to protest, then thought for a moment. "Yeah, you could call it that."

Bosk said, "After all we've done for this? You'd cinder the whole deal? You can't just fucking walk—"

Callaghan waved him down. "In the Hamptons, Thom, you said you were worried about security. Let me tell you what I'd do. You give me the numbers and authorized names on the accounts, I'll set up a chain of at least six companies. Your name, mine, and Bosk's will not appear in a single corporate document. The actual trades will be ordered by a South African company an associate of mine incorporated years ago and which hasn't been used for anything other than phantom trading. Another associate will approach a vice president at the bank and give him enough money to put his kids through Wharton to doctor the records so the firm will never see a decrease in balance. We'll also get the vp on tape, so if he has a change of mind later, we'll still have him on the hook. The funds will go out on Monday and be replenished by Thursday at the latest. I'll have two separate hedges going so we have another October '87, we can cut losses before we lose our balls."

Sebastian laughed with pure admiration.

"You like it, huh?"

Thom Sebastian's mind took in Callaghan's plan, raised a number of silent objections—analyzing as the SEC or FBI or Justice Department might—and found they were all disposed of. He said, "Brilliant," which was something he rarely admitted about any business deal and never would have said unless he meant it.

"How 'bout it, Thom?" Bosk said. "Come on. Let's burn, my man. Burn, burn, burn. Make some fucking-A money."

Sebastian turned to his friend and opened his mouth to respond. But he paused. His eyes swept over Bosk's jutting, handsome chin, his pudgy fingers (oh-so-fast on the buttons of the Quotron on his desk), his hungry eyes, and Sebastian realized that what he was looking at, the *only* thing he was looking at, was a very young boy fidgeting on a very expensive couch.

Sebastian turned back to Callaghan, who may have been a thief— and a vain, self-conscious one at that—but was at least a man. "I still have to say no."

Callaghan said, "Well, you know, Thom, you aren't going to make any money, I mean *serious* money, seven-figure money, without some risk."

"I've thought about that."

Bosk said angrily, "Jesus Christ, Thom, we've been working on this for months. After what the firm did to you, you said you wanted to get even. They fucked you over royal."

Again, Callaghan waved his hand to silence Bosk, then smiled. A man who knows the protocol of making money knows the protocol of not making it as well. "Thom," he said slowly, "you're a very smart young man. You're savvy, and you're a ball-buster. You could knock the business world on its ass."

Sebastian said, "But you have to understand, Callaghan—I'm a lawyer. That's all I am. That's all I want to be."

The man nodded. "I'm disappointed, but I can't force you into something you don't want to do."

Sebastian stood. He was waiting to feel joyous, freed, unburdened, exhilarated. He felt none of those. He walked to the door. "See you 'round."

Mitchell Reece closed his litigation bag and slid it under the seat of the Delta 727.

Still no call from Taylor Lockwood. He hadn't been able to reach Lillick after the paralegal had called and left the message that said simply, "Urgent." He wondered what Lillick had to tell him. He considered it for a moment, but then his thoughts fell back to the case he was working on, and after he had mentally organized some loose ends, he began, for some reason, to replay Wendall Clayton's funeral.

I recall one time when I happened to meet Wendall, it was a Saturday evening, late. We happened to be strolling up Madison Avenue together. He, from the firm. I, from some function at my congregation. . . .

The Episcopalian minister forsook the pulpit and, like a talk show host, walked down into his audience.

. . . and we passed a few moments in idle conversation, but I saw that there were striking similarities between his profession and mine. He voiced some concern for a young man or woman, a young lawyer at the firm, who was suffering from doubts. Wendall wanted to inspire this protégé. . . .

Hundreds of people. Most of the partners from Hubbard, White & Willis, many associates, many friends had attended. Reece had not spoken to the widow.

. . . just as I in my own way deal with spiritual doubt in our young people. . . .

One hell of a church, Reece recalled. Huge, pointy, Gothic, solid. All the joists and beams met in perfect unison—high, so high up in the air. Stone and wood and metal became one in the dark apogee of construction, that much closer to heaven. It was a fitting place for an aristocratic man to be eulogized.

Linda Davidoff's funeral, he decided, had been better. The church was tamer, the minister more upset. It seemed to Reece better to get more tears and fewer words from men of the cloth.

Clayton's minister had been correct about one thing, though: He and Clayton had indeed been cut from the same bolt—that of noblemen and medieval clergy. Pentacles would be their suit. *Choose this sign for dark men of power and money.*

Aggressive men.

The minister was seizing an opportunity to preach, just as Clayton, too, had seized a chance of his own—and had died as a consequence of his reach.

Reece thought of Linda again, a fast image. Then there was the sudden grind and windy slam of the plane's wheels coming down. The stewardess announced final approach. And as he glanced out the window, Reece thought it was ironic that he saw below him the huge cluster of the dense graveyards in Queens—a whole city of a graveyard, it seemed. He watched until it vanished under the wing.

As he walked down the ramp toward the terminal, Reece saw his last name on a card a limo driver held up.

"Is that for Mitchell Reece?" he asked.

"Yes, sir. You have luggage?"

"Just this."

The man took his bags.

"I'm going to the Hubbard, White office. You know where that is?"

"I think we're supposed to stop someplace else, sir."

"What do you mean?"

"I believe there's some kind of problem."

Reece climbed into the back of the Lincoln. "What kind of problem?"

"An emergency of some kind. There's a phone inside, sir. You're supposed to call this number." He handed Reece a slip of paper and got into the car. The door closed with a heavy chunk, and before Reece had picked up the cellular phone, the car had pulled away from the curb.

· · ·

The driver wasn't sure where the entrance was. The limo drove past three doors that said *Manhattan General,* but they all seemed to have smaller signs Reece couldn't read. Maybe: *Authorized Personnel Only* or *Drug Rehab Program.*

The driver pulled up in front of pale-yellow-painted doors. It looked like the entrance to a grade school. Reece left his suitcase and the litigation bag in the limo and walked into the hospital and up to the admissions nurse. He asked about Taylor Lockwood, and she solemnly pointed him down a corridor, old and musty.

In a dingy room, with a greasy chicken-wire–impregnated window, he found her. She was lying on her back, covered up to her neck with a white sheet. Her hair was pulled back, though whether it had just fallen that way or been arranged by a nurse or attendant, he didn't know.

Her face was gray.

Reece sat down next to her.

Taylor opened her eyes in surprise. "Oh, Mitchell, it's you. Kiss me, then see if you can scarf up some ice cream. I'm starving to death."

thirty-one

"**S**uck on ice," Reece said when he returned five minutes later. Taylor frowned.

"I asked them what you could have to eat. They said you should suck on ice."

She nodded at the IV. "Glucose. It's pure carbohydrates. I'm dying for a hamburger."

Reece gave her a Life Saver. "How do you feel?"

"Like I had a run-in with a truck, and the truck won."

"You look, well, awful."

"Awful is a compliment, considering how I did look. The nurse tells me I've recovered incredibly well. I was also lucky. Whoever tried to kill me used too much culture. It was so tainted, I got sick—brother, I'm talking Mount St. Helens—before I ingested much of the bacteria."

"Tried to kill you?"

Taylor nodded. "I got careless. I think there was a bug in my phone. Or somebody noticed me going through Wendall's desk after all."

"Was it Donald?"

"Oh, Mitchell, I think it was. There were some appetizers from a party Donald and his wife held for clients. Somebody put a plate of them out for Sean and me."

"Did he get sick, too?"

"No, but I ate all the shrimp. And the doctor said it would be real unlikely for botulism to grow naturally in food like that. Mostly, the culture grows only in sealed containers."

"But it could just be a coincidence. How could he poison you? You can't just buy botulism at Pathmark."

She smiled. "Who's one of Donald's best friends? I'll give you a clue: Name a client he's had for twenty years."

Reece grinned like the winner of a turkey shoot. "The president of Genneco Labs."

"I was talking to a pathologist here. He told me Genneco does a lot of research into antitoxins, you know, like antidotes. I think Donald bribed somebody at the company to get some botulism culture and put it in the food he gave me. That's why I told him I was almost dead, in a coma."

"You *what?*"

"I was afraid he'd try again. I called and pretended I was my doctor."

Reece said, "That's it. We go to the cops."

She touched his hand. His was burning hot; she guessed hers was freezing. "Not yet. I'm scared, Mitchell. He's so powerful. You saw the connections he's got at the police department. I want to play dead for a few days more."

He considered, then nodded. "God, I can't believe he'd do it."

"I'm sorry about your loft. It's pretty messy. You aren't going to want me to stay over anymore."

"Oh, yes, I am. And you're coming home as soon as possible. When can you leave?"

"Tomorrow probably."

He paused. "Does Sean know about this?"

"No. I didn't want him involved."

"It's probably better not to tell him."

"Mitchell . . ." To her surprise, she started to cry. "I'm glad you're back."

Reece leaned forward and touched her face. "You're so thin. I'll have to fatten you up."

He bent forward to kiss her.

She waved him away. "Oh, I'm such a mess. Let me make myself pretty for you. Go on, get on home. Visiting hours are over."

· · ·

Surrogate's Court of the State of New York
County of New York

IN RE MATTER OF JUNE R., AN INFANT

Surrogate Lee—This is an action for a private adoption of a minor.

Upon testimony offered by petitioner, one Ralph Dudley, and by the proposed adoptive child, the court must deny petitioner's application.

The court is disturbed by the apparent lack of present care of the child and accordingly orders the child to be placed in custody of the state Department of Social Services.

The court shall also instruct the attorney general to appoint a guardian ad litem to represent the interest of the child in all future proceedings. Such guardian shall prepare a complete report on the circumstances under which the child came to be abandoned by her natural parents, and determine if they can be located.

The court has considered Mr. Dudley's oral application in court to be appointed such guardian, and though impressed with his arguments on the law, holds that it is more appropriate that a third-party guardian be appointed by the state.

Upon completion of such report, this court shall reconsider the petition for adoption.

Order signed.

· · ·

Taylor lay in her hospital bed all morning, watching game shows and occasionally feeling guilty about all the flowers that were arranged against the gray wall of her room. Taylor had forgotten that her friends might be a little troubled by her near-demise. She had warned her parents that she was not as sick as reports might show, but aside from Mitchell, no one else knew she was in the land of the conscious, and attorneys and fellow paralegals had sent dozens of thinking-of-you notes, accompanying hundreds of dollars' worth of roses and jonquils and baby's breath and other flowers. (The cheap carnations, she noted cynically, were from Donald and Vera Burdick.)

The dupe didn't need to last much longer, though; they were discharging her that afternoon. But she imagined that Burdick might already be wondering why her mother and father were not in town making funeral preparations or why no visitors were allowed to see her comatose and hooked up to life support. He might even be calling the real Doctor Sarravich at this very moment and getting an enlightening answer to his question about Taylor's current condition.

She was brooding about what to do after she was released from the hospital, when the kick in the teeth came—the TV reception started to go. She took the remote control, a chunky box on a heavy gray cord, and started jiggling it. The set started changing channels by itself and finally locked onto the network showing *General Hospital*. It would not let go.

Come on. . . .

Nothing wrong with soaps, of course, but this particular show reminded Taylor of boring summer vacations spent by herself (nobody plays with undertakers' daughters). She whacked the control one last time then shut off the set. She looked around for a paperback or something else to read.

There wasn't much. The hospital had put her purse in the safe but left her leather address book, which had interesting information in the back—holidays of various nations, time zones, toll-free numbers, foreign monetary units, temperatures in world capitals.

She got tired of this info pretty quickly, though, and was about to risk a walk to the newsstand, if there was a newsstand, when she saw a folded sheet of paper stuck in the back of the address book.

She unfolded the paper. It was the poem that Danny Stuart had given her. Linda Davidoff's poem, her suicide note. She quickly put it away, then, on impulse, opened the sheet and reluctantly read.

WHEN I LEAVE

By Linda Davidoff

When I leave, I'll travel light
and rise above
the panorama of my solitude.
I'll sail away, fast and high,
weightless as the touch of night.

When I leave, I'll become a light
that has no vision, has no voice.
We'll explain our love in clear, essential ways.
(After all, what is a soul but love?)
After all is cast aside, after all is burned away,
I'll travel light, transported home to you
in the buoyancy of pure and peaceful flight.

Taylor Lockwood thought of Linda, the beautiful, quiet, gypsy poet, and cried briefly, folding the poem and slipping it back into her book. She lay back in bed, dizzy from the simple act of sitting up. She wiped her eyes and blew her nose with a rough tissue from a plain white box the hospital provided, waiting for the headache to diminish. She closed her eyes, but after a moment she opened the address book and took out the poem.

She read the lines very slowly, and after five minutes she read them once more.

At one-fifteen the next afternoon, a time when Wall Street offices were nearly empty and the streets were brimming with the occupants of those offices, en route to luncheon clubs, Taylor Lockwood sat on a bench in front of the Hubbard, White building, wearing jeans, boots, and a brown leather jacket over a work shirt—and dark Perry Ellis sunglasses, through which she now watched Donald Burdick walk briskly out of the lobby and duck into his Lincoln Town Car limo. As soon as the car peeled away from the curb, she stood up and walked to the loading dock of the building. Taylor started up the stairs. At fifteen, she stopped and caught her breath, then slowly pushed open the back door, the latch on which was still—as Thom Sebastian had told Dennis Callaghan—taped open. (And was probably lousy with fingerprints. She hoped for his sake that Sebastian had given up his life of crime. He may have been a good lawyer, but he was a pretty incompetent crook.)

Through the open doorway, she surveyed the broad, main corridor on this floor. It was empty. She waited a moment or two, then pushed the door open and, unseen, walked quickly down the hallway to the file room. She stepped inside and closed the door behind her.

Taylor Lockwood had learned early the real power centers at Hubbard, White. One of these was a short, round-faced woman of sixty. Mrs. Bendix, the file room supervisor, had used her miraculous skills at memory and association to save the butts of almost every attorney and paralegal in the firm on more than one occasion. Taylor now stood over her spun-blue hair as the woman flipped through the three-by-five cards that were her computer. Taylor silently waited for her to finish. Mrs. Bendix—like Donald Burdick—was a person one did not interrupt. When she was through, she looked up and stared in astonishment. "You're sick. I gave two dollars for flowers."

"They were lovely, Mrs. Bendix. I recovered more quickly than they expected."

"They said you were almost dead."

"Modern medicine."

Mrs. Bendix was eyeing her clothes cynically. "This firm has a dress code. You're outfitted for sick leave, not work."

"This is a bit irregular, Mrs. Bendix. But I have a problem, and you're just about the only person who can help me."

"Probably am. No need to stroke."

"I need a case."

"Which one? You've got about two hundred to chose from."

"An old case."

"In that event, the possibilities are limitless."

"Let's narrow things down. Genneco Labs. Maybe a patent—"

"Hubbard, White does not do patent work."

"Well, how about a contract for the development of an antibotul-ism drug?"

"Nope."

Taylor looked at the rows and rows of file cabinets. Thousands of them. A thought fluttered past, then settled. She asked, "We ever represented a client that was a restaurant, hotel, food company, something like that?"

"Sorry, not a bell is rung, though in 1957 we did have a cruise line as a client. I got a discount and took a trip to Bermuda. I got a coral cut that got infected. But I transgress. You were asking?"

"Have we ever represented anybody who *sued* a restaurant or hotel for food poisoning? Soup company maybe?"

"Nope."

"You're sure?"

"I'm always sure."

In frustration, Taylor puffed air into her cheeks.

Mrs. Bendix said, "Don't look so forlorn, child. Let us recap. You're looking for a client that was either a plaintiff or a defendant in a food poisoning case."

"About a hundred percent right."

Mrs. Bendix said tantalizingly, "Since you said *client,* I assume you meant *client*. So—"

Taylor knew that when people like Mrs. Bendix bait you, you swallow the worm in its entirety. She said, "Maybe I was premature when I said client."

"Well," the woman said, "if it wasn't a client, I would harken back to"—she closed her eyes, creasing her gunmetal eyeshadow, then opened them dramatically—"Maxwell *v.* Quail Island Lodge. Six years ago. We represented an insurance company that intervened in the suit. Sick people all over the place. I understand it was the turkey."

"Insurance company," Taylor said. "I didn't think about that."

Mrs. Bendix said, "Apparently not."

"Now I have another one for you. An auto case. Car running off the road."

"Not fair, that's too easy. Hubbard, White handling a PI auto case? There's only been one in the past ten years. A former partner's son-in-law. That would be State Farm *v.* Billings."

"Mrs. Bendix, you are incredible."

"Yes," she said.

"One last question: Can you tell me if anyone checked out the files on those two cases in the past six months?"

This was beyond her brain. She pulled the logbook out and thumbed through it quickly, then held it open for Taylor to look at. Mrs. Bendix laughed. "Well, that's quite a coincidence, isn't it?"

"Not really," said Taylor. Then she said, "I'd like to check them out, too. The files."

Mrs. Bendix went to retrieve them while Taylor stared down at the log, her eyes following the stately curves of Donald Burdick's signature.

"Do you mind my saying? . . . I mean, will you take it personally if I say you don't look very good?" John Silbert Hemming asked.

Taylor Lockwood said, "I lost twelve pounds in two days."

"Hell of a diet. You should write a book."

"We couldn't market it. The secret ingredient ain't so appetizing. I'm feeling better now."

They were at Miracles Pub. She was probing at a bowl of Greek chicken soup flavored with lemon. It wasn't on the menu. Dimitri's wife had made it herself. She had some trouble with the spoon—she had to keep her fingers curled; her rings tended to fall off if she didn't.

Taylor said, "I need a favor."

Hemming, who was eating a hamburger, said, "If it's not illegal, and not dangerous, and if you agree to go to the opera with me a week from Saturday at eight o'clock sharp, I'd be happy to oblige."

She considered. She said, "One out of three?"

"Which one?"

"I'd like to go to the opera."

"That makes me very pleased. And very nervous. What's the favor?" He nodded toward his plate. "This is a very good hamburger. Can I offer you some?"

She shook her head and dipped her eyes toward the soup. "My first solid food."

"Ah." He resumed eating. He cut like a surgeon. A glistening, garlicky Caesar salad was set on the table next to theirs, and Hemming nabbed the waitress and ordered one. Taylor thought that since they had nearly identical eating habits, he and Willy Lansdowne would make good friends.

After a moment, she asked, "Why do people murder?"

"Temper, insanity, love, and occasionally for money."

The spoon in her hand hovered over the surface of the soup, then made a soft landing on the table. She pushed the bowl away. "The favor is, I want you to get me something."

"What?"

"A gun. The kind without any serial numbers."

The New York State Department of Social Services worked fast.

Junie had met with one caseworker, a savvy woman who reminded the girl of a hooker who turned tricks at the West Side Art and Photography Club. Junie looked at her seen-it-all eyes and no-bullshit smile, said, "Oh, fuck it," and reported in great detail how a little girl made thirty-five thousand dollars a year, part time.

The next day, Junie was in a foster home in upstate New York, and the West Side Club was the front-page feature in the evening edition of the *Post*. Though gentlemen did not read that particular newspaper, Ralph Dudley made an exception this once, since the *Times* wouldn't have the story until tomorrow morning. He now sat at his desk, lit only by a single battered brass lamp and paltry December dusk light bleeding into his office, and stared at the same article he'd already read four times.

Like all addicts, Dudley had an emotional as well as a physical relationship with his addiction, and as he gazed at the photo of the cops leading the girls out of the house where he had spent many hours and many tens of thousands of dollars, he felt as if a friend had died.

He wondered if Junie had or would say anything about him. She was, of course, in a position not only to destroy the delicate balance of his career, such as it was, but also to send him to prison for the rest of his life.

These possibilities he considered with remarkable serenity, sipping coffee from a porcelain cup. In his numb state, he was nothing more than curious about his fate. He weighed the possibilities and decided that he was probably safe. She would say nothing. Although she'd been badly used by life and had the indulgence and dangerous edge of those who learn survival before maturity, Junie was nonetheless motivated by a kind of justice. That had been one of the things that had attracted him to her. Also, he believed that she loved him, in her complicated and utterly flawed comprehension of that word.

Ralph Dudley had again escaped unscarred. He now felt an urge to cry.

His calendar was clean for today, though in one hour, he was scheduled to attend a cocktail party at the New York State Ballet, of which Hubbard, White & Willis was an endowing sponsor. Many potential clients would be there. He almost canceled, but then decided not to. He could not bear to sit home alone.

He looked at his fancy black telephone. It had a row of speed dialer buttons. He had never learned how to use the feature until just a few days before, though the telephones had been installed in the firm three years ago. He had only one name penned in, on the little card next to the top button: *Amanda Wilcox.* He wondered if she'd be going to the party tonight. Had they discussed it? He couldn't remember.

Ralph Dudley picked up the phone and pressed the button. As he listened to the fast musical burst of tones of the dialing circuit, he realized he had no idea what he was going to say. None at all.

Differences.

Taylor Lockwood thought about one difference between them, between her and Mitchell Reece, which was this: He could win and be satisfied solely with winning. Yet Taylor would need a smile of concession and acknowledgment from the defeated. *It's okay. You did the right thing. All is forgiven.* In victory, Reece would have only pride, not ecstasy. But neither would he have hatred for the defeated. He had no need to obliterate. He would win, and be content, and move on with his life. Whereas Taylor needed either to win over or to wholly destroy the souls of those she had conquered.

Taylor would never be able to master the art of mastery. Wendall Clayton had died because of her. Thom Sebastian had cringed before her, Ralph Dudley had been shamed. This was the use of power, and she didn't like it.

Taylor lay in Reece's morality-play bed, feeling the presence of the proud knights and gargoyles floating behind her on the headboard. She was leaning forward, breathing in shallow puffs, as if waiting for something—some occurrence, some presence, some person she hadn't yet identified. She would relax for a moment, then a few minutes later found herself straining again, waiting. Anticipation. A Victorian clock chimed. She wasn't paying attention and didn't count the number. She guessed it would be five P.M.

Near quitting time at the firm.

The end of another day at Hubbard, White & Willis. Files being stacked away, dress shoes being replaced with Adidas and Reeboks, places in law books being marked for the night, edits being dropped in the *In* box for the night word processing staff.

Taylor Lockwood picked up the scarred gray .38 revolver. She smelled it, sweet oil and wood and metal warmed by her hand. She hefted the small pistol, much heavier than she'd thought it would be.

Then she put the gun in her purse and walked unsteadily to Mitchell Reece's desk, where she found a pen and one of his pads of yellow foolscap. She thought she had the message all planned in her head, but when she actually began writing, she found it was much more difficult than she had thought. It took her almost a half hour to write one short paragraph, and she had several false starts. But she could not hurry; it was vitally important to her to be extremely articulate as she explained to Reece why she was going to the firm that night to kill Donald Burdick.

thirty-two

"Is it important?" Donald Burdick's staticky voice asked through the intercom.

Carol lifted her manicured hand off the button and looked up at Thom Sebastian. "He asks if it's—"

Thom Sebastian said, "Yes."

"He says yes."

"All right," Burdick said, grumbling.

She said to Sebastian, "He'll see you now."

"Thank you."

Sebastian entered, wondering how many times he'd been in this office. A hundred fifty, two hundred? He tried to remember the first time he'd walked into the room. That would have been six and a half years ago, as a young lawyer bristling with eagerness and untested dreams about the law.

How many billable hours ago?

Thousands and thousands and thousands . . .

"Hello, Thomas, come in." Burdick was solemn and deferential.

Sebastian sat in one of the leather chairs and crossed his legs. Their eyes met. For the first time in his years at Hubbard, White & Willis, Thom Sebastian felt he was the equal of Donald Burdick. He didn't

have to hang on every word that Burdick said. He didn't have to nod
and take desperate notes and skitter off to his desk to begin drafting
letters of credit and security agreements for delivery at the start of
business the next day. He could say *Don* if he wanted to. It would be an
insult, though, and he decided, after deliberation, that he did not want
to be insulting.

He smiled cordially and said, "Donald, I'm giving notice. I'm
leaving the firm."

Burdick was nodding. "Well, I'm very pleased you've found
something this soon. I know the partnership committee decided
against you, but I want to make absolutely clear that we had no
concerns about you as a lawyer. Your work was good."

Still, economies must be effected. . . .

"I wish I could say I understand, Donald. It's confusing to hear
you say that. I am a good lawyer. I've made the firm a lot of money, I've
saved our clients millions of dollars. And yet I didn't get the golden
ring."

"Ah, the golden ring. Is that how you look at it? See, perhaps
that's part of the problem. Partnership is not a reward, it's just an
opportunity. There are risks, there is responsibility."

Sebastian pretended to consider this for a moment, although in
fact he had rehearsed a dozen times words similar to what he was about
to say. "No, Donald, the *firm* made it a golden ring, not me. You hold it
out. You . . . tantalize. It's the system you've created. Your rules,
your games . . . But we could debate this endlessly." Pleased with
the peace in his voice, the self-assurance, he said, "I just wanted to let
you know I'm leaving. And to tell you, sincerely, that I've learned a
great deal from you and the other lawyers at the firm. I'm very grateful
for that."

Burdick appeared genuinely touched. "Well, thank you, Thom,
that's a very gentlemanly thing to say."

"Oh, I believe I qualify for my year-end bonus."

"Yes, of course, we'll see that you get it. I suppose you should talk
to the business manager about having your things shipped out. We'll
pick up the tab for that."

"Thank you." Sebastian lingered. He didn't have to lead any
further; Burdick asked the question: "And where will you be going?
Another firm?"

"No. A corporation. I'll be a senior vice president and chief general counsel."

"Ah, that's the way to go, son. Stock options, benefits, profit sharing. A company I know?"

"MacMillan Holdings."

Burdick slowly capped his Mont Blanc and set it on his desk. "You're going to become general counsel of Mac-Millan?"

"I've worked with them for years now. I know Steve Nordstrom and Ed Gliddick quite well. We play golf frequently."

Burdick's eyes narrowed. "MacMillan was the first client I brought to Hubbard, White."

Sebastian didn't say a word.

Burdick's eyes closed and he rocked back in his tall chair. Then, suddenly, he began to laugh. "I'll be damned. The firm's losing them, aren't we?"

Sebastian moved his head slowly in what he thought was a fair parody of an elderly partner's grave nod. "I'm taking most of the work in-house, and the jobs we need outside counsel for, I'll pick another firm. A cheaper one. Cost savings are reflected in the company's bonuses."

Burdick thought quickly, and his mind considered a number of complicated business and financial arrangements he might suggest to Sebastian to save some of the revenue that MacMillan paid to Hubbard, White. He said, "I suppose there isn't any way . . ." But his voice faded as he saw Sebastian's cocked head and polite smile.

Burdick laughed again, then rose. Sebastian did, too.

They shook hands, and each said good-bye to the other, but it was Sebastian who offered, "I wish you the best of luck."

After he left Burdick's office, Thom Sebastian went to his office and sat for five minutes, staring at the telephone. Three times he reached out for it, hesitated, and put his hands flat on the thick mass of papers covering his desk.

The night before, sitting in the Space, feeling numb from the crash of the music and thinking exclusively about Taylor Lockwood, he had resolved to act. He wasn't sure where she was; the rumor was that she was sick. She wasn't answering her phone, and he'd been glad she was out; it gave him more time for avoidance.

But now he couldn't delay any longer.

Sebastian could negotiate with the best of them and could stare down the orneriest partner in Wall Street, but to do what he planned, he now felt his courage pressed to the breaking point.

Sebastian stood up, paced in his office for a few minutes, then impulsively walked downstairs, wondering if he was making the biggest mistake of his life.

As Donald Burdick rose to walk into Bill Stanley's office and tell him that MacMillan Holdings was walking, his intercom buzzed. He picked up the phone receiver. His secretary said, "There's a woman on line two-eight. She won't give her name, and she says it's important."

"The important news I had five minutes ago cost this firm four million dollars. . . . Tell her to call back."

He was ten feet from his desk when Carol's voice called, "She said to say it's about Wendall Clayton's death. Is it a crackpot? Should I call the police?"

Burdick said abruptly, "I'll take it. And hold all calls."

Dead tired.

Mitchell Reece walked up the dark stairway of his building and wondered if the expression, which he felt applied to him tonight, meant dead as in no longer living, or dead in the British way, meaning very. Being a lawyer, he tended to analyze questions like these—verbal curios. Of no significance other than that there was a minor mystery behind them. He had to get to the bottom of things. He became irritated if he stumbled on a question that he couldn't immediately answer.

He began working his three locks, each opening with a small, satisfying hammer of metal on metal. *Dead tired.* He'd have to look it up. Then he pushed the huge metal door open and stepped inside, saying, " 'Lo, love."

The loft was empty.

He listened for running water, knowing how much Taylor liked to take baths. But he heard nothing. He didn't remember that she'd be out today. He'd told her when he left that morning that she had to stay in bed all day. He'd looked at her critically and told her that she hadn't gained nearly enough weight. She'd nodded in an exaggerated way, like an eager geisha, and then trotted back to bed.

Maybe she'd just run to the store. Or had she had a relapse?

He had just taken off his coat when he found the note lying open on the table, whose impassive carved faces gazed at him from knee level as he read.

He didn't actually read the whole thing. It was more a speed-read, where you get the gist and let the details fall by the wayside. But what he read was enough for him to pull on his coat and gloves in one smooth motion, and run out the door, which this time he didn't even bother to close, let alone lock.

Taylor Lockwood had never liked the big conference room. For one thing, it was always kept dim—a pastel room so underlit that the colors became muddy and unreal. For another, she associated it with the big meetings in which the paralegal administrator would gather her flock and give them all a big pep talk, which amounted to a plea not to quit just because the raises were going to be only 6 percent. Things would be brighter next year. And Bill and Connie and Stu and Courtney would look at each other and decide to go with it—for the good of the firm.

It was eight o'clock in the evening. Taylor sat in a large swivel chair at the base of the U, the chair Donald Burdick reserved for himself.

Then the huge teak doors to the conference room opened. Mitchell Reece ran into the room. He stopped when he saw the gun in her hand.

She looked at him with dulled surprise. "Mitchell, what are you doing here?"

"You leave me a note that you're going to kill a man, and you don't expect me to stop you."

"It's too late, Mitchell. We can't go to the police. We have no evidence. He's destroyed it all. Just like he'll destroy us if we don't stop him." Her voice droned. Her eyes were dull as milky ice.

"Taylor, are you crazy?"

She laughed briefly, with no humor in her voice. "Maybe," she answered.

"You think you're just going to aim the gun and shoot him? Just like that?"

She glanced up, over Reece's shoulder, and said, "We're about to find out." She hid the gun behind her back and called, "Donald, I'm over here."

Reece spun around.

A figure emerged from the dull light of the hallway into the deeper shadow of the end of the conference room. Burdick, in his perfect posture, walking with the gait of a ballroom dancer, stepped past the doors, which swung closed with a heavy snap. Footsteps sounded along the marble, then disappeared as the partner's shoes touched the carpet.

Burdick called from across the room, his voice ringing dully, like a bell through fog. "It *is* you, Taylor. The last I heard, you were at death's door. And Mitchell?" He walked to within ten feet of them and stopped. He remained standing.

Among the three of them, the distance expanded, and Taylor Lockwood became the center of the room's dark universe. She sensed, through the ventilation grilles, the rush of a white-noise sound. Or perhaps it was the humming of the blood through her vibrating temples. In the vague reaches of the room, abstract paintings sat like frozen nebulas, and the dots on the electronic panels and telephones in the corner glowed like red stars dying millions of light-years distant.

She looked at Burdick for a moment, then slowly lifted the gun.

His mouth opened. He blinked. "Taylor, is that a gun?"

She had a rehearsed speech. She forgot it entirely, and blurted in a choked voice, "You killed Wendall Clayton. You tried to kill me."

The partner gave a harsh bark of a laugh. "Are you mad?" He looked at Mitchell for help, his eyes deep reservoirs of bewilderment. "What's she saying?"

"You son of a bitch," she whispered. "You poisoned me. You shot Wendall. And I'm going to kill you."

"Taylor!" Reece shouted.

Burdick's hands were out in front of him. "No, please. I don't know what you think about me. I swear to God I never tried to hurt you. I promise you—"

"No!" she screamed and cocked the gun. Burdick backed against the wall, eyes huge disks of terror. Reece froze.

They stood in those positions for a hugely long minute. Taylor inhaled, staring at the gun, as if willing it to fire by itself. "I can't," she cried. "I can't do it." The gun drooped.

Reece stepped forward slowly and took the gun from her. He put his arm around her shoulders. "It's all right," he whispered.

"I wanted to be strong," she said, "but I can't do it."

Burdick said to them both, "I swear I had nothing to do—"

She pulled away from Reece's arm and faced Burdick in her fury. "You may think you have the police and the mayor and everyone else in your pocket, but it's not going to stop me." She grabbed a telephone off the table.

The partner shook his head. "Taylor, whatever delusions you have, you're wrong."

She had just started dialing when a hand reached over, lifted the receiver away from her, and replaced it in the cradle.

"No, Taylor . . ." Mitchell Reece said and lifted the gun, the muzzle pointing at her like a single black pearl. "No," he repeated softly.

thirty-three

S he laughed at first. With much the same sound that Mitchell
Reece had uttered when she told him a week ago that Clayton had
been murdered. Then her smile faded, and she said in bottomless
horror, "Oh, no." His face was stone, his eyes cold dots of metal.

"You, Mitchell?" she whispered.

Reece was silent, but the grim pressure of his closed lips answered
her question.

Donald Burdick said, "One of you tell me what's going on here."

Reece said to her, his voice choked with sorrow, "Why didn't you
stop when you should have, Taylor? Why? It was all planned out so
carefully. How could you ruin it?"

Burdick, horrified, said, "Mitchell, it was you?"

Taylor's eyes closed, and her hands covered her face.

Reece said, "Wendall killed the woman I loved."

Taylor saw cold pain in his face. "Linda?" she asked. "Linda
Davidoff?"

Burdick asked, "What are you saying?"

He said, "A man and a woman." His eyebrows lifted at the
simplicity of the tragedy, how apparent it was. "A man who'd never
had time for relationships, a woman who was beautiful. The two of

them, never in love before. That wasn't a good combination—an ambitious, tough lawyer. Best in law school, best at the firm. . . . The other, a poet, shy, sensitive. Don't ask me how they became close. Opposites attract, maybe. A secret romance. Oh, yes, Taylor, there are *some* secrets in a law firm. They dated, they fell in love. She got pregnant, and they were going to get married."

A moment passed, and Reece seemed to be hefting the words he would use next. Then he continued in his sonorous voice, "Wendall was working on a case one weekend, and he needed a paralegal. Linda had stopped working because of the baby, but she wanted to make some extra money. When Wendall asked her to do some weekend work, she said she would. He supposedly had a bunch of associates working with him up in Connecticut. She took the train up there, but there was no case at all. He tried to seduce her. She slapped him. She called me, crying. I told her to take a cab if she had to, but to leave. She asked Clayton to take her to her parents' summer place in southern Connecticut. When they got there, Clayton tried again. She ran from him. He claimed she accidentally fell over a railing on the back porch. I think he lost his temper and pushed her."

"He claimed?" Burdick asked. "You mean he confessed this to you? When?"

"The night I shot him," Reece said calmly. "After the trial."

"Oh, God," Taylor said, "the girl you were seeing? You weren't going to Westchester at all. You were going to Connecticut, you took flowers to Linda's grave."

Reece nodded.

Click, click. The nail of her index finger, right hand, touched the marble, and she gave a fast burst of a laugh, like a machine-gun spray, almost hysterical. "Oh, Mitchell, it's so clear now. It's so clear." She looked at Burdick. "Don't you see what he's done?" She turned to face Reece, who sat on the dark, dried-blood-red conference table, swinging his legs back and forth. The gun rested beside him, under his hand. Taylor said, "You broke into your own file cabinet and took the Hanover note, then hid it in Wendall's office. Then you arranged to bug your own office so you'd look as innocent as possible. You recorded some conversations, then planted the tapes with the note. You had me track him down."

She thought for a moment. "Then, at his party, I found the receipt from the security service. Upstairs, where *you* sent me to search—after you planted it there. . . . Finally I found the note." She laughed bitterly. "Though not as fast as you would have liked."

"You gave me a few bad moments at the trial," Reece said. "That's true."

Taylor continued, "You keep me with you all that day, then send me into hiding at the Algonquin. Why? Because Wendall can't find out he's been accused of a burglary he didn't commit before you've had a chance to kill him. The night of the trial, you didn't have dinner with the clients at all. You went to the firm and you shot him in the head. Where did you get the gun, Mitchell? From one of your criminal clients?"

"That night," Reece said calmly, "I called and asked him to meet me in the office about the St. Agnes case. I told him it was urgent. He met me at eleven. I took out the gun—I did get it from one of my clients, as a matter of fact, Taylor—and asked him to tell me how he'd killed Linda. He admitted what had happened, and I shot him. He died bravely. He didn't do anything desperate or silly. I was impressed." And she saw in his eyes, even now, a wisp of admiration for Clayton's courage.

Men of most renowned virtue . . .

Reece was gazing at her, impassive as a statue.

Eyes still on Reece, locked into his, Taylor said, "Donald was a big help, wasn't he?" She turned to the partner. "Nothing personal, Donald, but you laid a smoke screen like a presidential adviser." Her hands were shaking now. The numbness she'd felt at first was going fast, the image of Reece in bed, his mussed hair, the ski trip, playing with the buttons of his blousy shirt, they were overwhelming her. The tears started. "And as for me, well, you were keeping tabs. All you had to do was look across the pillow."

She saw motion in the plane of his face like the first cracks in spring ice. Reece took a Kleenex from his pocket and began rubbing the trigger guard and grip and frame of the death-colored gun. He nodded. "You won't believe me if I tell you what happened between us, that wasn't part of the plan."

"Not for a minute," she said, managing a damaged smile. "Because you tried to kill me, didn't you? The botulism was in your loft. Something you left in the refrigerator."

His eyes were wide. "I didn't want to hurt you! You should have stopped when you were supposed to!"

Burdick said, "But Mitchell, how could you risk it? You love the law. You'd jeopardize everything for this, for revenge?"

He smiled with a look as bleak as a hunting field in December. "Don't you know me by now, Donald? You think I'd get caught? Every nuance was planned. Every action and reaction. Every move anticipated and guarded against. There was no way it wouldn't work." He sighed and looked at Taylor. "Except for you, of course. You were the fatal flaw . . . such a persistent little girl. You couldn't cope, could you? It was all too much for you."

No, Mitchell, not that, don't say that.

"Your father knows about death, Taylor. It doesn't make him crazy. To him it's just a part of nature, all in a day's work. How come his . . ."

Don't hurt me any more than you have, Mitchell. Don't—

". . . little girl goes to pieces because some bastard dies? People die all the time. Good ones and bad ones. This was a bad one. Why are you so concerned?"

"You used me!"

His attention dipped for a moment to the gun. He flipped it open expertly and saw six cartridges in the cylinder. Then from his pocket he took the note that Taylor Lockwood had written. The note about going to kill Donald Burdick. She watched him rub it with another Kleenex to obliterate his fingerprints. He folded it into a tight square.

He's going to use that, isn't he? To make it look like I shot Donald, then killed myself. I've written my own suicide note.

"I don't know how to explain it to you, Taylor. I don't think I can so that you'd understand. Someone like you can't comprehend it. I had to kill Wendall. There was no power on earth that would save him when I decided he had to die. Winning is my whole life. I simply cannot lose."

She leaned forward. "It's happened, hasn't it? It's all caught up with you. Pushing, pushing, pushing . . . years and years of it. Win the case, win the fucking case—that's all you see, all you care about! You don't know what the law is anymore. You've turned it inside out."

"Don't lecture me," he said wearily. "Don't talk to me about things you can't understand. I live with the law, I've made it a part of me."

Burdick said, "There's no way you can justify it, Mitchell. You killed a man."

Reece rubbed his eyes. After a moment, he said, "You get asked a lot why you go to law school. Did you go because you wanted to help society, to make money, to further justice? That's what people always want to know. About justice . . . there's so little of it in the world, so little justice in our lives. Maybe on the whole it balances out, maybe God looks down from someplace and says, 'Yeah, pretty good, I'll let it go at that.' But you know the law as well as I do, both of you. Innocent people serve time, guilty ones get off. Wendall Clayton was as guilty of Linda's death as if he'd slipped pills into her drink, or shot her."

Taylor said, "The fake suicide note, Clayton's, the one you typed the night you killed him and sent to Donald. 'Men of most renowned virtue . . .' How does it go?"

Reece said, " 'Have sometimes by transgressing most truly kept the law.' "

"You meant it about you, then, not Clayton."

Reece nodded solemnly. "It's about me."

"And you're going to have to kill us now, aren't you?" she asked, and she wondered if, just before he died, Wendall Clayton's voice had been as calm as hers was now, she wondered if fear anesthetized as deeply as did betrayal.

"Mitchell," Burdick whispered, "just put the gun down. We'll go to the police. If you talk to them—"

But Reece pushed off the table and walked slowly over to Taylor. He stood two feet away. She didn't move.

"No!" Burdick shouted. "Don't worry about the police. We can forget what happened. There's no need for this to go beyond this room. There's no need. . . ."

Reece glanced at him briefly but didn't speak.

Mitchell Reece touched Taylor Lockwood's hair, then her cheek. He nestled the muzzle of the gun against her breast.

"I wish . . ." He cocked the gun. "I wish . . ."

Taylor wiped the thick tears. "But it's *me*, Mitchell. Look at what you're about to do."

"Please, Mitchell," Burdick said. "Money, do you want money? A fresh start somewhere?"

But it was Taylor who raised her hand to silence the partner. "No. He's come too far. I understand that now."

At last there were tears on Reece's face. "It's not working the way I'd planned it. It's not working. I don't have any choice. Oh, Taylor . . ." The gun wavered. For a moment, it seemed to be levitating; he might have been going to touch the chill muzzle to his own temple. But his deeper will won, and he lowered it to her once more.

Taylor Lockwood was still. There was no place to go. All she could do was close her eyes, which she did.

Reece pulled the trigger.

The metallic click was as loud as the gunshot would have been.

Reece's eyes flickered for a moment. He pulled the trigger three more times. Three more clicks echoed throughout the room. His hand lowered.

"Fake," he whispered with the incredulous tone of someone questioning a terrible accident. "It's fake?"

Taylor wiped the streaming tears from her face. "Oh, Mitchell . . ."

Burdick stepped forward slowly and lifted the gun away from him.

Taylor said, "The gun is real, Mitchell, but the bullets are just props. All I had was speculation, Mitchell. I needed proof that you were the one."

Reece leaned against the wall. "Oh, my God."

Taylor called, "John . . ."

Motion from the shadows, and John Silbert Hemming stepped out of a corner conference room, shutting off the Sony tape recorder he held in his hand. Reece glanced at him, then back to Taylor. The private detective said to Taylor, "You could have stopped earlier. We had enough on tape for a conviction."

She stared at Reece and said in a whisper, "I had to know if he'd do it."

The handcuffs went on quickly, with a crisp, ratchety sound.

Reece was staring at Taylor. "How?" he whispered. She'd never seen such shock in anyone's eyes, pure, uncomprehending astonishment.

She said, "Her poem, Linda's poem. When I read it, I didn't think it was a suicide note at all. It was a love poem. It's not about killing herself, it's about leaving solitude and loneliness. Somebody who was going to kill herself wouldn't leave that as a note."

He was shaking his head. "Impossible. You couldn't make that kind of deduction."

"I thought about everything that happened. About the kind of strategist you were, about Clayton's womanizing, about how it would be easy for you to get a gun from one of your clients, about where you were the night Wendall was shot, about your trips to Westchester. Hard evidence? I couldn't find any. Until I found the files. The botulism case file, the Quail Island Lodge case, with the expert witness from American Biological Supply. I figured you called him last week and bribed him for some botulism culture. Then there was the State Farm file, the one where a car went off the road and looked like it was going to sink in a reservoir but ended up on a ledge of rock that kept the car from going down. In exactly the same place we drove into the reservoir that night. You needed to make it look like Clayton was desperate enough to kill us, so he'd be desperate enough to kill himself. You wrote Donald's name in the log when you took out the files, but they had your fingerprints on them. I wasn't sure about you and Linda. It was a guess. I called Donald and we arranged this, to find out for sure."

Reece said softly, "It wasn't enough, was it? You couldn't just accept an insignificant death. No, not you. Your father gave them what he could, dressed them in their finest, made them up with greasepaint, turned them into harmless caricatures of themselves, and put them to sleep in their little boxes. Well, that and a few tears are about all most of us can muster up, Taylor. Life goes on. But not you, no. That wasn't enough. You have to bring back the dead, don't you?"

Her voice was as calm as his. "Mitchell, you wind people up, they may not always do what they're supposed to do. That's what you hadn't quite figured on. That it might bother me to cause someone's death. That I might feel bad about it, might want to pay condolences." She wondered if she would scream, or slap him, or even reach for his throat with her hands, which she felt had the strength, a thousand times more than enough strength, to end his life right now. But she did none of those. She felt no cold swelling of hate. It was so curious: Reece's betrayal and the—what had she felt?—not love she knew now, but passion maybe or obsession, they were both perfectly balanced, had canceled one another out. She felt nothing. Like stepping into body-temperature water. Taylor looked at Mitchell Reece and she felt nothing.

"Taylor, I—"

"I don't want to hear anything more." But she was speaking only to John Silbert Hemming, who nodded solemnly and, hunched down over Reece, escorted him out into the lobby.

Donald Burdick lifted the telephone, and after a pause dialed 911 for the second time in two weeks.

Sean Lillick had finished copying his elaborate musical lead sheets and returned to Halsted Street. He halted abruptly in the middle of the corridor. "Taylor! You're out of the hospital?"

Spinning lazily in the chair of her cubicle, she glanced at him with weary eyes. "Back from the dead."

"You're all right?"

"In a manner of speaking."

He continued up to her desk and handed her the thick sheets of manuscript paper. "Take a look. My latest opus. It's about Wendall Clayton."

She stared at the ledger lines without reading them.

He asked, "What's the matter?"

"Mitchell Reece killed him." Odd how the act of simply saying a few words could bring physical pain.

"What? Who?"

"Wendall."

"Jesus!" Lillick sat in his chair, and she told him the story. His fingers formed brackets and supported his temple. When she finished, he whispered something, but she didn't hear; she was noticing his ear.

The earring.

The tiny red-purple dot of a hole in his right ear. The boy Junie had told her about. "Sean, you were with Clayton in the firm a couple weeks ago. That Saturday night. *You* were the one?"

"Maybe I was. So what?"

"What were you doing?"

He shuffled his music. "Helping him with the merger."

"And?"

"Nothing." He was looking away from her face, and she wondered what stern or frightening persona he had seen.

"Oh, for God's sake, tell me." She gripped his arm.

His eyes widened in sudden surprise at the toughness in her voice. He said, "I needed money. He was paying me to, like, go through file cabinets and desks, find things. Embarrassing things, you know, on people who were against the merger."

"You were his spy?"

He stared down at the Plexiglas carpet protector under her chair. "I told him about Donald's meeting in Florida with the MacMillan people. I told him about Dudley's girlfriend. . . . I know I shouldn't have. . . ." He shrugged like a little boy caught lifting change from his father's dresser and hoping for forgiveness.

Taylor wasn't in the mood to comfort him. She said coolly, "Guess it doesn't matter now, does it?" He was talking to her, quickly, justifying what he'd done, giving her the story of a neglectful father, a passion for music, a fear of everydayness. . . . Taylor wasn't listening. She was following the music on the sheets of paper she held. On the first page at the top was written: *The King of Wall Street, An Opera in One Act.* She sight sang a few bars in her head. "You wrote this?"

Lillick didn't know where his answer was going to lead. He said, "It's not finished."

She handed them back, and wrote a name and phone number on a piece of foolscap.

"Who's this? Willy Landsdowne?"

"Career counseling."

"What's he?——"

"Just call him. Tell him I sent you, and show him those lead sheets. He'll take care of the rest."

"Okay, sure."

"Do it before you apply to law school."

He shrugged. "Who is?——"

"Just do it."

It was then that she noticed an envelope addressed to her, sitting on her lamp. She opened it, and looked at a scrawled note, signed by Thom Sebastian. She read the note, then laughed, a short, high burst that caught Lillick's attention.

"What's up?"

"I just got proposed to."

"As in marriage?"

"Cake, ring, honeymoon in Europe."

"No shit. In a letter?"

She said, "At least it wasn't a fax."

"Who's the lucky groom going to be?"

Taylor laughed again, then looked up at Lillick and shook her head.

"Okay, so who's the heartbroken son of a bitch?"

"That's for me to know."

He leaned forward toward the letter, but she folded it away from him and slipped it into her purse.

"You've sure got your secrets, Taylor."

"Secrets in a law firm?" she asked quietly. And Lillick sensed it was a joke, but she wasn't smiling when she said it.

He pulled on his battered Bob Dylan jacket. He said, "I'll be at the Plastic Respect tonight, you want some company."

"Doubt it," she said and watched him leave. She pulled on her raincoat and walked through the still, half-lit corridors. The Slavic cleaning women in their blue uniforms moved from office to office with their wheeled carts; Taylor could hear the whine of vacuums coming from different directions. She imagined she could smell a sour gunpowder scent, as if Reece had in fact fired real bullets from the heavy pistol. But she realized, as she passed a conference room, that it was just a residue of cigar smoke. Earlier in the evening, a deal had closed. Or maybe it had fallen apart. Or postponed till tomorrow. Some client was richer, or poorer, or left uncertain for another day.

She pushed the elevator button and leaned her head against the cool marble.

Outside, Wall Street was nearly as quiet as the halls of Hubbard, White & Willis. This was a daytime place. It worked hard and curled up early. The offices were mostly dark, the bartenders had stopped pouring drinks. The streets were sparsely populated with lone cabs and limousines. A sluggish breeze was pushing snow-rich clouds over the harbor.

Occasionally someone in a somber overcoat would appear, then vanish into a cab or down a subway stop. Going to who knew where—

maybe to one of Sebastian's clubs, or to pursue some private lust like Ralph Dudley's, or maybe just to retreat to their Upper East Side enclave of an apartment for a few hours' sleep before the grind began again tomorrow.

The police had gone, Burdick had gone. The partner would need some rest; he'd have plenty to do in the morning. More favors would be required. Taylor suspected, though, that Donald Burdick would have a sizable inventory remaining.

One A.M.

Taylor got into a cab and gave the driver her address. She slouched down in the seat, staring up at the greasy Plexiglas divider. *Thank you for not smoking. 50-cent surcharge after 8 P.M.* The cab was a block away from her apartment when she changed her mind. She rapped on the window and told him to drive to an address in the West Village.

"Yeah?"

"Yeah."

"This time of night?"

"This time of night."

Taylor Lockwood sits in the spotlight.

Dimitri twists his curled hair and leans over the microphone. (His habitual suspicion left when she told him, "I'll play for free. You keep the receipts. All of them. The tips, too. Just one thing, Dimitri. No satin touch. Not tonight, okay?")

"Ladies and gentlemen . . ."

She whispers, "Dimitri."

". . . it is my pleasure to present Miss Taylor Lockwood at the piano."

She touches the keys, cold and smooth as mirrors, and feels their yielding resilience as she begins to play.

After half an hour, Taylor looks up into the cockeyed light, a brilliant starburst beaming at her, so bright she can't see the patrons. Maybe the wobbly tables are all occupied. Or maybe just the opposite. In any event, if anyone is in the audience, they listen silently.

She smiles, not to them, but only for herself, and sways slowly, the way an enraptured concert pianist would, as she plays a medley of Gershwin that she herself has arranged, all revolving around *Rhapsody in Blue.* Tonight she improvises frequently, playing jazzy harmonies and risky variations, allowing the music to carry itself, the notes soaring and regrouping, then flying to altitudes that Willy Lansdowne or Sean Lillick would approve of. But Taylor Lockwood never lets go completely and is careful to alight at regular intervals on the theme; she knows how much people love the melody.

Jeffery Wilds Deaver is a former attorney and journalist. He is the author of the popular Rune series of mysteries from Bantam, one of which—*Manhattan Is My Beat*—was nominated for an Edgar Award by the Mystery Writers of America. The most recent, *Hard News*, has been called "peerless entertainment" by *Kirkus Reviews* and "totally recommended" by *The Drood Review*. Deaver's next book, *The Mystery of You*, is being published by Doubleday in January 1993.